Just When You Thought It Was
Safe For a Little War—It's *Back!*

One of Balser's men dashed into the great hall from the courtyard beyond, crying, "Lord king! Lord king! Aragis! Aragis the Archer!"

Gerin sprang to his feet with an oath. "Aragis has crossed over the border?" he demanded.

"Aye, lord king, He's here, lord king."

"What, with his army?" Gerin said. "By the gods is there fighting out there? How did he get here, with no word beforehand?" He looked at his armor, hanging on the wall.

Balser's man stunned him again, saying, "No, lord king. He's here by his lonesome."

Gerin ordered the drawbridge lowered, and Aragis' chariot crossed over it. Aragis the Archer seldom showed hesitation about anything, which was one reason the Fox wondered why they weren't already at war.

Without waiting for the chariot to stop, Aragis hopped out of it and strode briskly over to Gerin, like a hunting dog following an exciting scent. Abruptly, he stuck out a hand. "I greet you, lord king,"

"I greet you, lord king," Gerin said, accepting the clasp. "You don't mind my asking, why aren't we trying to kill each other right now?"

"Don't worry, I thought we'd be doing just that by this time, too." Aragis bared his teeth. "I think I'd have won, too. But something more important's come up."

"More important than which of us ends up ruling the northlands?" Gerin said.

"The Empire's come back to the northlands," Aragis answered.

Baen Books by Harry Turtledove

FOX AND EMPIRE

HARRY TURTLEDOVE

FOX AND EMPIRE

Copyright © 1998 by Harry Turtledove

A Baen Books Original

Baen Publishing Enterprises
P.O. Box 1403
Riverdale, NY 10471

ISBN: 0-671-87858-1

Cover art by Darrell K. Sweet

First printing, January 1998

Distributed by Simon & Schuster
1230 Avenue of the Americas
New York, NY 10020

Printed in the United States of America

I

Up in the watchtower, the lookout winded his horn: a long, unmelodious blast. "Two chariots approach from the south, lord king!" he bellowed.

From the courtyard far below, Gerin the Fox, king of the north, cupped a hand to his mouth and replied: "Thanks, Andiver. We'll see who they are when they get here."

"Aren't you going to go up on the palisade and have a look?" the sentry demanded indignantly.

"In a word, no," Gerin answered. "If two chariots' worth of warriors can conquer Fox Keep, either they're gods, in which case looking at them won't do me any good, or else we're all such cowards that the men who are on the palisade now would be running away, and that's not happening, either. So I'll wait for them down here, thanks very much."

Andiver said something the height of his perch kept Gerin from understanding. The Fox decided it was probably just as well.

His son Dagref smiled at him. "That was very logical," he said. Dagref, at fourteen, was as remorselessly logical as the most terrifying Sithonian philosopher who'd ever made a living lecturing in the Elabonian Empire. Up until twenty years before, Gerin's kingdom, as well as the rest of the land north from the High Kirs to the

1

River Niffet, had been a frontier province of the Empire. Elabon, though, had abandoned the land north of the mountains in the face of the devastating werenight caused by all four moons' coming full at the same time and, almost incidentally, the barbarous Trokmoi swarming south over the Niffet.

"It was indeed," Gerin said. "So what?"

Dagref stared at him. Man and youth shared a long face, long nose, and swarthy complexion. Dagref, though, had only fine down on his cheeks and chin, and his hair was a brown almost black. Gerin's neat beard and his hair were gray, and getting grayer by the year: he was past fifty now, and often knew it by the creaking in his bones.

"Logic is the greatest tool, the greatest weapon, in the world," Dagref declared.

"That depends on what you're doing," Gerin replied. "If you're in the middle of a brawl, you can't slay a Gradi or a Trokmê or one of Aragis the Archer's jolly henchmen with a well-aimed syllogism. That's why we carry these things every now and then."

He hefted his sword. The sun glinted, red as blood, from the polished edge of the bronze blade. Dagref held a sword, too. He enjoyed fencing with it much less than fencing with his wits. He was very dangerous with the latter, only somewhat so with the former.

"Come on." Gerin made as if to attack him. "If some big ugly lug carves chunks off you, it doesn't matter that he's never heard of the law of the excluded middle. You won't be around to instruct him afterwards."

Dagref parried the slash. His answering cut made Gerin give back a pace. They did not work against each other as often as Gerin would have done had he not been left-handed: learning how to fight him went only so far in teaching Dagref how to fight others. His son was left-handed, too, which gave Gerin the rare chance to see what others faced when they met him.

"Keep the blade up!" the Fox cautioned. "You don't keep the blade up, I can do something like this—" He snapped a cut at Dagref's head, so quick and sharp that his son had to stagger back. "Or even this." The Fox feinted another head cut; if he hadn't stopped his thrust, he would have put it into Dagref's chest.

"Yes, I see." Dagref nodded. And he did see, too. He had the makings of a good swordsman; he had long arms and quick feet and didn't do the same thing wrong over and over again. But he didn't automatically do the right thing, either, and, when he did do it, he didn't do it fast enough. Only years of patient practice would give him the speed he needed. Intellectually, he realized that (he was very good at realizing things intellectually). "Let's try it again, Father."

Those were the words Gerin wanted to hear. Before he could go through the passage again, though, one of his men up on the palisade called a challenge to the approaching chariots: "Who comes to Castle Fox?"

The answer made Gerin forget about swordplay and hurry up onto the palisade after all: "I am Marlanz Raw-Meat, emissary of King Aragis the Archer, come to have speech with King Gerin."

"Hello, Marlanz," Gerin called once he reached the walkway and could peer over the tops of the palisade timbers. "Come in and be welcome. I'll listen to whatever Aragis has to say, though I don't promise I'll do anything about it."

At his command, the gate crew let down the drawbridge over the ditch around the palisade. Marlanz's chariot rattled into Fox Keep. King Aragis' representative was a big, burly man in his late thirties; from previous encounters with him, Gerin knew he was smarter than he looked. "Hello, lord king," Marlanz said as the Fox came down to greet him.

When Gerin clasped hands with him, Marlanz's big paw (a word that came naturally to Gerin's mind, as Marlanz had a were streak in him) almost engulfed his own. "What brings you north this time?" the Fox asked, though he had the bad feeling he already knew.

And sure enough, Marlanz said, "Lord king, Aragis bids me tell you that he is not going to stand idly by if Balser Debo's son swears homage and fealty to you. He warns you not to pursue that further."

The Fox looked down his nose at Aragis' ambassador, no mean feat since Marlanz was three or four digits' width taller than he. "Aragis has no business telling either Balser or me what sort of relationship we can have. Balser was never Aragis' vassal, nor was his father before him. Balser styles himself baron, nothing more, but he's as free a man and as independent a lord as I am—or as Aragis is."

"Yes, and Aragis intends that he remain free, and not come under your influence," Marlanz said.

"If, of his own free will, he wants to declare himself my vassal, Aragis has not the right to forbid it."

Marlanz Raw-Meat folded thick arms across his broad chest. "Lord king, King Aragis is strong enough to enforce his will on Balser—and on you."

In the end, it came down to strength, Gerin thought. Adiatunnus the Trokmê, a rival now a vassal, had first declared the Fox king of the north after he'd beaten the Gradi pirates back to a single keep on the edge of the Orynian Ocean. Aragis had started calling himself king a little later, his claim springing from his being the only noble left in the northlands with strength enough to stand against Gerin.

"If Aragis tries that, he will get the war he's been saying

he doesn't want ever since the days right after the werenight," Gerin answered. "Tell him that, Marlanz. Make sure he understands it. And tell him that, if he does try it, I believe he'll end up being the sorriest man ever born."

Marlanz scowled. He'd known Gerin long enough to know the Fox did not casually make such boasts. In Marlanz's younger days, he'd been more a bruiser than a diplomat. He'd gained skill with years. These days, Aragis probably trusted him further than anyone else— not that Aragis trusted anyone very far. Trying to strike a conciliatory tone, Marlanz said, "You have to see how things are, lord king. Balser's holding points like a knife straight at the heart of the lands that acknowledge King Aragis' suzerainty. If it comes under your control, you're halfway to invading his domain right there."

Gerin scowled back. In Aragis' sandals, his acquisition *would* look that way. "I don't want to use the holding as a knife. I want to use it as a shield against Aragis," the Fox said. "It's hardly less dangerous to me in his hands than it is to him in mine. You might remind him that he was the one who paraded chariots past Balser's border to frighten him into yielding. I can't help it if Balser started talking to me instead."

"It might be best if we could keep Balser neutral between you and Aragis, inclining neither to the one nor the other," Marlanz said.

"That would have been fine," Gerin said. "It *was* fine, while it lasted. I wasn't the one who changed it. Now Balser doesn't think he can trust Aragis to keep his hands where they belong. Am I supposed to tell him, 'No, I'm sorry, I won't protect you from your neighbor, even if you want me to'?"

Marlanz looked unhappy. "I knew that was foolish," he muttered; Gerin didn't think he was supposed to hear.

Aragis' envoy gathered himself. "Lord king, I'm sorry, but I don't have a lot of room to wiggle here. King Aragis has told me to tell you that, if Balser becomes your vassal, it will mean war between the two of you."

"Then it will be war." Gerin slapped Marlanz on the back and waved him toward Castle Fox. "We don't have to start killing each other quite yet, I don't think. Why don't you come into the great hall and drink some ale with me, eat some bread, and we'll see what else we can scare up for you."

"I'll do that right gladly," Marlanz said. "You brewed a fine ale the last time I was here, lord king, and you're not the sort to let something like that slip. And you have a name all through the northlands for feeding your guest-friends well."

"I probably earned it when I managed to get you out of my keep before you ate the larder empty—just before," Gerin said. Marlanz laughed, although, like most of Gerin's jokes, that one had a hard core of truth. "Come on," the Fox urged, and they walked into the great hall side by side.

Van of the Strong Arm, Rihwin the Fox, and Carlun Vepin's son sat at a table near the hearth, and near the altar to Dyaus Allfather in front of it. A tarred-leather jack of ale sat in front of each of them. Van was also gnawing a roast rib of mutton. As Gerin and Marlanz walked in, the big outlander tossed it into the rushes on the floor to watch a couple of dogs squabble over it.

"By all the gods, it's Marlanz Raw-Meat," Van rumbled, recognizing Aragis' envoy. He rose from the bench and strode up to clasp Marlanz's hand. As they did whenever they met, the two big men studied each other. Gerin studied them both. The golden-haired outlander was taller and broader through the shoulders, but he was also older, being within a year or two either way of the

Fox's age. At his peak, he'd been stronger than Marlanz—he'd been stronger than anyone Gerin had ever known. But Marlanz, a decade younger, was closer to his own peak, which had also been formidable. If the two of them fought . . . Gerin didn't know what would happen. That was strange. In the more than twenty years since Van had come to Fox Keep, he'd always been sure his friend could best anyone merely human. Now—

Now we're getting old, Gerin thought. *Strength goes.* He smiled to himself. *Guile, though, guile endures.* Aloud, he said, "Marlanz says Aragis will go to war with us if Balser gives me homage and fealty."

"He's welcome to try it," Van said. "I don't think he'll be so happy afterwards, though." A few years earlier, he would have whooped with glee at the prospect of a fight. He still didn't shrink from it—Gerin couldn't imagine him shrinking from a fight—but he no longer rushed toward it like a man rushing toward his beloved.

"My king is not happy about it now," Marlanz answered, "but he will not shrink from it, not if that means seeing his own rights overthrown."

That made Rihwin the Fox speak up: "In good sooth, King Aragis has no right pertaining to the holding of Balser Debo's son, it never having been a fief of his."

"I said the same thing," Gerin told him, "but not half so prettily."

"You have not the advantages of a noble upbringing south of the High Kirs," Rihwin replied, as if forgiving his fellow Fox for flaws beyond his control. After two decades in the northlands, Rihwin still clung to the elaborate phrasing he'd learned at the heart of the Elabonian Empire, and to the gold hoop he wore in his left ear, an affectation to which the rest of Gerin's vassals had never quite accommodated themselves.

Marlanz looked from Rihwin to Gerin and back again.

"As I have noted before, he has the right to keep a stronger neighbor from taking advantage of a weaker one."

"As *I* noted before," Gerin said pointedly, "if Aragis weren't a strong neighbor liable to take advantage of a weaker one, Balser wouldn't be interested in having me as his lord."

"If you told him as much out there," Van said, "did you bring him in here to tell it to him over again?"

"As a matter of fact, I brought him in here for some ale and some bread and whatever we can pry out of the kitchen in the way of meat," Gerin said. He slapped Aragis' vassal on the shoulder again. "Sit you down, Marlanz. If Aragis and I have to fight, we'll fight. Meanwhile, you're my guest-friend."

Servants brought Marlanz a drinking jack, a round of flatbread, and some ribs like the one Van had been gnawing. Carlun Vepin's son, Gerin's steward, looked as if he was calculating the cost of everything. And so, no doubt, he was: the Fox wouldn't have wanted him for the job if he didn't keep track of every jar of ale, sack of beans, and barrel of salt pork.

Whatever Carlun thought, he kept it to himself while warriors other than Gerin were around. He was no fighting man. He'd been the headman of the serf village close by Fox Keep till Gerin caught him cheating on the records there, trying to hold back produce from his overlord's notice. That had earned him both a promotion and a warning about what would happen if the Fox ever caught him cheating again. Either he hadn't cheated since or he'd done it too well for Gerin to have noticed. The Fox didn't think Carlun was clever enough to get away with that; he almost but not quite hoped he was wrong.

Marlanz made eyes at one of the serving women. Gerin

happened to know she was newly married, and happy with her husband. She kept on serving Aragis' envoy, but did nothing to encourage him, and twisted away before he had the chance to pull her down onto his lap.

He glanced over to Gerin. "You always did give your serfs a lot of say in what they should do to keep your guests happy."

"I haven't changed," the Fox answered. "Far as I can see, forcing them to bed men they don't want only causes trouble. If she's interested in you, Marlanz, that's fine. If she's not, maybe you can find someone else who is."

Marlanz didn't make an issue of it. Gerin remembered how he'd been inclined to do just that, the first time he came up to Fox Keep. Yes, he'd learned a thing or two over the intervening fifteen years. And, of course, since he was fifteen years older himself, he didn't burn so hot as he had then, either.

"I passed the night at your son's holding on my way up to your keep here, lord king," Marlanz remarked, changing the subject with a smoothness he hadn't had as a younger man. "He seems to be shaping into a fine baron in his own right."

"For which I thank you," Gerin said. "Aye, I think Duren's a splendid lad. Of course, being his father, I'd think that even if it weren't so."

"Well, it is," Marlanz said. "And I didn't see any signs that his vassal barons are anything but what they ought to be, either. You had some trouble with that, as I recall."

"A bit," the Fox admitted. Duren held his holding as grandson to the previous baron, Ricolf the Red, not as Gerin's son. Ricolf's petty barons had been anything but enthusiastic about accepting him, partly because they feared Gerin's influence and partly because, with Ricolf gone, they'd had hopes of escaping vassalage altogether and setting up on their own. As far as Gerin could see, the hope had obviously been foolish, but that hadn't kept them from having it. A lot of the hopes men had were obviously foolish to everyone but them.

"Aye, Duren's a fine young fellow." Marlanz cocked his head to one side. "Is he the heir to your kingdom, or is that Dagref whom I saw out in the courtyard with you?"

"Yes," Gerin answered, and let Marlanz make whatever he would of it. Duren was his son by Elise, Ricolf's daughter. He hadn't seen her since Duren was a toddler; she'd run away with a traveling horse doctor. Dagref, his sister Clotild, and his brother Blestar were his by Selatre, the former Sibyl at the farseeing god Biton's shrine down at Ikos. The Fox sighed. Life was never so simple as you wished it would be.

"Yes to which?" Marlanz demanded: he was, Gerin knew, persistent. The Fox just smiled at him. After a bit, Aragis' vassal figured out he wouldn't get a straight answer. He smiled back, shrugged, and emptied his jack of ale. A serving woman—not the one he'd tried to paw—refilled it for him.

Gerin took a pull at his own ale. He wondered where Dagref had gone. His eldest child by Selatre had a curiosity as fierce and ruthless as a longtooth: he should have been besieging Marlanz with every sort of question. The Fox wondered what he'd found more interesting than the arrival of a near-stranger.

Had it been Duren at the same age, Gerin would have guessed he was off with a girl. But Dagref's curiosity was, as yet, more of the intellect than of the body. One day soon, the Fox suspected, a serving girl would kick his feet out from under him. What happened after that would be interesting.

No sooner had Gerin thought of his son than Dagref, as if summoned, came running into the great hall. He spared Marlanz Raw-Meat no more than a hasty glance. "Father, come quick, out back by the stables," he exclaimed. "It's Ferdulf again."

"Oh, by the gods," Gerin said, which, where Ferdulf was concerned, had alarmingly literal implications. The Fox sprang to his feet. Dagref, the message delivered, was already dashing away. Gerin pounded after him, aware with every step that he wasn't as fast as he had been.

Behind him, he heard Van and Rihwin exclaiming, too. A moment later, they followed the Fox. And Marlanz came right on their heels. He hadn't a clue about what was going on, but he wanted to find out.

Dagref sprinted around Castle Fox, then pointed with a dramatic forefinger. "There!" he said.

There were Clotild and Blestar. There too were Maeva and Kor, Van's children. Maeva, though a year younger than Dagref, was already blossoming into ripe womanhood—but womanhood of heroic proportions. Van's blood told in her temperament as well as her size and strength; she wanted to be a warrior, and Gerin, rather to his own alarm, thought she would make a good one. Kor was even more alarming. He also had his father's build, but took his incendiary temper straight from Fand, the Trokmê woman with whom Van lived in something less than wedded bliss.

And there were Geroge and Tharma. The two monsters towered over all their companions, even Maeva. They were large and hairy and remarkably ugly, with clawed hands and feet, low foreheads, little eyes under beetling brow ridges, and long jaws full of big teeth (though Geroge's right upper canine was of gold rather than being a natural fang). They both waved to Gerin, who had raised them from . . . he supposed *cubs* was the best word.

He didn't see Ferdulf. And then, just before Dagref said "There!" again, he did. The preternaturally beautiful four-year-old had doffed his tunic and was walking around in the air about twenty feet off the ground.

"Magic?" Marlanz asked from behind Gerin with what was, under the circumstances, commendable calm.

The Fox shook his head. "Not exactly." He raised his voice to Ferdulf: "Come down from there this instant, before you—" He stopped. *Before you hurt yourself* didn't work, as it had with his own children. Ferdulf wasn't going to hurt himself. Gerin wasn't sure Ferdulf could hurt himself. He tried a different tack: "—before you drive everybody down here crazy."

"What do I care?" Ferdulf stood on his head, supported by exactly nothing. His voice was not a four-year-old's, but the same rude, rich baritone he'd had since he was a newborn babe.

Marlanz said, "Lord king, will you please tell me what's going on here?" He took Geroge and Tharma in stride; he'd met them before. Ferdulf, however, was new to him. Like most men in the northlands, he viewed the new with suspicion.

Gerin didn't, in most cases. With Ferdulf, he made an exception. Trying to sound casual, he answered, "That's Mavrix's son by Fulda, a peasant woman here. Now do you understand?"

For a moment, Marlanz didn't. Then he did, and his eyes got wide. "Mavrix?" He tried his best to imitate Gerin's flat, unemphatic tones, but didn't have much luck. "The Sithonian god of wine?" Calm crumbled into astonishment: "You've got a god's get here, lord king?"

"Yes, the little bastard," Gerin said, which, in dealing—or trying to deal—with Ferdulf, had proved true in any number of ways.

Dagref plucked at his father's sleeve. "I brought you

out here so you could do something about him," he said
pointedly. "The last time he started going around up in
the air this way, he piddled on all of us, and I wanted
to see if we could keep that from happening again." The
glare he gave the Fox said his father's reliability had
just come down a peg for him.

"What exactly do you want me to do?" Gerin asked
in some exasperation. "I can't lean a ladder against the
air, the way I would against the palisade." He cast a
cautious eye up toward Ferdulf's little pecker. Mavrix's
get had divine powers and a four-year-old's sense of
humor; the Fox was hard pressed to imagine a more
terrifying combination.

Dagref took a deep breath. "If you don't come down
from there this instant," he told Ferdulf, "none of the
rest of us is going to play with you for a long time." His
voice broke in the middle of the threat, so he didn't
sound so fierce as he might have, but he did sound as if
he meant what he said. He always sounded as if he meant
what he said. He gestured to his comrades. Clotild and
Blestar nodded. So did Maeva and Kor. And, a beat late,
so did Geroge and Tharma.

"Oh, all right," Ferdulf said sulkily, sounding very much
like his own father, who raised petulance to an art. He
came floating down and put his tunic back on.

"That was bravely done," Maeva said. She eyed Dagref
with a thoughtful interest to which he as yet remained
in large measure blind.

"That *was* bravely done," Gerin agreed; telling Ferdulf
what to do took nerve. Well, his son had never lacked
for that. Sense, possibly, but not nerve. The Fox went
on, "But why did you call me when you could handle it
by yourself?"

"I didn't know if that would work," Dagref answered,
"and I thought you would have a better idea. When you

didn't—" He raised one eyebrow, as Gerin might have done. *You* should *have had a better idea*, he said without words.

In a much more cautious voice than he'd used till now, Marlanz Raw-Meat asked, "What all can the little godlet do besides fly?"

"What all?" Gerin clapped a hand to his head, as if it ached. When he thought about Ferdulf, it soon did ache. "Who knows? I'll tell you this much: I went to see him as soon as I got word he'd been born, and he said hello to me in that same voice you heard him use now. Life hasn't been dull since, believe me."

"Is his mother a goddess, too, or a demon, or—?" Marlanz fell silent, seeming to guess how little he could guess.

Gerin's smile was ironic. "I told you, his mother's name is Fulda. She still lives down in the village close to the keep here. She has a pretty face and a ripe body, which is why I used her when I was summoning Mavrix against the Gradi—which, in case you're wondering, was a good idea that didn't work. Ferdulf listens to her when he feels like it and ignores her the rest of the time, which is about what he does for everybody else."

"You told me you'd summoned Mavrix the last time I came up here," Marlanz said, remembering. "You didn't tell me he'd got a woman with child."

"Ferdulf hadn't been born then," the Fox answered. "I didn't know then what I'd get. For that matter, I still don't know what I have. Why don't we go back to the great hall and have another jack of ale, and we can talk some more about it?"

"Good enough, lord king." Marlanz hurried back to the hall, as if he feared Ferdulf and was trying to conceal it from everyone, especially from himself.

✧   ✧   ✧

Selatre had been working in the kingdom's library—an overstatement of what one upstairs room of Castle Fox held, but an overstatement Gerin had been making ever since he'd succeeded his father as local baron, more than twenty years before. She came down for supper.

When she did, Marlanz bowed before her. "Lady, seeing as you were Sibyl at Ikos, and seeing as the farseeing god spoke through you there," he said, getting around to his question a clause at a time, like a lawyer south of the High Kirs, "does that mean this Ferdulf you've got here pays any special heed to what you say?" He spoke of Mavrix's son as he might have of a dangerous wild beast, which struck Gerin as fitting enough.

Selatre gave the question grave consideration, almost as if she expected Biton to speak through her here and now. After scratching the side of her pointed chin for close to a minute, she delivered a short answer: "Not very often."

Marlanz stared, then started to laugh. "Well, that's straight, and no mistake," he said, his last couple of words blurring into an enormous yawn. He turned back to Gerin. "If you'll be kind enough to have somebody show me up to my bedchamber, I'll thank you for it. I've spent a good many days on the road, coming up from Aragis' keep."

"I can do that," Gerin said, and waved for a servant, who led Aragis' envoy away. The warriors who had accompanied Marlanz would sleep in the great hall; the Fox had made sure they had plenty of blankets to stay comfortable. No one at Fox Keep had to fear night ghosts, for he made a point of giving them the blood they needed to keep from molesting mortals.

Once Marlanz was gone, Selatre put on that thoughtful expression again. "Do you suppose we *could* find a way to use Ferdulf?" she said in a low voice.

"Against Aragis, you mean?" Gerin asked, as quietly. His wife nodded. He said, "I never thought about it before. I never imagined Ferdulf doing anything but whatever he wants." He looked around. None of the men who'd come to Fox Keep with Marlanz seemed to be listening, and a couple of them were already asleep, but Gerin had not grown as old as he had—*older than I ever thought I'd be*—by taking unnecessary chances. The necessary ones were quite bad enough. "Let's talk about it upstairs."

"All right." Selatre rose from the bench in one smooth motion. She and Gerin walked up the wooden stairway hand in hand.

In the chamber nearest the top of the stairs, Van and Fand were arguing. The outlander and the Trokmê woman looked on quarrels as most folk looked on meat and drink. Gerin met Selatre's eye. Wryly, he shook his head. After Elise had left him, before he'd met Selatre, he'd shared Fand's affection—and her temper—with Van for a while. No wonder he did his best to keep his even-tempered wife that way. He had standards of comparison.

He and Selatre shared the next bedchamber with their children. Since he didn't feel like explaining everything to Dagref (however much his son thought himself entitled to explanations), and since Clotild might well also still be awake, he led Selatre past that door, too. She nodded, understanding his reasons without his having to spell them out. *One more reason to love her*, he thought.

Rihwin had the chamber on the other side of the Fox's. Since Rihwin could no more keep secrets than Fand could keep calm, Gerin walked by his room. The next bedchamber held Marlanz. Across from it was the library, to which Gerin and Selatre were both drawn like feathers gliding toward rubbed amber.

Few in the northlands knew their letters. Selatre hadn't,

not till Gerin taught them to her after bringing her to Fox Keep. He'd thought to give her a useful place here, not knowing he would fall in love with her in short order—and she with him, too, which struck him as stranger and more marvelous. She'd also fallen in love with books. That, unlike falling in love with him, he understood completely. He'd done it himself.

He opened the door, then gestured for her to go in ahead of him. She did—and started to laugh. When he followed her into the chamber, he laughed, too. There sat Dagref in front of a lamp, his nose in a scroll.

Gerin glanced over at Selatre. "Anyone would think he was our child," he said.

Dagref looked up at his parents. "Of course I'm your child," he said testily, "and I'm sure you came in here so you could talk about something you think is none of my business."

"You're right," Selatre told him.

"It isn't fair," he said. "How am I supposed to learn what I need to know if you won't let me find out about it?" He started to stalk off, then stopped under Gerin's glare. When he went back, rolled up the scroll, and replaced it in its proper pigeonhole, his father stopped glaring.

"That was good," Selatre said with a smile after her son did depart. "He figured out why you were unhappy."

"Something, anyway," Gerin agreed. "Tell him the same thing four hundred times in a row and he will start to listen—if it suits him. If it doesn't . . ." His scowl said what happened then. After a moment, he went on, "And yet, if it's something he *wants* to learn, he'll soak it up the way dry ground soaks up the first rain of the year."

Selatre gazed at him with amused fondness. "Anyone would think he had you for a father," she murmured.

The Fox tried to glare again, but ended up laughing

instead. "You know me too well—and you have altogether too little respect for your king." That made Selatre laugh, too. But Gerin quickly sobered. "*Can* we use Ferdulf as a weapon against Aragis if we do go to war?"

"I would be happier trying it if he were the son of any other god than Mavrix," Selatre said.

"Why do you say that? Because Mavrix is about the least predictable god in anyone's pantheon, or because he's shown he isn't fond of me in particular?"

"Yes," Selatre said, as Gerin had with Marlanz. He made a face at her. Despite her joke, though, both halves of the question could legitimately be answered *yes*. Mavrix was the Sithonian god of wine, beauty, fertility, creativity . . . and of the chaos accompanying all those. He did not know, from one moment to another, what he would do next, nor did he care. And his encounters with the Fox over the years had mostly ended up alarming both the god, who was a coward at heart, and the man, who was anything but.

Gerin said, "For once, I'd like to use a weapon against my foes that isn't stronger than I am, so I won't have to spend so much time worrying whether it will turn in my hand and end up being worse than simply losing whatever fight I happen to be making."

"The question, then, it seems to me, is, if we go to war with Aragis, whether we can beat him without resorting to . . . extraordinary means," Selatre said.

Gerin paused a moment to admire the precise phrasing of that. He tried to answer with similar precision: "We can—if everything goes right. If Adiatunnus chooses to remember he's my vassal, and doesn't take the fight as an excuse to throw off his allegiance and set up on his own, for instance."

"He'd better not," Selatre said with no small anger, "not when he's the one who first proclaimed you king."

"He's been a good enough vassal since, too," Gerin admitted, "but he's a Trokmê, which means he's almost as fickle as Mavrix. If he sees the two greatest Elabonian lords in the northlands going at each other, the temptation may be too much for him to stand. And there are the Gradi, too."

The seafaring invaders from the chilly lands north of the Trokmê forests had tried to establish themselves and their grim gods in the northlands a few years before. Fear of them was what had made Adiatunnus remember he was Gerin's vassal. Fighting together instead of against each other, Elabonians and Trokmoi had pinned the northerners against the Orynian Ocean. More than that they could not do, not when Gradi galleys controlled the sea.

Because Voldar, the chief Gradi goddess, and the rest of the northerners' gods contemplated making the northlands into a frigid copy of the home from which they'd come, a land too cold for even barley to grow there, Gerin had managed to persuade Baivers, the Elabonian god of barley, beer, and brewing, to join with the ferocious powers of Geroge and Tharma's kind and battle those Gradi gods. He didn't know whether that battle on the spiritual plane had been won or lost. His best guess was that it still went on, five years after its beginning: time, for the gods, was not as it was for men. What he did know was that, without help from their gods, the Gradi hadn't been able to stand against him. That was the only thing that mattered.

No, not quite the only thing. "If Voldar and the other Gradi powers ever manage to pull loose from the battle I found for them, they won't be very happy with me."

"They haven't done it yet, and it's been a long time now." Selatre spoke with her usual brisk practicality. "And, if they do, you'll come up with something."

That wasn't practicality; it was, as far as Gerin could see, madness. "Everyone else expects me to have all the answers and pull them out of my beltpouch whenever I need them," he growled. "I thought you knew better."

She looked steadily back at him. "You forget, I've been living by your side these past fifteen or sixteen years. I know what you can do. Everyone else just guesses." When that drew nothing more than a sardonic snort from the Fox, Selatre went on, "You *would* come up with something. I know you too well to doubt it. Maybe, with Ferdulf here, you could use him to call on Mavrix, and—"

"That would be wonderful, wouldn't it?" Gerin said. "Mavrix likes me about as well as Voldar does. Trying to use one god who can't stand me to head off another one who can't stand me, either . . . I think I'd be better off jumping out of the watchtower and hoping I broke my neck when I hit. Besides, Voldar's stronger than Mavrix. I found that out."

"Well, you'd do something else, then." Selatre still sounded confident. "I thought of Mavrix because we were talking about Ferdulf."

"So we were," Gerin said. "The best thing I can think of to do with him is to hope that his being here frightens Aragis, and to hope Aragis never finds out how much his being here frightens me."

"You're the king of the north." Amusement glinted in his wife's eyes. "Nothing is supposed to frighten you."

She was poking him in the ribs to make him jump. He knew as much, but answered seriously: "No, that's Aragis. As far as I've ever seen, nothing does frighten him—and that frightens me. He's very simple, like a hunting hawk. He goes straight for what he wants, knocks it down, and kills it. The only reason he's never gone after me is that I've always looked too big to knock down. Maybe I don't, not any more. I don't think Marlanz is bluffing."

"No. Aragis doesn't want you becoming Balser's overlord," Selatre agreed. She cocked her head to one side and studied him. "Wouldn't you say that means he's afraid of you?"

Gerin started to say something, then stopped. What he did say, in tones of appreciation, was, "I think I've just been outargued."

Selatre was still studying him, but now in rather a different manner. "And what do you propose to do about that?" she inquired.

He got up, walked over to the door, and barred it. He'd had a serf skilled in carpentry install the bar and the brackets that held it a couple of years before. At about the same time, he'd taken to storing a bolt of thick woolen cloth in one corner of the library. That had perplexed Dagref, who'd noted, pointedly and accurately, that nothing else but books ever got stored in that room. "It's not doing any particular harm there, so let it alone," Gerin had told him. That was also true. Dagref had grumbled about it for a while, but then, as is the way of such things, he'd got used to it. He probably didn't even notice it was there any more.

The other thing he didn't notice, however alert he was to connections between events around him, was that that bar and the roll of cloth had appeared in the library at about the same time he and Clotild grew to the point where they didn't sleep much more than Gerin and Selatre did. The Fox's bedchamber had only one large bed in it. Private moments there got harder and harder to find.

"What *are* you doing?" Selatre asked now, though her tone of voice suggested she knew perfectly well what he was doing—and that she might have done it herself if he hadn't.

"Who, me?" Gerin unrolled the cloth on the floor. When he'd doubled it over onto itself, it was a little longer than a woman, or even a man, might be, lying at full length.

Selatre came over and stood beside him. As if altogether of its own accord, his arm slid around her waist. She moved closer. Her voice, though, was thoughtful as she said, "It's really not quite so soft as the bed, is it? And you don't always remember to keep your weight on your elbows instead of on me." She let out a small sigh that might have proclaimed she was resigned to his iniquities.

Some pleasant little while later, Gerin murmured, "There. You can't say I'm squashing you now." Selatre, astride him, nodded agreement altogether too solemn for the moment. Both of them started to laugh—quietly. Gerin slid his hands along her smooth, warm length. "Is this better, then?"

"Better?" Her shrug was delightful. Even then, though, the answer she gave was carefully considered: "I don't know. It's not the same, and you're not squashing me. That's enough." She began to move, and the answers she and Gerin found were not expressed in words.

Once he'd put on his linen tunic and wool trousers, Gerin rolled up the bolt of cloth and slung it back in its corner. In the light of the single lamp still burning in the library, it looked altogether mundane: just one more thing for which there hadn't been room anywhere else in the crowded castle.

Suddenly, Selatre started to giggle. The Fox raised an interrogative eyebrow. She said, "I wonder what Ferdulf would have thought if he'd been walking in the air outside the window just then."

There was an aspect of Ferdulf's unusual abilities Gerin

hadn't contemplated till then. "Maybe he would have learned something," he said, which made Selatre laugh again. He went on, "Considering which god he's the son of, maybe he wouldn't have, too." He and Selatre both laughed at that. Were they a little nervous? If they were, they both kept quiet about it. He unbarred the door. Selatre blew out the lamp. They went off to bed.

Marlanz Raw-Meat looked as if he'd bitten into something sour. "It's still no, is it?" he said, and swigged at the ale which, with bread and honey, made up his breakfast.

"It's still no," Gerin said firmly. "If Balser Debo's son acknowledges that he is my vassal—and I expect he will—I'll protect him from all his neighbors, including Aragis the Archer."

"I'm sorry to hear that, lord king," Marlanz said. "I'll take your words down to King Aragis. After that, I expect I'll see you in the field." He put down the loaf on which he'd been gnawing and made cut-and-thrust motions. "Guest-friends don't slay each other, of course, but that doesn't hold for your men."

"I know," Gerin said. "Tell Aragis also that I have no quarrel with him if he has no quarrel with me. Tell him I don't aim to use Balser's land against him. Tell him he and I have managed to keep from going to war with each other up till now even though we've been the two strongest men in the northlands for most of the past twenty years. I'm in no great hurry to change that."

"I'll tell him everything you say, lord king." Marlanz upended his jack, then looked into it as if amazed it held no more ale. "I'll tell him, but his mind's made up. If Balser claims you for his overlord, Aragis will go to war. When he says something like that, it's as sure as the sun coming up tomorrow."

From everything Gerin had gleaned by intently watching his rival over the years, Marlanz was telling the truth. When Aragis said he would do something, he *would* do it, no matter how appalling it might be. He was not a man who deviated from his declared purposes. That made him more dangerous than someone who might be intimidated, but also made him more vulnerable because he was more predictable.

But the lands he controlled and those acknowledging the Fox's overlordship already marched over a long stretch of the northlands. If he went to war with Gerin, he could pick the spot for the first assault. "Tell Aragis one thing more from me," the Fox said, and Marlanz Raw-Meat nodded attentively. "Tell him that if he starts this war, I will finish it, and he won't care for that."

By Marlanz's expression, he didn't care for it, either. "I will take your words to him just as you say them, lord king," he promised. His face got longer yet. "I don't think it will help, but I'll do it."

"All right. I'll tell you one thing, too, Marlanz," Gerin said: "I don't hold this against you personally. You're doing as a good vassal should, following the orders of your suzerain. I think you'll be sorry for doing it even so."

"That's in the hands of the gods," Marlanz said, and then looked as if he wished he could have the words back. They must have made him think of Ferdulf, and from Ferdulf go on to Mavrix. He wouldn't know Mavrix was none too well disposed toward Gerin. Aragis did know that—or had known it some years before. But Aragis had also seen Gerin cozen Mavrix into doing what the Fox wanted him to do. He might well reckon that meant man and god had patched things up. With luck, the prospect—even if it wasn't a true prospect—of facing an irate god would give even the Archer pause.

The prospect of facing an irate god had given Gerin pause several times. That didn't mean he hadn't done it. It didn't mean he hadn't got away with it, either. He had no reason to assume Aragis couldn't get away with it, too. He wished he did have such a reason.

"Try to make Aragis see that I don't want this war, will you?" the Fox persisted. "If I did want it, I'd hold you here, and the first thing Aragis would know was that my men were coming over the border at him."

"As I say, lord king, I'll pass on everything you say to me," Marlanz replied. "I don't think it will do much good, as I told you before. King Aragis will answer that it only means you don't want war now, right this minute, not that you don't want war at all." He sat a little straighter, a little more defiantly. "Can you tell me my king would be wrong?"

"Yes," Gerin said. "If I'd wanted war, I could have had it whenever I chose, and I've never chosen war with Aragis, not down through these past twenty years." He sighed; he was blessed—or perhaps cursed—with the ability to see the other fellow's point of view. "And he'll say the only reason I didn't do it was because I wasn't ready all this time, and now I finally am." He felt tired. "Go on home, Marlanz. Pretty soon Aragis and I can try killing each other, and then we'll find out who's better at that."

The warriors who had accompanied Aragis' envoy up to Fox Keep had their chariots ready for the return journey. Gerin's resignation to the prospect of war ahead seemed to reach Marlanz where his earlier denials had been brushed aside. As Marlanz stepped up into his car, he spoke urgently: "I'll urge him to hold the peace— by Father Dyaus, I swear it. Whether he listens to me . . ."

"If he doesn't listen to you, maybe he'll listen to edged bronze." Gerin waved to the gate crew. "Let down the drawbridge." The men in the gatehouse turned the capstan. Bronze chain rattled out, a link at a time. Down went the bridge. The Fox waved again, this time to Marlanz Raw-Meat.

Marlanz looked to be on the point of saying something more. Instead, he bowed stiffly and tapped his driver on the shoulder. The fellow flicked the reins. The horses got moving. The chariot's axle squeaked as it began to roll. The other car, the one with a crew of warriors, followed. Horses' hooves thundered and wheels boomed on the drawbridge. Marlanz was still peering back over his shoulder at the Fox when his driver swung south and took the car out of the narrow line of sight the gate offered.

Gerin could have mounted to the palisade and watched Marlanz till he was out of sight, but what point to that? He went back into the great hall and called for ale instead. Carlun Vepin's son sat in there, cutting a length of sausage into identical bite-sized chunks before he ate them. He looked up from that fussily precise task and said, "There will be war then, lord king?"

"I'm afraid there will," Gerin answered. "I don't see how I can turn Balser down. Evidently Aragis doesn't see how he can let me accept Balser's vassalage. If that's not a recipe for war, I don't know what is."

Carlun stabbed one of those chunks of sausage with the knife he'd used to cut it. He brought it up to his mouth, chewed, swallowed. Only then did he deliver his verdict: "It will be expensive."

"Thanks so much—I hadn't realized that," Gerin snapped. The steward choked on another bite of sausage; he'd always been vulnerable to sarcasm. Gerin slapped him on the back. "Steady there—expensive, yes; fatal, no."

"I suppose not, lord king," Carlun said. "Nothing else

you've undertaken has been fatal—though the gods can drop me in the hottest of the five hells if I understand why not." He cocked his head to one side. "Maybe it's magic."

Gerin turned his most enigmatic stare on the steward. "Maybe it is," he answered, which made Carlun look nervous. Gerin had studied sorcery down in the City of Elabon before the Elabonian Empire severed itself from its fractious northern province. He'd had to return to the northlands with his magical studies, like all the rest, incomplete: the Trokmoi had slain his father and brother, leaving him baron, a job he'd wanted about as much as a longtooth wanted an aching fang.

Despite insatiable curiosity, he hadn't intended to practice much sorcery after coming back to the north. The only thing more dangerous, commonly to himself, than a half-trained mage was . . . The Fox backed up and started that thought again, because he couldn't think of anything more dangerous than a half-trained mage.

That didn't mean he hadn't practiced magic every now and again. *Amazing what desperation will do*, he thought. When faced with a Trokmê wizard bent on destroying him for a fancied slight, or with the eruption of the monsters from under Biton's temple down at Ikos, or with the invasion of the Gradi and their ferocious gods, the risks of sorcery suddenly seemed smaller.

He hadn't killed himself yet. That was the most he could say for his sorcery. After a moment, he shook his head, rejecting false modesty. In hair-raising fashion, the magic had done what he'd wanted it to do. Balamung the Trokmê mage was destroyed, the monsters—except Geroge and Tharma—were made to return to their gloomy caverns, the Gradi were pinned back to a single castle at the edge of the ocean.

And because Gerin hadn't killed himself once—*though*

not for lack of effort, he thought—both his friends and his foes had conceived the notion that he really was a formidable wizard in his own right. So long as he didn't conceive the same foolish notion and try to act on it, he figured he'd be fine. Thinking he had a true sorcerous talent also made people think twice about crossing him.

As now: Carlun said, "Then I will prepare for war sure everything will turn out right, even if I don't see how."

That went too far. Gerin shook his head again. "Prepare as if you think everything will go wrong. In your mind, make things look as black as you can. Figure out how we'd come through that. Than, when something works out better than you expect—if anything works out better than you expect," he added from the depths of a deeply pessimistic nature, "you can take it as a bonus."

"I understand, lord king." Carlun hesitated, then said, "Forgive me, lord king, but in a lot of ways you think more like a serf than how I thought a noble would think. I always thought nobles had so much, they never needed to worry about what to do when things go wrong."

"Only goes to show you were born a serf and not a noble," Gerin answered. "The only people without worries are the dead ones and the ones who haven't been born yet. Nobles don't worry about their overlords' taking too much of the harvest away and making them starve, they worry about their neighbors' taking their lands away and killing them. Comes out about the same in the end, I'd say."

"Maybe so," Carlun said, "but nobles press on peasants all the time, and on their neighbors only now and again."

"Nobles in my domain had better not press on peasants all the time, or on their neighbors, either," Gerin said. But he understood what Carlun meant: that was how things commonly worked in the northlands, and how they had worked for generations. He wondered if he ought to despair when his own steward seemed to think the changes he was making were anomalies that wouldn't last.

He got no time to contemplate that gloomy notion, which might have been just as well: Herris Bigfoot, the headman of the peasant village close by Fox Keep, came running into the great hall, crying, "Lord king! Lord king! Come quick, lord king! Ferdulf's at it again."

"Hullo, Herris," said Carlun, who was the headman's brother-in-law.

"Hullo." Herris grudged his kinsman by marriage the one word, but then gave his attention back to the Fox. "Will you come, lord king?"

Gerin had already risen to his feet. "I'm coming, Herris, though by all the gods I'm not certain what I can do to rein in Ferdulf that you couldn't manage for yourself."

"But, lord king, that's your job," Herris said.

The Fox sighed. It *was* his job, which didn't mean he relished it. How was he supposed to impose his will on a four-year-old demigod? Rather more to the point, how was he supposed to do it without regretting it afterwards? In weary resignation, he asked, "What's he gone and done this time?"

"Uh, lord king, you'd better come see for yourself," the headman answered.

People had been saying that about Ferdulf since the day he was born. He'd spoken to the midwife while she was cutting the cord that had linked him to his mother. He'd greeted Gerin when the Fox came down to the village to see what Mavrix had begotten on Fulda. And he'd only become more alarming since, as his power had grown with his body.

Out of Fox Keep and over the drawbridge strode Herris and Gerin. The village was only a short walk south of the keep. The peasants lived in thatch-roofed huts of wattle and daub. Smoke issued from the holes in the center of several of those roofs: women cooking, no doubt. Other women were working in the vegetable gardens by the huts or feeding the chickens that ran around as if they thought the place belonged to them, not to the Fox.

Most of the men were away from the village, either tending to cattle and sheep or weeding in the fields of growing wheat and barley. Gerin didn't notice any signs of unusual chaos, which wasn't always the case when Ferdulf got into mischief. He noticed as much, with something approaching hope in his voice.

"You'll find out, lord king," Herris Bigfoot said.

He led the Fox toward Fulda's hut. Before they got there, Fulda came outside. She might well have been the best-looking young woman in the village; the long tunic she wore lessened but could not hide the impact of her figure. Rihwin the Fox had chosen her at Gerin's urging, to help attract Mavrix to Fox Keep to fight the Gradi gods; after failing in that fight, Mavrix himself had chosen to impregnate her.

"Lord king," she said now, "I'm sure he didn't mean it."

When that phrase got stuck to the mischief of an ordinary small boy, it meant said mischief was worse than it had any business being. When it was applied to the mischief of a small demigod . . . "What's he gone and done now?" Gerin asked, not sure he wanted to find out. No, that wasn't true. He did want to find out. He wished he didn't have to find out.

"You'd better see for yourself," Herris and Fulda said in the same breath. They looked at each other and laughed. The headman's eyes lingered on Fulda. Any man's eyes had a way of lingering on Fulda. Seeing that, Gerin thought it was liable to cause trouble one of these days. It would, however, be trouble of an ordinary sort, trouble he'd seen many times before, trouble he knew how to handle. The kind of trouble Ferdulf caused was something else again.

"What's he gone and done?" the Fox repeated.

"He was playing in the mud by the pond, and he—" Fulda began. She gave up. Her shrug was magnificent. "You'd better see for yourself," Herris said again.

Gerin loudly exhaled through his nose. Spinning on his heel, he stalked off toward the pond close by the village. Herris and Fulda hurried after him, both expostulating. None of the expostulations made much sense. That didn't surprise him; had things made sense to the villagers, they wouldn't have needed him to straighten them out.

He strode past the last hut. There was the pond: not much of a pond, perhaps, to a connoisseur of such, but enough. Ducks swam in it. In the mud by its edge, the village pigs wallowed. Their happy grunting filled the Fox's ears, much as the gabble from Herris and Fulda had done not long before. But not all of that grunting came from the edge of the pond, nor were all the quacks that punctuated it from ducks on the water.

After a second, more careful, look at the peaceful scene ahead, Gerin turned back to the village headman and the demigod's mother. "I owe you an apology," he said, not a common admission for a lord to make to a couple of serfs.

"What are we going to do, lord king?" Herris Bigfoot demanded.

"I—don't—know." Gerin stared out at the pond. Most of the ducks there were of the ordinary sort, the males with shiny green heads, the females drab and brown all over. A couple of them, though . . .

A couple of them, Gerin's eyes confirmed, were ducks

only from the neck down. From the neck up, they were pigs. Because their heads were smaller than they had any natural business being, the grunts those heads admitted sounded strange, but they were undoubtedly piggy grunts.

And, sure enough, one of the piggy bodies by the pond sported an outsized green head with a flat bill, and another a head similar but brown. *Neither pork nor fowl*, the Fox thought dazedly.

"What are we going to do?" It seemed to be the sort of day where everyone repeated himself: Herris' turn again.

"I don't know." Gerin was echoing his own words, too. Then he found something new to add: "Hope they breed true, maybe."

Herris and Fulda both stared at him. He'd succeeded in startling them, anyhow. Well, they—and Ferdulf— had succeeded in startling him, too. Suddenly, the village headman started to laugh. "I wonder if they'll lay eggs or have live young," he said.

Fulda voiced a more immediately pragmatic consideration: "I wonder what they'd taste like."

Gerin tried to imagine a flavor halfway between duck and pork. His stomach rumbled; he didn't know whether his imagination was accurate, but it was vivid enough to make him hungry. He said, "If you find out what they taste like now, you won't find out later whether they lay eggs or not."

"You're right, lord king." Fulda didn't seem to have thought so far ahead.

But Herris Bigfoot said, "Lord king, what will you do to Ferdulf on account of this? Even if he is a god's son, he's got no business changing things around so. What if he starts putting the wrong heads on people next?"

"A lot of people are wrongheaded enough without

getting switched around," Gerin said. But that was a quip, not an answer. Knowing it was necessary, the Fox went on, "I'll have a word with him." *And what if he decides to put the wrong head on* me? There was a thought the Fox wished he hadn't had. Pretending— most of all to himself—it had never crossed his mind, he turned to Fulda. "Is he back at your house?"

"Yes, lord king," she said. She hesitated, torn between a mother's love for her child and the certain knowledge the child she had borne to Mavrix was not of the ordinary sort. "Whatever you do, lord king, be careful."

That was good advice. It was such good advice, in fact, that Gerin wished his career had given him more chances to take it. As things had worked out for him, though, had he been careful, he probably would have been dead several times over.

He started back toward the hut where Fulda lived. She and Herris trailed after him. He discovered Ferdulf had come out while he was staring at the pigducks in the pond and the duckpigs by it. Ferdulf was whacking at something in the grass with a stick, for all the world like any other four-year-old. But he was not any other four-year-old. He looked up at Gerin and spoke in his mellow baritone: "I wonder how *you'd* look with a big green duck's head." He frowned in concentration.

Nothing happened, for which the Fox was duly grateful. "Probably pretty silly," he replied after considering. He refused to let Ferdulf put him in fear—or rather, he refused to let Ferdulf see he put him in fear. In the same mild, thoughtful tones he'd just used, he went on, "I wonder how you'd look with your backside all red and sore."

"You wouldn't dare," Ferdulf said. "You know whose son I am."

Gerin did know, only too well. "I've spanked you before, when you earned it," he answered, which was also true. He didn't tell Ferdulf he'd gone back to Fox Keep and got drunk afterwards, to celebrate surviving the experience.

Ferdulf frowned. "I was littler then. I didn't know all the things I could do."

"Just because you *can* do something doesn't mean you *should* do it," Gerin said. If Ferdulf thought he was coming into his full powers at four, what would he be like at fourteen? At thirty-four? The Fox did his best not to think about that. He also did his best not to think about how unlikely it was for Mavrix's get to understand what restraint meant.

"Why not?" Ferdulf asked with what sounded like genuine curiosity. Sure enough, he didn't understand Gerin's point.

Patiently, Gerin explained, "Because some of the things you can do either frighten people or make them unhappy."

"So what?" Yes, Ferdulf was Mavrix's son, all right.

"How do you like it when someone frightens you or makes you unhappy?" Gerin asked.

"You're about the only one who ever tries to do anything like that," Ferdulf answered. He looked thoughtful. "I wonder if I could stop you."

The Fox felt fingers prying in his mind: that was how he recalled the sensation later, at any rate. It showed him that Ferdulf, however strong he was by merely mortal standards, was weak by those of the gods—Mavrix had rummaged through Gerin's thoughts and memories like a man going through a beltpouch in search of a pin.

"Stop that!" the Fox said, and tightened his mental muscles. He wasn't sure that would do any good, but had no intention of yielding to the little demigod without first putting up whatever fight he could.

Ferdulf looked astonished, as he usually did when things failed to go as he'd thought they would. "How are you doing that?" he demanded. "You're supposed to be thinking about what *I* want you to think about, not what you want to think about." By his tone, that latter wasn't worth contemplating.

Those probing mental fingers groped harder. Gerin grunted. Ferdulf had told him his resistance had some success (something an older, wiser foe would have known better than to do), so he kept on resisting, as the palisade to Fox Keep had withstood a Trokmê siege.

He got the feeling resistance wasn't enough, not by itself. "Here," he said. "You're going to think about what I want *you* to think about." He couldn't reach out and touch Ferdulf's mind, not directly. But there were other ways of gaining the demigod's attention. Gerin grabbed Ferdulf and flipped him over his knee.

Ferdulf let out a squeal of pure outrage. "I said you wouldn't dare!" he cried. The probing fingers vanished from Gerin's mind. If nothing else, the Fox had managed to distract him.

"Just because you said it doesn't make it so." Not without a certain amount of trepidation, Gerin brought down the hand that wasn't restraining Ferdulf.

The demigod's howl was quite satisfactory. Ferdulf tried to rise straight up into the air, as he had while playing at Fox Keep. He did rise, too, but not very far, not with the Fox holding onto him.

"Have I got your attention yet?" Gerin asked. Even with his feet off the ground, he retained enough presence of mind to administer another dose of the medicine he had chosen. "Why don't you put us both down, and we can talk about it some more instead of fighting?"

"Oh, very well." Ferdulf's petulant tones were an echo of those Mavrix used when, as did happen once in a while, the Sithonian god was compelled to change his ways.

"Thank you," Gerin said, most sincerely, when his feet touched the ground again.

"You're welcome," Ferdulf answered, an unexpected bit of politeness he must have acquired from his mother. He gave the Fox a dirty look. "Why are you so much harder to change than pigs and ducks?"

As the implications of that sank in, Herris Bigfoot and Fulda gasped. Gerin gulped. Ferdulf *had* been trying to give him a duck's head, then. "I don't know why," he said. "I'm just glad I am. And I want you to remember I am. The next time you try to change me— or anything else—you're going to be in trouble. Have you got that?"

"Yes, I've got it." Ferdulf didn't look happy about it, either, which was a long way from breaking Gerin's heart. The little demigod glared up at him. "How come you get to tell me what to do, when you're only a mortal?"

"Why?" The Fox considered that. "I can think of a couple of reasons. One is, I may be just a mortal, but I've been around a lot longer than you have. I know more about the world than you do."

The first of those statements was undoubtedly true. The second would undoubtedly have been true were Ferdulf an ordinary four-year old. Were Ferdulf an ordinary four-year-old, though, he wouldn't have tried flying off with the Fox, and he wouldn't have tried decorating him with a mallard's head, either.

Whatever else Ferdulf was, he wasn't trained to catch logical flaws. He accepted what the Fox told him more readily than Gerin would have. "That's one," he said. "What's two?"

"Two is very simple," Gerin answered. "I just showed you I'm strong enough to do it, didn't I?"

Besides being Aragis' argument over Balser's allegiance, that also had its logical flaws. How long would Gerin go on being stronger than Ferdulf? What would happen when he wasn't stronger any more? Gerin didn't know the answers to those questions. He could think of things liable to be more pleasant than discovering what those answers were.

But Ferdulf, though a demigod, was a four-year-old demigod. As with any other four-year-old, things as they were now seemed close to the way they would be forever. "Yes, you're stronger," he said, angry resignation in his voice. "But not everybody is."

If that aside didn't want to make Herris, and maybe Fulda, too, run somewhere far, far away, maybe it should have. Gerin carefully chose a different issue. "I'm not the only one who's stronger than you, Ferdulf. What about Selatre, my wife?" Despite her disclaimer to Marlanz, Ferdulf had been known to heed what she said.

"That's not fair!" he exclaimed now. "The god she knows still keeps an eye on her, and my father won't pay any attention to me."

"You can tell that farseeing Biton still holds Selatre in his mind?" Gerin asked.

"Of course," Ferdulf said. "Can't you?"

He didn't altogether grasp how limited the ordinary human sensorium was. He'd also said something else interesting, though he probably didn't know it. So Mavrix was less than attentive to his offspring, was he? That didn't surprise Gerin, though he hadn't known it before. A god of unbridled fertility didn't strike the Fox as likely to make the most devoted parent for any one child.

"Will you behave yourself?" he demanded of the little demigod.

"I suppose so," Ferdulf answered.

"No more pigducks or duckpigs?" Gerin said. Having Dagref in his household, he'd learned better than to leave loopholes open: "And no more mixing any other creatures—or people—together, all right?"

"All right," Ferdulf said, not too much sulk in his voice. Gerin didn't trust his promise very far, but didn't altogether discount it, either. From what he'd seen of Ferdulf, the promise was worth about as much—and as little—as that of any other child of the same age. Sooner or later, the demigod would forget he'd made it and do something else appalling. That was how children behaved, even children of large powers. But the Fox didn't think Ferdulf would go out and deliberately break his word.

"Fair enough," he said. "We have a bargain, then." Ferdulf nodded and went off to play. Gerin didn't think he walked a couple of feet off the ground intending to intimidate. More likely, he just wasn't thinking about what he was doing.

Herris Bigfoot, by now, took such minor impossibilities in stride. He said, "Thank you, lord king. We are grateful to you, believe me, for keeping him under what control you do."

Gerin looked him straight in the eye. "Quack," he answered seriously. "Quack, quack, quack." Herris looked horrified. Fulda gasped in dismay. Gerin let both of them stew for a moment, then started to laugh.

"That wasn't nice, lord king," Fulda said, sounding more sorrowful than angry.

He thought about it. When Ferdulf terrorized the villagers, he didn't know any better. Gerin did. "You're right, of course," he told Fulda. "I shouldn't have done it. I'm sorry."

If anything, the apology—the second in the space of

a few minutes—disconcerted her more than the quacks had. "You're the king," she blurted. "You don't have to say you're sorry to the likes of me."

He shook his head. "No, you're wrong. It's Aragis who never needs to say he's sorry. That's the difference between us, right there." Fulda didn't understand. He hadn't expected she would.

II

"Who comes to Fox Keep?" called the sentry up on the palisade.

"I am Balser Debo's son," came the reply from the chariot outside the keep. "I am here to give homage and fealty to Gerin the Fox, the king of the north, to acknowledge him as my suzerain and overlord of my barony."

The sentry whirled to see where Gerin was. As it happened, he was standing in the courtyard not far away. "Did you hear that, lord king?" he exclaimed, his voice going high and shrill with excitement. "Did you hear that?"

"I heard it," the Fox answered. He'd been waiting for this moment for some time, waiting for it and at the same time half hoping—maybe more than half hoping—it would not come. Now that it was here, though, he would have to make the most of it. He raised his voice: "Balser Debo's son is welcome at Fox Keep. Let him enter!"

Bronze chain clattered as the gate crew lowered the drawbridge. Balser's chariot rolled into the courtyard. The driver reined in the fine two-horse team. Balser got down from the car and walked over to the Fox. He was a young man, dark, slim, not very tall but well put together, who wore his beard in the forked style that had long been out of date but was suddenly all the rage again.

Like the first stone sliding down a mountain to start an avalanche (Gerin remembered how the Elabonian Empire had blocked the last pass through the High Kirs with just such an avalanche, leaving the northlands to their own devices when the Trokmoi invaded), Balser was going to cause a lot more trouble than he ever could have accounted for by himself. His coming here, in fact, was no doubt the beginning of the rockslide.

Well, no help for it. Gerin hurried to meet him halfway. The two men clasped hands. "I greet you, Balser Debo's son," the Fox said as his men gathered to watch the drama unfold. "Use my keep as your own as long as you are here."

"I thank you, lord king," Balser replied. "If you should ever come south, my keep is likewise yours."

Gerin nodded. He was glad to make a new guest-friend. Webs of host and guest, guest and host, each bound by the sacred ties of friendship to do no harm to the other, stretched across the northlands. Without them, feuds among barons would have been even worse than they were.

But Balser had not traveled here to become a guest-friend, however pleasing that might have been for the southern baron. "You're certain you want to become my vassal?" Gerin said. "You don't care to stay your own lord, as your father and grandfather were before you?"

"My father and grandfather never had to worry about Aragis the Archer." Balser sent Gerin a curious look. "Is it that you don't want my vassalage, lord king? That's not what you gave me to understand before."

"No. It isn't that. Aragis has threatened you. Aragis has tried to scare you out of your breeches, as a matter of fact." The breeches in question were dyed in bright checks of maroon and yellow, a Trokmê mode that had grown fashionable among men of Elabonian blood, too. Scaring Balser out of them would, in Gerin's opinion, have improved his wardrobe. That, however, was not of the essence. "I don't blame you for wanting me to protect you from him, and I'll do just that."

"The gods be praised—and you, too, lord king, for your generosity," Balser said. "That's exactly what I want. I'm not strong enough to hold him off on my own— he's shown me that. You let your vassals remember they're men; I'd sooner go with you than have him swallow me down."

"For which I thank you." The Fox didn't want to thank Balser, not really. He wanted to kick him. He wanted to kick Aragis, too, for frightening Balser into his own arms. He wanted to kick Aragis for being too arrogant to blame himself for frightening Balser, too. Had Aragis shown only a little more restraint, Balser would have stayed neutral.

But the only man in all the northlands who had ever made the Archer show restraint was Gerin. Precisely because Gerin worried him, he could not bear to have the Fox ruling Balser's barony, which lay close to his own. Another round of war was the last thing Gerin wanted, but that had nothing to do with anything. War had come up to Fox Keep, riding in Balser's chariot.

Balser's name had brought Van and Rihwin out of Castle Fox—and Selatre, too, a few paces behind them. Gerin didn't know where Dagref materialized from: one moment, he wasn't anywhere to be seen, but he stood at his father's elbow the next. Van's daughter Maeva had a quiver on her back and a bow in her hand; she must have been practicing her shooting. Unlike Dagref, she hung back a little from her elders. But Balser's name drew her, too— she knew it meant fighting, and that was what she wanted.

As the crowd grew, Balser said, "I'll do it here and now if you like, lord king. We seem to have enough witnesses."

"Oh, indeed," the Fox said. "It's getting anything done without witnesses that's hard around here." Geroge and Tharma came ambling around the corner of the castle. Gerin didn't think Balser's name had attracted them. But, when they saw people gathering, they hurried up to find out what was going on. They were people, too— or they were convinced they were.

Balser didn't look so sure. "Lord king, I'd heard you kept a couple of those monsters at your keep, but I hadn't believed it."

"You may as well, because it's true. I'm quite fond of them, as a matter of fact." Gerin offered no compromise there whatever. If Balser didn't like it, he could go back to his barony. That would disappoint Maeva, who wanted a war, but not the Fox, who didn't.

But Balser showed no signs of packing up and leaving. "Are they your vassals, too?" he asked. "I do like to know the company I'm keeping."

One of Gerin's eyebrows rose at that display of sangfroid. "Stepchildren, more like," he answered, and had the satisfaction of startling Balser in return.

"Why is everybody standing here?" Geroge asked. He pointed at Balser with a clawed index finger. "And who is this strange gentleman?"

Hearing him speak and make good sense startled Balser again. The baron could have remarked on Geroge's being a strange gentleman himself. Gerin gave him points because he didn't. Instead, he answered the question seriously: "I am Balser Debo's son, and I have come to give homage and fealty to your . . . stepfather."

Geroge and Tharma both clapped their large, hairy hands together. "Oh, good!" they said.

Seeing that everyone who dwelt at Fox Keep took the monsters for granted helped Balser do the same. He turned back to Gerin, saying, "Where were we, lord king?" He answered his own question by going to one knee before the Fox.

Rihwin coughed and said, "Meaning no offense, son of Debo, but the ritual of offering submission to the king, he being of rank superior to that enjoyed by other sorts of overlords, requires the vassal to rest both knees on the ground."

Gerin hadn't intended to make an issue of it. As far as he was concerned, one knee would have been as binding as two. Balser, fortunately, didn't seem inclined to make an issue of it, either. "Very well," he said, and went from one knee to two, at the same time offering his hands to Gerin, palms pressed together. The Fox enclosed Balser's hands with his own. Balser gave him homage: "I, Balser Debo's son, own myself to be your vassal, Gerin the Fox, King of the North, and give you the whole of my faith against all men who might live or die."

"I, Gerin, King of the North, accept your homage, Balser Debo's son, and pledge in my turn always to use you justly. In token of which, I raise you up now." The Fox pulled Balser to his feet and kissed him on the cheek, sealing the ceremony of homage.

"By Dyaus the father of all and the other gods of Elabon, I swear my fealty to you, lord king," Balser said with a bow.

Gerin bowed to him in turn. "By Dyaus the father of all and the other gods of Elabon, I accept your oath and swear to reward your loyalty with my own."

"I am your man, lord king," Balser said: not a formal part of the ceremony, but a truth nonetheless.

"So you are," Gerin said. "We'll feast tonight to

celebrate"—not that he felt much like celebrating—"and then tomorrow I'll send out messengers to some of my other vassals, telling them your lands need protecting against Aragis. I want warriors down there as fast as may be."

Balser looked less than delighted at that prospect, but in the end nodded. He seemed to be realizing for the first time what all having an overlord entailed. Gerin's men were going to be overrunning his holding, and he couldn't do anything about it. They wouldn't burn and loot and kill, as Aragis men would have done (at least not to anywhere near the same degree), but they would be there, and the holding would no longer be his in the sense it had been for so long.

And, of course, the presence of the Fox's men in Balser's holding was liable to bring Aragis' army over the border, in which case the Archer's men would do the burning and looting and killing Balser had come to Gerin to prevent. The Fox thought he saw the moment in which Balser figured that out, too. His new vassal wasn't so good as he might have been at holding his face straight.

"Second thoughts?" Gerin asked him.

"Some," Balser answered, which bespoke a certain basic honesty. "I couldn't go it alone any more, and I couldn't stomach bending the knee—bending both knees—to Aragis. That left bending the knee—the knees—to you."

"For which ringing endorsement I thank you," Gerin said. Balser's worried expression made him hold up a hand. "Don't fret. You haven't offended me. You knew what you were doing and why you were doing it. That's more than a lot of people ever manage. Now come on." He waved Balser toward Castle Fox. "We'll enjoy ourselves for the time being, and then—"

Van broke in from the crowd of onlookers: "—And then we'll go off and fight ourselves one bloody big war."

He didn't sound so eager as he would have in his younger days, but he did sound very sure. No one who heard him claimed he was wrong, either.

Gerin shouted for ale, and ordered an ox slain. Carlun Vepin's son grimaced at that. Gerin took no notice of him, telling the cooks, "Lay the fat-wrapped thighbones on Dyaus' altar and set them afire, so the smoke will rise up to heaven and the Allfather will favor what Balser and I have done today." Actually, by everything he'd seen, by everything other gods had told him, Dyaus hardly bothered noticing what went on in the material world. Gerin shrugged. He still had to make the effort.

Fand came downstairs to see what the commotion in the great hall was about: a big, rawboned Trokmê woman, still more than handsome though gray streaked her once-fiery hair. She carried a couple of pieces of cloth she'd been sewing into a tunic and a long bone needle.

She'd heard Van's last remark. "Go off and fight a war, will you now?" she said, advancing on him. "Leave me behind, will you now?"

The outlander scowled. "I will," he rumbled, and pointed to the needle. "There's a weapon for piercing cloth, not flesh."

Fand scowled right back at him. "You've got a weapon in your breeches for piercing flesh," she jeered, "and better nor half the reason you're so wild for going off to battle is that along the way you find some pretty young things to stick it into, girls who aren't after hearing your lies a thousand times, the way I have."

"Better than half the reason I'm wild to go off to battle is that you aren't carping and cawing at me while I'm away," Van retorted.

Fand shouted at him again. He shouted back. Each one's opening shot had made the other angrier, no doubt because both contained a painful amount of truth. Gerin eyed with some concern the needle Fand was holding. She'd stabbed a Trokmê lover before she turned up at Fox Keep. She and Van occasionally quarreled with more than words, but neither of them had ever seriously damaged the other. The Fox wanted that to stay true.

Balser glanced over at him. "They must care for each other," Gerin's new vassal remarked, "else they'd try and kill each other over some of the things they're saying."

That marched very well with Gerin's own thoughts. "Some people enjoy quarreling," he said. "I've never seen the sport in it myself."

In the midst of her own tirade, Fand heard his quiet comment. She spun away from Van and toward him. "Sure and I'm not quarreling for nobbut the sport of it, lord king Gerin the Fox." She loaded his title and name with the familiar scorn that could only have come from a former lover. Pointing at Van, she went on, "I'm quarreling for that he willna keep his trousers on the instant he's out of my sight."

"Am I the only one?" Van shouted. "By the gods, it's hardly better than luck my children look like me."

Instead of coming to blows, they went upstairs a few minutes later. Gerin breathed a silent sigh of relief. He'd seen them do that a good many times before, too. They found being angry added spice to their lovemaking. That bemused the Fox, too. It wasn't the way he worked.

Rihwin the Fox said, "As a calm descends over the battlefield . . ." He winked.

"If you had a wife, she'd be after you the same way," Gerin said.

"Without a doubt, you have reason, lord king." Rihwin gave a bow that was only slightly mocking. "Therefore I was wise enough never to wed."

"Therefore you've got bastards in half the peasant villages in my domain," Gerin said, which was also true.

"I am not a eunuch," Rihwin said with dignity, "and I do all I can for my byblows." Gerin had to nod. Rihwin was erratic and extravagant, but not badhearted.

"Never a dull moment around these parts, is there?" Balser Debo's son was looking a trifle walleyed, as if he hadn't expected anything like the turbulent stir of personalities he'd found at Fox Keep. Maybe he was having more second thoughts about becoming Gerin's vassal. Too late now.

In all seriousness, Gerin replied, "I do keep trying for them, but I haven't had much luck." Balser laughed, wrongly thinking he'd made a joke.

Riders went out of Fox Keep the next morning to summon Gerin's vassals to bring their retainers to his holding for the likely campaign against Aragis. "So many men climbing up on horses' backs," Balser said, as bemused by the show of equitation as by what had gone on in the great hall the night before (which, to the Fox's way of thinking, had been on the mild side). "Always something new here, eh, lord king?"

"I hope so," Gerin answered. That, he saw, startled Balser anew. He went on, "Don't you think life would get dull if we kept doing the same things the same old way forever, the more so as a lot of those old ways don't work as well as they might?"

Balser plainly hadn't thought about it at all. As plainly, he would have been quite happy to go on not thinking about it at all, and to see the same old ways go on forever if he could. Most people were like that, as Gerin had discovered to his continued disappointment.

"About this business of horseriding," Balser said, "we don't hardly see it down in my part of the northlands." He'd steered clear of openly arguing with his new overlord, and was turning the conversation back toward the comment he'd made first: not a bad performance, Gerin thought. Aloud, he said, "It's been more than twenty years now since one of my vassals, Duin the Bold, came up with those footmounts—*stirrups*, we call 'em— that let a man stay mounted while he uses both hands for archery, and let him charge home with a spear without having to worry about going back over the horse's tail the instant he strikes home. We had good luck using mounted men against the Gradi; I think the chariot is on the way out."

"For traveling, I can see that it might be," Balser said. "Easier to ride than to harness up a car every day, and you don't have to worry about your axle or your wheels breaking, either." Suddenly seeming to realize what he'd said, he scratched his head. "I've just spoken well of the new, haven't I?"

"I'll not tell if you don't," Gerin said solemnly.

"That's a bargain." Balser laughed, but then held up a hand. "I don't speak well of everything new, mind you. Are you saying riders will take the place of chariots in war, too? I have trouble believing that. A man on horseback isn't nearly so frightening to his foes as a chariot thundering down on them."

"Maybe not," Gerin said, "but riders can go places chariots can't, and can fight on ground that would have chariots tipping over. And with chariots, remember, your driver has to tend to the horses. He can't do much fighting. With men on horseback, you're not wasting one in three."

"But every rider has to tend to his horse," Balser returned. "I don't see that the gain's worth it."

"One way or the other, we'll find out," Gerin said. "There will be a lot of chariotry in the force I bring down to defend your land—there'll have to be, because a lot of my vassals don't like the idea of riding any better than you do. I'll have a good many horsemen along, too, though, and we'll see how they fare against Aragis' chariots. They gave the Gradi plenty of trouble, as I've said, but the Gradi fight on foot. This will be a different test."

"A . . . test?" Balser Debo's son tasted the words: a fitting comparison, for he went on, "You sound as if you're trying out different ways of brewing ale."

"As a matter of fact, Adiatunnus the Trokmê gave me one, not so long ago," Gerin answered. "His people have taken to roasting the barley malt almost to the point where it's burnt. I'd lay long odds they did it by accident the first time, but it makes a pretty good brew: black as rich earth and full of flavor."

Balser threw his hands in the air. "I might have known you'd have something of the sort to tell me," he exclaimed, and then looked at the Fox from under lowered eyelids. "You haven't given me any of this funny black ale."

"I don't like to spring it on people as a surprise," Gerin said. "It does take a bit of getting used to, or so most folk find. But if you're game for something new, I have a few jars down in the cellar."

Balser was more willing to contemplate novelty in ale than he was in ways of fighting. After he'd downed a jack of the Trokmê-style brew, he smacked his lips a couple of times and said, "That's not too bad. I don't think I'd care to drink it all the time, but for now and again it'd be fine. It'd go right well with blood sausage, I'd say."

"Now that you mention it, it does," Gerin said, and called for some to prove the point. While they were eating, he went on, "You ask me, the more choices you have in anything, the better. If you're bedding a woman, for instance, you don't want to just climb on top and pound away all the time."

Balser looked as astonished as he had at the idea of fighting from horseback rather than in a chariot. "What other way is there?" he demanded.

Gerin spent a moment silently pitying his new vassal's wife, if Balser had one. But then, the Fox, while a student down in the City of Elabon, had become acquainted with a scroll that got copied and recopied as it passed from hand to hand and from generation to generation. The text had been educational, the illustrations even more so.

He didn't go into great detail. The more he talked, though, the wider Balser's eyes got. Balser could see possibilities if you pointed them out to him. "Lord king," he burst out, "I'd've become your vassal for this all by its lonesome—to the five hells with anything else."

"I never thought of getting vassals like *that*," the Fox said with a laugh. "More flies end up stuck in honey than in vinegar, though, don't they? I wonder if Adiatunnus would have given me less trouble over the years if he'd spent more time figuring out all the different postures he could bend the Trokmê girls into."

Balser ran his tongue over his lips. "I'm from far enough south that I haven't had much dealing with the Trokmoi— or their women. Are the wenches as loose as I hear?"

"Well, no," Gerin answered, and Balser looked disappointed. The Fox went on, "Their ways are freer than ours. You'll never find a Trokmê who's shy about telling you what he—or she, very much *or she*—thinks. If they like you, you'll know about it. And if they don't like you, you'll know about that, too."

"Ah," Balser said. "Well, that's not too bad, I suppose." He was young enough, and of rank high enough, to assume that women *would* like him. Maybe he was even right. On the other hand, given how much he'd shown he didn't know, maybe he wasn't.

On the other hand . . . Gerin sighed. "On the other hand," he said, "there's Adiatunnus. He's as good at hiding what he thinks as any Elabonian ever born. He's learned from us, too, since he brought his band of woodsrunners south over the Niffet. If he hadn't had me for a neighbor, he might be the one styling himself king of the north these days."

"He sounds like trouble," Balser said. "You should have killed him."

"He is trouble," Gerin answered. "He *was* trouble, anyhow. I did try to kill him. It didn't work. If it hadn't been for the Gradi, I'd have tried again, and that probably wouldn't have worked, either. The past five years, he's been as good a vassal as a man could want. He even came to Fox Keep so I could teach him his letters."

"A woodsrunner?" Both Balser's eyebrows shot up. "Why on earth did he want to do that? I never felt the need myself."

"He's always thought we Elabonians were more civilized than his people, and so aped us, though he'd never own as much out loud," Gerin said. "I'll teach anyone who wants to learn. I don't mind having serfs able to read and write. For one thing, it makes keeping track of what they have and what they owe easier. For another, some of them are sharp—my steward used to be a serf, for instance."

"I've heard some things about that." Balser didn't say whether he thought those things good or bad.

Gerin didn't much care, one way or the other. He also wasn't quite ready to change the subject. "But I was talking about Adiatunnus. Trokmê or not, he never shows ahead of time how he'll jump. He's my biggest worry in going to war against Aragis, as a matter of fact."

"How's that, lord king?" Balser asked. "Afraid he'll jump you from behind?"

"That's just what I'm afraid of." The Fox looked at Balser with somber approval. The baron from the south might not think much of reading, but he was not a fool. "And that's why I'll be waiting and watching to see what he does now that I've asked him for men. If he gives me all I've asked for, well and good. If he comes himself at their head, better than well and good. If he sends me excuses instead of men . . . in that case, I have to leave more men behind myself."

"But then you won't be able to do a proper job of defending me!" Balser exclaimed.

"I won't be able to do a proper job of defending you if I'm fighting a big war up here, either," Gerin pointed out. He held out his hands as if they were the pans of a scale and moved them slowly up and down. "It's not a matter of doing all one thing or all the other. It's finding a proper balance between them."

Balser didn't say anything. The noise he made in the back of his throat, though, did not sound like agreement.

"Of course, we may be fretting over shadows," Gerin said. "It depends on Adiatunnus."

Balser made the same noise, rather louder.

By dribs and drabs, vassals started coming into Fox Keep. They slept in the rushes of the great hall, they slept in the courtyard, and, as the army grew, they began setting up tents on the meadow near the keep and sleeping there. Every time a new contingent arrived, Gerin would look delighted and Carlun Vepin's son appalled. The Fox thought of them as fighting men; to his steward, they were but extra mouths to be fed.

"I'll tell you what they are," Van said one day after a dozen or so warriors led by a young baron named Laufram the Lean stared in wonder at the nondescript keep of their overlord, and at the swelling host. "They're peculiar, that's what."

"How do you mean?" Gerin asked.

"I don't quite know," the outlander confessed. "But they're different from the way they used to be when I first came to Fox Keep."

"*We're* different from the way we used to be when you first came to Fox Keep," Gerin said. "We were young men ourselves then, or near enough."

Van shook his head. With some impatience, he answered, "I know that. It's not what I mean. I've taken it into account, or I think I have."

"All right." Gerin spread his hands. "But if that isn't what you mean, and you can't tell me what you mean, how am I supposed to make sense of it?"

Van shrugged a massive shrug and walked off muttering into his beard. A little while later, though, he came up to Gerin at a pounding trot. "I have it, Captain!" he said; he'd never called his friend *lord* or *lord prince* or *lord king*. "By all the gods, I have it!"

The Fox raised an eyebrow. "Do you suppose taking a physic will cure you of it?" When Van made as if to hit him, he laughed and said, "All right, you have it. Now that you have it, what is it?"

"It's this," the outlander said importantly: "Back in the old days, your vassal barons would just as soon spit in your eye as look at you. Is that so, or isn't it?"

"Oh, it's so, all right," Gerin agreed. "A lot of them had been used to dealing with my father. To them, I was nothing but a puppy sitting in the big dog's place. I had to prove I belonged there every day." The smile he wore was slightly twisted. Some of his memories of the early days after he took over the barony were fond ones, others anything but.

"That's right." Van's head bobbed up and down. "That's

exactly right. But these troopers coming in now, and the barons leading them, too—what do they treat you like? To the five hells with me if they don't treat you like a king."

Gerin thought about it. Then he too slowly nodded. "Maybe they do," he said. "The ones who are lordlets now are the sons and grandsons, most of them, of the lords who held those keeps back twenty-odd years ago. You and I, Van, we've outlived most of the men who started with us."

"We haven't outlived Aragis," Van said. "Not yet, anyway." His big fist folded around the hilt of his sword in grim anticipation.

"No, nor Adiatunnus, either." Gerin plucked at his beard. Outlasting the competition wasn't a very dramatic way of gaining the upper hand, but it worked. How many young men died long before they were able to show all they could do? How many times had he nearly died himself? More than he cared to think of, that was certain.

"Ah, Adiatunnus." Van spoke with a certain fond ferocity. Gerin often heard the same note in his own voice when he talked about the Trokmê chieftain. The outlander went on, "And what will you do if himself himself"—he put on a Trokmê lilt for a moment—"doesn't care to come when he's called, as a good vassal should?"

"Worry," the Fox answered, which made Van laugh. "It's not funny," Gerin insisted. "I was talking about this with Balser, too, and fretting over it before I talked with him. If Adiatunnus waits till I'm all tied up with Aragis and then rises against me . . . I don't think I'd enjoy that much."

"Neither would he, after you were through with him," Van said. Gerin thought that even his friends got the idea he could do more than he knew to be humanly possible. Van continued, "If he betrays you, you could loose the Gradi against him."

"Oh, now there's a fine notion!" Gerin exclaimed. "If you have a sore toe, take an axe and whack off your foot."

"Well, you could make him think you were going to do it," Van said.

And that, when you got down to it, wasn't the worst idea in the world. Ferocious as they were, the Trokmoi feared the Gradi, who had often beaten them in battle and whose gods had trounced their own. If they hadn't feared the Gradi so much, Adiatunnus would have gone to war against Gerin years before, instead of asking him for aid. Nevertheless—

"I hope I don't have to think about it," Gerin said. "I hope he shows up here with a whole great whacking unruly lot of Trokmoi in chariots." He laughed at himself. "And if I'd said anything like that a few years back, everyone would have been sure I was out of my mind."

"Don't you fret about it, Captain," Van reassured him. "Everyone was sure you were out of your mind anyhow."

"It's such ringing endorsements that have made me what I am today," the Fox said, "which is bloody fed up with people who use friendship as an excuse to insult me."

He did not intend to be taken seriously, and Van obliged him. "Don't fret about that, either. I'd insult you even if we weren't friends." Both men laughed.

Gerin laughed even more four days later, when Adiatunnus and a whole great whacking unruly lot of Trokmoi in chariots did show up at Fox Keep. He had all the relief off his face by the time the Trokmê chief swaggered over the drawbridge and into the courtyard.

Or so he thought, at any rate. After the bows and the handclasps were over, Adiatunnus tilted his head back to look down his long, thin nose at the Fox. He blew out a long breath through his luxuriant, drooping mustachios and said, "Sure and I'll wager you're not sorry to set eyes on me at all, at all."

"Well, if you're bright enough to see that, you're bright enough to see I'd be lying if I said anything else," Gerin answered. "You're not the sort of man I can take for granted, you know."

Adiatunnus preened. Like a lot of Trokmoi, he was vulnerable to flattery. But Gerin hadn't been lying, either. He would much sooner have had the woodsrunner under his eye than behind his back.

"So you're finally going after Aragis the Archer, are you now, lord king?" Adiatunnus said. "About time, says I. Past time, says I." His pale eyes gleamed in his knobby-cheekboned face. "For years I waited for the shindy 'twixt the two of you to start, so I could put paid to you once for all." He shook his big fist at Gerin in anger not altogether assumed. "And you, you kern—you wouldna fight him!"

"You were one of the reasons I never did," Gerin said, again truthfully. "I knew you'd land on my back if I got into it with Aragis—till you and I made peace with each other, that is." He said not a word about any worries he'd had on summoning Adiatunnus as a vassal this time. If the Trokmê chief didn't already have ideas in his head, the Fox had no intention of putting them there.

Adiatunnus, as it happened, already had them. "Oh, aye: I thought on doing it the now, but I held myself back, indeed and I did."

"That's . . . interesting." Gerin felt a drop of sweat slide down his back. "Why, if you don't mind my asking?"

"Not a bit," Adiatunnus answered. "Two reasons, in all. The first is, you came to my aid against the Gradi when you were right on the point o' going to war against

me instead. What a blackhearted spalpeen I'd be to forget
it."

"Well, by the gods!" the Fox exclaimed. "Gratitude's
not dead after all." He bowed to Adiatunnus. "Now you've
put me in your debt. But go on. Two reasons, you said,
and you gave only one. What's the other?"

The Trokmê scuffed his foot against the ground, more
like an abashed boy than a man who'd ably led his clan
for more than twenty years. "Sure and I'm shamed to
own it, but I'm shamed to lie, too. Here it is, Fox, and
to the crows with you if you brag of it: I was after fearing
that, did I hit you whilst you looked the other way, you'd
still somehow or other make me sorry I ever was born.
I say that, mind, and I reckon myself not the least tricksy
man living these days, nor the weakest, either."

Gerin considered. "Mm, I don't know whether I could
have or not. I tell you this, though: I would have tried."

He doubted he could have done much to Adiatunnus,
not if he was embroiled against a foe as formidable as
Aragis at the same time. Again, he did not mention his
doubts to the Trokmê. Ideas about how dangerous he
was were ones he wanted Adiatunnus to have.

"When do we move against Aragis?" Adiatunnus asked.
"Whenever it is, my warriors will be ready."

"Likely tell!" Gerin gave him a saucy grin. "I'll set the
day for you two days before the one I tell my Elabonians,
so we can all set out at the same time."

Adiatunnus glared. "Is that a tongue you carry in your
mouth, or a woodworker's rasp? We're not so slow as
all that, indeed and we're not, for you'd fret over less
an we were."

"Fair enough," Gerin said. "Come drink some ale with
me now, and your warriors and mine can get drunk
together and tell lies about all the different times they
tried to kill each other."

"And some of the tales they tell won't be lies at all, Fox darling," Adiatunnus said. "Widin Simrin's son would be here, for instance, I'm thinking? He wasna in his own keep when I passed it by on the way hither."

"Yes, he's here," Gerin answered. "Remember, he and you are both my vassals now. You can't go having your own little wars for the fun of it."

"Indeed and I'd never think such a thing!" The sparkle in Adiatunnus' eyes said he didn't expect Gerin to believe a word of it. "But I do recall the days when we went after each other, and not a doubt have I got that they're in his memory as well. Hashing them out over some ale will be safer nor going through them ever was."

"Truth that," Gerin agreed, falling into the Trokmê tongue for a couple of words. Like a lot of Elabonians who'd grown up on the border, he used it almost as readily as his own language.

Adiatunnus held up a forefinger. "One more question, before I drink deep and forget I meant to ask it: have you had more of your books copied out, that I might buy them of you?"

"Yes," Gerin answered: "a chronicle and a poem."

"Ah, that's fine, that's fine indeed," the Trokmê chieftain said. "When you told me you'd teach me the art of reading, I bethought myself I'd learn it as I learned to use a tool or a weapon. The more such things you know, the better, after all. But, you omadhaun, you, why did you not tell me beforehand it'd be near as much fun as futtering?"

"Why?" Gerin's eyes were wide and innocent. "If I had told you that—beforehand, mind you—would you have believed me?"

"Nay, I wouldna," Adiatunnus admitted. He gave the Fox a sudden, suspicious stare. "Don't go thinking you're civilizing me the now, or whatever you're after calling it. A Trokmê I am and I remain, and proud of it."

"Of course," Gerin said, more innocently still.

"Lord king, I beg you, put the army in motion soon," Carlun Vepin's son said. "You have no idea how fast they're going through the stores you've built up over the years."

"I have a very good idea how fast they're doing it," Gerin returned. "I ought to. And the reason you build up stores in the first place, Carlun, is to be able to use them at times like these."

Normally, that sort of answer would have silenced the steward. Now, though, he shook his head and said, "Truly, lord king, you must see this for yourself. Come down into the storerooms under the castle. Look at the empty shelves. Look at the empty chambers, by the gods! See what this campaign is doing to Fox Keep."

The Fox sighed. The trouble with Carlun, as with any good steward, he supposed, was that accumulating got to be an end in itself for him, not a means to an end. Shouting at the former serf had produced no lasting relief. Humoring him might buy Gerin a longer quiet stretch. "All right, let's go have a look," he said, and rose from the bench in the great hall he and Carlun had been sharing.

After exclaiming in glad surprise, Carlun rose, too. Pausing in the kitchen only to light two clay lamps at a cookfire, the steward handed Gerin one of them and then led him down into the cellars below Castle Fox. The air was cool and damp down there, full of the yeasty smell of ale and a greener odor suggesting that, somewhere back among those corridors, a crock of gherkins had gone over.

Carlun pointed to a bare wall. "Look, lord king! We had jars of ale set there not so long ago."

"I know that," Gerin said patiently. "If we all started drinking river water, the first thing it would do is make all my vassals and all *their* vassals and all *their* retainers hopping mad at me. The second thing it would do is give about half of them a flux of the bowels. That's not really what you want if you expect to fight a war sometime soon."

"And here," Carlun said dramatically, paying no attention whatsoever to him. He held the lamp close to another row of jars, so the Fox could see they had the lids off and were empty. "These were full of wheat, and these over here were full of barley, and these—"

"And you, Carlun, you're full of beans." Gerin's patience was breaking now; when it broke, it left sharp edges. "If I don't feed my soldiers, that will get me talked about worse than not giving them ale."

The steward still was not listening. The steward was determined not to listen. In the darkness all around, the flickering lamplight gleamed off his pale, set face. Gerin had seen less battle-ready faces coming at him over shields. Carlun pointed toward a corridor down which they'd not yet gone. "And the peas, lord king! When you think what's happening to our peas . . ."

What Gerin was thinking was that this wasn't working as he'd hoped. No matter what he did, Carlun wasn't going to stop nagging him about how much the warriors were eating. Wearily, he said, "All right, show me the peas, Carlun, and then we'll go back upstairs. The men aren't eating any more than I thought they would, and the stores don't look to be in any worse shape than I thought they were."

Carlun rounded the corner. Gerin followed close behind him. With a gasp, the steward stopped in his tracks. Gerin had to stop in a hurry, too, lest he walk up Carlun's back and perhaps set the steward's tunic on fire. Then the Fox's hand flew to the hilt of his sword, for he heard two other gasps from farther up the corridor.

He took his hand away from his sword as fast as it had gone there. He started to laugh. Down here, two gasps didn't mean thieves. They meant two people surprised when they wanted privacy. He had fond memories of some of the corridors in the cellar, not this one in particular but some nearby. He knew his son Duren had amused himself down here, too.

"Sorry to disturb you," he called into the gloom at the end of the passage, wondering if he'd interrupted Dagref at a moment in his education he couldn't possibly have acquired from a book.

From out of that gloom came a deep voice: "You startled us, lord king. We didn't think anyone would be down here."

Gerin clapped a hand to his forehead. He knew that voice. It wasn't Dagref's. "Carlun and I will go up to the great hall now," he said. "When the two of you have put yourselves back together, I want you to come up there, too. We have some talking to do, I'm afraid."

"Aye, lord king," came the answer from the darkness.

"Come on," Gerin said to Carlun, who was still staring down the passageway. "Let's go."

The steward looked back toward him as if he'd gone mad. "But, lord king, we're not nearly through the vegetables, and we haven't even begun on the smoked meats and, er, sausages."

"To the five hells with the vegetables and the smoked meats." Gerin didn't mention the sausages. If he didn't think about them, maybe he wouldn't think about . . . . On the other hand, maybe he would. He grabbed Carlun by the arm. "Come on, curse you. Do you want to annoy them, hanging about down here?"

That got Carlun moving, as the Fox had thought it

would. It got Carlun moving so fast, he tripped on the stairs going up to the kitchens not once but twice. Once up in the kitchens, he hurried out through them. Gerin followed more slowly. He wondered if Carlun would wait in the great hall to discuss beans and radishes and smoked pig's knuckles. When Carlun chose to find something else to do out in the courtyard, the Fox nodded without any particular surprise. He hadn't hired his steward to be a hero.

He sat down at the bench where he and Carlun had been talking. A couple of troopers started to come into the great hall. The Fox waved them out again. A serving girl walked over to him with a pitcher of ale. He waved her away, too, wanting both a clear head and no audience for the discussion he knew he was going to have.

A couple of minutes later, Geroge walked out of the kitchens, looking as nonchalant as he could. Gerin nodded and slapped the bench beside himself. Some of the monster's nonchalance evaporated as he came over and sat down.

Gerin nodded again. He didn't say anything, not until Tharma came out of the kitchens, too. She didn't even try for nonchalance. Worry twisted her face as she joined Geroge and the Fox. "Well, well," Gerin said, then, as mildly as he could. "How long has this been going on?"

Geroge and Tharma were too hairy for him to tell whether they blushed. By the way they wiggled on the benches, he thought they did. "Not long, lord king," Geroge answered. He did more talking than Tharma.

The Fox glanced over to the female monster. "You're not with child, are you?"

"Oh, no, lord king!" she said quickly. "I would know."

"That's good," he said, and wondered where to go from there. Geroge and Tharma had been raised as brother and sister. He thought they *were* brother and sister; the peasant who'd found them as cubs and brought them to him said they'd been together. But discussions of incest seemed out of place when they were the only two of their kind above ground in the northlands. He'd actually thought this moment would come sooner than it had.

"Are you angry at us, lord king?" Geroge asked. Reading his expression and tone of voice weren't easy, but he seemed more worried about the Fox's anger than one of his own children would have been. Gerin shook his head. If that wasn't irony, he didn't know what was.

With a sigh, he answered, "No, I'm not angry. You're the only two like yourselves in these parts, and you're . . . a man and a woman." He knew no better way to put it. "What else are you going to do?"

"Oh, good," Tharma said. "I hope I do get to be with child before too long."

Gerin coughed. "I'm not so sure that's a good idea," he said, one of the better understatements he remembered making in some time.

"Why not?" Tharma asked. "You could marry us the way you or the headman does for the serfs, and then the children wouldn't be bastards."

"We wouldn't want that, lord king," Geroge added seriously.

The Fox was tempted to pound his head against the top of the table at which he was sitting. All things considered, he was more proud of himself than not over how he'd raised them. They earnestly wanted to do everything the right way, the proper way. The only trouble was, they didn't see enough of the picture, a failing anything but unique to their kind.

He explained as gently as he could: "You know how people who don't know you get upset when they first see you, because you remind them of the trouble that happened around the time when you were born?" He couldn't come up with a politer way of putting that. The monsters had done their horrific best to overrun the northlands, and that best had nearly proved good enough.

"Oh, yes, we know about that," Geroge answered, nodding his large, fearsome head. "But once people get to know us, they see we're all right, even if we don't look just like them."

Part of the reason people saw that—a big part—was that the two monsters were under Gerin's protection. Another part, the Fox admitted to himself, was that, as monsters went—even as people went—Geroge and Tharma were good people. And another big part of the reason they got such tolerance as they did was that they were the *only* two monsters above ground.

"I don't know how happy regular people would be if you started raising a family," Gerin said carefully. "They might worry that the things that happened when you were born would start happening again."

"That's foolish!" Tharma bared her prominent teeth in indignation. "We know how to behave. We should. You taught us yourself. And we'd teach our little ones the same way."

"I'm sure you would." Gerin was absurdly touched at the faith they put in his teachings. No, his own children didn't pay nearly so much attention to them. "Even so, though, people would worry, and they might get nasty. I don't want that to happen."

"You're the king," Geroge said. "You could tell them to stop it, and they'd have to listen."

That was how the monsters had lived to grow up in the first place. Gerin didn't know if he could stretch it to a family of them. He didn't really want to find out. He'd contemplated getting rid of Geroge and Tharma when they reached the age where they could reproduce their kind. He hadn't done it. The reason he hadn't done it, he now discovered, was that he couldn't do it. He'd raised them as his stepchildren, and they *were* in essence his stepchildren.

"By all the gods, be careful," he told them. He might have told Dagref the same thing. One of these days soon, he *would* be telling Dagref the same thing. He gestured sharply. Geroge and Tharma hastily rose from their seats and went out into the courtyard.

Gerin stared after them. He bunched his right hand into a fist and brought it down hard on the tabletop. He'd known this day was coming. He was a man who prided himself on acting with decision. Now the day had come and gone, and all he had to show for it was ambiguity.

He looked down at his fist and willed it to unfold. When it did, he started to laugh. It was not amusement, or not amusement with anything but the human condition: the part of it that had to do with the difference between the way men thought things would work and the way they actually turned out, and with making the best of that difference.

"Twenty years ago," he muttered under his breath, "twenty years ago, I thought I was going to slaughter every Trokmê on the face of the earth." He'd had good reason to think that, too. What better reason than the woodsrunners' killing his father and older brother and making him leave the City of Elabon to return to the northlands he'd learned to despise? He'd taken vengeance as great as any man could have done, and now . . .

And now Adiatunnus walked into the great hall, waved, walked over and sat down beside him, and clapped him on the back while shouting for ale. And the Fox was genuinely glad to have the Trokmê with him. He was too honest to try to pretend otherwise to himself.

"Life," he observed with a profound lack of originality,

"is a much stranger and more complicated thing than we think when we first set out on it."

"Truth there," Adiatunnus agreed, "or would I be after calling a cursed southron like your own self a friend and meaning it?" That so closely mirrored Gerin's own thought, he blinked in startlement. Adiatunnus went on, "But not a chance at all have we of making the pups believe it. I've given up, I have. They think everything's simple, sure and they do. A grave, now, a grave's a simple thing. What comes before—nay."

"You should have gone down to the City of Elabon, to study philosophy," Gerin said. "You'd have made the Sithonian lecturers work for a living, I think."

"Philosophy? We're getting old, you and I. Is that philosophy?"

"It will do, till something better comes along." Gerin called for ale himself.

Carlun Vepin's son stood beaming from ear to ear. The army Gerin had assembled was leaving Fox Keep. The soldiers wouldn't stop eating and drinking, of course. But they would stop eating and drinking where the steward could see them doing it, and where he could see the results of their depredations. To Carlun, nothing else mattered.

Dagref drove Gerin's chariot. Concentration turned the youngster's face masklike. This was his first campaign, and he was determined to make no mistakes. He would, of course, despite all his determination. Gerin wondered how he would deal with that. The only way to find out was to let him have the chance and see what happened.

Van had another thought. Setting a hand on Dagref's shoulder, he said, "I rode to war with your brother at the reins not so long ago."

"Yes, I know," Dagref answered. "Duren is older than I am, so of course he got to do all these things first."

"Of course," Van echoed, and winked at Gerin. The Fox nodded. That qualification was Dagref to the core: not only precise but also just a little slighting to anyone who dared presume he wasn't precise.

Gerin said, "When we get down to Duren's holding in a few days, he'll be surprised how much you've grown."

"Yes," Dagref said, and fell silent again. Five years earlier, Dagref had wanted to be like Duren in every way he could. Now he was his own person, and increasingly insistent that everyone acknowledge him as such.

No doubt he also thought about Duren in a different way these days. One of them would succeed the Fox. Duren was Gerin's firstborn, but Dagref was his firstborn by Selatre. Duren already ruled in his own right the barony that had been his grandfather's. Dagref, as yet, ruled nothing and nobody. In another five years, though, or ten . . .

Since Gerin had yet to decide who would succeed him, he didn't blame Dagref for having the question a good deal in his mind, too. He wished he could send the lad down to the City of Elabon. Even more than himself, perhaps, Dagref was made for the scholar's life. The Fox sighed. He hadn't been able to stay a scholar, and there was no guarantee Dagref would, either. Life, as Gerin had learned, did not come with a guarantee.

That was a lesson serfs sucked in with their mothers' milk. Most serfs, seeing an army on the move, whether made up of the enemy or of their overlord's warriors, ran for the woods and swamps with whatever they could carry. Women ran faster than men—and had better reason to run.

The serfs who labored in the Fox's holding, though,

watched the chariots come forth from the keep without fear. A few of them even waved from the fields and vegetable plots where they labored. Slowly, over the years, they'd let Gerin convince them his soldiers were likelier to mean protection than rapine and rape.

As Dagref drove past the village, a small figure came out of one of the huts there and trotted after his chariot. No child should have had any business gaining on a two-horse chariot. This one did so with effortless ease. "Father," Dagref asked in a small, tight voice, "did you intend for Ferdulf to campaign with us?"

"Of course not," Gerin answered. He waved to the little demigod. "Go back to your mother!"

"No," Ferdulf answered in his utterly unchildlike tones. "The village is boring. And with you and all your soldiers gone from the keep, it'll be boring there, too. I'll go with you. Maybe you won't be boring." He sounded as if, with some reluctance, he was giving the Fox the benefit of the doubt.

Gerin's reaction was that life with Ferdulf wasn't likely to be boring, either, but that didn't mean it would be more enjoyable. "Go back to your mother," the Fox repeated.

"No," Ferdulf said, in his stubbornness not only childlike but godlike, a point in common between the two aspects of his nature Gerin had noticed before. Ferdulf stuck out his tongue. Like Mavrix, he could stick it out improbably far when he wanted to. "You can't make me, either."

As if to emphasize that, he leaped into the air and flew along ten or fifteen feet above Gerin's head, jeering all the while. "If the little bugger doesn't knock that off," Van muttered behind his hand, "he's liable to find out just how close to immortal he is when he comes in for a landing."

"I know what you mean," Gerin said. He didn't expect Van to try wringing Ferdulf's neck, or to succeed if he did try. He understood—he understood down to the ground—the reasons the outlander had for contemplating semideicide.

Glaring up at Ferdulf, the Fox declared, "If you don't come down from there this minute, I'll tell your father on you."

"Go ahead," Ferdulf answered. "He doesn't like you, either."

"That's true," Gerin said calmly, "but he wouldn't pick such foolish ways of showing it." He thought he was even telling the truth. Whatever else could be said about him—and a great deal else could have been said about him—Mavrix had style.

Ferdulf did hesitate. In his hesitation, he fell a few feet—almost low enough for Gerin to reach up and try plucking him out of the air. At the last minute, he thought better of it. He'd laid hold of Ferdulf on the ground, and had got away with it there. Doing the same thing from a moving chariot struck him as imperfectly provident.

Dagref spoke over his shoulder: "Aren't you going to make him go back to the village?"

"I'm open to suggestions," Gerin snarled. "Right now, I'd be satisfied with making him shut up."

"Oh, I can do that," Dagref said. "I thought you wanted what you said you wanted in the first place."

"One of these days, you'll learn the difference between what you want and what you'll settle for," Gerin said, to which his son responded with only a scornful toss of his head. Nettled, the Fox snapped, "What forfeit will you pay if you don't make the little bastard shut up?"

"Why, whatever you like, of course," Dagref replied.

Van whistled softly. "He's asking for it, Fox. You ought to give it to him."

"So I should." Gerin tapped Dagref on the shoulder. "Go ahead. Do it. Now."

"All right," Dagref said. "What forfeit will *you* pay if I do?"

"Whatever you like, of course." Gerin spoke in mocking imitation of his son.

"Hmm." Dagref looked up to Ferdulf, who was still flying along making a hideous racket. "You know, right now you'd annoy my father much more by keeping quiet than you do with all that noise."

Silence.

After a minute or so, Van broke that silence with a thunderous guffaw. Gerin glared up at Ferdulf, who flew along, still silent, but made a horrible face back at him. Merely human features could never have accommodated that sneer. Of course, a merely human being wouldn't have been flying along above the chariot, either.

"Have I won, Father?" Dagref asked.

"Aye, you've won," Gerin admitted, more than a little apprehensively. "What will you ask of me?"

He'd promised too much. He knew he'd promised too much. Now he had to deliver. If Dagref said something like *Declare me your successor on the spot*, he didn't see how he could do anything else—unless he could talk his son out of it. Talking Dagref out of anything was no easy task.

He couldn't see his son's face; Dagref was concentrating on driving the chariot. More silence stretched. Gerin knew what that meant. Dagref was thinking things over. One thing he seldom did was speak too soon. In that he was very like his father. Gerin had broken his own rule, and now he would have to pay for it.

"I don't know right now," Dagref answered after that pause for thought. "When I decide, I'll tell you."

"All right," Gerin said. "You'll know best. Whatever

it turns out to be, make sure it's what you really want now and what you really want years from now, too."

"Ah." Dagref rode on for another little while, then said, "You're not going to tell me you were only joking and you didn't really mean it?"

Had he and Dagref been having a purely private argument, Gerin might have tried telling him just that. With a demigod as witness, he thought the consequences of granting whatever Dagref asked for would be less than those of trying to break his word. "No, I'm not going to tell you that," he said. "I'm going to count on your good sense."

Van poked him in the ribs. He grimaced. The outlander's face bore an unseemly smirk. The Fox knew what he was thinking: at Dagref's age, good sense was hard to come by. With anyone of that age but his contemplative son, he would have had little hope himself. As things were, he had . . . some.

Dagref said, "All right, Father." His chuckle was eerily like the one Gerin would have used under the same circumstances. "I'm not likely to get another promise like that out of you, am I?"

"You weren't likely to get the first one," Gerin answered. "That was a sneaky bit of business you used, playing Ferdulf off against me."

"I learned it from you," Dagref said. "You've been playing foes off one against another for years now. Sometimes they even notice you're doing it, but never till too late."

He spoke matter-of-factly. He knew what he knew. That Gerin's foes—all of them men grown—had failed to see it till too late was their misfortune, not his. In his own rather withdrawn way, he was formidable.

Rihwin and a squadron of his riders came up and surrounded the chariot just then. Gerin was glad to watch them for a while. They took his mind off both Dagref and Ferdulf. The horseriders were staring up at Ferdulf and exclaiming; not all of them had paid the little demigod much heed till now. Ferdulf responded with a series of aerial maneuvers that would have left an eagle dizzy. The riders clapped and cheered. Ferdulf's face bore a smug grin. Like Mavrix, he was vain.

Dagref, having used Ferdulf to score his point against his father, paid no more attention to him. He watched the riders, too. Gerin understood that: most of them were young men, a good number hardly older than Dagref. Gerin hadn't seen so many nearly smooth cheeks and chins since his days in the City of Elabon, where shaving was the custom.

Even the riders who had raised beards looked absurdly young to the Fox. One of them, though very fuzzy, made Gerin wonder if he had even Dagref's years. The Fox shook his head. He'd been thinking more and more lately that the whole world was looking too bloody young.

But then he saw Dagref eyeing that very young-looking horseman too, and decided his eyes and wits hadn't been playing tricks on him after all. He said, "Son, I can tell that riding horses is the coming thing. You won't have to spend all your time driving a chariot. You can learn what you need to know."

Dagref looked away from the rider. "Umm—" he said, rather foolishly, as if his mind had been somewhere else. That was unlike him. Then he gave his usual serious notice to what Gerin had said. "Oh, it's all right," he said. "I can ride a horse now—Rihwin's been teaching Maeva and me and some of his own bastards when they come to Fox Keep. I haven't done any fighting from horseback yet, but not a lot of men have."

"You're right," the Fox said. "I don't think it will go on being so much longer, though. If we fight Aragis now, everybody in the northlands will know what horsemen can do. And if they do what I think they will, everybody in the northlands will want to have his own riders by this time next year."

"Now there's an interesting question, Father," Dagref said. "You could profit by sending out men to teach your neighbors how to fight from horseback, but that would also be teaching them to fight better against you. Would it be worthwhile, do you suppose?"

"Yes, that *is* interesting," Gerin said. "Do I sell a man the axe he wants to use to chop off my head? I suppose I'd have to decide one case at a time instead of laying down a blanket rule beforehand. Some I'd think I could trust, some of the ones I couldn't trust I'd be sure I could beat, and some I wouldn't want to help any which way."

"Ah." Dagref considered that, then nodded. "You're saying that making a rule is like making a promise: once you've made it, you have to stick by it, whether that looks like a good idea or not." He coughed a couple of times, then added, "I wish you'd have said that more often when I was smaller."

Straight-faced, Gerin answered, "I haven't the faintest idea what you're talking about." Dagref turned to give him an irate stare. After a moment, they both started to laugh.

When evening came, the army was still on land that had been in the Fox's family for generations. Peasants who lived near the roadway came up to the army with sheep and pigs and chickens to sell. Adiatunnus watched the dickering with no small astonishment. "They run toward you, not away," he said to Gerin. "It's not that they stay in their fields, the which is strange enough, but they run *toward* you." By the way he spoke, the peasants might have practiced some unnatural vice.

"They've seen me lead armies south on campaign a good many times," the Fox answered. "They know we won't rob them or take any woman who doesn't want to be taken."

"Doesna seem right," the Trokmê chieftain said. "If they dinna fear you, how can you rule them?"

"Oh, they fear me—if they get out of line, they know I'll make them sorry for it," Gerin said. "But they don't fear that we'll steal or rape for the amusement of it. The idea is to make them feel safer with me over them than with anyone else they might think of." Adiatunnus walked off shaking his head.

As the sun neared the horizon, Tiwaz's waxing gibbous disk, halfway between first quarter and full, grew brighter. Golden Math, a day before full, crawled over the eastern horizon. Ruddy Elleb and pale Nothos were not in the sky; both a little past third quarter, they would rise not long after midnight.

Just before sunset, Gerin's men dug several short, narrow trenches on the outskirts of their encampment. They wrung off the chickens' heads and cut the throats of the other animals they'd got from the peasants, letting the blood spill into the trenches: an offering for the night ghosts that might otherwise have driven them mad.

The ghosts came forth as soon as the sun disappeared from the sky. Gerin had been trying all his life to grasp their shape, trying and failing. Nor could he understand their cries, which dinned in his mind. Grateful for the boon of blood, they tried to give him good advice, but he perceived it only as wind and noise.

"I've heard 'em howl worse," Van remarked.

"I was thinking the same thing," Gerin said. "We've fed 'em well, and we've got good-sized fires going to hold 'em away from us a bit, but I've heard 'em a lot louder and more frightening than they are now. I know what part of the answer is, or I think I do."

Van grunted. "I've seen it myself, around your keep and in the village close by. It's that Ferdulf, isn't it?"

"I think so," Gerin said with a sigh. "The ghosts are just ghosts—spirits that never found their way into the five hells. They're stronger than we are—stronger in the nighttime, anyhow—because they haven't got any bodies to worry about. But stack them up against a demigod, and they know they'd better walk—uh, flitter—small."

"Belike you're right." Van made a fist and smacked it into his open palm. "But I tell you this, Captain: there's been plenty of times I wanted to slaughter the nasty little bugger, no matter whose son he is."

"Heh," Gerin said, and then, "You know I don't set much stock in being king, not among friends I don't. This time, though, I'm going to claim my rank. If anybody tries killing him, it'll be me first."

"Wait till after we've fought Aragis," Van said.

"Well, yes, that thought crossed my mind, too," the Fox admitted. "I do wonder why Ferdulf decided to come along, though. What worries me is that he *is* half a god—"

"The wrong half," Van put in. "The wrong god, too, come to that."

"Maybe. But what does he know that I don't, and how does he know it?"

The outlander's jaw worked, as if he truly were chewing that over. And, as if he didn't like the taste of the answer he got, he spat on the grass. "Bah!" he said. "Best I can tell you is, we're all liable to be better off if we never find out."

"Can't argue with you there," Gerin said. "But my guess is, we're *going* to find out, one way or the other. I dare hope Ferdulf is here so that, if we do need some strange sort of help against Aragis, he'll be able to give it to us."

"Aye," Van said. "I hope that, too. And if we're wrong, and he's along to let Aragis have some help against us, he'll give it to us then, too, right up the—"

"Yes, I know. I understand that," Gerin broke in hastily. "It's the chance we take, that's all. I've taken a lot of chances, these past twenty years and more. What's another?"

"The one that kills you, could be," Van said.

"Well, yes." The Fox shrugged. "There is that."

III

Every time a chariot came up the Elabon Way from the south, Gerin tensed, wondering whether this would be the one that brought him word Aragis had swarmed over the border into Balser's holding—or whether Aragis had swarmed over the border in some other place altogether, in which case he would have to change his line of march in a hurry.

But no such news came. On the fifth day after setting out from Fox Keep, the army reached the castle from which Gerin's son Duren ruled his holding. The pace was slower than the Fox would have liked, but an army on the march, of necessity, moved no faster than its slowest parts.

Holding the keep by descent from his grandfather, as Duren did, he maintained full formal independence from Gerin. Gerin had asked his eldest son's leave before entering his barony at the head of a fighting force. He would have been astonished and dismayed had Duren refused him that leave, but Duren did nothing of the sort. The border guards he still maintained at the frontier between his holding and the lands over which the Fox was suzerain stood aside as the warriors came past them. Their eyes got wide when they saw how many men Gerin had with him.

Gerin could not see the eyes of the sentry on the wall of Duren's keep, but he would have bet they were wide, too. The fellow's voice sounded more than a little awestruck as he hallooed: "Who comes to the castle of Duren Ricolf's grandson?"

He knew perfectly well who came, but the forms had to be observed. A great many men, Gerin had seen over the years, got very upset when jolted out of the smooth routine of their everyday lives. And so, as if he were an unexpected arrival, he answered, "I am Gerin the Fox, king of the north, come to guest with my son, Duren Ricolf's grandson." He didn't blame Duren for using Ricolf's name after his own: on the contrary. He found it a clever touch.

"Enter, lord king, and be welcome as lord Duren's guest-friend, and as his father," the sentry replied. The drawbridge to the keep was already down; with his holding altogether surrounded by the Fox's lands, Duren feared no sudden assault. Gerin tapped Dagref on the shoulder. Duren's half brother drove the chariot across the drawbridge, over the moat, and into the keep.

Duren was waiting in the courtyard, as Gerin had been sure he would be. Coming into this keep, Gerin saw ghosts that had nothing to do with the ones that came forth when the sun went down: Ricolf the Red and Elise and his own younger self. He saw Duren's younger self, too, coming here at about the age Dagref had now to claim this barony and make it his own. That, over these past five years, Duren had done.

He was nineteen now, and looked enough like a young version of the Fox to make Gerin wonder for a crazy instant if he hadn't somehow slipped back across the years to his own early days. Oh, Duren was a little fairer, a little stockier, but the biggest difference between him now and his father at the same age was that his face held not the slightest trace of dreaminess. Gerin had been a second son, able to afford such luxuries as thinking about whatever he chose. With five years as a baron already under his belt, Duren worried about essentials first and everything else afterwards.

That did not mean he wasn't smiling. "Good to see you, Father, by Dyaus and all the gods!" he said, his voice deeper than Gerin's. He folded the Fox into a bear hug when Gerin got down from the car. Then he nodded to Dagref, who still held the reins. "You've got him learning the trade, I see, same as you did with me at the same age. How does it feel, Dagref?"

His half brother weighed that with deliberation he'd probably got from Selatre. "Too much to do, not enough time to do it in," he answered. "Probably would be more if I were better at what I did."

"You will be," Duren told him, then turned back to Gerin. "He's shaping well, seems like." He spoke thoughtfully, in a way Gerin hadn't heard from him before. The Fox knew what that meant: the succession was in his mind. Well, he would have been a fool if it weren't. The awkward moment passed quickly. Duren went on, "Mother's well, I trust?"

He meant Selatre. He knew she hadn't birthed him, of course, but she was the only mother he remembered; he hadn't been weaned long when Elise ran off with the horseleech. "Yes, she's fine," the Fox said, nodding. "Clotild and Blestar, too."

"And my pair as well," said Van, who had got down to stand beside Gerin and beam at the young man who was as near his nephew as made no difference. "You've grown up, that you have. Beard's thicker than mine was at the same age, I'd say."

"It's darker," Duren said judiciously, "so it will look thicker than a yellow one like yours. Come into the great hall. Drink some ale with me. So you're finally going to war with Aragis, are you, Father?"

"No," Gerin said. "He's going to war with me, or he says he is. Marlanz Raw-Meat told me he'd stopped here, so you'll have heard Aragis' side of the story. He frightened Balser into going over to me, and now he'll try to punish Balser and me both. He's welcome to try."

"Coming back from your keep, Marlanz didn't seem very happy," Duren said.

"Good," Gerin said. "He shouldn't be happy. Neither should Aragis. The Archer is strong and tough and dangerous. He can pick his time and his spot to start the war. And once he's done that, I aim to lick him."

"I'm sure you will," Duren said—as usual, more confident than the Fox himself. "What help do you want with me?"

"If your vassals will send a few chariots south with the rest of the army, that would be fine," Gerin answered. "If they don't want to do that, though, I'm not going to lose any sleep over it. They don't love me, some of them, and they can say it's not their fight."

"Do you want me to go myself?" Duren asked.

"As I say, I won't turn you down, but I don't see any great need for it, either," Gerin said. He nodded toward Dagref. "You said it yourself: it's your brother's turn to learn the trade. You already know."

"Yes." Duren didn't say anything more. His eyes narrowed. Gerin's mouth tightened. Things would never be the same for Duren and Dagref. They'd be watching each other—and watching him—till the day he died. After that, regardless of the provisions he'd made, they were liable to square off against each other. For that matter, if Gerin lived long enough, Blestar was liable to square off against both of them.

Duren said, "I'll feast your leaders tonight. Will you be swinging off the Elabon Way and heading over to

Ikos to find out what Biton has to say about the fight against Aragis?"

"I hadn't planned to, no," Gerin said. "When the Sibyl speaks the prophetic verses, they usually stay obscure until after the fact. And even when they aren't obscure, some people will try to make them so. You ought to know that for yourself."

"Oh, I do," Duren said. "My loving vassals, doing everything they could to keep from admitting the god had said I was meant to be baron of this holding after all." He snorted. "They've got used to the idea by now—or if they haven't, they keep quiet about it."

"That will do," Gerin said. "It will have to do. You can't control how they think, only what they do—and only so much of that." He raised an eyebrow. "A feast, eh? What does your steward have to say about that?"

"He says it will cost too much," Duren answered. "As best I can tell, that's what stewards always say." The Fox laughed and nodded.

He ate bread and honey and smoking beef ribs and berry tarts in the great hall a little later, and washed them down with ale. As he ate and drank, he thought of other, long-ago feasts he'd had in this place. Rihwin the Fox sat across the table from him. He'd feasted here, too, when he was courting Elise. With a mischievous grin, he asked, "Shall I dance for you, lord king?"

"Go howl!" Gerin exclaimed. If Rihwin hadn't got drunk and danced an obscene dance, Ricolf the Red would have wed Elise to him, and then . . . Gerin didn't know *and then what*. The world would have been vastly different for him. He did know that.

The chamber Duren gave him for the night was only a couple of doors down from the one in which he'd slept twenty-one years before, the one in which Elise had begged him to help her escape from a marriage to Wolfar of the Axe, a marriage that, most sensibly, she did not want. Before too long, she'd been wed to the Fox, which also turned out to be a marriage she did not want. Duren couldn't have known where his father had stayed on that earlier visit. Gerin had no intention of ever telling him.

Van had been in the next room then. He was in the next room now. He'd brought a serving girl in there then. He'd brought a serving girl in there now. (The walls were thin; Gerin had no doubts.) He'd been unattached then. He was married to Fand now. Gerin hoped he wouldn't bring her back an itemized list of his infidelities on campaign, as he'd been known to do. Life was hard enough already.

The outlander didn't have the stamina he'd enjoyed two decades before. Quiet returned now sooner than it had then. Gerin took advantage of the quiet to go to sleep. He woke up in the middle of the night. In the next room, Van was snoring. So was the girl. They kept Gerin awake almost effectively as they would have, making love. After a while, he did drift off again.

He woke the next morning with a headache that wasn't quite a hangover. A jack of ale and some bread and honey made it retreat if not disappear. Van washed raw cabbage down with his ale, suggesting he had more morning pain than Gerin did. Seeing the Fox watching him, he grinned and said, "I keep reminding myself what a good time I had last night."

"Last night, I kept reminding myself how miserable I'd be today if I let myself drink too deep." The Fox felt smugly virtuous for feeling as good as he did.

"There's the difference between us, all right," Van said. "I had the good time, and I'll take the bad that goes with it. You miss the bad, aye, but you miss the good, too, sometimes."

"Some people like mountains and valleys," Gerin

replied. "Some people like flatlands better. Me, I'm one of them. Besides, I don't really want any woman but Selatre—mm, not enough to do anything about it, anyhow. And," he added with considerable dignity, "I don't snore."

"Honh!" Van said. "That's what *you* think."

When Adiatunnus didn't come out for breakfast as soon as Gerin thought he should, the Fox asked Duren to send a servant to pound on his door. Adiatunnus duly emerged, looking much worse for wear than Van did. "You see, son?" Gerin said to Duren. "He was slow getting up when we campaigned against the Gradi, and he still is."

"I'm not slow, Fox darling," the Trokmê said, in the cautious tones of a man who does not want to hear himself talk too loud. "What I am is dead. Be after having some respect for the corp of me."

He shuddered at the first taste of ale, but looked more lifelike after he'd downed a couple of jacks. "Since you may not have to bury him in the courtyard after all," Gerin said to his son, drawing a glare from Adiatunnus, "we'll be off soon."

"I don't know, Fox," Van said. "Remember, the rest of the woodsrunners are liable to be as sleepy as this one is. We may not be out of here for two or three days."

"And to the corbies with you as well," Adiatunnus said. "Remind me once more we're allies, so I don't go cutting your throat from the sheer high spirits of it."

"You and which army?" Van returned politely.

They were just warming to the debate, and still on this side of sword and axe and mace and spear, when Gerin said, "Slaughter each other some other time, if you must, but remember for now that we have to take on Aragis first."

"Sure and it's all the fun out of life you're stealing,"

Adiatunnus said, and Van rumbled agreement. The two of them united, quite happily, in complaining about the Fox till the army left Duren's keep and headed off to the south.

Balser Debo's son's driver brought his chariot up alongside the Fox's. "Now we're getting close to my lands," Balser said. "Better country, if you'll forgive my saying so, than what you've got up around your own keep."

"Maybe," Gerin answered. "The timber's a little different—you've got more elms and beeches and such down here, not so many pines. And your peasants can plant a few days earlier in spring and won't have to worry about frost quite so soon in the fall."

"Better country, as I said." Balser sounded smug.

"Maybe," Gerin said. "Or better some ways, might be a truer way to put it. You'll grow a few things we don't. But the Elabon Way here has gone back to gravel, because peasants and local lords plundered the stone paving when there was nobody around to tell 'em they couldn't or shouldn't." As if to prove his point, gravel kicked up from one of the wheels to Balser's chariot and hit him in the hand. He grunted. "Wasn't even gravel here when this land first came under my suzerainty."

Balser coughed. "Well, lord king, the way that works is, you do what you think you have to do for the moment, and let later on take care of itself."

Gerin knew what that meant. It meant Balser and his vassals—and his serfs, too, if they thought they could get away with it—had been plundering the Elabon Way in his holding for building stone whenever they needed it. He wouldn't do anything about that, not when it had happened before Balser was his subject. He did say, "No more pulling up paving stone. That's all over now. If the road weren't here, Balser, we wouldn't be able to get to your holding fast enough to do you any good about Aragis."

"I suppose not." Balser, plainly, hadn't looked at it in that light before. Just as plainly, he didn't care, either.

"I mean it," the Fox said. "This is part of what you bought when you gave me homage and fealty. The Elabon Way is the one good thing the Empire left behind when it pulled back from the northern lands. I've done everything I could to keep it in good shape. It's turning into the backbone for my own kingdom."

"Well, yes, I have seen that you care about it," Balser admitted. "It's only a road, though, after all." He and Gerin looked at each other with complete mutual incomprehension.

"You'll have to get used to some new ways of doing things, now that you are my vassal," Gerin said, and let it go at that.

"Yes, lord king." Balser didn't sound dutiful. He sounded resigned. The Fox had no doubt about what he was thinking: something on the order of, *How many of those new ways of doing things will I really have to get used to, and how many will I be able to ignore?* Every one of his new vassals had thoughts like that. After a while, they—or most of them, anyhow—got the idea that the new ways—or most of them, anyhow—worked pretty well.

When Gerin had come by this road years before, on his way down to the City of Elabon with Elise and Van, he'd thought the barons here well away from the River Niffet were soft. They hadn't trimmed the brush back from the road as well as they should, they hadn't kept their castles in good repair, they'd half forgotten they were supposed to be fighting men.

The past twenty years and more had changed that.

The Trokmê invasion, the eruption of the monsters from under Biton's shrine, and endless rounds of strife among the Elabonians themselves meant barons who weren't alert didn't live long. The ones who did live made sure no one ever got the chance to take them by surprise.

"*Still* no move from Aragis," Gerin said when they made camp that evening. "That's not like him. He's never been one to bluff and then back down. If he says he'll do something, he does it. He's a bastard, but a reliable bastard."

Not far away, an Elabonian fell on his face, as if he'd tripped over a stone in the grass. But there were no stones in the grass; the meadow was as smooth as an ornamental lawn in front of a high functionary's residence in the City of Elabon. Ferdulf giggled.

Gerin scowled. "Van said it—he does tempt you to find out just how nearly immortal he really is."

"Compose yourself, lord king," Rihwin said. "Could it not be that, by mere rumor of his presence, the demigod intimidates and inhibits Aragis the Archer from trying conclusions with you?"

Remembering how thoughtful Ferdulf had made Marlanz Raw-Meat, Gerin had to nod. "Ferdulf certainly intimidates and inhibits me," he said. "It would be nice if he did it to everyone else."

Van looked around to see if Balser Debo's son was in earshot. Not spotting him, the outlander chuckled and said, "Balser's going to be mighty unhappy if you bring this army down to his holding, eat every storeroom he has empty, lay tight hold on the land that was his, and then don't even have to do any fighting."

"Myself, I wouldn't mind that a bit," Gerin replied. "Fighting is wasteful. But you're right. Balser became my vassal so I could protect him. If he doesn't need protecting—"

"But, had he not come to you for protection, Aragis could have swallowed him at his leisure," Rihwin pointed out.

"That's so," Van agreed, "but he won't think about it. He'll think he never should have come to the Fox at all."

"If wheat and barley were as thin on the ground as thankfulness, we'd all go hungry most of the time, and that's a fact," Gerin said. "Still and all, the crop does grow. Adiatunnus told me one of the reasons he set out on this campaign with me instead of revolting—"

"Being a Trokmê, he's revolting almost by definition," Rihwin broke in.

"You keep quiet," Gerin told him, which, aimed at Rihwin, was good advice almost by definition. "As I was saying, or trying to say, one of the reasons he set out on this campaign was that he was grateful I'd gone to his aid against the Gradi five years ago."

"Aye, that was one," Van said. "The other, if I recall, was a nasty hunch you'd turn around and kick him in the ballocks if he tried stabbing you in the back."

"I never claimed gratitude was the only reason he chose to bring his men along with ours, just that it was *a* reason," Gerin said. He started to elaborate, but both his old friends were laughing too hard to pay any attention to him. After a moment, he gave up and started laughing himself.

They reached Balser's keep the next morning, eight days after setting out from Fox Keep. Math and Tiwaz floated in the sun-pale sky, the one at the third quarter, the other a waning crescent not far from the sun's skirts. Seeing the keep still undisturbed, Balser, who was riding at the head of the army with Gerin, let out a sigh of relief. "We won't have to try to take it back from Aragis, the gods be praised," he said.

"I hadn't thought we would," Gerin said. "The country-side, maybe, but not the keep. He hasn't had anywhere near the time he'd need to starve it out, and storming a castle is expensive even if you win. If you lose, trying it is likely to ruin you."

He looked east, then west. If Aragis the Archer hadn't come charging straight into Balser's holding, he'd probably gone and hit the Fox somewhere else along their border, with the news not having reached him yet. Try as he would, Gerin couldn't make himself believe Aragis really would stay quiet after giving such a blunt warning that he would go to war if Gerin accepted Balser's vassalage.

A look at Balser's keep suggested why Aragis might have thought it wise to launch his attack somewhere else. The keep perched atop of knob of high ground that the baron had scrupulously swept clear of all undergrowth above ankle high. A kitten would have had trouble approaching unseen. No man could have, not even afoot.

"Strong place," the Fox observed.

"Your strong place now, lord king," Balser said, "and you didn't even have to win it at war." Was that bitterness? It might have been. In Balser's shoes, Gerin, seeing peace and tranquillity in the holding, would have been wondering whether he could have gone on playing his two bigger rivals off against each other instead of finally yielding to one of them.

Balser had alert men in his keep. They were on the walls and ready long before the army came into archery range. Nor did they assume it was friendly for no better reason than its coming from the north. With Aragis for a neighbor, Gerin would have been alert, too.

The men on the wall raised a cheer when they recognized their overlord. They raised another cheer

when he told them Gerin's warriors had come to protect
them from anything Aragis might try to do. The second
cheer was not so lusty as the first; perhaps they hadn't
looked to be quite so thoroughly protected. But, at
Balser's shouted command, they lowered the drawbridge
and let the Fox's forces into the keep. As far as Gerin
was concerned, that finally proved Balser's good faith.

"I am your vassal, lord king," Balser said, thinking along
with him. "What is mine is yours, and you have handsomely
met your obligations to me."

Gerin had no doubt met those obligations altogether
too handsomely to suit Balser, whose holding now lay
in his hands. "I'll send some men down toward your
frontier with Aragis," he said. "Most of the army will
camp outside here. We won't pack the keep too full,
and we'll try not to eat up everything you own. This is
the business of the whole kingdom now, not just of the
lands you rule. The whole kingdom's resources will help
support it."

"Thank you, lord king." Balser bowed. "That you say
such a thing is why I would sooner be your vassal than
Aragis'."

Balser's men came out to help the Fox's warriors deal
with their horses and chariots. They exclaimed to see
so many men on horseback. Rihwin's troop galloped over
the flatlands and drew more exclamations and applause
at the way they handled their animals. Afterwards, Gerin
and Van started to head up into Balser's keep. The Fox
looked around for Dagref, to bring him along, too.

He spotted his son talking with one of the improbably
young, implausibly fuzzy riders: the one he'd noticed
early in the marches as being both younger and fuzzier
than anyone had any real business being. Dagref seemed
to sense Gerin's eye on him. He made a hasty farewell
and hurried up to the Fox.

In the great hall, Balser served up stewed trout and apple tarts and ale flavored with honey. He introduced to the Fox his wife, a plump young woman named Brinta. "She'll be glad of what I've learned from you, too, lord king," he said.

"I do hope so," Gerin answered, resolutely keeping his face straight. No, Balser hadn't forgotten their talk on different ways of doing things.

Just at that moment, the dogs in the great hall, who had been happy enough to root around in the rushes for scraps, all seemed to decide at once that soldiers' legs were the long-lost objects of their affection. The soldiers, for some reason, did not share that opinion. A great racket of shouts and yelps erupted. "What on earth—?" Brinta said with a giggle.

Gerin looked this way and that till he spotted Ferdulf. The little demigod was giggling, too, nastily. Catching his eye, Gerin shook his head. Ferdulf stuck out his tongue. The Fox sighed. Ferdulf had already worked his mischief; nothing to be done about it.

A serving maid was sitting on Van's lap. Gerin suspected she'd be sitting on the outlander's lap again, or in some other posture, as soon as the two of them found some privacy.

And another serving girl was hovering over Dagref, and doing it so obviously that he couldn't help but notice. She was older than he, but not by a great deal, and looked more friendly than calculating. Dagref himself looked . . . interested, and surprised at himself for being interested.

Yes, your body will surprise you, Gerin thought, watching while seeming not to watch. If Dagref was going to discover just what his flesh could do, Gerin was as well pleased that he should do it away from Fox Keep, with a woman he probably wouldn't see again. She wouldn't want so much to put on airs for being his first, and he'd be less inclined to imagine himself in love with her for no better reason than discovering what she hid between her legs.

"Oh, by the gods," Gerin murmured, "when I make calculations like that, I know I've been a ruler a long time. Too bloody long, maybe."

"I'm sorry, lord king?" Balser said. "I didn't quite hear that."

"It wasn't anything, really," the Fox answered turning toward him. "Only the fuzz that gathers if you don't dust your brains every now and then."

Brinta laughed a little; she understood what he was saying. A frown slowly spread over Balser's face—he didn't. And then, a moment later, he did, and enlightenment slowly replaced confusion. He had, by then, drunk enough ale to keep him from doing anything in a hurry. "That's well put, lord king," he said.

"I thank you," Gerin answered. Courtesy of any sort, he'd found, was uncommon enough to deserve encouragement.

"Well put," Balser repeated. His breath was enough to get a man drunk. "Reminds me of a story that—" The story, as he told it, had not much point and went on for so long, Gerin wished he hadn't encouraged it.

When at last it ended, he looked around the hall again. Van and his new friend had disappeared. Gerin had expected nothing less. He wondered what Fand was doing back in Fox Keep, and with whom. When this campaign was over, he'd probably find out in alarming detail.

And Dagref and the young serving girl were gone, too. Gerin stared down at the table. His son would be different when the sun rose tomorrow, in ways he didn't yet suspect. Being Dagref, he was liable to be different in ways Gerin didn't yet suspect, too.

He still hadn't said what he wanted from Gerin as a

forfeit for making Ferdulf keep quiet. With some people, the Fox might have taken that to mean he'd forgotten about it. As far as he could tell, though, Dagref never forgot about anything.

Gerin realized he'd been woolgathering when he looked up again and discovered Balser and Brinta had gone off to bed without his noticing. He poured down the ale left in his drinking jack. The woman who refilled it said, "Lord king, if you're weary, I'll take you up to your bedchamber now."

Maybe he'd been doing more than woolgathering there. Maybe he'd been dozing. He picked up the jack and said, "Maybe that's a good idea."

"Lord Balser has put you in the chamber next to his own," she said. "Up these stairs here . . . down this hall"— as she spoke, she guided him—". . . and it's this door right here." She worked the latch. A lamp was already burning on a stool set by the bed. She hesitated, then asked, "Lord king, do you want me to go in with you?"

"What?" Gerin said, and then felt foolish. The young woman had made *what* perfectly plain. The Fox smiled a lopsided smile. "My thanks. That's kind of you, but no. I don't forget I have a wife when I'm away from home."

He waited to see how she would take that. He'd had such offers a good many times. When he said no, as he habitually did, about half the time he ended up offending the woman whose company he'd declined. Some people fondly imagined they were irresistible, and that their beauty could move even a king. Had he been half his age, a lot of them probably would have been right.

This time, though, the serving girl just shrugged and nodded. "However you like, lord king. Sleep well, then." She went back toward the stairway, not even waggling her rump to show him what he'd be missing.

He went into the bedchamber, took off his sandals, and stripped down to his undertunic and drawers. After he'd used the chamber pot, he lay down on the bed and blew out the lamp. He didn't go to sleep right away; the walls here were no thicker than those at Duren's keep, and the noises from the chamber next door distracting. By the sound of things, Balser was intent on trying out every variation on an ancient theme about which he'd learned in Fox Keep. And, by the sound of things, Brinta also found the experiments . . . interesting.

For a little while, listening to them amused the Fox. After that, he just wished they'd shut up so he could doze off. He tried not to listen to them, which was like trying not to think about the color red: the more he tried, the more he failed. Finally, about the time when he should have got thoroughly annoyed, he fell asleep instead.

His first thought on waking up to early morning sunshine was to wonder if Balser and Brinta would be at it again: his new vassal was a young man. But things next door were quiet. Either Balser had worn himself out, or he'd already gone downstairs. The Fox splashed water from a basin onto his face, got into his clothes, and went downstairs himself.

Balser was sitting in the great hall, drinking ale and looking absurdly pleased with himself. A couple of tables over sat Van, who was also drinking ale and looking absurdly pleased with himself. And a couple of tables over from him sat Dagref, who was drinking ale and looking thoughtful—but a long way from displeased with himself.

Gerin started to go over to him, then decided that wasn't the best idea he'd ever had. If Dagref thought he was prying, he not only wouldn't get anywhere, his son would also be more inclined to hide things later.

So the Fox remembered from his own youth, anyhow.

He called for ale and he called for a couple of apple tarts and he made a point of not looking in Dagref's direction while he ate and drank. After a little while, Dagref got up and came over to him. "Good morning, son," the Fox said, concealing the pride he took in the success of his restraint.

"Good morning, Father," Dagref answered, and seemed at a loss how to go on from there. Gerin hadn't asked if he'd slept well, against which he could have reacted—one way or another. After a moment, the youth brightened. "Could you break me off half of that tart, please?"

"Certainly," Gerin said, and did. He kept on eating his own breakfast. When he spoke again, it was of business: "We'll probably pass today here, too. Tomorrow, I'll send men down along Balser's border with Aragis, to show the Archer we are here and we do intend to protect this holding."

"That sounds good enough." Dagref had no trouble talking about things that would happen away from the keep. "It's not as if we've tricked Aragis in any way. We let him know what we were going to do before we did it. He has no proper cause for complaint I can see."

"Ha," the Fox said. "Just because you can't see it doesn't mean Aragis can't see it."

"But in justice—" Dagref began in his most didactic tones. Then his tongue clove to the roof of his mouth. That startled his father, who had seen him in a great many states, but confusion seldom among them. Gerin's gaze followed Dagref's, and all grew clear. Coming out of the kitchen was the serving girl who'd stayed close by Dagref the night before. Exactly how close by him she'd stayed, Gerin suspected he was about to find out.

The girl looked as if she hadn't had a whole lot of

sleep, but she was also of an age where she could get through a day without much sleep. She also looked tousled and happy, a look often harder to counterfeit than passion at the moment itself.

She came over to Dagref and stood behind him. Of itself, his hand found hers. He sent Gerin an alarmed look, as if realizing he'd given away the game. He didn't realize he'd given it away sometime earlier. A little more slowly than he should have, he also figured out he needed to say something. "Father," he announced, "this is Rowitha."

"Hello, Rowitha," the Fox said gravely.

"Hello, lord king," she answered. Her hand tightened on Dagref's; she found the moment almost as awkward as he did. At last, she managed, "Your son, he's . . . very nice."

Dagref's face went as hot and red as the fire in the hearth. "I think so," Gerin said, grave still. "I'm glad you do, too. I'd also say" —he nodded to Dagref— "he thinks you're very nice."

"Yes!" Dagref agreed with great fervor. Now he squeezed Rowitha's hand. Gerin hoped he wasn't going to decide he was in love with her. Dagref clung to his opinions as tenaciously as fresh-water mussels clung to rocks. That was fine, when those opinions had some rational basis. Gerin didn't reckon bedding a woman for the first time any such rational basis. Convincing Dagref it wasn't, however, was unlikely to be easy.

Then he stopped worrying about how to deal with the beginnings of his son's love life, for one of Balser's men dashed into the great hall from the courtyard beyond, crying, "Lord king! Lord king! Aragis! Aragis the Archer!"

Gerin sprang to his feet with an oath. "Aragis has crossed over the border?" he demanded.

"Aye, lord king," Balser's man replied. Balser and Van

were on their feet, too, and so was Dagref, Rowitha for the moment forgotten. "He's here, lord king."

"What, with his army?" Gerin said. "By the gods, is there fighting out there? How did he get here, with no word beforehand?" He looked around for his armor, which hung on the wall not far from the fireplace.

And Balser's man stunned him again, saying, "No, lord king. As far as anyone on the wall can tell, he's here by his lonesome."

Down went the drawbridge. As soon as it had thumped onto dry land on the other side of the moat, Aragis' driver crossed over it and into Balser's keep. *No hesitation*, Gerin thought, standing there in the courtyard with Balser and Dagref and Van and some of his leading vassals. But then, Aragis the Archer seldom showed hesitation about anything, which was one reason the Fox wondered why they weren't already at war.

Without waiting for the chariot to stop, Aragis hopped out of it and strode briskly over to Gerin. He was a slim, hawk-faced man of about the Fox's age who leaned slightly forward as he walked, as if he were a hunting dog following an exciting scent.

Abruptly, he stuck out a hand. "I greet you, lord king," he said. As an obvious afterthought, he nodded to Balser. "Baron."

"I greet you, lord king," Gerin said, accepting the clasp. Aragis' grip was firm and hard, as it had been for as long as the Fox had known him. "You don't mind my asking, why aren't we trying to kill each other right now?"

"Don't worry, I thought we'd be doing just that by this time, too." Aragis bared his teeth in what was as much snarl as smile. "I think I'd have won, too. But something more important's come up."

"More important than which of us ends up ruling the

northlands?" Gerin said incredulously. Aragis' head jerked
up and down in a sharp, emphatic nod. Gerin whistled
softly under his breath. A few times in his life, he'd been
at the very edge of spreading news, the outermost
boundary between those who knew and those who didn't.
Aragis, plainly, was such an outer ripple now. The Fox
said, "You'd better tell me, then, hadn't you?"

Aragis nodded again. "It's not a question of which of
us ends up ruling the northlands any more," he said.
"It's a question of whether we can keep our heads on
our shoulders."

"By your five Elabonian hells, what are you talking
about?" Van boomed.

"The Empire's come back to the northlands," Aragis
answered.

For a few heartbeats, that didn't mean anything to
the Fox. Save for memories of his student days down
in the capital, he hadn't thought much about the
Elabonian Empire in the more than twenty years since
it had closed itself off from its former northern province.
He'd thought about it as little as he could get away with
in the days before it had done so, too; he hadn't paid
the tribute required of him because he hadn't got the
protection the tribute was supposed to earn.

But if the Empire had returned . . . "Father Dyaus,"
he whispered.

"That's the way of it, all right," Aragis the Archer agreed.
"They've cleared two of the passes through the High
Kirs, and they're sending soldiers through 'em. I don't
know what all's been happening down there these past
years, but it surely looks as though they've got a lot of
soldiers to send."

"Father Dyaus," Gerin said again. He'd worried about
Aragis. He'd worried about Adiatunnus and the Trokmoi.
He'd worried about the monsters from the caverns under

Biton's shrine at Ikos. He'd worried about the Gradi. He'd worried about Ferdulf. Worrying about the Empire of Elabon, long vanished from the northlands, had never crossed his mind.

Dagref spoke with his usual precision and accuracy: "Something might perhaps be done against the Empire if you two kings joined forces."

Aragis turned his clear, cold-eyed gaze on Dagref, but spoke to his father, saying, "No fools in your family, are there, Fox? This wouldn't be the lad who was kidnapped, would it, the one I got back for you from that cursed minstrel?"

"No, that's Duren, his older half brother," Gerin answered. "This is Dagref, whom I present to you with the warning that you'd better not ever be wrong in his presence, or you *will* hear about it."

"Ah, one of those," Aragis said, and then paused, the small grin he'd put on slowly fading. He gave Dagref another long look. "Mm, no, maybe not. Most of that kind think they know it all and turn out not to know a thing. If this one says something, he'll have a good notion of what he's talking about. You'd have been the same way before your beard sprouted, eh?"

"Oh, yes," Gerin answered, putting an arm around his son, who looked as if he could have done without the attention. "I was always sure in those days. I wasn't always right, mind you, but I always thought I was."

Dagref squirmed under the Fox's arm. "Let me be," he said indignantly. "The only other way either one of you could come through this mess would be to ally with the Empire against the other, and how far do you suppose you could trust the imperials? They'd use you and then sweep you aside."

Both Gerin and Aragis stared at him then. Gerin was pretty sure he eventually would have reached that same conclusion himself, but not with his son's effortless ease and ruthless clarity. Aragis made a sharp, short bow to Dagref. He said, "I came here to propose alliance to your father. You help me see I chose right. I am in your debt."

"Don't let it worry you," Dagref said tranquilly. "My father's in my debt, too. You didn't lose a bet to get there."

Aragis turned a speculative eye on Gerin. "Don't ask me about that now," the Fox said. "More important things to think about."

"As you say." Aragis the Archer managed a thin smile. "Still, anyone who gets the better of you at anything needs careful watching. Shall we speak, then, of what needs doing against the Empire?"

Balser Debo's son said, "Use my great hall as your own, lord kings." Of all the people in the courtyard, he was the only one who sounded delighted at the news Aragis had brought. Gerin had no trouble figuring out why: it meant Aragis and he wouldn't be fighting their war through Balser's holding. The noble might not even have to feed his new overlord's large, expensive army very long. If the warriors headed south to fight against the Elabonian Empire, they'd end up on Aragis' lands.

"They want the land back," Aragis said after he'd sat down and had a jack of ale pressed into his hand. "As far as they're concerned, it's as if they've never been away. The one who came to my keep said I could stay on—as baron, mind you, not as king—if I paid twenty-one years' worth of back tribute."

"Dyaus Allfather!" Gerin exclaimed. "Did you let him live?"

"I'm afraid I did." The Archer sounded faintly embarrassed at the admission. "I wasn't ready to fight in the south then—I had all my strength shifted north to go to war with you." He spoke as if Gerin should have expected nothing else. Since the Fox *had* expected nothing else, he only nodded. Aragis went on, "I just sent him out of my lands naked, to let the Empire have a clue as to how much it could ever expect to take away from me."

"Well done!" Van boomed. Adiatunnus clapped his hands. Gerin admired Aragis' gesture, too, but probably would have handled the imperial envoy rather differently himself.

Before he could decide whether to say as much, Dagref did it for him: "Being less abrupt with the fellow might have proved more prudent." Dagref was still at the age where, if something seemed obviously true to him, he let the world know about it without troubling his head about things like tact.

"I thought about that later," Aragis said. After pausing to down his ale and hold out the jack for a refill, he went on, "At the time, all I thought about was that the arrogant bastard had angered me, and so I was going to anger him right back, by the gods."

"Are you fighting with the imperials down on the southern border of your kingdom, then?" Gerin asked.

Aragis shook his head. "They're holding some of the territory that's rightfully mine, the whoresons. I don't know whether you know it or not, but these days I rule almost down to the foothills of the High Kirs." Again, his smile was one that a wolf might have offered. "Easier pushing south against the odds and sods there than coming north against you, Fox."

"Good." Gerin gave back that same display of teeth. Aragis' concern about him was the only thing that had kept them from clashing years before. "So you want my help against the Empire, do you?"

"It's your neck, too," Aragis answered steadily. "If they beat me by myself, do you think they'll stop at the northern border to my realm? And if they look like beating me, do you think I wouldn't go over to them, as your boy says, and save what I can by helping them smash you flat?"

"No and no, respectively," the Fox admitted. Aragis gave him that fierce smile again. He sighed. "Equal allies, as we were against the monsters fifteen years ago?" Aragis nodded, as if that went without saying. From his perspective, no doubt it did. Gerin might have tried extorting more from him, since he was the one more threatened, but didn't bother. Aragis had a notoriously long memory for slights. Thinking as much, Gerin realized that, while he intimidated Aragis, Aragis also intimidated him.

Adiatunnus realized the same thing at the same time. "You're giving him better terms than ever you offered me," the Trokmê said indignantly.

"You've been my vassal the past fifteen years, and of your own free will, too," Gerin retorted. "Of course, you spent a lot of that time forgetting it of your own free will, but that doesn't make it any less so." Adiatunnus didn't look any less aggrieved, either. *Too bad for him,* the Fox thought.

Aragis the Archer coughed. "There's one thing more," he said.

Gerin didn't care for his tone. Of course, Gerin hadn't care for his tone since he'd come into the courtyard, or for any of the news he'd delivered. Wondering what he was saving for last, the Fox asked, "And that is?"

"They've got wizards with 'em," Aragis answered glumly. "Real wizards, I mean, trained in that Sorcerers' Whatchamacallit of theirs, down in the City of Elabon."

"Collegium," Gerin said, and Aragis nodded; he'd forgotten the unfamiliar term. "Well, isn't that jolly?" Gerin went on. "I don't think there's a single sorcerer like that in all the northlands. And they'll have more than one along, sure as sure. Thank you, my friend. I didn't think I could feel any worse. Now I find I'm wrong. They'll know what they're doing, too—really *know*." Every spell he'd tried, he'd tried knowing he was liable to make a horrid botch of it.

He needed a couple of heartbeats to recognize the expression on Aragis' face. For one thing, it didn't sit well there; Aragis had for years molded his features to project harsh certainty and very little else. For another, he hadn't thought the Archer granted him so much respect in this particular area. But Aragis said, "Another reason I want you with me, Fox, is the skill *you've* shown as a mage since the days of the werenight."

"You haven't got any idea what you're talking about," Gerin said, his voice not far from a groan.

Aragis went on as if he hadn't spoken: "And when Marlanz Raw-Meat came back from your keep, he told me you had a god's son living in the village close by. If we have a god's son with us, even those cursed imperials will have to sit up and take notice." The Archer grew eager. "Did this—Fergulf, was that his name?—come south with you to campaign against me? Can we use him against the Empire?"

"Ferdulf," Gerin corrected absently. "Yes, he came along. He didn't come to campaign against you so much, I don't think. He said he came because Fox Keep would be boring once the army left." Aragis looked blank. Gerin sighed. Looking around Balser's great hall, he didn't see Mavrix's annoying son. He turned to Dagref. "Go track down Ferdulf, would you please? My fellow king here had better get a good idea of what he's pinning his hopes on."

Dagref took a deep breath, as if about to argue: he didn't want to miss a single word of what passed between his father and Aragis the Archer. Seeing Gerin's face, though, he sensibly decided arguing here wouldn't do him any good and would land him in trouble. He got up with no more than a small grimace and hurried out into the courtyard.

He came back soon enough, Ferdulf at his side—and, for a wonder, walking on the ground. Ferdulf, as the Fox had seen to his own discomfiture, got on with Dagref better than he did with almost anyone else. Gerin wasn't sure what that said about his son's character, and wasn't sure he wanted to find out, either.

Dagref pointed Aragis out to Ferdulf. The demigod strode up to him, inspected him, and shook his head. "This is supposed to be another king?" he said. Aragis' eyes widened when he heard the deep voice coming out of the small body. Ferdulf sniffed. "Doesn't seem so much of a much to me." His gaze swung toward Gerin. "Of course, you're not so much of a much, either."

"I'm so glad I have your respect," Gerin said.

Aragis stared from one of them to the other. Gerin already knew the Archer tolerated much less in the way of back talk and disrespect from subjects than he did himself. And now, despite having heard about Ferdulf, despite having heard for himself that Ferdulf was not the ordinary four-year-old his body made him out to be, he made the mistake of treating him as if he were: "You, boy!" he said, as he might have to any serf. "Who was your father again?"

Gerin could have told the Archer he'd just done something foolish. Before he got the chance, Ferdulf demonstrated it. As usual, showing proved more effective than telling. Ferdulf walked over to Aragis. Then he walked up Aragis' legs, treating their vertical as a horizontal. Then he walked across Aragis' lap. And then he walked up Aragis' chest, treating that in the same fashion as he had the Archer's legs. Planting his feet on Aragis' collarbones, he looked across—effectively, down—at his startled face. "My father, *man*, was the god Mavrix of Sithonia. Who was yours, or didn't your mother know, either?"

Aragis had courage. Not even his worst enemy would ever have denied that. So, now, he heard only the insult, and forgot a demigod had delivered it. Grabbing Ferdulf by the ankles, he tried to throw him away. That didn't work; Ferdulf refused to be budged. Snarling an oath, Aragis sprang to his feet and grabbed for his sword.

Everyone who was anywhere near him snatched at his arm to keep him from drawing the bronze blade. "Enough!" Gerin said sharply. "My judgment is that dishonors are even here."

"What gives you the right to judge?" Aragis and Ferdulf said the same thing at the same time, then glared at each other for having done so.

"Aragis, I've put up with you since just after the werenight, and you, Ferdulf, I've put up with you for as long as you've been around—it only seems like forever," Gerin said. "If I haven't got the right to judge, who does?"

"No one." Again, demigod and king spoke together. Again, they glared at each other. Neither was fond of the Fox. Each was fonder of him than of the other.

"Get off King Aragis, Ferdulf," Dagref urged. "Standing on him like that won't do any good."

"It does me plenty of good," Ferdulf said, but he took a step off Aragis' chest into midair, then drifted to the ground like a chunk of thistledown. Aragis rubbed at his collarbones; he must have felt the weight of the demigod on him.

"Ferdulf, you haven't got much use for Elabonians, have you?" Gerin asked, a question whose answer seemed obvious.

"Would you, were you I?" Ferdulf returned, rolling his eyes.

"Oh, I don't know." Gerin spoke musingly now. "After all, you're half Elabonian yourself."

"All the more reason to despise that half," the demigod said. "Without it, I'd be altogether divine."

Without it, you wouldn't be here at all, Gerin thought. But he didn't bother mentioning that. Instead, he said, "Well, from what King Aragis here tells me, the Empire of Elabon is coming. The Emperor wants to make this part of the world do as he says when he's down in the City of Elabon. He wants to make this part of the world obey him the same way that Sithonia has to obey him."

Even after more than four years, he didn't know just how much instruction Mavrix had given Ferdulf about Sithonia, or how much knowledge of his father's homeland Ferdulf had inherited, or whatever the process was by which Ferdulf knew what he knew. He did know Ferdulf knew enormously more than any purely human four-year-old had any business knowing. Would that be enough? He could but hope.

Ferdulf had disappointed his hopes a good many times, and blasted them a few more. This time, he lived up to them. "The Elabonian Empire will never do to this land what its overmuscled morons have done in and with and to fair Sithonia," the little demigod cried, his big voice echoing back from the roof beams of the great hall. "It shall not come to pass. I shall not permit it."

Aragis started to say something. Gerin caught the Archer's eye and shook his head ever so slightly. For a wonder, Aragis listened to someone other than himself. He kept quiet.

"I shall destroy the Elabonians, root and branch! I shall smite them, hip and thigh!" Ferdulf thundered. Some of Balser's men broke into applause. Aragis the

Archer looked as if he was about to join them.

Gerin caught his eye once more. The Fox shook his head again, a gesture even smaller than the first one. As slightly, Aragis' ever so erect shoulders slumped. Gerin was glad Ferdulf wanted to take on the forces of the Elabonian Empire. He didn't think Mavrix's son would be able to beat them singlehanded. Elabon had ruled Sithonia for hundreds of years, no matter how much the Sithonians looked down their noses at their overlords. Divided into quarreling city-states, the Sithonians also looked down their noses at one another. Their gods squabbled among themselves. If all their men and all their gods hadn't been able to keep the Elabonians out of Sithonia, one bad-tempered little demigod wasn't going to keep the Empire out of the northlands, not by himself he wasn't.

As long as he despised the Elabonian Empire more than he despised either Gerin or Aragis, though, having him along wouldn't hurt.

"What are we waiting for?" Ferdulf demanded. "The sooner we strike these bronze-bound blockheads, the sooner we send them scurrying back into the south! When we fight, let us give no quarter."

Every once in a while, when trying to work magic, the Fox had a spell succeed too well. He hadn't worked magic here, not in the strict sense of the word, but got something of that feeling nonetheless. What would happen if and when Ferdulf discovered he couldn't beat the Empire by himself? Would all his joy in trying disappear? Would he turn on Gerin and Aragis instead?

This once, Gerin wished he weren't quite so good at coming up with unpleasant questions long before he had any answers for them.

Aragis said, "Are we allies against the Empire, then, you and I and Ferdulf here?"

"You and I are," Gerin said. "I already told you that. Having the Empire on my border I like even less than having you on my border." Aragis showed his teeth again in that snarling smile. The Fox went on, "As for Ferdulf—" He turned to the demigod. "Will you join with us against the Elabonian Empire?"

"_I_ am against the Elabonian Empire," Ferdulf said. "If you want to stand against it, too, _you_ may join with _me_."

Gerin remained of the opinion that one god's son, no matter how arrogant, was not going to prove a match for all the soldiers and, if what Aragis said was true, all the mages of the Empire of Elabon. But he did not feel like quibbling about definitions with Ferdulf. Instead, he held out his hand. Aragis clasped it. A moment later, the demigod set his warm little palm over both their hands. Gerin had made a good many unlikely alliances in his time. This one struck him as being as improbable as any.

Balser Debo's son looked mutinous. "By the gods, lord king, why should I furnish you with twenty chariot crews? All the fighting you aim to do will be off my land."

"That's not the point." Gerin might have borrowed his hard, harrowing smile from Aragis the Archer. "The point is that you owned yourself my vassal. True, you did it because you wanted me to help protect you. But that doesn't mean your obligations go away when the danger to your holding disappears. I have the right to ask this of you, and ask it I do."

"It's outrageous!" Balser exclaimed. "Why should I send my men off to fight farther south than they'd ever have any natural reason to go?"

"Because if you don't, they're likelier to be fighting here sooner or later anyhow," Gerin answered. "The idea, if we can bring it off, is to beat the Empire as far south as we can. If we can do that, the imperials may never get up here at all."

If all the fighting turned out to be in the south, Aragis' lands would suffer far more than his own. That might end up giving him a decisive edge on the Archer: so declared the calculating part of his mind that never slept.

"I suppose *my* twenty men are going to make the difference between beating the imperials and losing to them," Balser said scornfully.

"By themselves? I doubt it, or else we're in worse trouble than I think," Gerin said. "But if you leave yours home and Widin Simrin's son leaves his home and Adiatunnus leaves his home . . . You didn't much like the idea of Adiatunnus' leaving his men home when you thought Aragis was going to land on you like a load of rocks, did you?"

Balser had the decency to turn red. "All right, I see what you're saying, lord king. Bah! To the five hells with me if I like it."

"Oh, I'm just dancing with glee myself at the idea of taking on the Elabonian Empire. Dancing with bloody glee!" The Fox did a few rather awkward steps.

Balser stared at him. Kings were supposed to be serious, even solemn, people. Gerin didn't fit the bill. He hadn't intended to be a king. He hadn't intended to be a prince, or a baron. If he wasn't always what the world thought he was supposed to be, that was the world's hard luck.

But he wasn't always a funny man, either. "One more thing for you to think about," he told Balser: "How many men do I have on your lands right now?"

That got through to his new and now reluctant vassal. Balser looked as if he'd bitten into a pear about three days after it should have been tossed into a swill bucket for the pigs. "Lord king, when I became your vassal, you promised you'd respect my rights," he said reproachfully.

"So I did," Gerin agreed. "And, when you became my vassal, you promised you'd live up to your duties. This is one of them. I am within my rights to ask it of you. You are not within your rights to refuse it to me."

Plainly, Balser Debo's son did not agree. As plainly, he couldn't do anything about it. "Very well." He spat out the words one by one. "Twenty chariots and their crews, to go with you when you leave my land."

"I do thank you for them," the Fox said. "They will help. And there's one other thing you need to remember: the sooner you furnish them to me, the sooner we will be able to leave your land, and the sooner we stop eating your storerooms empty."

"Ah," Balser said. "I was wondering if you'd be able to come up with a reason for me to give you the crews and cars in a hurry. You have, by the gods."

"I thought that might be so," Gerin said.

Balser sighed. "Get caught up in the quarrels of neighbors bigger than you are and you find they make you do things and then expect you to like it."

"I don't expect you to like it," Gerin told him. "I do hope you'll see the need." He got a shrug from Balser, which was about as much as he'd thought the baron would give him. Then he shrugged, too: the Elabonian Empire was forcing him into a position not far from the one in which he'd put Balser. He hoped he'd have better luck than Balser getting out of it.

Aragis the Archer studied Gerin's assembled forces. "I'll tell you this much, Fox," he said: "I'm gladder to have you with me than I would have been fighting you. You've got more men here than I thought you could raise."

"I've never picked a quarrel with you," Gerin answered. "I wasn't picking a quarrel with you over Balser's holding, either, however you chose to take it. But I wasn't going to back away, either."

"Leave that aside, since I'm not such a fool as to call my ally a liar," Aragis said, which let him call the Fox a liar even as he said he was doing no such thing. "You've put a lot of men on horseback here, too. You always were one to try things no one would have looked for."

"Maybe." Gerin raised an eyebrow. "You came here all by your lonesome, and you say I do things nobody would look for? What would have kept me from dropping you off Balser's wall on your head?"

Aragis shrugged. "I counted on your good sense. Biggest worry I had was that some of your troopers would do me in before I got the chance to tell you what the Empire was up to. But your men are well disciplined, too—maybe not quite so tight as mine, but well enough."

"Your idea of discipline is to make your men fear you worse than any foe," the Fox said.

"Well, of course," Aragis said, as if surprised Gerin contemplated discipline of any other sort. "It's worked, too. Tell me it hasn't."

Gerin couldn't tell him that. Whether it would work for Aragis' successor was a different question. Maybe Aragis didn't care. Maybe he thought one of his sons was as fierce as he—an alarming idea if ever there was one.

"My way works, too," Gerin said, and Aragis could not deny that. The Fox went on, "We'll see—or our sons will see, or our grandsons—whose way ends up working better."

By way of reply, Aragis only grunted. Gerin hadn't expected much more from him. Other times he'd talked with Aragis about anything further away than the immediate future, he'd got only incomprehension in return. Within Aragis' range of vision, he was most effective; beyond it, he didn't seem to see at all.

"How determined did the imperials seem to be about taking back the northlands?" the Fox asked Aragis. "If we give them one set of lumps, or maybe two, will they go back over the High Kirs and leave us alone? Or do you think they'll keep coming after us no matter what we do?"

"I don't know the answer to that," Aragis answered. "I do know one thing: if we don't give them a set of lumps, we've lost the cursed fight." He paused, as if waiting for Gerin to disagree with him. When Gerin didn't say anything, the Archer picked up again: "They're every bit as arrogant as I remember them being, and that's saying a lot."

"So it is," Gerin agreed. "Down in the City of Elabon, they'd look down their noses at you for wearing trousers instead of robes, and for coming straight out and saying what you mean instead of talking all around it from four different directions at once." He looked up at the sound of hoofbeats. "And a good day to you, Rihwin. What can I do for you?"

Atop his horse, the noble from the City of Elabon tossed his head in anger more assumed than real. "I heard that last remark of yours, lord king, and I desire you to know that it filled my heart with resentment, that I reject it as a slanderous and scurrilous assault on my former homeland, that it bears not even the slightest relation to truth of any sort, and that, furthermore, your syntax in framing the said remark, being both slipshod and leaden, causes me to—"

"—Prove the point of everything I was saying?" Gerin suggested.

"Oh, I am wounded. Wounded!" Rihwin cried, clapping

a hand over his heart. Gerin snorted. By the expression on Aragis' face, he wouldn't have put up with Rihwin's flamboyant nonsense for a moment. There were times when Gerin wondered why he put up with his fellow Fox's nonsense himself. But, over years, Rihwin had— narrowly—convinced him he was worth keeping around.

And then his friend did his best to unconvince him. Rihwin's face took on a look almost of transfiguration. In soft, reverent tones, he said, "With the Empire returned to the northlands once more, surely commerce between us and the long-sundered south will soon revive."

As soon as Rihwin spoke of commerce, Gerin knew what he had in mind. Gerin would have liked to see commerce revived, too, commerce in books and fine cloth and other such luxuries the northlands had trouble producing for itself. Rihwin, however, would be thinking of only one such luxury. "You don't mean commerce. What you mean is wine."

"And wherefore, I pray you, should I not?" Rihwin demanded.

"For one thing, you get into trouble when you drink wine," Gerin answered. "You get into trouble when you drink ale, too, but you get into worse trouble when you drink wine. For another, with wine comes Mavrix, lord of the sweet grape. Do you truly want more dealings with him?"

That did give Rihwin pause. The first time he'd ever invoked Mavrix, just before the werenight, the Sithonian god had permanently taken away his ability to work magic. Their meetings since had not been marked with any great warmth, either; Mavrix disliked and distrusted not only Gerin but also anyone who had anything to do with him.

But Rihwin was made of stern stuff—either that or he had a marvelously selective memory. He said, "It should be all right, lord king, and for the chance to taste

wine once more, what risk could be too great?" He struck
a melodramatic pose on horseback.

"I like wine well enough," Aragis said, "but ale suits
me." He stuck out his chin and folded his arms across
his chest in a different sort of melodrama, the pantomime
of demanding obedience.

As Gerin could have told him, getting obedience out
of Rihwin the Fox was an uphill fight. Loftily, Rihwin
observed, "Some people are of the opinion that, for no
better reason than something's suiting them, it should
suit everyone, a proposition easily demonstrated to be
fallacious."

Aragis blinked. Gerin watched him sort through
Rihwin's sentence a clause at a time. He watched him
scowl when he got to the end of it. "Some people," Aragis
rumbled, "are of the opinion that anyone else cares about
their opinions to the extent of dumping a pisspot."

"Yes, some people are," Rihwin agreed. He and Aragis
glared at each other. Gerin would have bet the two of
them were likely to rub each other the wrong way. When
he made bets of that sort, he usually proved right. When
he bet something would go well, on the other hand, he
was wrong dishearteningly often.

That afternoon, his army reached the border between
Balser's holding and the lands Aragis the Archer ruled.
The border guards cheered. "Kick Aragis the Arrogant's
arse!" one of them shouted. The rest offered even more
creative advice. They all cheered Gerin.

Aragis tapped his driver on the shoulder. His chariot
broke out of the swarm and rattled over to the border
station. One of the guards recognized him, and went
from jeering to white-faced and shaky in the space of a
heartbeat. At his whispered comment, the other warriors
shut up one by one.

"I thought I would give you the chance to say to my

face what you say to my back," Aragis told them. "I see you have not the belly for it. This surprises me not at all." At his order, his driver took him back up alongside Gerin.

"That took nerve," the Fox said. In his own cold-blooded way, Aragis had style.

The Archer shrugged. "Most men are dogs. They yap loud enough when nothing bigger and fiercer is around. When challenged, though, they sniff your backside and then roll over."

"Use them as men and you'll find them likelier to behave as men," Gerin said. Aragis shook his head. They rode on in silence after that. Gerin would have been happier had he been more nearly certain he was right and his royal rival wrong.

IV

Gerin had not been down in the lands over which Aragis the Archer ruled for more than twenty years. For some time, he'd been busy far closer to Fox Keep. Then, after his attention reached so far south, the only way he could have come was at the head of an invading army. Here he was at the head of an army, but, to what would have been his astonishment up until a couple of days before, he wasn't invading.

Before the Empire of Elabon withdrew beyond the High Kirs, the lands closer to the mountains had been more nearly a true part of the Empire than the raw frontier up by the River Niffet. Some of the villages hereabouts had almost deserved to be called towns. Close by the Elabon Way, especially, trade had flourished. It was, in fact, the condition to which the Fox aspired to lift his own holdings.

And Aragis, who had such splendid underpinnings for his kingdom, was letting them slip. Maybe Gerin remembered these lands as having been more prosperous than they really were because he'd been so much younger the last time he'd been through them. But he didn't think so. He hadn't been so young as all that. He could see signs of change, too, and not for the better.

Several villages had buildings standing empty—not just houses, but smithies and potters' works and taverns

116

as well. Some had fallen down into rubble. Some were being torn down to patch other buildings still in use. And only weeds and bushes grew in the blank spaces between houses where others had presumably stood.

Some fields weren't being cultivated, either. In them, scruffy wheat and barley fought what was going to be a losing fight against brambles and saplings and plain, ordinary grass. "You don't seem to have quite so many people as you did," Gerin remarked to Aragis, sounding as casual as he could.

"Just have to make sure the ones who are left work harder to take up the slack." Past that, Aragis was indifferent. Gerin wanted to grab him by the front of the tunic, lift him into the air, and shake some sense into him. *What are you doing, you fool?* he wanted to shout. *Don't you see that, if this goes on a while longer, the peasants you have left won't be able to feed all your warriors? Then it won't matter how strong your armies are, or would be, because you won't be able to keep them in the field.*

Aragis wouldn't listen. Aragis wouldn't have the vaguest idea what he was talking about. Aragis would get angry. Knowing all that, Gerin walked away instead of screaming at him.

Van followed the Fox. "If you could have seen the look on your face there when the Archer said, 'So what?'—" the outlander began.

"If he saw it, he didn't know what it meant." Gerin kicked at the dirt. "If he had known what it meant, he wouldn't have let this happen to his lands in the first place." Gerin kicked again. "I wouldn't have had to fight him. In another few years, all this would have fallen under its own weight."

"Maybe," Van said. "Or maybe, if he heard the creaking, he would have fought you. If he won, he'd have your lands to ruin over the next twenty years. Even if he lost, he wouldn't have so many fighters to feed."

Gerin studied him. "That's a cold-blooded way of looking at things. It's more the way I'd look at them than how I'd expect you to."

"And who's been living beside you in Fox Keep these twenty years and more?" Van returned. He shook his head. "I wouldn't have thought that way when I first came there, not when I swam the Niffet with the Trokmoi shooting arrows at me till I got out of range. I'd spent so many years wandering, I didn't expect I'd ever put down roots." His head went back and forth again. "Never would have thought I'd stay attached to the same woman so long, either."

"You don't let that worry you, not when you're off someplace where Fand can't see what you're up to."

"And so what?" Van said. "If I get the itch, by the gods, I scratch it." His chuckle was mordant. "And if I didn't, I'd get no credit for holding back. One campaign we fought over in the southwest, years ago this was, I kept my prong in my breeches the whole time, and when I got back to Castle Fox I said as much to my lady love. What happened? Do you remember what happened, Fox?"

"Sorry," Gerin answered. "You and Fand have had enough dustups that that one doesn't stick in my mind."

"No, eh? Well, it does in mine. She thought I was lying, is what she thought. That put more fire under her cookpot than she gets when I tell her about all the pretty girls I rumple. So I ask you: what am I supposed to do?"

"I don't know," the Fox said. As far as he could see, Van and Fand quarreled as much because they enjoyed quarreling as because they really had anything about which to quarrel. He'd suggested as much to the outlander once or twice. Van had agreed with him, which was alarming, and had done exactly nothing to change his ways, which Gerin found even more alarming.

Dagref trotted by on horseback. He waved to the Fox and to Van. Loping along beside the horse, barely visible over the beast's back, was the fuzzy-bearded youngster Gerin had noticed once or twice before as the army moved south. He didn't wave. *Has to be from some keep out in the middle of nowhere,* Gerin thought. *The king's son isn't far from his own age, so he can be easy with him, but with the king and his old friend—no.*

Van said, "One of these days before long, Kor will be coming with us when we go to war, too. Won't be long, not the way time goes by now."

"You're right about that," Gerin said. "He'll be something to watch out for on the battlefield, too."

"That he will," Van said proudly. "My size, or most of it, and Fand's temper, or worse. I tell you the truth, the gods had better help anybody fool enough to stand in his way by the time he's seventeen. And if Maeva were a lad, I'd have two grand warriors to leave behind me when I go." He scratched his chin. "I wonder how many brats I've got that I don't know the first thing about? A few, I shouldn't wonder, but I've never been like Rihwin, ready to keep track of 'em all."

"Rihwin's almost as good at keeping track of his bastards as Carlun is at keeping track of beans," Gerin agreed. He spotted his fellow Fox not far away, and raised his voice a little: "The only thing Rihwin can't keep track of is Rihwin."

"Are you speaking to me or of me or against me?" Rihwin asked. "In sooth, I was but enjoying a vision, a memory of days long past, and nights as well, nights spent in the pursuit of knowledge, nights spent comparing the color and bouquet of one glorious vintage against another, and—"

"—Mornings spent wishing you were dead," Gerin broke in. Rihwin looked indignant. With his flexible features, every expression he assumed was, in a small way, a work of art. Gerin took no notice of him, but pressed ahead: "All you remember about wine is the parts of the drinking of it you enjoyed. The parts that weren't so much fun, you forget."

Rihwin shook his head. "There was," he insisted, "nothing about drinking wine that failed of enjoyment for me. I was a connoisseur." He struck a pose of exaggerated estheticism that would have made Mavrix proud.

"Fanciest word for *drunk* I ever heard," Van said.

Rihwin looked indignant all over again, giving a rendering full of even more virtuosity than the previous one. Before he could protest out loud, though, Gerin spoke up in agreement with the outlander: "You weren't much of a connoisseur the day we met you down in that horrible dive in the City of Elabon, the one not far from the Sorcerers' Collegium. What you were was somebody trying to climb into a wine jar through the little hole in the neck, and you didn't care a lick about the vintage you were drinking."

"After all these years, I must confess to remembering little about the occasion," Rihwin said with dignity.

"Yes, passing out will do that to you, won't it?" Gerin replied.

"You were as cold as a carp on a snowbank," Van added.

"If you grand and magnificent gentlemen, who of a certainty have been sober every moment of every day of your lives, insist on reviling me and casting imputations upon my character, I shall be forced to take myself off and drown my sorrows—in ale, worse luck." Rihwin marched away, nose in the air.

Behind him, Gerin and Van both started to laugh.

"There's nothing we can do with him," Gerin said, and his voice held only admiration. "Not a single thing."

"How about a good swift kick in the arse?" Van suggested.

"If all the knocks Rihwin's taken over the years haven't let in any sense, one more kick won't do the job," Gerin said, and Van laughed again. Nonetheless, Gerin kept a thoughtful eye on Rihwin the Fox. When Rihwin got particularly vehement on the subject of wine, strange things had a way of happening. Gerin didn't want strange things to start happening. Life, at the moment, was quite complicated enough without them. Unfortunately, he had not the slightest idea what he could to do prevent them.

Most of Aragis' warriors were down in the southern part of his lands, keeping an eye on the forces of the Elabonian Empire. Even so, more detachments joined the army the Fox was leading. Aragis' peasants and villagers might have had their troubles, but his kingdom did seem to support an astonishing number of soldiers, every one of them well armed, well equipped, and to all appearances a rugged customer.

"I would have put even more men into the south against the Empire," Aragis remarked to Gerin when yet another contingent of his warriors came rattling up in their chariots to join the army, "but I had to hold a good many back to fight you in case you decided to jump on me and then worry about the Empire."

"To the five hells with me if you don't have enough fighting men to tackle two big wars at once," Gerin said.

"If your Trokmê neighbor had decided to forget he was your vassal, you wouldn't have brought so many of your own troopers down to Balser's holding." Aragis spoke with as much certainty as if he'd announced that

Math moved through the sky more slowly than Tiwaz.

Since he was right, Gerin changed the subject: "Who's commanding the force you've got facing the Empire?"

"My eldest son, Aranast, with Marlanz Raw-Meat to hold him steady should he falter," Aragis answered. "Aranast has never tried leading that big an army before. If he's up to it, well and good. If he's not, I don't aim to let him throw away the kingdom."

"That's sensible," Gerin agreed, though he wondered how happy Aranast was at having Marlanz looking over his shoulder. Then something else occurred to him: "The first time you sent Marlanz up to treat with me, you had an older man with him, too, to hold him to the road if he tried wandering off."

"You have your son with you here," Aragis said, nodding to Dagref. "One day, he'll lead men on his own. For now, he's still learning."

Gerin nodded, but still thought the two principles not quite the same. Dagref plainly lacked the experience he needed to lead now. In a while, he would as plainly have it. Aragis seemed to make a habit of using a man with such experience alongside one who was just on the edge of having it. The idea was a long way from the worst one Gerin had ever met.

That evening, as the steadily growing army was encamping by the side of the Elabon Way, a chariot came pounding up the highway, wheels clattering on stone paving, the driver whipping on the horses to wring every last drip of speed from them.

The fellow in the car with him sprang down as soon as the chariot halted. "Lord king—" he gasped, and then paused for a moment to catch his breath. He was swaying a little; if he'd come a long way in a chariot going hells for leather, solid ground probably felt unsteady under his feet. Gerin came over to hear what he had to say. Aragis frowned at that, but said nothing. The messenger resumed: "Lord king, uh, lord kings, there's an imperial coming behind me. You'll meet him on the road tomorrow, I've no doubt, but I can tell you what he's going to say."

"Good," Aragis said briskly, and Gerin nodded. "Say on, Sandifer." The Archer glanced at the Fox and shrugged a small shrug, acknowledging that this business concerned both of them.

Sandifer said, "Lord, uh, kings, he's going to give you ten days to disperse your forces, or else there will be war: voluminous war, I heard him say, whatever that means."

"It means he talks like a southerner," Gerin said. "They like to throw in a fancy word every now and then, whether they use it the right way or not."

"I heard that," Rihwin called.

"If they want volumes of war," Aragis said, ignoring Rihwin (as did Gerin), "we'll give them enough to fill the Fox's library."

That wasn't using *voluminous* the right way, either, but Gerin was not inclined to undertake literary criticism on his fellow king's utterances. "If it comes to war— no, when it comes to war," he said, "do you aim to go back into your keeps and make the Empire dig you out one castle at a time?"

"Only if I have to," Aragis answered at once. "If I were fighting the imperials alone, I might do that, for they'd have far more strength than I do by myself. But they'd ravage the countryside, so that even beating them back now might mean losing to you next year. My lands shield yours here, you'll notice."

"That's what you get for living south of me." Gerin scratched his head. Aragis could see that having the Elabonian Empire devastate his territory would weaken him to the point where he'd have trouble withstanding the Fox. He wasn't stupid, nor anything close to it. But the idea that he was doing to his own lands over the course of years what the Empire would do in a single campaigning season had never entered his mind. It wasn't immediately apparent, and so wasn't there at all for him.

The Archer said, "With you beside me, Fox, I aim to fight those imperial bastards as hard as I can and as far south as I can. One thing I will say about you: now that you've said you will fight alongside me, I don't think you'll turn on me instead of the Empire. There are others in the northlands to whom I'd not trust my back."

Gerin bowed slightly. When it came to judging how things ran in the short term, Aragis was as good as anyone he'd ever know—as good as he was, probably. Could he trust Aragis at his back? The only answer he could come up with was . . . *sometimes*. He said, "Knowing which enemy to pick counts for a good deal."

"Oh, indeed." Aragis bared his teeth in one of his alarming smiles. "Did I not rely on you to understand the Elabonian Empire was more dangerous to both of us than we are to each other? Did I not put my life in your hands on that understanding and no more?"

"You did." Gerin wondered whether he would have done that in reverse if, say, the Gradi had been on the point of beating him five years earlier. Maybe. Maybe not, too. Because Aragis lived so close to the here-and-now, every crisis was liable to seem a matter of life and death to him. Gerin was better at waiting than his hard-charging fellow king.

"We cast defiance in the envoy's teeth, then, and smash the Empire's army on the battlefield." Aragis' eyes had a fierce falcon's glint in them, too. He believed every word of what he was saying. Maybe that would help him make his belief real. Maybe it would make him try to do more than he really could. Gerin shrugged. He'd find out soon.

When the chariot bearing the envoy of the Elabonian Empire and those in which his retinue rode came into view, Gerin felt—not for the first time since leaving Fox Keep—he'd fallen back in time through close to half his life. Not since his last trip down to the City of Elabon, more than twenty years before, had he seen men dressed in the flowing robes the imperials south of the High Kirs affected.

Adiatunnus saw them, too, and did not know what to make of them. "Is the Empire after sending women to treat with us the now?" he asked, not quite in jest.

"No, that's just their style down there," the Fox answered. "And they shave not only their cheeks and chins, the way you Trokmoi do, but their upper lips as well. I did it myself, when I lived down in the city."

"But you had the sense to go back to a better way," Adiatunnus said.

Gerin shrugged. "Sometimes different is just different, not better or worse."

He looked around for Ferdulf. When he spied the little demigod, he waved for him to come over. Ferdulf came, looking suspicious. More often than not, Gerin was doing his best to make him go away. "What do you want?" Ferdulf growled.

"See those fellows up ahead?" The Fox pointed. "That's the envoy from the Elabonian Empire and his friends."

Ferdulf's lip curled in splendid scorn. "So? What do you want me to do about it? Miserable imperial—" His voice faded down into a scatological mumble.

That was just what Gerin wanted. "They probably won't like you any better," he said with a grin he did not show: Ferdulf seemed to have forgotten he too was an Elabonian. "They're the ones who hold down Sithonia, after all."

"I wonder what I can do to them," Ferdulf mused. Dagref looked back over his shoulder at Gerin. Gerin wished he hadn't done it; the look might have alerted Ferdulf to the notion that he was being manipulated. If Dagref did have to give Gerin a look, though, a look of approval was the one the Fox wanted. Dagref, as his father had learned to his own discomfiture, was better than anyone else at manipulating Ferdulf.

Up came the Elabonian chariots. The one in the lead had a shield painted in green and white stripes mounted on the pole between the two horses: a shield of truce. That chariot and the one behind it pulled away from the rest and approached the army that had set out from Fox Keep. "I am Efilnath the Earnest," the fellow in the fanciest robe called, "commissioner to his majesty Crebbig I, Emperor of Elabon. I see here Aragis the Archer, who presumes to make the error of styling himself king. Rumor has it that others in the province are equally rash. Be any such others present, that I might treat with and dismiss all such false claimants simultaneously?"

"I am Gerin the Fox," Gerin announced, "king of the north. I am here in alliance with Aragis. I note, Efilnath, that if you call claims false and say ahead of time you will dismiss them, you are not treating with those who make them, only disposing of them. I also note that they—and we—are not to be disposed of so readily."

He wondered who Crebbig I was. On his last journey down to the City of Elabon, Hildor III had reigned there: an indolent excuse for a monarch. Whatever Crebbig's faults—and, being a man, he was bound to have them—indolence did not seem to be among their number.

"As the Elabonian Empire does not recognize that

this land has ever been anything but an imperial province, so naturally we cannot recognize any men styling themselves kings, save in recognizing them as rebels and traitors," Efilnath said.

Aragis the Archer growled something angry under his breath. Gerin was about to growl something out loud when his eye chanced to fall on one of the men in the chariot behind Efilnath's. The fellow was nothing special to look at—not too tall, not too wide, not too handsome—and wore a robe that would have been altogether ordinary in the City of Elabon. Nonetheless, perhaps by the way he carried himself, perhaps by a certain look in his eye, Gerin knew him for what he was: a wizard from the Sorcerers' Collegium.

And he recognized Gerin, too—not as an equal, as one who had completed the same arduous training, but as one who had some part of it. Those oddly compelling eyes of his widened, just a little; plainly, he had not expected to come across anyone in the northlands who shared even a fragment of his arcane expertise. Gerin understood that. The Elabonians south of the High Kirs reckoned the northlands a barbarous backwater. He knew they had a point, but not so much of one as they thought they did.

He smiled at the wizard, a bleak display of acknowledgment and warning. The Elabonian got down from his chariot and hurried over to Efilnath's. He whispered in the envoy's ear. Whatever he said—and the Fox had a pretty good notion of what it would be—Efilnath seemed unimpressed. "Come what may, a backwoods baron remains a backwoods baron," he said, a distinct sniff in his voice.

"Oh, Ferdulf," Gerin called sweetly, "come and say hello to these nice people, would you please?"

"What nice people?" Ferdulf snarled. "All I see is a

bunch of Elabonians who think they're smarter than they really are—idiots who think they're halfwits."

As if his rumbling baritone wouldn't have been enough to alert the southerners that he was something out of the ordinary, he also strolled along a couple of feet off the ground. Efilnath gaped at him. So did the wizard, in a different, more intensely concentrated way. "Who are you?" he demanded, and then, a moment later, "*What* are you?"

By way of reply, Ferdulf stuck out his tongue. It went out improbably far. The tip wiggled like a serpent's tongue for a moment. Then he drew the whole thing back in with a wet *plop*. He smiled unpleasantly at the Elabonian sorcerer.

Sweetly still, Gerin said, "Lord Efilnath, lord wizard—"

"Call me Caffer," the wizard said. As the Fox knew, it was not his real name. Wizards warded those, to keep enemies from working magic with them.

"Lord Efilnath, lord Caffer, then," Gerin resumed, "allow me to present you to Ferdulf, the son of Mavrix, who, when he is not accompanying me, dwells in the village by Fox Keep."

"A son of the lord of the sweet grape, here?" Efilnath exclaimed. "Impossible!"

"Not impossible," Caffer said. "It is truth." He and the Elabonian envoy conferred again, more urgently this time.

Gerin hoped the idea that Ferdulf was at least in some measure under his control would get through to the imperials. Ferdulf didn't help, remarking, "And a bloody boring hole that village is, too."

"Yield to the Empire's might, pay the tribute long owed us, and all shall be forgiven concerning these usurpations of authority you have perpetrated," Efilnath said with what he obviously thought was true generosity. "Return to your own barony, abandon any false claims to suzerainty over your neighbors, and live under the beneficent splendor of Crebbig, justly styled the Magnificent."

"Pay twenty years' tribute?" Gerin shook his head. "Not likely, not when the Elabonian Empire wasn't here for a day of that time."

"Twenty years' tribute, yes," Efilnath said, "plus whatever you may have owed prior to that time. Our records indicate that you northern barons were shockingly lax in paying your dues even before such time as we temporarily fell out of touch with you."

"That's a nice way to put it," Gerin said. "Before you forgot all about us, you mean. Before you left us to the tender mercy of the Trokmoi, you mean. Before you weren't here to help us fight the monsters or the Gradi, you mean. And if you go away again now, you'll expect us to pay you again for being gone, won't you?"

Ignoring the sarcasm, Efilnath said, "You did not, as I have noted, contribute your fair share before we temporarily fell out of touch with you."

With a shrug, Gerin answered, "It all depends on how you look at things. I never saw any imperial soldiers on the Niffet helping me hold the Trokmoi at bay. If the crops failed, I never saw any grain hauled up from south of the High Kirs to help us. I don't know about you, Efilnath, or about your Emperor Crebbig, either, but I'm not in the habit of paying for what I don't see."

"Crebbig is your Emperor as well as mine." Efilnath sounded shocked—artfully shocked—that Gerin could imagine otherwise.

Caffer broke in: "Speak to me of the Gradi, lord baron. South of the High Kirs, we know less of them than we would like."

"The Fox's style is *lord king*, even as is mine," Aragis

said. "Best you remember it, lest he take your rudeness to heart and avenge himself on you."

Aragis was likelier than Gerin to do something like that. Gerin started to say he wasn't offended, but then checked himself. Why not give the imperials something else to worry about? He laughed scornfully instead. "I'll answer," he said. "They think they can rule this province, and they don't even know who lives in it."

"They temporarily fell out of touch, that's all," Dagref said. He struck the perfect tone. It wasn't even scorn. It said the Empire's envoy and wizard didn't rate scorn, only amused disdain.

It struck home, too. In a voice less suave than he had used before, Efilnath demanded, "Lord baron, will you then yield to the authority of the Emperor Crebbig and beg his forgiveness for the autonomy you have usurped?"

"In a word, no," Gerin answered. "This would look to be a word you people don't know well, since your comrade heard it from Aragis without listening to it."

Ferdulf's yawn was as extravagant and as anatomically unlikely as the distance to which he'd stuck out his tongue. "Go away, you foolish people," he said. "You only prove how dull Elabonians can be." And then, without warning, all the gentleness disappeared from his mockery. "Begone. Get out of this land. You have no right to it. I, a god's son, so declare."

Efilnath flinched. Gerin would have flinched, too, had an angry demigod growled at him. But the Empire's envoy was not without spirit. "The gods of Elabon say otherwise, and I serve them and the Emperor."

"What do you suppose the gods of Elabon do say, Father?" Dagref whispered to Gerin. "Efilnath and his friends here are Elabonian, but so are we. How do the gods choose one side or the other?"

"My guess is, they probably don't," the Fox whispered back. The gods of Elabon, from everything he'd seen, intervened in human affairs as little as they possibly could. Most of the time, that suited him fine. Against the Gradi, whose own gods were as aggressive as they were, he'd wished the Elabonian deities had done more. Now, he'd be just as well pleased to have them keep on doing nothing in particular.

While he and Dagref talked, Efilnath and Caffer were also holding their own low-voiced colloquy. Gerin couldn't make out what the Elabonian envoy was saying. Whatever it was, Caffer agreed with it: he nodded several times, each more vigorously than the one before.

"Quit jabbering, the two of you," Ferdulf growled at the men from south of the High Kirs. "I told you once, get out of here. Now I tell you twice. Leave while you can still take your clothes with you, which is better luck than the last imperial envoy had, isn't it?"

Now Efilnath nodded to Caffer. The wizard pointed in Ferdulf's direction. His lips moved. So did his right hand, in passes Gerin knew he would never be able to match for swift fluidity. As Aragis had said, this was a mage from the Sorcerers' Collegium, the most highly trained and skilled band of sorcerers this part of the world knew.

Ferdulf shouted in rage. "Try and silence me, will you?" he roared, and suddenly, despite staying the same size, seemed much larger and fiercer than he had a moment before. He pointed two fingers at Caffer, a vulgar gesture straight from the alleys of the City of Elabon.

It was a vulgar gesture with power behind it. Caffer staggered, and had to snatch at the rail of Efilnath's chariot to keep from falling. He looked astonished that his sorcery had failed. The one flaw Gerin had sometimes noted in trained Elabonian wizards was a belief that, because they could do so many things, they could do everything.

But Ferdulf looked astonished, too. He, evidently, had expected to flatten the Elabonian wizard.

"Enough, both of you!" Gerin said sharply. "We met here behind a shield of truce. Shall we fall to blows now, and save the waiting?"

"No," Efilnath said. Caffer gave a shaky nod to show he agreed with his superior. Ferdulf, on the other hand, looked ready—looked eager—to continue the battle of powers. Gerin glared at him. He glared back. His eyes blazed with more power than the Fox had ever seen in them. Resolutely, Gerin kept staring. To his everlasting relief, Ferdulf finally nodded, too.

"Go back to your soldiers, then," Gerin told the imperial envoy. "When we meet again, we shall be at war."

"I said this earlier, to your other ambassador," Aragis added. "Now my fellow king confirms it. If you want this land, you will have to take it from us—and from the god's son here." He beamed at Ferdulf. Gerin had never seen him beam before. It was, when you got down to it, a pretty alarming sight.

"We have powers of our own," Caffer said. His voice wasn't as certain and bright as a new-stamped coin, though. After that first clash with Ferdulf, doubts had entered his mind. Doubt was the enemy of strong sorcery. The thought made Gerin beam, too, in Caffer's direction. The mage from the City of Elabon looked as if he could have done without that sunny smile.

Efilnath the Earnest tapped his driver on the shoulder. The fellow steered the horses in as tight a circle as he could. They went off the Elabon Way for part of it, their hooves kicking up clumps of dirt and grass. Then they got back on the road and clattered off down the paving stones. In precise order of precedence, the rest of the chariots in Efilnath's party followed, Caffer jumping up into his car when it came past him.

As that car rolled away, Caffer looked back over his shoulder at Gerin—or perhaps at Ferdulf, who stood nearby. Ferdulf snarled, like one tomcat warning another to go away. Caffer stared steadily back at him—a stare that proclaimed *I will not be cowed*—until the soldiers in another chariot got between him and Mavrix's son.

"It will be war." Aragis the Archer spoke with a certain somber satisfaction. "If the imperials will not heed words, let them heed the flight of arrows and the thunder of chariotry."

"It will be war," Gerin agreed. He looked around. "I don't think Efilnath or his men were paying much attention to our riders. That's to the good, in my view. May they prove an unpleasant surprise for the imperials."

"So may it be," Aragis said, though sounding more as if he hoped it would be so than as if he expected it.

"Let's follow the imperials as close as we can," Gerin said. "If they're as proud of themselves as they always used to be, they'll expect us to cower and wait for them to come to us. The more we can rock them back on their heels, the better off we'll be."

"Oh, aye, no doubt of that. If I'd had only a few more men of my own—or if I hadn't worried that you'd jump me instead of joining me, I'd have done as much myself," Aragis said. He turned his harsh gaze on the Fox. "And now for what you'd likely call an interesting question: who commands?"

"Interesting indeed," Gerin said, almost as lightly as he'd hoped he could. "Well, it's easy enough to answer: you do."

"Just like that?" The Archer stared. He'd been ready for an argument.

But Gerin said, "Just like that. For one thing, this is

your land. You know it, and I don't. For another, you also know—or you'd better know—I'll take my men out of the fight if you try to harm them with your orders. That should be enough to keep you honest, or close to it."

Aragis weighed the words, then nodded with his usual abrupt decision. "Very well. Let it be so. Had you insisted on taking the lead, I likely would have yielded, but I'd have given you a harder time than you sound as though you'll give me."

"That also crossed my mind." Gerin grinned at the other king in the northlands. "I didn't feel like arguing with you every time I turned around, either. Life is too short for that. You're a perfectly good general; I've seen as much. I doubt we'd do a whole lot better with me giving orders than with you."

"Why do you make me think you've won a victory when I see you yielding?" Aragis asked suspiciously.

"Sometimes you can do both at once," Gerin told him. The Archer shook his head, like a man bedeviled by gnats he couldn't see. The only victories he understood were the ones where he went out and smashed something. Gerin nodded to himself. With luck, there would be plenty of that sort. *There had better be*, he thought.

More and more of Aragis' men joined the army as it moved south in the wake of the imperial envoy and his entourage. At Gerin's suggestion—to which the Archer agreed after a sour look—the newcomers rode at the head of the army. "That way," Gerin said blandly, "if the imperials have spies in your land, they'll have a harder time spotting all our riders."

"If the Elabonians have spies in our land, I'll crucify them." Aragis obviously meant what he said. Down south of the High Kirs, the Empire crucified miscreants. The headsman's axe mostly settled them in the northlands. But, for spies, Gerin would not have been surprised in the least to learn that Aragis might take the trouble to run up crosses.

Marlanz Raw-Meat sent a charioteer back to Aragis and Gerin to let them know the imperial envoy had passed his army and returned to the host the Elabonian Emperor had sent into the northlands. "And," the messenger added, "he says the horseman you sent to warn him this Efilnath was coming got there ahead of the cursed imperial even though he went cross-country, as a chariot couldn't do. No man afoot could have run fast enough to outdo a car, either."

"Isn't that fine?" Gerin said.

"Isn't that splendid? Isn't that magnificent?" Rihwin the Fox said.

"Oh, shut up," Aragis the Archer said. Gerin and Rihwin both laughed at him till he looked so fierce, they stopped. Rihwin probably wouldn't have stopped even then, but Gerin contrived to tread on his toes. He wanted Aragis angry at the Elabonian Empire, not at his own allies.

He might make Rihwin stop laughing. Making Rihwin shut up was another matter. In his best didactic tones, Rihwin lectured Aragis: "So you see, lord king, judicious employment of men riding horses does in good sooth have the potential to smite the foe when and where he least expects it."

"I see a man who talks too bloody much, is what I see," Aragis rumbled, and worked a small miracle: Rihwin did fall silent. Aragis kept right on scowling, not so much at Rihwin as at the world around him: "We're going to eat this country empty, curse it."

"Could be worse," Gerin said cheerfully.

"Oh? How?" The scowl remained, now turned full force on Gerin.

He said, "Easy enough. Could be the imperials eating your countryside empty. For that matter, could be the imperials burning out your countryside so nobody'd be able to eat from it."

Aragis pondered that, then looked surprised. "Well, you're right. It could be worse," he said gruffly. "That doesn't make this any too good, though."

"I didn't say it did." Gerin resolutely kept his tone light. That wasn't too hard for him. His land wasn't facing invasion—yet. His land wasn't facing being eaten empty—his land had already had an army feeding off it, when he'd thought he was going to war against Aragis rather than the Elabonian Empire.

The next afternoon, Gerin's force came up to the encampment where Aragis' main army kept an eye on the imperials. Marlanz Raw-Meat rode out to greet the Fox. "Well met, lord king," he said, clasping Gerin's hand. "I'm happier to see you fighting with me than fighting against me, if you know what I mean, heh, heh."

"Oh, yes," Gerin said. "I never wanted to fight a war with your king, either, and now I won't." *I'll fight a war with the Elabonian Empire instead, and I would have wanted that even less, had it occurred to me not to want it.*

Marlanz said, "Lord king, I present to you Aranast Aragis' son."

"Lord king," Aranast said politely, bowing. He looked like Aragis, right down to the cast of features that warned nobody had better disagree with him for any reason whatever. Gerin didn't think he had the force of character that would let him back up that cast of features, but he wasn't very old yet, either. He couldn't have had more than a couple of years on Duren.

Thinking of Duren made the Fox wish he'd accepted more support from his own eldest son. He hadn't thought he'd need it against Aragis the Archer. The Elabonian Empire had rather greater resources than his rival king. He didn't know what part of those resources the Empire had committed or would commit to reconquering the northlands, but he'd find out soon enough.

Aranast said, "We've all . . . heard a great deal about you, lord king."

"That's nice," Gerin said blandly, playing the simpleton to see how Aragis' son would respond.

Aranast drew back half a pace, struggling to reconcile the ruler who'd held his father at bay for two decades with this fellow who sounded as if he had not a brain in his head. After a moment, he smiled a smile that matched any of Aragis' for icy precision. "Much of what we've heard is how self-effacing you are. I see that's so."

All right, then: he wasn't a fool. That disappointed the Fox. With a smile of his own, Gerin said, "If I wanted to stay in hiding, I wouldn't have come south."

"We're glad you did, whatever your reasons were," Marlanz said hastily. "The Empire won't be so glad." He paused. "Is . . . that Ferdulf . . . with you?" As he had up at Fox keep, he spoke of the demigod as if Ferdulf were some kind of wild animal.

"Oh yes, he's here," Gerin answered.

"Good!" Marlanz said with heartfelt relief—one of the rare times Ferdulf had ever inspired that emotion, or indeed any emotion save inchoate, or sometimes not so inchoate, fury in anyone.

As if to prove he was there, Ferdulf strolled over, rose into the air till he could look Marlanz in the face, and said, "I remember you. You're the man who's made out of raw meat."

"Most men are," Marlanz replied with what Gerin thought of as commendable calm. He stared back at Ferdulf. "I expect you are, too."

"Well, yes," the little demigod admitted, "but not raw meat of such a gross and repellent sort as yours or the Fox's here; of that I'm comfortably certain."

"No doubt you're right," Gerin said in a voice of elaborate unconcern. "When you go in the bushes, it's daisies and violets that come out, not the stuff that makes them grow."

Ferdulf gave him a look full of such concentrated loathing, he had to brace himself to stand against it. The demigod stalked off through the air. "He does dislike the Empire more than he dislikes us, doesn't he?" Marlanz asked anxiously. "I had hoped he would, ever since I learned the imperials were coming over the mountains."

"He did, anyhow," Gerin said, which made Marlanz look more anxious still and Aranast downright alarmed. The Fox laughed. "It will be all right. He and I have been carving chunks off each other for as long as he's been around. He's used to it. He'll get over it. But he despises the Elabonian Empire with a fine bright loathing that should be good for a long time to come."

"Do you plan to move straight against the Empire, lord king?" Marlanz asked the Fox.

Gerin pointed to Aragis. "You'd better put that to your own overlord, Marlanz," he replied. "He's in overall command here."

Aranast looked as if he'd already assumed that. Marlanz looked surprised, then tried to look as if he hadn't. It didn't work: Aranast had noticed. Marlanz would probably be unhappy after Aragis found a chance to speak with him in private. Had the Archer been operating against Gerin, he would have been delighted. Since they were on the same side, he wasn't.

Aragis said, "They are here. They have no business being here. My fellow king agrees they have no business being here." He turned his fierce gaze on Gerin, as if daring him to disagree. He couldn't disagree. Aragis came to a conclusion as obvious to him as a Sithonian geometer found the proof of two triangles' congruence: "And so, we attack."

A mounted scout came galloping back to the army of the northlands. "Lord kings!" he shouted to Gerin and Aragis, who rode at the head of their conjoined forces. "The imperials aren't far south—just back of the next rise south from the one I rode over here. They're in column, but they aren't asleep—look like they can deploy in a hurry whenever they take a mind to."

"We'll hit them anyhow," Aragis said. At his order, his driver reined in. Gerin had Dagref pull to a stop beside his fellow king. Aragis waved to gain the attention of the troopers behind him. "Left and right!" he shouted. "Form line of battle! Left and right!"

Cheers rose, from his men and Gerin's both. They were going to get the fighting so many of them craved. The Fox hadn't understood anyone's being eager for battle, not since his first one, but a lot of people were. The warriors peeled off across the fields to either side of the Elabon way to make a ragged line that would only get more ragged as they advanced against the Empire.

"What about the horsemen?" Gerin asked, when Aragis didn't give them any special orders.

The Archer frowned. "That's right," he said—sure enough, he'd forgotten about them. After a moment's thought, he issued the command: "Let them go off around to the right. Maybe they can take the imperials in the flank, since they won't be looking for anything like that."

He spoke as if he didn't expect that to happen, as if he was sending Rihwin's riders out of the way so he could get on with the main battle. Gerin didn't try to change his mind. No matter why he'd issued the order, it made good sense. Gerin waved for Rihwin, drew his attention, and relayed it.

"Aye, lord king, we shall essay it," Rihwin replied. He glanced over to Aragis the Archer with an expression that said he too knew Aragis didn't expect much. "Perhaps we shall disabuse doubters of their dubiety."

"Talk fancy like that when you get near the imperials," Aragis said. "Maybe they'll think you're one of them long enough to help you hurt 'em."

"I shall, lord king, and I thank you for the suggestion," Rihwin said. He surveyed Aragis with respect no less real for being grudging.

But the Archer hadn't finished: "If you don't fool them, maybe you can bore them to death."

"Thank you again, lord king, so much," Rihwin said tightly. He rode off to rally his men and take them in the direction Aragis had commanded. Gerin wondered whether Aragis had insulted him for the sake of being insulting or to inspire him to fight harder. Gerin also wondered whether Aragis bothered drawing such distinctions.

"Where's that Ferdulf?" Aragis demanded, looking around. "I want him front and center against the Empire."

Front and center Ferdulf came. He and Aragis made allies more unlikely than Gerin and Aragis. "Back over the mountains with them!" Ferdulf shouted, and rose above the front rank like a living battle standard. The troopers—especially Aragis' men, who knew him only as a demigod and not as an obnoxious brat—raised a cheer.

"Forward!" Aragis shouted. With another cheer, with a rumble of wheels and squeaks from ungreased axles, the chariots rolled ahead.

In the car with Gerin and Dagref, Van said, "Ah, well, another brawl." He hefted his spear. "Now to make the other fellows sorry their mothers ever bore 'em."

Aragis shouted again: "Our cry is, 'The northlands!' " A third cheer rang out from his men and the Fox's, louder than either of the other two.

Gerin set a hand on Dagref's shoulder. "Drive as I command you, or as seems best to you if I'm too busy fighting to give you any orders. The gods keep you safe."

"And you, Father. And all of us," Dagref answered. Then he frowned. His back was to Gerin, but the Fox recognized the expression by the way his son's shoulders hunched forward a little. After his usual pause for thought, Dagref went on, "But, of course, the gods won't keep all of us safe. Why make the prayer, then?"

If Dagref was worrying over philosophical questions, he wasn't likely to panic when the fighting started. Gerin had never gone into battle with that sort of preparation. He didn't think Duren had, either. But if philosophy helped keep his eldest by Selatre on a steady course, the Fox would not complain.

Over the first low rise rolled the army. The chariots were just coming down the far slope when over the crest of the second rise the scout had mentioned came the lead chariots of the force the Elabonian Empire had sent out to reclaim the northern province it had abandoned a generation before.

At the sight of their foes, Gerin's men and Aragis' raised a great shout: derision and hatred all commingled. "Hold the line steady!" Aragis yelled. "By Father Dyaus, I'll cut the balls off the first chariot crew I see charging ahead all on their lonesome. Hold steady."

And the line did hold steady. In the short run, fear worked well enough to keep men obedient. More and more imperial chariots came up over the crest of the second rise. They were deploying as they advanced; their line got wider as the Fox watched. He wished his men and Aragis' had been closer to them, to hit them before they shook themselves out into line. Wishing got him what wishing usually got.

Dagref said, "All their chariots look just alike. Isn't that peculiar?"

"Not when you think about it," Gerin answered. "Down in the City of Elabon, the Empire has an armory where smiths and carpenters and such make weapons for the whole imperial army. They have a pattern for spears and a pattern for helmets and a pattern for chariots, too. It's not the way it is here, where each keep will have its own carpenter or wheelwright with his own notions about how to do things."

"Then these cars will likely be better than some of ours but worse than others," Dagref said. "If they keep on making them to the same pattern long enough while we test worse against better, sooner or later all of ours will be better than theirs."

"Or else we'll try something different altogether." Gerin looked west to see if he could spot Rihwin's troop of horsemen. He was, on the whole, glad to discover he couldn't: trees screened them from what would momentarily become the battlefield. If they got round that screen, they were liable to give the imperials a nasty surprise.

"Elabon! Elabon! Elabon!" The foe was shouting, too, in rhythmic unison very different from the great incoherent roar that came from the men of the northlands. The imperials were much more uniform in appearance than Gerin and Aragis' troopers, each of whom equipped himself as he could afford and as he thought best. The men from south of the High Kirs put the Fox in mind of the warriors Ros the Fierce had used to conquer this province in the first place, a couple of hundred years before. That comparison worried him; Ros' warriors, by all accounts, had been as tough as any ever made.

"This'll be the biggest chariot fight I've ever seen," Van said as more and more imperials came over the rise.

"Biggest chariot fight this part of the world has ever seen," Gerin answered, "unless there were bigger ones when we Elabonians conquered it in the first place." No sooner were the words *we Elabonians* out of his mouth than he found them odd. He thought of himself as an Elabonian. He spoke the Elabonian language. He worshiped Elabonian gods. He revered Elabonian civilization (not least the parts borrowed or stolen from Sithonia). And now he was going to do his best to defeat the soldiers of the Elabonian Empire.

Of course, they'd kill him if he didn't. That was a powerful argument in favor of fighting.

Ferdulf floated high overhead, screaming abuse at the imperial army. Gerin didn't know what the little demigod could do beyond screaming abuse. Even that would help, with his being so obviously supernatural. Maybe Ferdulf didn't know himself whether he could do anything. Maybe he wouldn't know till he tried it and it either worked or it didn't.

To Dagref, Gerin said, "If you see the Empire's wizards, steer toward their cars. If we can get rid of them, we help our own cause more than we do by putting paid to ordinary troopers." Dagref nodded.

Gerin reached over his shoulder, pulled an arrow from his quiver, and set it to his bowstring. The two armies were closing fast. Already the first few arrows had begun to fly. They fell far short of their targets. There were always soldiers who couldn't wait till they had some reasonable chance of hitting something before they started to shoot.

Closer and closer came the enemy cars. Gerin's own mouth felt dry. His heart pounded. He understood why the overeager troopers had begun to shoot too soon. It made them feel the battle had started and the waiting was over. Beside the Fox in the jouncing car, Van was muttering, "Come on. Come on. Come on." Gerin didn't think he knew he was doing it. He wanted to get into the fight, too, but carried no bow.

Straight ahead was an imperial with a gilded corselet and helmet. That made him an officer of some sort, and also a good target. Gerin set himself, drew the bow to his ear in one smooth motion, and let fly. The bowstring lashed the leather brace on his wrist. He grabbed another arrow, nocked it, and let fly again.

The officer in the gilded armor did not fall. Shooting from a chariot took a lot of luck, even for the best of warriors. Of course, with enough shafts in the air, some of them were bound to be lucky. Here and there, screams rose from both lines. Men crumpled and fell out of their cars as those bounded over the fields. Horses crashed down, too, sending chariots slewing sideways and, once or twice, crashing into one another and bringing more men to ruin.

Buzzing like an angry bumblebee, an arrow flew past the Fox's ear. He shook his head, as if at a veritable insect. Indeed: with enough shafts in the air, some *were* bound to be lucky—and unlucky for him. An old, pale scar puckered his left shoulder. He knew what wounds were like.

"Here we go," Van said. Aragis wasn't being subtle about what he did: he was throwing his army straight at the imperial forces. Maybe he thought they would break and flee—they were effete southerners, after all. The commander the Elabonian Emperor had sent over the mountains was taking the same approach to the warriors from the northlands. Maybe he thought they would break and flee—they were half-barbarous rebels, after all.

Neither side broke. Neither side fled. Neither side did much in the way of maneuvering. Gerin aimed for the driver of the chariot that was thundering toward him. His arrow caught the luckless Elabonian right in the neck. The fellow dropped the reins and clutched at himself as he fell out of the chariot. A wheel thumped over him. He lay very still.

One of the bowmen in that imperial chariot snatched for the reins. He missed. They dragged along the ground. The horses, no longer under anyone's control, slowed from gallop to walk. Dagref steered past them, so close that Van was able to use his heavy spear. He let out a great shout of fierce glee as he watched the imperial soldier crumple.

Some of the chariots of the opposing sides shot past one another. Others pulled up to avoid collisions. The fight turned into a melee. What had been neat lines turned into a confused jumble of chariots and horses. Some men kept on shooting arrows at their foes. Others, at closer quarters, drew swords and axes and slashed away at one another.

"Pull back, in the Emperor's name!" an imperial officer shouted to his men. "We'll form line again and smash through these savages."

But the troopers of the Elabonian Empire could not pull back and re-form. They were locked together with the warriors from the northlands as tightly as if held in a lover's embrace.

"Smash 'em!" Aragis yelled. "Smash 'em to pieces!" Gerin wondered how he'd grown so strong with no better notion of strategy than that. Maybe ferocity had had more to do with it than strategy. Any of Aragis' men who gave ground would have to face him afterwards. That meant giving ground was anything but a sure way to escape from danger.

An imperial chariot pulled close to the one Dagref was driving. One of the warriors in it turned and cut at Gerin with his sword. The Fox leaned away from the blade, which flew past him. He snatched an axe out of a bracket set into the side of his chariot and smashed it into the trooper's ribs. It bit through the scales of his corselet. Blood gushed from the wound. With a bubbling shriek and an outraged expression, the soldier toppled.

Van boomed laughter. "You do that once every fight, Captain, seems like," he said. "They never expect you to be left-handed, and that's a mistake they never get to make twice."

Gerin started to answer, but shouted "Watch yourself!" instead. An imperial trooper with an axe ran toward the chariot from the side. Many horses on both sides were down; many drivers had been hit; many chariots had overturned. Some men kept fighting on foot.

Van jumped down from the car and, with a roar that might have sprung from a longtooth's throat, rushed at the soldier of the Elabonian Empire. The soldier was close to a foot shorter than the enormous outlander, whose helm and the nodding horsehair crest above it made him seem taller still. When Van thrust with his spear, the imperial did not wait to try conclusions with him, but spun on his heel and ran away to find a foe for whom he was more nearly a match. Shouting laughter, Van sprang back into the chariot.

Dagref managed to get out of the press and send the car, at Gerin's direction, toward several imperial chariots whose crews were pressing hard against some of Aragis' men and some of his own. A couple of the Empire's chariots also pulled loose and quickly moved to block his path.

Suddenly, Ferdulf flew down from the sky and screeched in the faces of the imperials' horses. One team ran wild, thundering out of the fight. The other team didn't run at all. The horses reared and screamed in terror. The Elabonian warriors clung to the rails of their car. That was all they could do to keep from being spilled out onto the ground.

That also made them easy meat for Gerin and Van. The Fox shot one at close range; Van speared another. The third did dive out of the chariot then, and so preserved himself.

"Well done!" Gerin shouted to Ferdulf. "Keep it up— you'll drive them crazy."

Floating in midair, Ferdulf grinned at the Fox, who, with the Elabonian Empire as the new standard of comparison, looked better to the obnoxious little demigod than he ever had before. "I've found something else new to do to them, too," Ferdulf said.

He drifted up above the fight, tugged his tunic up over his belly, and . . . It wasn't really something new. It was the disgusting game he'd been playing at Fox Keep when Marlanz Raw-Meat came to visit. Then, it had been nothing but disgusting. Now, if a soldier of the Elabonian Empire unexpectedly got pissed on from out of the sky, he was liable to be distracted for a few crucial moments, during which he could neither attack nor defend himself very well. Several soldiers paid with their lives for such distraction.

Ferdulf seemed to have an unlimited supply of his nasty weapon. Gerin had never thought that one of a demigod's attributes might be the ability to piss endlessly without having to load up on water or ale. That was not the sort of ability on which the Sithonian mythologizers and their Elabonian imitators dwelt. They had their minds on higher things. Ferdulf didn't.

Another attribute of his, one the mythologizers might actually have mentioned in writing, was his uncanny ability to avoid arrows. He got plenty of chances to use that ability, too. Plenty of outraged imperials sent shafts his way, and he was not floating so high as to be anything but an easy target. Nevertheless, every arrow missed. Gerin couldn't tell whether the arrows went wide or Ferdulf dodged. However that worked, none struck home. He took unpleasant revenge on the men who shot at him, too.

And then, with a squawk of surprise and indignation, he tumbled out of the sky not far from the Fox. "Oh, a pestilence!" Gerin exclaimed. "Caffer or one of their other cursed wizards found a spell that would bite on him after all. Dagref!"

"Aye, Father," Dagref said, and then looked back over his shoulder at Gerin. "Are you really sure you want to rescue him?"

"Don't tempt me, lad," Gerin said. He would have liked it better had the words come out of his mouth sounding more like a joke. But, while he wouldn't have cared to explain himself to either Ferdulf or Mavrix, the idea of leaving the Sithonian god's irksome little bastard to his fate held an appalling appeal.

Even though Ferdulf wasn't flying, arrows still wouldn't strike him. They dug into the ground all around his little feet, but none pierced his flesh. "Finish him!" an imperial shouted—sure enough, there was Caffer, looking indecently pleased with himself.

"Steer toward the sorcerer!" Gerin shouted, and shot an arrow at Caffer. The wizard deflected it with an absent-minded pass. He could not do so without effort, though, as Ferdulf could, and, while he was momentarily distracted, the demigod floated off the ground. As soon as the arrow had gone by, the mage from the City of Elabon renewed his spell, and Ferdulf, shouting in fury, found his feet on the ground again.

Gerin shot at Caffer once more. Once more, the wizard made him miss. An imperial warrior jumped out of a chariot and ran toward Ferdulf, who, after another leap into the air while Caffer was otherwise engaged, had again returned to earth. Cursing, Van sprang down and dashed to the demigod's aid. Unlike the other trooper, this one stood and fought.

The Fox had scant time to watch that fight. Dagref, by then, had driven quite close to Caffer's car, close enough for him to snap his whip at the wizard. The whip wasn't so easy to deflect as Gerin's arrows had been. Caffer did manage to evade it, then howled a spell. The lash changed to a serpent in Dagref's hands. The serpent hissed, twisted, and tried to bite.

That, however, did not work so well as Caffer had hoped. Like a lot of boys his age, Dagref was fond of snakes. This one was bigger than any Gerin had seen around Fox Keep, but that did not seem to faze his son. Dagref grabbed it behind the head. He had to use both hands to control its writhing length. Gerin snatched up the reins to keep the horses from running wild.

"Thank you, Father," Dagref said. Then he shouted to Caffer: "You made it—now see how you like it!" He threw the snake into the wizard's car.

Caffer had had a spell handy for turning whip to snake. He did not seem to have one for turning a snake back into a whip. He and his driver and the warrior in the chariot with them all shouted and stomped and slashed at the serpent, which, like every other serpent, proved extremely reluctant to expire.

Dagref took the reins back from Gerin as calmly as if

nothing had happened. The Fox shot a third arrow at Caffer. The wizard knew nothing of this one till it rammed its way between two ribs and pierced him almost to its fletching. He straightened up and screamed, a long wail of agony and surprise mixed. Since men, like snakes, could prove reluctant to die, Gerin shot him again, this time in the face. He spilled out of the chariot like a sack of peas.

With a shout of joy, Ferdulf floated above the field once more. Gerin looked around to see if Van needed help against his foe. The imperial warrior lay on the ground, thrashing toward death. Van's spear dripped blood. "Fool was brave," the outlander said as he got back into the chariot, "but that doesn't make him any less a fool."

"Father, I'm sorry, but I haven't got a whip any more," Dagref said.

"Considering what you did with it, I think I'll forgive you," the Fox answered, his voice dry. "That was quick thinking."

Dagref's shoulders went up and down in a shrug. "I didn't see anything better I could do with the thing."

Van looked around the field, then nudged Gerin. "Fox, are we winning this confounded fight or losing it?"

Gerin looked, too. "To the five hells with me if I know," he said. "They aren't running, and we aren't running, and we're all mashed together." With a certain sardonic pride, he added, "The fights I make are *neater* than this, anyhow. Aragis has no sense of tidiness."

"You can tell him that when everything here is done," Van said with a grin. "Wait till I'm around, though, if you'd be so kind. I want to hear what he says to you afterwards."

Dagref managed to keep the chariot moving as he wanted even without a whip to speed the horses along.

What to do on the battlefield did not come naturally to him, as it did, say, to Van, and to Duren, too. But he thought well, and did not let himself get rattled. All that counted, too.

And he managed to keep everything that was and should be going on straight in his mind, which a good many men who reckoned themselves great captains had trouble doing. He said, "Shouldn't Rihwin and his horsemen ride in from the flank sometime soon?"

"Father Dyaus!" Gerin exclaimed. His head whipped around toward the west. "I'd forgotten all about them. Where are they, anyhow?"

Van looked west, too. "Probably in amongst the trees," he said, "trying to figure out which side is which. Like you said, Fox, this is about as untidy a brawl as I've ever seen."

"Well, one way for them to neaten things up would be to attack right about now," Gerin said. "Our men know who they are, and the imperials don't, except to figure out that they aren't friends, and—"

He shut up. Neither Dagref nor Van was paying attention to him. They were both staring west. Gerin took another look in that direction, too. His sour expression disappeared, to be replaced by an enormous grin. Sounding more serious than he often did, Van said, "You ever by any chance think of going into the prophet business?"

"I leave that to my wife and farseeing Biton, thanks," Gerin answered.

Regardless of whether or not he'd foretold their arrival, Rihwin's riders approached the battlefield at something close to a gallop. Gerin's men, and Aragis', cheered. The imperials either cursed or laughed.

More slowly than he should have, the officer who led the Elabonian Empire's army figured out that the horsemen, however peculiar they looked to him, might represent a real threat. He detached a squadron of chariots from his main force—no easy task, considering how heavily engaged against the men of the northlands his army was—and sent them against the new foes on horseback.

When other imperials weren't trying to kill him, Gerin watched with great interest the clash of the old way and the new. To his vast astonishment, it went exactly as Rihwin the Fox had predicted it would. He'd known Rihwin more than twenty years; in all that time, he couldn't recall thinking such a thing before. What he thought now was that Rihwin had picked a splendid time to be right.

The chariots thundered across the fields toward the horsemen, bumping and jouncing as they always did. The warriors in the bumping, jouncing cars shot arrows at Rihwin's men. Rihwin's men shot back. Not only that, they rode around the chariots as if the latter were nailed to the ground. They shot back at the imperials from all directions at once; anyone who tried to lift a shield against a shaft coming from the right was apt as not to be pierced by one coming from the left or the rear.

Dagref said, "We're watching the end of a whole way of fighting. I didn't think it would happen quite so easily."

"Neither did I," Gerin said.

"Neither did anybody," Van said.

But happen it did. Before long, the chariots the imperial commander had sent out against the horsemen were swept off the field as if by a broom. Rihwin's riders began showering the men in the main imperial force with arrows. Some rode close, to use sword and spear against their foes.

Where the men of the Elabonian Empire had fought Gerin and Aragis' chariots to a standstill, the shock of the new alarmed them far more than its actual effect on the battlefield and the number of horsemen would have warranted. At first by ones and twos and then in larger numbers, they broke off the fight and withdrew to the south. They weren't routed; they fought back fiercely when the men of the northlands pursued. But they weren't going to fight on that field any more, either.

Rihwin rode up to Gerin. His sword had blood on it. So did his face; an arrow had nicked one cheek. But his face also bore an enormous grin. Gerin didn't blame him—he'd earned the right to grin. "How about that, lord king?" Rihwin said. "How *about* that?"

"Well, how about it?" Gerin asked, deadpan. Rihwin stared, then started to laugh. So did Gerin. Why not? They'd won.

V

"It's a battle," Gerin said for the eighteenth—or was it the twenty-third?—time that afternoon. "It's not the war."

This particular time, he happened to be talking with Adiatunnus. The Trokmê chieftain gave him an impatient look, as if he were quibbling over trifles. "They're licked the now, and we'll see them no more, is it not so?"

"No, curse it, it's not so," the Fox said wearily. "Or rather, it's so that we beat them, but there's no way of knowing whether that means they've had enough or whether we'll be in another battle day after tomorrow."

Adiatunnus said, "You're after telling me, then, that the Elabonians from over the mountains are even more stubborn nor the lot of you kerns we Trokmoi have been coping with all along?"

"As stubborn as we are, anyhow: we're a branch off that trunk," Gerin said. "The other part of the bargain is, they're drawing on the resources of a land bigger than this province, and all of it under the rule of one man; it's not split into fragments the way the northlands are. If the Emperor orders this army to keep fighting, it will. If he orders another army up over the High Kirs, we'll have to fight that one, too."

"Maybe this whole business of civilization isna the fun I thought it was." Adiatunnus walked off shaking his head.

Gerin went back to what he had been doing: helping to care for the injured. Study and more practice than he wished he'd got had left him as good a battlefield surgeon as anyone else in the northlands. He dug out arrowheads, stitched up slashes, helped set a couple of broken bones, and urged anyone with any sort of wound to wash it out with ale. "It helps clean," he said, "and a clean wound is less likely to go bad than a dirty one."

"Wine would be better," said an imperial trooper who had been pitched out of his chariot and captured while he was stunned.

"So it would, if we had any," the Fox agreed. Spotting Ferdulf strolling along not far away, he waved and called the demigod's name.

Rather to his surprise, Ferdulf came to him. "What do you want?" Mavrix's son asked, sounding less hostile than Gerin was used to. Maybe Ferdulf had figured out that he ought to be grateful. And maybe the Fox would flap his arms and fly to Fomor. He'd borrowed the image from the Trokmê tongue; Fomor was the name the woodsrunners gave the moon Elabonians called Tiwaz.

Hoping to take advantage of what passed for good nature with Ferdulf, Gerin said, "Do you have any healing powers, by any chance?" Mavrix had great power over flesh, but Gerin thought it wiser not to mention that, lest Ferdulf grow angry at being reminded, however indirectly, that he was only half a god.

The question seemed to take Ferdulf by surprise. "I don't know," he answered. "I don't think I ever tried. Why should I try, anyhow? Even if I can, all I'd be doing would be healing Elabonians, and I don't like Elabonians."

"You'd be healing warriors who could fight against the Elabonian Empire again," Gerin pointed out.

"There is that," Ferdulf admitted grudgingly. His small shoulder shrugged. "Oh, all right, I'll see what I can do. I don't know if I can do anything, you know. Sometimes, when I try to do something, I find I can. Sometimes I can't. That makes me angry."

"Be angry at the Empire, for causing these wounds in the first place," Gerin suggested. "Don't be angry at our men who are hurt. It's not their fault."

"No?" Ferdulf said. "If they were better soldiers, maybe they wouldn't have got hurt to begin with." But, having said that, he went over to a man who was cursing as blood from a wounded arm slowly soaked the bandage wrapped around the injury.

"What's he going to do?" The soldier looked at Ferdulf as dubiously as the demigod was looking at him.

Ferdulf reached out and touched the bandage. The warrior exclaimed in delight. Ferdulf exclaimed, too, and jerked his hand away. He grabbed at his own arm, in the spot where the warrior had been wounded. His lower lip stuck out in petulant dismay. "It hurts! It hurts as if the arrow had gone into me."

"But it took my pain away," the warrior said. "While you were holding me, it didn't hurt any more, and I thought I felt it getting better, if you know what I mean. But when you took your hand off the wound, it hurt again."

"And I stopped hurting," Ferdulf said, as if that were much more important. To him, no doubt, it was.

Gerin said, "Could you try a little more, even so? This would be a great help in the war against the Empire, if you could do it."

"It hurts," Ferdulf repeated. Gerin, though, had chosen the right hook with which to catch his fish. Ferdulf might have been reluctant, but he set his hand on the warrior's wound once more. The fellow let out a great, luxuriant sigh as his pain vanished again. Ferdulf grimaced and whimpered, but did not let go.

Then the soldier said, "Dyaus Allfather, will you look at that?" With his good arm, he pointed to the demigod.

Gerin stared. Forming on Ferdulf's little arm, even as he watched, was what looked as if it would be a wound of the same sort as the trooper had suffered. Gently, the Fox said, "Ferdulf, you don't have to go on any more. In fact, it might be better if you didn't."

When Ferdulf looked down at himself, he gasped and jerked his hand away from the wounded man. Along with Gerin and the warrior, he stared at his arm. Slowly, what would have become a wound faded from his flesh.

"You made mine better, little fellow, and I thank you for it," the soldier said. "It doesn't hurt near so much now. But I wouldn't have wanted you to go on any more, not when you were going to start bleeding yourself any minute there."

"Too high a price to pay," Gerin said regretfully. He clapped Ferdulf on the back as if the little demigod were a man. "You did what you could, and I thank you for trying."

"If I were all god, I could have done it." Ferdulf scowled. No, that thought was never far from his mind. "I feel the power in me, but I can't keep it from doing what it does to me. My body won't bear what it should."

The Fox suspected that problem would plague him all his life, which was liable to be a very long life indeed. Being only a man, Gerin had only human abilities, which did not overtax his merely human frame. Ferdulf's abilities outstripped the body containing them, as if a squirrel, say, were to be suddenly endowed with human intellect.

While Gerin was pondering that, Aragis the Archer came up to him. He looked as happy as he ever did, which wasn't very. "Your men fought well, Fox," he said, nodding to Gerin. "Better than I thought they would, and I've never thought they couldn't."

"I understand that, or you'd have attacked me," Gerin said, to which the Archer, unabashed, nodded again. Gerin went on, "Nothing wrong with the way your soldiers did their job, either, but I've always known any men you led would fight hard."

"If they didn't, *you'd* have attacked *me*," Aragis said. That was what he would have done, and he judged others by his own standards. After a few heartbeats, he added, "You got more out of those riders than I thought you would, too. Always up for something new." What came next was half bark, half chuckle. "Keeps your neighbors on their toes."

Gerin raised an eyebrow and grinned a lopsided grin. "That's the idea."

"Oh, I know. I understand as much," Aragis said. "Even so, I never thought you'd put a woman on horseback." He turned that coughing chuckle loose again. "Women are for being ridden, not for riding."

"What in the five hells are you talking about now?" Gerin demanded. "I haven't got any women—"

And Aragis threw back his head and guffawed. Gerin was as astonished as if the High Kirs had suddenly stood up on little spindly legs to dance a sprightly Trokmê dance. "By the gods, there's something you didn't know," the Archer said. "Haw, haw, haw! Who would have guessed it? The Fox with something going on right under his nose, and he had never a clue. Haw, haw!" He wiped his streaming eyes.

The last time something had gone on under Gerin's nose without his noticing, Elise had run off with the horseleech. After close to half a lifetime, that memory remained bitter as horseradish. Holding his voice under tight control, he said, "You'd better tell me just what you mean."

"I mean what I say." Aragis' face bore an utterly

uncharacteristic grin. "I generally do, which is more than some people I might mention can claim. And what I say is this—if one of your riders tries to piss standing up, it'll run down her leg. And if you didn't notice, you ought to take your eyes to a smith and get 'em sharpened."

"You're not joking," Gerin said slowly. That was foolish, and he knew it. As far as he could tell, Aragis never joked. The Fox pointed toward the riders, who, as they usually did, stayed a little apart from the rest of the warriors. "Show me this woman you say is there."

"Father Dyaus, if you don't know a woman when you see one—" Aragis didn't merely guffaw, he giggled. Gerin wondered if a demon had taken possession of him. It would have to be a very silly demon, to get a giggle past Aragis' lips. The Archer took him by the arm. "All right, come on, then. If you need showing, I'll show you. While I'm about it, shall I tell you how to make children, too?"

"I have the hang of that, thanks," Gerin said through clenched teeth. "Now do as you said you would."

"Come on, then." Aragis was still chuckling as he headed for Rihwin's riders. Gerin, following, fumed. The Archer's head went this way and that. Gerin was about to start jeering when Aragis' arm shot out. "There, by the gods. Talking to your own son, she is. Did he bring her along to keep himself amused on campaign?"

"That's not a—" The words clogged in Gerin's throat. The rider standing there talking with Rihwin was the very young-looking fellow with the very fuzzy beard he'd noticed a couple of times on the way south from Fox Keep. He'd thought that an improbable beard for such a young men to have. Now that he took a closer look, he saw it was improbable because it wasn't real. Recognizing that it wasn't real, he took a closer look at the face under it. "Maeva!" he exclaimed.

❖   ❖   ❖

Van's daughter whipped her head around. Dagref spun toward his father and Aragis, then, resigned, turned back to face Maeva. Gerin caught a few words of what he was saying: "—bound to happen sooner or later."

"Well, Fox," Aragis said, chuckling still, "is that a woman, or have you forgotten what they look like?"

"That is a woman," Gerin agreed seriously. "That is a woman who, now that you've found her out, is liable to kill you for doing it."

Aragis started to laugh some more, then looked at him. The Archer looked at Maeva, too. She stood a couple of digits taller than he did, and was wider through the shoulders, too. And, as Gerin had recognized her face, Aragis recognized her name. "Considering who her father is, you're likely the one who isn't joking now," he said.

"Not even a little bit," the Fox answered. "I tell you, my fellow king, I shouldn't want her angry at me." He raised his voice: "Maeva, come here, if you'd be so kind. Dagref, you'd better come, too. You seem to have known what was going on."

"Yes, I knew, Father," Dagref said with impressive artificial calm. "What of it? You never forbade Maeva to come on campaign with us, and—"

"I never thought I'd have to forbid her to come on campaign with us," Gerin said, "because I never thought she'd do it."

Dagref talked right through him: "—and she killed at least one imperial, and wounded three more. If that doesn't show she can hold her own on the field, what *does* she have to do to prove it?"

Gerin started to answer that, then stopped when he realized he had no good answer handy. He turned to Maeva. "What will your father say when he finds out you've come to war?"

She shrugged, which only made her shoulders seem

wider. "He'll probably shout and scream at me," she answered, "but what *can* he say now? I'm here, and I've already fought. He would have done the same thing. He *did* do the same thing, back when he was my age."

"Younger," Gerin said absently. "But he was a man. You're—"

"—Here and alive and with a dead foeman," Dagref put in. "That is what you were going to say, isn't it, Father?"

Aragis snorted. Gerin gave him a dirty look and Dagref another. Then the Fox spotted a tall, nodding horsehair crest of crimson. He waved in that direction. Van waved back. Gerin waved again, this time to bring his friend over. "I'm not going to say anything right now," he said as Van ambled toward him. "I'll leave that to Maeva's father."

Maeva herself gave him a look he would sooner not have had. But she stood straight and waited for Van to arrive. He towered over her, but he towered over almost everyone. "Hello, Fox," he boomed. "What do you need me for now? I was just about to . . ."

He followed Gerin's glance toward Maeva. For a moment, the Fox didn't think he'd recognize her under the false whiskers she'd stuck to her face. Gerin was ready to twit Van for that before remembering he hadn't penetrated Maeva's disguise, either. And then Van did. His gray-blue eyes got very wide. He started to say something, but all that came out of his mouth was a wordless, coughing croak of astonishment.

"Hello, Father," Maeva said. By then, she had her voice under control. It was a strong contralto that could easily have been mistaken for the treble of a youth whose voice hadn't broken—although such a youth probably wouldn't have sprouted so thick a beard.

Still, Gerin wasn't altogether astonished she'd managed

to pull off the imposture. Most people saw what they expected to see, heard what they expected to hear. Maeva was as big as a man, she was in a place where only men were expected to be, she handled her weapons like a man, so what else but a man was she likely to be? *An illustration of the difference between what's likely and what is*, the Fox thought.

Van finally found words: "What are you doing here?" They weren't the best words, perhaps, but Gerin would have been hard pressed to come up with better on the spur of the moment.

Maeva had had the chance to compose herself. "Why, spinning thread and baking bread, of course," she answered with irony she must have learned from Dagref.

Van stared and spluttered. Dagref, sounding helpful when in fact he was anything but, said, "She's one of Rihwin's riders. She killed an imperial, and wounded a couple of more."

"What will your mother say?" Van demanded of his daughter. That made Gerin stare. He couldn't ever remember hearing Van use Fand's name in such a fashion before.

Evidently, Maeva couldn't, either. With a shrug, she replied, "When you go on campaign, you don't pay attention to what Mother says. Why do you think I'm going to?"

Listening with an analytical ear, Gerin admired that. It assumed Maeva had as much business going on campaign as anyone else. The Fox waited to see if Van would accept, or even notice, that unspoken assumption.

The outlander shook his head, like a bear bedeviled by bees. "It's not the same, not the same at all," he said. "Fine woman that your mother is, there's only so long I can stand being in the same place with her."

"Do you think it's any different for me?" Maeva asked.

Van coughed, then turned red beneath his bronzed hide. "Well, aye, it's some different," he answered, and let it go at that rather than explaining how it was different. That would have involved explaining how adultery ranked alongside fighting as his favorite campaign sports. He coughed again, then said, "Now that I know you're here, I'll say you've had your fun, and now you're to go back to Fox Keep where you belong."

Maeva set her chin. "No," she said, a reply remarkable for simplicity and succinctness.

Somehow, the shade of red Van turned was different this time. "I am your father, I'll have you know, and what I tell you, that you shall do."

"No," Maeva said again. "Did you pay any attention to what your father told you once you'd killed your first man?"

"He was dead by then," Van said, an answer that was not really an answer. He turned to Gerin. "You're the king, Fox. If you tell her to go home and keep herself safe, she'll have to do it."

Gerin suffered his own coughing fit then. In all the years he'd known Van, the outlander had never appealed to his authority till now. Thoughtfully, he said, "I don't know. Isn't a lone girl on the road liable to face more danger than one in the middle of our own army?"

"She can take care of—" Van began, and then, a couple of words too late, stopped in his tracks.

Dagref, as was his way, drove home the logical flaw with a mallet: "If she can take care of herself, what point to sending her home?"

Maeva sent him a grateful look. The one Van sent him was anything but. Gerin said, "I don't think you're going to win this one, old friend. If she were a boy, you wouldn't be trying."

"But she's no boy, which is the point to the business," Van said stubbornly. "I know soldiers, and—"

"Wait." The Fox held up a hand. "I know Maeva, too. Don't you think anyone who tried to touch her if she didn't care to be touched would end up a eunuch like the priests of Biton, and that bloody quick?"

Van kept frowning. "Not right," he said again. "Not even close to right." After a moment, Gerin figured out what was likely troubling him. No doubt Maeva could protect herself if she didn't want to be touched. What if she *did* want to be touched, though? That had to be in Van's mind.

Aragis said, "You're not going to send her home." He sounded as if this was the first time he'd imagined that possibility.

Gerin bowed to him. "Lord king, there she is." He pointed to Maeva. "If you think you can order her home and make it stick, go ahead. Me, I don't like to waste orders that won't be obeyed. It weakens every other order I give after that."

"One way to do it would be to forbid her from any future fighting here," Aragis said, "and to post guards around her to make sure she cannot join it."

He was not a fool. He would never have done so well for himself had he been a fool. Maeva's face fell. Gerin could indeed do that. Van saw as much, too. Where his daughter wilted, he beamed. "That's the way, by the gods," he said, and bowed to Aragis. "I thank you, Archer. That's just the way."

"Oh, yes, a splendid suggestion," Dagref said. Had Gerin loosed his own sarcastic tones quite so freely when he was younger? On reflection, he decided he had. No wonder no one had liked him much. Dagref went on, "Not only does it take one proved fighter out of the army, it takes half a dozen or however many more out to watch her and make certain she doesn't do what she's already shown she's good at doing."

Maeva had eyed him with a certain speculation back at Fox Keep. He hadn't noticed then. If he didn't notice now, he was blind. Besides, his education in such things had advanced since then.

But maybe he didn't after all, for Aragis was eyeing him, too. "I am a king, young fellow," the Archer said coldly. "Do you cast scorn on me?"

"On you, lord king? Of course not," Dagref answered. "But a king can spout foolishness like anyone else. If you don't believe me, listen to my father for a while."

Aragis pursed his lips, then turned back to Gerin. "If that one can fight as well as he talks, he will be dangerous—if you let him live."

"Honh!" Van broke in. "We've said the same thing about Ferdulf, close enough. No wonder those two get on pretty well."

Dagref took no notice of that. He spoke to Gerin, who hadn't managed to get a word in edgewise about Aragis' suggestion: "Father, one of the things you always talk about is giving people the chance to do what they're good at. Why else would you have made Carlun your steward?"

"Because you weren't old enough yet to do the job?" the Fox suggested, perhaps a fourth in jest.

His son ignored him. His son was good at ignoring him, and getting better. "Why else do you teach peasants to read and write? If Maeva's good at fighting and wants to do it, why shouldn't she have the chance?"

"You can't get maimed with a pen and a scrap of parchment in your hands, curse it," Van said.

Gerin still hadn't said anything. No matter what he did say, he realized, he was going to make people he cared about unhappy. He hated having to speak in circumstances like that. Too many times, though, he had no choice. This was one of them. Slowly, he said, "Maeva *has* proved what she can do. That she came south with us proves she wanted to do it. Much as I'd like to, I can't see any justice in sending her back."

"Thank you, lord king," Maeva said quietly. Dagref looked as pleased as if he'd invented her. Van looked like a thunderstorm about to spill over. Maeva went on, "Now I peel this fuzz off my face."

"Were I you, I wouldn't," Gerin said. "With the beard, you look like any other northern warrior, near enough. Without it, the imperials will see you're something out of the ordinary and take special care against you. That's the last thing you ever want on the battlefield. I've got rid of a good many foes who didn't think I was dangerous till too late."

"I don't know," Van said. "I want 'em afraid of me." With his tall-plumed helm, his gleamingly polished corselet of solid bronze, and his great size and bulk, he smashed Gerin's principle to smithereens. He had the strength and skill to get away with it, too.

Dagref said, "A lot of the southerners shave their faces. They might not take Maeva for a woman, just for a northerner who does likewise."

"If you'll remember, son," Gerin said with a certain relish, "I didn't say they were liable to take her for a woman. I said they were liable to take her for something out of the ordinary. A man from north of the High Kirs without a beard is out of the ordinary, too."

"Why, so he is," Dagref said. "You're right, Father." He was not least disconcerting because he had no trouble admitting he was wrong.

Gerin rubbed his own chin. He'd shaved his face when he came back up from the City of Elabon, but harsh, ceaseless teasing had made him—and Rihwin, too—conform in outward appearance, if not in what lay beneath.

"Thank you, lord king," Maeva said again. "I will do everything I can to show myself a worthy warrior for you."

"I shall have words for you presently, young lady," Van said, and stomped off. Somehow, that particular salutation seemed out of place when aimed at someone in a leather shirt with bronze scales sewn into pockets on it.

"You handled that smoothly," Aragis said to Gerin; the Fox supposed he meant it for a compliment. "I wouldn't have decided as you did, but I can see how and why you did it, which I never would have guessed when I spied . . . your new warrior." With a nod to Maeva that might have been ironic or might not, he took himself off, too.

Maeva went back toward the rest of the riders. Gerin expected Dagref to follow her, but the youth stayed. "I want to thank you, Father, for keeping Maeva with the army," he said. "If you'd ordered her back to Fox Keep, I would have used the promise I won from you to make you change your mind."

"Would you?" Gerin said, and his son nodded. Half the Fox—maybe more than half—wished he *had* ordered Maeva back. That would have rid him of the promise at a price he could afford. Now— Who could say what Dagref would come up with now? Gerin eyed his son in a speculative way. "You must think a lot of her, if you'd give up the promise for that."

"She's like a sister to me," Dagref said. Then, a moment later, he turned pink. With characteristic honesty, he corrected himself: "Maybe not quite like a sister." He didn't so much leave as flee. Rubbing his chin once more, Gerin stared after him.

The next morning, Gerin's men and Aragis' moved south after the imperials. The pursuit went slowly. Gerin had expected it would, but it was even slower than he'd looked for. In their withdrawal, the soldiers of the Elabonian Empire had manhandled boulders onto the Elabon Way and scattered caltrops not only on the road but in the fields to either side of it.

"We may have won a battle, Fox, but we haven't won the war," Aragis the Archer said. "They'll be ready to take us on again before long."

"I thought as much from the way they pulled back," Gerin answered. "I said so, to whoever would listen. Nobody much listened. I wish I'd been wrong."

Every so often, he would roll past wreckage of the army he had beaten: a chariot fallen to pieces; a dead horse; a hastily dug grave, brown against the green of the fields, to mark the final resting place of some imperial trooper who'd died slowly instead of quickly. Every time he spotted a grave, he wondered if Maeva had seen it. That probably didn't matter. No one her age believed anything bad could happen to her. The years taught you otherwise, sooner or later—more often sooner.

A rider came trotting back from around a bend in the road. "Lord king!" he shouted, and then, remembering himself, "Lord kings!"

"What have the imperials gone and done now?" Gerin asked.

"Lord king," the scout answered, seeming relieved to be speaking to a single sovereign, "lord king, there's a wall across the road."

Gerin pictured a barricade of rocks and logs, perhaps with a few dismounted archers behind it to give approaching warriors a greeting less friendly than they might have wanted. "Did you ride around it?" he asked. "Do they have an ambush somewhere back of it?"

"Couldn't ride around it, lord king," the horseman said.

"It's too wide to ride around." He stretched out his arms as far as they would go.

"What's he talking about?" Aragis demanded irritably.

"I don't know," the Fox admitted. "Best thing I can think for us to do is go have a look for ourselves." He tapped Dagref on the shoulder. "Forward. We'd better find out."

As soon as the chariot rounded the bend, he saw the horseman had been telling the truth. His own visualization had been at fault. The wall was of red brick, about ten feet high, and stretched off to east and west as far as the eye could see. Van said, "The imperials couldn't have built that."

"Of course not," Gerin agreed, "or their soldiers couldn't have, anyway. It's sorcerous, without a doubt."

"Maybe it's an illusion," Van said hopefully. "Maybe if we go up to it, we can go right through it."

It looked very solid. Of course, an illusion that didn't look solid wouldn't have been much of an illusion. Gerin jumped down from the chariot. He walked up to the brick wall and slapped it with the palm of his hand. It felt very solid, too. Suddenly suspicious, he closed his eyes and walked forward. He bumped his nose, not too hard, because he wasn't going too fast.

He opened his eyes. He was staring at bricks, up so close they were blurry. He backed away. The bricks became sharp and clear. They didn't disappear, no matter how hard he wished they would.

More and more of the army came round the bend in the road. Gerin heard the exclamations of surprise that rose from his men and Aragis'. Some were just exclamations of surprise. He could deal with those. He was surprised himself. Others, though, ones that came mostly from his men, were full of confidence that he could get rid of the wall in short order.

Van had his own ideas about how to do that. Saying,
"Don't be shy with the cursed thing," he shouted for a
hammer. When he got one—a stout bronze-headed tool
that looked about as deadly as the mace he carried—
he slammed it into the wall with all his strength. Nothing
happened, except that he grunted in pain and rubbed
at his shoulder. "Didn't even dent it," he said in disgust.

"You wouldn't," Gerin said. "It's magical."

"Really?" Van said, packing enough sarcasm into the
word to prove he'd lived a good many years in Fox Keep.

Aragis the Archer said, "This is why I wanted you with
me, Fox, not against me."

Gerin glared at him. "Why? So I can look like an idiot
in front of your men and mine both?" Aragis' expression
was one of stolid incomprehension. He was convinced
Gerin was a marvelous mage. Nothing would unconvince
him except watching the Fox fail. In that case, he was
liable to get unconvinced in a hurry. Hoping to sidestep
the issue, Gerin looked around and shouted, "Ferdulf!"

"What do *you* want?" the little demigod demanded.
He was back to being surly. Most of the time, Gerin
wouldn't have let that bother him. Now he would have
been glad for a little of the grudging gratitude Ferdulf
had shown right after the battle against the Empire.

Since he didn't have it, he went ahead without: "Can
you fly up over the wall and tell us what's on the other
side of it?"

"Grass," Ferdulf said. "Trees. Cows. Elabonians. Go
far enough and there are mountains. I don't need to fly
over it to tell you that."

Gerin exhaled through his nose. *I will not let the little
divine bastard get my goat*, he thought. With as much
patience as he could, he said, "Knowing exactly where
the imperials are might be good for us. We'll probably
fight them again once we get past the wall, you know."

"Oh, all right," Ferdulf said sulkily, and hopped up into the air. What happened next made everyone who saw it exclaim in surprise and alarm. As Ferdulf rose, so did the wall in front of him.

He exclaimed, too—angrily. He didn't much care about obeying Gerin. Having the Elabonian Empire thwart him was something else again. But as fast as he flew, as high as he flew, whichever way from side to side he flew, the wall rose to keep him from passing over it. When he flew lower, it shrank, as if it, or the wizard in charge of it, could sense exactly how high he was at any given moment.

When he returned to the ground, the wall went back to being what it had been before he started flying: ten feet high, and very solid-looking. Gerin rubbed his nose. It felt as solid as it looked.

"You ought to knock it down," Ferdulf said. "A wall like that has no business existing in the first place."

"Van didn't have much luck. And if it's magical, I'm not sure we *can* knock it down," Gerin said. "For instance, how thick is it?"

"I don't know," Ferdulf answered. "I think you're pretty thick yourself, though, if you stand here and let it baffle you."

Rihwin the Fox came riding over to Gerin. "Nice piece of work, isn't it?" he said with the tones of one admiring a fellow professional's achievement even when that achievement inconvenienced him. He'd studied sorcery down in the City of Elabon till a jape played on a senior wizard got him expelled from the Sorcerers' Collegium. Despite that expulsion, he'd been a better mage than Gerin up to the moment when Mavrix took away his sorcerous powers. He still knew magic well, even if he couldn't work it any more.

"I'd like it better if it weren't so nice," Gerin said.

"Oh, but it's as pretty a use of the law of similarity as I've ever seen," Rihwin protested, "not only in building the wall, but also in making detection of the keystone— or rather, in this case, the key brick—as difficult as possible."

"What nonsense is he spouting now?" Aragis demanded irritably.

Gerin took no notice of his fellow king. "Father Dyaus," he whispered. "I do believe you're right."

"Of course I'm right," Rihwin said. "When have you ever known me to be mistaken, pray tell?"

"Only when you open your mouth," Gerin replied, which reduced Rihwin to irate splutters. Gerin ignored those, too. He walked up to the wall and examined it brick by brick. Sure enough, each brick was identical to all its neighbors: not just similar to them, but identical. Each one had a chip near the center, each had a scratch at the upper left-hand corner, and each, over to the right, had embedded in it a tiny crystal or flake of mica that sparkled when the light caught it at the right angle. "Isn't that interesting?" he murmured.

"Now you're the one full of drivel," Aragis complained. "Tell me at once what's going on."

"One of their wizards took a brick and sorcerously duplicated it about as many times as there are drops of water in the Niffet," Gerin answered. "If I could find out which brick is the real one, I wouldn't have any trouble—well, not much trouble—making the wall disappear."

"Ah," Aragis said, and then, "All right. I was beginning to wonder whether you were able to talk sense or not. I see you are. Good. As I told you, I wanted you on my side because of the wizardry you know. Now—find that brick and get rid of it."

Rihwin had the grace to give Gerin a sympathetic look.

"It's not quite so easy as that, I'm afraid," Gerin said. "One of these bricks along the bottom row is sure to be *the* brick, but which one? Go ahead, lord king—you tell me which one it is."

"You're the wizard," Aragis said. "You're the one who's supposed to know things like that. Now get to work, curse it." He might have been ordering a lazy serf to spread manure over a field.

"I can't tell which brick it is by looking, any more than you can," Gerin said. "That means I've got a couple of thousand to choose from. And that's liable to mean we'll be here for a while."

"Can we go around the bloody thing?" Aragis asked.

"Maybe," Gerin said, "but I wouldn't bet anything I cared to lose on it. My guess is that, if the wall can go up and down to keep Ferdulf from flying over it, it'll go from side to side to keep us from getting by it."

"That makes more sense than I wish it did," Aragis said. "How do you go about finding out which brick is *the* brick, then?"

"You have not put forward an easy question, lord king," Rihwin the Fox said. "The essence of the law of similarity centering on resemblance, distinguishing between prototype and likeness is by its nature a daunting task."

"If it were easy, the cursed imperials wouldn't have bothered running up the wall in the first place," Aragis retorted. He folded his arms across his chest and looked over toward Gerin. "Well?"

"Well, my fellow king, much as I hate to disappoint you—and to disappoint myself, I might add—I haven't the faintest idea which one is *the* brick," Gerin answered. "I told you that once already. Maybe I can figure out some sort of sorcerous test, though the gods only know how long that'll take or whether it'll work. You'd need a god to tell you which one brick out of thousands is the real one and . . ." His voice trailed away. "You'd need a god—or maybe a demigod. How about it, Ferdulf?"

"You want something *more* from me?" Ferdulf said indignantly. His sigh declared that he was put upon far beyond anything his powers might have made acceptable. "There are times when I wonder why the gods ever bothered creating mortals in the first place."

"Some Sithonian philosophers wonder whether mortals didn't create gods instead of the other way round," Gerin said, which made Ferdulf, despite being descended from a Sithonian deity, give him a horrible look. He wished he'd kept his mouth shut. Since he hadn't, he went on in smoothly ingratiating tones: "Be that as it may, can you use your own great powers to see what we cannot? It would give you another chance to have a go at the Elabonian Empire, and embarrass the imperial wizard who put up the wall thinking it would stop us so easily."

"Oh, all right." Even in agreement, Ferdulf was petulant. In that, he took after his father. He floated up a foot or so into the air and drifted along to the west a couple of hundred yards. "It's this one right here." He didn't raise his voice—or Gerin didn't think he did—but it came as clear as if he'd been standing by the Fox. A helpful soldier ran forward and set his hand on the brick after Ferdulf left it.

Gerin trotted over to it, ignoring the weight of his bronze-and-leather armor. To look at, it was just another brick in the wall. He'd expected nothing different. He turned to Van, who'd followed him. "Will you do the honors?"

"I will, and gladly," the outlander answered. He smashed at the brick with the bronze-headed hammer. When a chip flew from it, chips flew from all the others along the wall. Soldiers cheered. Van hit the brick again and again, till it cracked in three places. The rest of the bricks cracked, too. Van pushed at one of the pieces with his foot. It came away from the rest of the brick—and the wall vanished.

About a hundred feet behind it stood a fellow in a fancy robe who looked absurdly surprised to be staring all at once at the entire army of the northlands. "That's a wizard!" Gerin exclaimed as the man turned to run. "Don't let him get away."

"I'll take care of that," Van growled. He snatched up a piece of the brick he had broken and flung it at the sorcerer. It caught him between the shoulderblades. He went down on his face with a dismayed squawk. Before he could get to his feet again, Dagref and a couple of other men who'd run after him jumped on him and frogmarched him back to Gerin and Aragis.

"Hello," the Fox said mildly. "I gather you're to blame for this latest bit of unpleasantness?" The wizard didn't answer. Gerin clicked his tongue between his teeth in mock dismay. "And I remembered manners south of the High Kirs being so much smoother than they are here in the northlands. Tell us what to call you, anyhow."

"Lengyel." The sorcerer replied to that without hesitation. It was, after all, only his use-name, not his hidden true name.

"Well, Lengyel, suppose you start answering my questions," Gerin said, still sounding mild but looking anything but.

"Well, Lengyel, suppose you start answering questions or we'll see how long you last up on a cross," Aragis added. "You'll have a cursed hard time working magical passes with your hands nailed to the wood." Sounding mild was beyond the Archer, but he did seem more matter-of-fact than menacing. To Gerin, at least, that made him more frightening, not less.

It seemed to have the same effect on Lengyel, who

did not look to be in a good position to work passes anyhow, not with Dagref jamming one arm up behind his back and the other held tight against his side. After licking his lips, the wizard said, "Tell me what you want to know."

"You were the fellow who made this wall?" the Fox repeated.

"Yes," Lengyel said, and then spoke in some exasperation: "And I certainly did not expect a pack of semibarbarous backwoods bumpkins to penetrate its secret quickly. I did not expect you to penetrate them at all, in fact."

"You keep a civil tongue in your head if you want to keep any tongue in your head," Aragis said, in about the tone Gerin would have used to tell Blestar to get down off the table.

"Don't worry about it, Archer," Gerin told him. "That's how the Empire thinks of the northlands. It's how the Empire has always thought of the northlands. Since the Empire hasn't had anything to do with us for the past twenty years, you can't expect them to have changed their minds during that time."

"How did—?" Lengyel's face suddenly twisted in pain. "Stop that!" he hissed.

"Then you stop wiggling your fingers," replied Dagref, who had given the wizard's arm a yank. "I don't know what sorcery you were trying, and I don't care to find out, either."

Lengyel bowed his head. For the first time, he seemed to realize the sorcerous wall hadn't come down and he hadn't been caught by a lucky accident. "You northerners are . . . more clever than I'd expected," he said slowly.

"We're clever enough to know we're better off out of the Empire than in it, anyhow," Gerin said. "Of course, you don't have to be very clever to figure out that paying taxes and not getting anything for them—no soldiers when the barbarians come over the border, no grain when the harvest fails—isn't the best bargain in the world."

"You people have paid no taxes the past twenty years, and you didn't pay many before that," Lengyel returned. "Why you deserve to be rewarded for not doing what you should have is beyond me."

"Even when we did pay, back a long time ago, the City of Elabon forgot everything this side of the High Kirs," Gerin said.

"That isn't the point," Aragis said. "The point is, where in the five hells is the imperial army we thrashed? Once we thrash it again, and maybe one more time after that, you southerners will figure out that you ought to leave us alone."

"This is the territory of the Empire of Elabon," Lengyel said. "We shall not abandon what is ours."

"I think you'd be wise to answer King Aragis," Gerin said. "If you don't answer, he's liable to get insistent, and you wouldn't care for that. Believe me, Lengyel— you wouldn't."

Lengyel looked at Aragis. He licked his lips again. Gerin hadn't said what Aragis would do to him if sufficiently displeased. He'd figured Lengyel's imagination would come up with something more horrific than anything he might suggest. If studying Aragis' hard face didn't start a frightened imagination working at a gallop, nothing ever would.

To make matters worse, Aragis smiled. The Fox would not have wanted to be on the receiving end of that smile. By all appearances, Lengyel didn't, either. His larynx worked a couple of times before he said, "The army—my army— will be most of a day's journey south of here, no doubt regrouping to face you reb—uh, you northerners—once more, and this time come away victorious."

"No doubt," Gerin said dryly. "Now—will the other wizards with the army know this wall has fallen, or will we be able to give them a surprise greeting?"

Lengyel licked his lips again. Gerin saw evasion forming in his eyes. Dagref must have sensed the same thing, for he gave the wizard's arm another jerk upwards. "Aii!" Lengyel yelped. "Have a care. You'll break it."

"Answer my father, then," Dagref said pleasantly.

"Yes." Lengyel's voice was sullen. "They will know."

"Too bad," Gerin said. "I'd have like to drop in on them unannounced. But, as Aragis has said, we will beat them, one way or another."

Van pointed at Lengyel. "What are we going to do with him now? Keeping a cursed wizard captive in our midst could mean trouble for us."

"So it could," Gerin said. "I hope it won't, though." He raised his voice: "Ferdulf!"

"What do you want to annoy me with now?" Ferdulf asked, as touchy as he usually was. He drifted through the air toward the Fox—and toward the captured imperial wizard. Lengyel's eyes almost bugged out of his head as he stared at the demigod. Ferdulf went on, "What do you think I'm able to do that you're too stupid to manage for yourself?"

"I want you to keep an eye and an ear and whatever other senses you happen to need on this fellow here." The Fox pointed at Lengyel. "If he tries to make a nuisance of himself with magic, stop him. If you can't stop him, shout for the guards. I expect they'll stop him for good."

"Yes, I'll do that," Ferdulf said, a look of nasty anticipation on his face. "I don't like Elabonian wizards, not even a little. I don't like what they can do, either." He hadn't cared for landing with a thump in the middle of the battle between the imperials and the men of the northlands. He hadn't been able to do anything about it, though, not till Gerin dealt with Caffer by means altogether unsorcerous.

Much as the late, unlamented (certainly by the Fox) Caffer had, Lengyel asked, "What manner of creature is this . . . Ferdulf, is that right?"

Before Gerin could answer, Ferdulf shouted, "I am not a creature, wretch! You are the creature. And a miserable creature you are, too, I'll have you know. I am the son of a god. Kindly grant me the respect due my station."

Lengyel was not in a good position to grant anyone respect, and Dagref and his other captors did not loose their grip on him anyway. The wizard spoke to Gerin: "He won't be enough to hold back the might of the Empire of Elabon. Nothing will be enough to hold back the might of the Empire of Elabon. Do what you will with me for saying so, but it remains true."

"No, it remains your opinion," Gerin answered. "My opinion—and I know the Empire better than you know the northlands, I assure you—is that you have no idea what you're talking about." He nodded to his son. "Take him away."

By the time two more days had passed, Gerin began to wonder how well he'd really known the Elabonian Empire after all. The imperials responded to defeat far more resolutely than he'd expected. They hadn't relied only on their sorcerous wall, but had had scouts and skirmishers out south of it. The skirmishers, when they clashed with Gerin's men, fought hard.

"They wouldn't have acted like this in Hildor's day," Aragis said. "Of course, in Hildor's day they stayed down in Cassat under the mountains and didn't bother with the rest of the northlands at all. This new Emperor of theirs must be a real meat-eater."

"I'm afraid you're right," the Fox said gloomily. Ahead in the distance, the latest party of imperial skirmishers fled back toward their own main force, some of Rihwin's riders and a few chariots offering pursuit. Gerin clicked his tongue between his teeth. "I hope they aren't trying to lure our people into an ambush."

"You don't think they would, do you?" Dagref sounded far more alarmed and far less rational than usual.

Gerin needed only a moment to understand why: Maeva was liable to be among the riders. If he said something about that, he'd only make his son angry at him as well as worried. What he did say was, "Well, it's not beyond the bounds of the possible, you know."

Dagref nodded. "Yes, that's true," he admitted, as much to himself as to the Fox. "I hope they don't, though."

"All right, son. I hope they don't, too," Gerin said. "I do want to remind you, our captains didn't get to be captains because they were so generous and trusting, they'd follow the enemy wherever he went without another thought in their heads."

"Yes, that's also true," Dagref said. "Of course, if all captains were as clever as you make out, no ambush would ever work, and we know that's not so."

Van boomed laughter. "He's got you there, Fox. I never thought I'd see the day when you were outlogicked, but your sprout can do it now and then."

"You're right," Gerin said, and let it go at that. Van evidently hadn't figured out what Dagref had: that his daughter was liable to be riding into danger. Gerin supposed that meant Dagref had outlogicked the outlander, too. Had he been Dagref's age himself, he would have pointed it out. Being the age he was, he kept quiet. Not all the things the years had brought were welcome, but discretion often came in handy.

Before long, the riders and chariots returned. No ambuscade had awaited them, and, for that matter, Maeva was not among them. Dagref had the grace to look sheepish. Some little while later, as the chariot rattled south along the Elabon Way, Van let out several startled oaths.

"What's biting you?" Gerin asked.

"What? Nothing. Never mind." Van shook his head and looked determined not to answer. The Fox decided pushing him right then would probably be a bad idea. The outlander had taken a while to work out what Dagref saw right away, was his guess, and didn't care for it any more than Dagref had.

Nothos, Elleb, and Tiwaz were in the sky when the army camped that night, the first pale moon a thin crescent, swift-moving Tiwaz a much fatter one, almost at first quarter, and ruddy Elleb a couple of days before full. Rihwin said, "I think they'll fight us again soon, tomorrow or the day after. If they wait much longer, we'll be down to Cassat."

"You're likely right," Gerin said. He caught one yawn, then let another one loose. "They won't fight us tonight, though. With the ghosts abroad, traveling by night will be more dangerous to them than we would."

"There you speak sooth, lord king," Rihwin answered. He yawned, too. "I shall have a good night's rest, the better to lay waste the imperials come morning, and the better to forget I was once a man from south of the mountains myself."

"Yes, you had better forget that, hadn't you?" Gerin said pointedly. He yawned again. "Me, I'm going to forget everything but my bedroll."

Morning dawned bright and clear. It also dawned without Lengyel. Both his guards were asleep and remained so despite repeated efforts to shake them awake. "Some drug or other, I judge," Gerin growled, examining the prostrate men with no small annoyance. "Maybe he had it secreted on his person, or maybe he found an herb he could use when he went behind a bush. Either way—" He raised his voice to a shout: "Ferdulf!"

"What *now*?" the demigod demanded, drifting over from some distance away.

"The wizard escaped," the Fox snapped.

"I didn't know anything about it," Ferdulf said. He looked at Lengyel's unconscious guards, too. "He didn't use magic to do it. That's what I was looking for. That's what you told me to look for, if you'll recall."

Gerin exhaled angrily. "I don't care if the whoreson bored them to sleep reading bad poetry. I didn't want him loose."

"That's not what you said," Ferdulf replied with considerable aplomb. "I can't keep track of everything at once, you know. I'm only superhuman."

In the abstract, Gerin admired the line. He had scant time to worry about the abstract. "Since you let him get away—"

"I did no such thing," Ferdulf retorted.

"You were charged with keeping him here," Gerin said.

"I was charged with making sure he did not escape by magic," the demigod said. "I did as I was charged, and he did not escape by magic. If a couple of witless mortals let him up and wander off when he didn't even have to bother with sorcery, that's hardly my problem, now is it?" He folded his skinny arms across his narrow chest and floated off the ground till he was staring the Fox straight in the eye.

The expression on his face ached for a slap. Regretfully, Gerin held off from delivering it. Instead, keeping his voice light, he said, "It depends on how you look at things, I suppose. If you don't mind taking the chance that his magic will do worse things to you than Caffer's did, you may be right."

Ferdulf might have had a god for a father, but he wasn't much better than any other four-year-old at looking ahead to the likely consequences of things he did—and things he didn't do. He was unhappy enough at what Gerin said to let his feet scuff the dirt once more. "All right—what should I do about that?" he asked in tones much less toplofty than he usually used.

"Now that he has escaped, can you use your powers to hunt him down, or to help some troopers hunt him down?" Gerin asked.

"I don't think so." Ferdulf frowned. "Or maybe I can. I could try, anyway." Gerin nodded.

He rose into the air now, till he drifted high above the encampment like a bad-tempered cloud. He twisted his body so that he faced due west, then slowly began bearing ever more to the south. Gerin wondered what sort of sense he was using to feel for the vanished Lengyel. Had it been a sense the Fox possessed, he could have done the search himself.

Up in the sky, Ferdulf suddenly stiffened. He dropped a few feet, as he had a way of doing when he wasn't paying full attention to his flying. Were he wholly divine, no doubt he wouldn't have had to worry about such things. Were he wholly divine, Gerin would have had to worry much more about him.

"There!" he called down to the Fox, pointing southwest. "He's going that way."

That way was the direction in which Gerin was almost certain the bulk of the imperial army lay. "How far away is he?" he shouted up to Ferdulf. "Can you tell?"

"Hard to be sure," Ferdulf answered. "I wasn't sure I could find him at all, you know."

"Yes, yes," Gerin said. "But is it worth my while to send a few men after him, or has he got back safe to the enemy's main camp?"

The little demigod dropped a few feet more. "I can't tell," he said, sounding angry at Gerin, Lengyel, and himself. "I wish I could, but I can't."

"A pestilence," Gerin muttered. "I wish you could, too." He looked around for Aragis. The Archer wasn't far away. "Shall we send men after the wizard?" Gerin asked him. "Were it up to me, I'd say yes, but you're the overall commander. If you want to hold back and let him go, I won't quarrel."

"Are you daft?" Aragis growled. "Of course, send men after him. Bringing him back is worth the risk. Send some of your riders. It's the sort of thing they'd be good for—they're faster than men afoot, and they can go places where chariotry can't. Chase him till he wishes he'd never run away."

"Good enough." As Gerin shouted for Rihwin, he reflected that the best way to fight Aragis was liable to be leading him into a trap, a place where he'd think he had an easy victory, but where in fact more foes waited than he'd expect. For the moment, though, he was an ally.

"How many men would you have me send, lord king?" Rihwin asked. "And shall I take Ferdulf?"

"If he'll go with you, certainly," Gerin answered. "That'll make it harder for Lengyel to turn your troopers into toads." He raised an eyebrow. "You're going to lead this chase yourself?"

"By your leave, I am," Rihwin said. "Since I could not even detect the presence of a woman warrior among my men, I'd fain reassure myself that I am on occasion capable of seeing beyond the end of my nose."

"Fair enough," Gerin told him. "But don't just have your eyes open for Lengyel. Remember, the imperials are liable to be waiting for you somewhere out there, too." He hesitated, then asked, "And how did Maeva seem to you?—as a warrior, I mean."

"Oh, I understood you; you need not fret over that." Rihwin looked chagrined. "Had Aragis not noticed what she was, I doubt I should have done so. This, you must follow, disturbs me for not one but two reasons: first, that she performs in every way so much like a man, and second, that I of all people simply failed to note her femininity."

"And what would you have done if you had?" Gerin asked, and then answered his own question: "If she didn't make you sing soprano for trying to do that, her father would have."

"I do not molest women who find my attentions unwelcome," Rihwin replied with dignity. "Given the number who find those attentions most welcome, I have no need to bother, or bother with, the others." What with the number of bastards he'd fathered over the years, that comment held no small grain of truth. With more dignity still, he went on, "In any event, the charms of a woman—or, I should say, a girl—of that age hold little appeal for me."

"All right, I'm persuaded," Gerin said. "Now go off and—"

But Rihwin, once begun, was not so easily headed. "Maeva may well be attractive to someone with fewer years than myself. Your son, for example, immediately springs to mind."

"Aye, he does, doesn't he?" Gerin said, which seemed to disconcert Rihwin—maybe he'd expected indignant denials. Gerin waved his fellow Fox forward. "Go on, get after that wizard. Don't stand around gabbing all day."

Rihwin and a squadron of his riders went trotting south a few minutes later. Ferdulf went along with them. Gerin wouldn't have wanted to be an imperial mage the little demigod flushed out of hiding. On the other hand, he wouldn't have wanted to be Rihwin using Ferdulf as a hunting hound, either. Most hunting hounds had the sovereign virtue of not talking back.

Rihwin and his men had been gone only moments when someone spoke to Gerin in a reedy tenor: "Lord king?"

He turned and found himself facing a fuzzy-bearded youth. He needed a heartbeat to remember the beard was false and the tenor in fact a contralto. "What is it, Maeva?" he asked cautiously.

"When you sent the riders out just now," Van's daughter asked, "did you tell Rihwin not to put me in that squadron?"

"No," Gerin answered. "Maybe I would have if it had occurred to me, but it didn't. I didn't tell him anything one way or the other. Did he say I did?"

"No, he didn't say that," Maeva said. "But when he didn't choose me, I wondered. Can you blame me?"

"I suppose not," the Fox admitted. "If you're going to do this, though, there's something I want you to think about, all right?"

"What?" Either in her own proper person or disguised as a man, Maeva was no one to trifle with.

"This," Gerin said: "Just because you *can be* chosen to do this, that, or the other thing doesn't mean you *will be* chosen all the time or that you *have to be* chosen. It may just mean you *weren't* chosen this one time, and you *may be* the next."

Maeva considered that with almost the grave intensity Dagref might have shown. At last, she said, "All right, lord king, that's fair enough, as far as it goes. But if I'm *never* chosen for anything dangerous, then it doesn't go far enough. If that happens, I'll get angry." Her eyes blazed, as if to warn that getting her angry was not a good idea.

Being acquainted with her parents, Gerin could have—indeed, had—figured that out for himself. He considered her words in turn. "You're with the army, Maeva. You're fighting. If you think none of the imperials could have killed you in the last battle, maybe I should send you home after all."

She tossed her head, a feminine gesture odd when combined with the false beard stuck to her chin and cheeks. "Nobody knew—well, nobody but Dagref knew—who I was, what I was. I was just another trooper. It's not going to be like that any more. It can't be like that any more. I wish it could."

"I'm not going to send you back, no matter how much your father wishes I would," Gerin said. "That means you're going forward. You'll get more fighting, believe me you will." He paused. "What will your mother think when you come home?" Fand was formidable, but not in the same way Maeva was.

"My mother? You heard me tell my father I didn't worry about that much, but . . ." Maeva thought it over. "My mother would probably say I didn't need to put on armor and carry a bow if I wanted to fight with men."

Gerin laughed. "Yes, that probably is what she'd say."

He wondered whether Maeva knew he and Fand had been lovers for a while, in the dark time between Elise's leaving him and his meeting Selatre. If she did, he wondered what she thought. He saw no way to ask. He didn't really want to find out. Some curiosity was better left unsatisfied.

He let out a small snort. Rihwin would surely disagree

with him there. But then, Rihwin didn't believe in holding back on anything.

"What's funny now, lord king?" Maeva asked.

"Sometimes the things you don't do are as important as the things you do," he answered. Maeva cocked her head to one side, no doubt wondering how that could possibly be amusing. Would Dagref have understood? Maybe. Maybe not, too. The Fox couldn't think of anyone else so young who might have.

When Gerin didn't seem inclined to explain further, Maeva went off scratching her head. He was unoffended. He'd sent his vassals off bemused more times than he could count. Most of those times had worked out all right. That gave him reason to hope this one would, too.

He peered south and kicked at the dirt. He also hoped Rihwin's chase after Lengyel would work out all right, but he had no particular reason to believe it would. Rihwin could perform far better than anyone who knew him only slightly might imagine. He could also perform far worse. Until he did whatever he did on any given day, no one could guess what that would be.

Trees blocked Gerin's view; he couldn't see as far as he would have liked. He couldn't see Ferdulf in the air any more, either. What was happening, out there where he couldn't see? How foolish had it been to let Rihwin and Ferdulf, each erratic by himself, go off together? How sorry would he be when he found out how foolish he'd been?

Was that a bird in the sky, down there to the south? No—no bird had ever flown with such a smooth, effortless motion. That was Ferdulf. (And what did the birds think of the little demigod who invaded their domain? Gerin would have bet they found him as annoying as everyone else did.) He was coming this way.

And, out from behind those trees, here came horsemen.

They had people on foot with them. Gerin took that for a good sign. Also promising was the way Ferdulf kept flying down and darting into the faces of the men on foot, as if they were chariot horses of the soldiery of the Elabonian Empire. The Fox wondered if Ferdulf was doing anything disgusting to them from on high. That didn't seem the best way to treat . . . prisoners, he supposed they were.

Gerin trotted toward the returning horsemen. So did Aragis. So did a good many ordinary soldiers. A lot of people were still curious to learn what the riders could do.

A horseman detached himself from the rest and approached the Fox at a rapid trot. After a moment, Gerin saw it was Rihwin. "We have him!" Rihwin shouted as soon as he was close enough for his voice to carry.

The soldiers cheered. Gerin clapped his hands together. Aragis looked astonished, and didn't bother hiding it. Gerin called, "Who are all the others you have there?"

"A round dozen of the fanciest whores off the streets of the City of Elabon," Rihwin answered. Gerin blinked. The soldiers burst into louder cheers. Rihwin waved them down. "Would it were so, but alas, it isn't. They're imperial troopers at whose forward camp Lengyel was staying. They offered no resistance, for we not only outnumbered them two to one but also came on them by surprise, thanks going almost entirely to the aid Ferdulf furnished."

"You probably wouldn't have been able to do it in chariots, would you?" Gerin asked, and Rihwin shook his head.

Aragis said, "I never denied horsemen had their uses, Fox. I even said this was one of them. Don't twit me here." He didn't sound so angry as he might have; he couldn't have expected Rihwin to succeed as fully as he had.

Here came Lengyel, looking even more dejected than he had when the men of the northlands captured him the first time. "Hello again," Gerin greeted him. "Aren't you glad we're barbarians and don't know what we're doing?"

"Delighted, I'm sure," Lengyel said sourly, which made Gerin respect him for the first time as a man rather than simply as a dangerous sorcerer.

Rihwin said, "And, lord king—lord kings—we have booty that may prove as valuable and delightful as our victory itself has been." He pointed to the mounts of some of his riders; the animals had skins tied on behind the horsemen. Grinning, he went on, "Here we find precious treasure scarcely seen in the northlands for a generation of men."

"Rihwin, you didn't—" Gerin began.

"Oh, but lord king, my fellow Fox, I did," Rihwin broke in. "Did you think that, after so long, I could resist the allure of so much splendid, glorious, magnificent wine?"

VI

"You idiot," Gerin said to Rihwin. "You clodpoll. You jackanapes. You bungler. You cretin. You jobbernowl. You madman. You fool. You loon. You twit. You lout. "You—"

"Thank you, lord king; I have by now some notion of your opinion, so you need not elaborate further," Rihwin said.

"Oh, but I was just warming up," Gerin said. "I hadn't even begun to discuss your ancestry, if any, your habits, and how lovingly the demons of the five hells will roast you after you die—which may be far sooner than you think, for I'm bloody tempted to murder you myself."

"Be reasonable, my fellow Fox," Rihwin said, a request to which Gerin might usually be expected to respond well. "Could you imagine I would pour the blood of the sweet grape out onto the uncaring ground rather than bringing it home in triumph?"

"And what about the lord of the sweet grape, Rihwin?" Gerin shouted, too furious for reason to hold any appeal. "What about Mavrix? Do you want to deal with Mavrix? Do you want Mavrix to deal with you? What happens when Mavrix and Ferdulf make each other's acquaintance? How far away would you like to be when that happens? Can you get to a place so far away?"

"I don't know," Rihwin said, an answer more inclusive than specific.

"Why didn't you bother thinking about any of those things ahead of time?" Gerin demanded, though he knew the answer only too well: at the sight of wine, anything resembling thought had fled from Rihwin's head.

Rihwin said, "Lord king, imagine if you'd been without a woman for most of the last twenty years and then found not one but half a dozen beautiful maids, all of them not only willing but eager. Would you leave them behind? Would you spill *their* blood out on the ground instead of enjoying them?"

"It's not the same, and don't you try to distract me," Gerin said. "You haven't exactly been pining away; you've made do quite well with ale."

"A man who wants women can, without them, make do with boys," Rihwin replied. "He can even, if his temper runs that way, make do with sheep. Making do, though, will not stop him from wanting women."

"I ought to spill this wine right now," Gerin grated.

He'd meant that to alarm Rihwin. Instead, it made the transplanted southerner brighten. "You mean you *shan't* spill it out?"

"Not right now," Gerin answered reluctantly. "Not till I think it through, which is a cursed lot more than you ever bothered doing."

"Blessings upon you, lord king!" Rihwin cried in fervent tones. He seized Gerin's hand, which alarmed his overlord. Then he kissed it, which alarmed Gerin even more. "Have no fear," Rihwin said, his eyes sparkling with amusement. "I am not one of those who, wanting boys, make do with women, of that you may rest assured." He changed notes yet again: "Er, lord king—*why* aren't you going to spill the wine out on the ground?"

Gerin let out a weary sigh. "Because I've seen, more

often than it suits me—much more often than it suits me—that you and wine and the will of the gods are somehow all tied together. The only reason I can think of to make it so is that your head is altogether empty inside, which means they have no trouble filling it with their desires."

"I loved the blood of the sweet grape long before I made Mavrix's acquaintance," Rihwin said. "I should have been as glad not to make that acquaintance, and I should have gone on loving wine had I not made it."

"All of that is no doubt true," Gerin replied. "None of it has anything to do with how many pits of wheat are buried around the village by Fox Keep, and none of it, I fear, has anything to do with why you found that wine and why you decided to bring it back here to our camp."

"This may be so, lord king," Rihwin said. "Let us assume it is so. If it be so, if I act at the will of the gods rather than pursuant to my own will, how is it you are furious with me, when I was but the empty-headed conduit through which they manifested their will?"

"Because—" Gerin stood there with his mouth hanging open, realizing he had no good answer. At last, he said, "Because you're handy, curse it," adding a moment later, "and because you'd have brought back that wine even without a god whispering in your ear, and you bloody well know it."

"Such a claim is all the better for proof," Rihwin said loftily. "If you do not purpose spilling the wine, what will you do with it?"

"Set a guard over it so you can't guzzle it," Gerin replied at once, and watched Rihwin's face fall. "And so no one else can, either," he said for good measure, but that did little to cheer his fellow Fox.

"You take all the fun out of life," Rihwin complained.

"I hope so," Gerin said, which made Rihwin angrier yet.

The wine stayed under guard. Rihwin kept right on grumbling. He wasn't the only one, either. Most of those grumbles, Gerin simply ignored. He couldn't ignore the ones from Aragis the Archer.

"Well, go ahead, my fellow king," the Fox said. "If you want to see what will happen, go ahead. If you want to meet Mavrix face to face, go ahead. You're a king. You can do as you please—till a god tells you otherwise, anyhow."

"Suppose I drink it and nothing happens?" Aragis demanded.

"Then you get to call me a fool," Gerin said. "Suppose you drink it and something happens? Will there be enough left of you for me to call a fool?"

Aragis muttered something into his beard that Gerin didn't catch. The Archer stomped off, making a point of kicking at the grass at every stride. He did not drink any wine. Gerin thought about teasing him, then thought better of it.

And then he got a request for wine from someone else, in a fashion he had not expected. Ferdulf came up to him in as nearly a polite way as he'd ever seen from the demigod. "May I please have a taste of the blood of the grape?" he asked.

Gerin stared. As far as he could remember, he'd never heard *please* from Ferdulf before. Not least because of that, he didn't say *no* right away. Instead, he asked, "Why do you want it?"

"Why do you think?" Ferdulf replied, with some—but not all—of his usual irritating sense of superiority. Gerin had an answer, or thought he did, but didn't speak it. He waited. The arrogance leaked out of the demigod. In a voice much smaller than Ferdulf usually used, he said, "If I drink wine, perhaps it will bring my father thither."

That was the possibility that had occurred to the Fox, too. It was not one that much appealed to him, whatever Ferdulf thought of it. "If your father does come," he asked cautiously, "what would you do?"

Ferdulf looked confused and unhappy, as opposed to malicious and intent on making everyone around him unhappy, his more usual aspect. "I don't know," he answered, something else he hardly ever said. "I think I'd like to ask him why he brought me into the world and what he intends of me, though—that for a beginning, and who can say from there?"

Why did he start you? Gerin thought. *As best I can tell, for no better reason than to annoy me.* Mavrix had certainly succeeded there. Aloud, the Fox said, "Why are you asking leave of me? You have the strength to overcome the guards I've set—I'm sure of it."

"Oh, yes," Ferdulf said carelessly. "But I know it might cause trouble, so I thought I had better ask before I do anything."

That didn't sound like Ferdulf, either. If nothing else in the world intimidated him, Mavrix did. Gerin said, "I don't really think the time is ripe now. Tell me the truth: do you?"

The little demigod sagged. "Maybe not," he said, and walked off with his feet on the ground, his head down. Then, suddenly, he turned back, hopping half his height into the air as he did so. "If my father were to be summoned, though, would he not take our side against the Empire of Elabon, which has inflicted such indignities on Sithonia over the centuries?"

"He might," the Fox admitted, and let it go at that: adding more would have reminded Ferdulf that the men of the northlands were as much Elabonians as the imperials. He went on in a different vein, saying, "Remember what the imperial wizard told us, though— the Empire of Elabon has ruled Sithonia for all those years, and the Sithonian gods haven't been able to do anything about it except slander the imperials. That being so, how much good will Mavrix do us?"

Ferdulf descended to the ground once more. He didn't answer, but went off in the direction he'd chosen before his afterthought. Gerin concluded he didn't think Mavrix would do much good. Seeing a humble Ferdulf was as novel an experience as any the Fox had had lately.

He looked in the direction of the wineskins and the guards around them. They'd drawn a fair-sized crowd. At first, that alarmed him. Then he relaxed a little. If a lot of people were hanging about the wine, that would make it harder for any one man—Rihwin's smiling face popped into his mind—to sneak away with any of the blood of the grape.

While the Fox was thinking thus, Van came up to him and said, "By all the gods, Captain, it's been a long time since I slugged down any wine. If I could just undo the tie on one of those skins, now— Wait, Fox! What in the five hells do you think you're doing, looking at me like that? Curse it, Fox, put your sword back in its sheath. Have you gone mad?"

"No, it's the whole world around me," Gerin answered. Van examined him closely for signs he was joking. By the way the outlander walked off shaking his head, he didn't find any.

The next morning, the army of the northlands rolled through another of those villages that had trembled on the edge of being towns and were now falling back unmistakably into the lesser status. Gerin had no time to do anything but mournfully note as much, for, a couple of bowshots south of the village, imperial scouts riding chariots with fast horses began pelting his men and Aragis' with arrows.

"Ha!" Aragis exclaimed. "They aren't as smart as they think they are." Without waiting for Gerin's advice, he shouted, "Rihwin! Forward the riders!"

"Aye, lord king," Rihwin said, and shouted orders of his own.

Out rode the horsemen. Gerin looked to see if he could spot Maeva among them, but had no luck. By the way Dagref's head followed the evolutions of the riders, he was looking for Maeva, too.

With roughly equal numbers, the horsemen routed the charioteers, as they had at the first big battle between the imperials and men of the northlands. The riders were faster and more maneuverable than their foes. They shot no worse than the men in the chariots. Before long, those chariots streamed back toward the southwest in headlong retreat.

"I think we ought to form line of battle," Gerin told Aragis. "We're liable to run into the whole imperial army any time now."

Aragis frowned. "If we don't run into the imperials, moving forward that way will slow us down." After a bit of thought, though, he nodded. "Let it be as you say. If we do run into them before we're ready, they'll make us sorry for it." As he had before the earlier battle with the forces of the Elabonian Empire, he halted the army and shouted, "Left and right! Form line of battle! Left and right!"

As they had then, his men and Gerin's cheered. That still left the Fox bemused, though he supposed he should have been used to it. Why didn't they think forming line of battle meant they were about to get maimed or die painful, lingering deaths? If they thought like that, and if their opponents fought the same way, nobody would fight wars. And then . . .

And then—what? Then they would not die painful, lingering deaths in battle, which was not, as Gerin's logical mind noted, the same as saying they would not die painful, lingering deaths. Fever might take them from life raving, or they might die of a wasting sickness that ate them from the inside out, or they might fall over from a fit of apoplexy and linger, perhaps for years, unable to speak and with half their bodies dead in life.

When you got down to it, there weren't any good way ways to die, only bad ones and worse ones. When measured with that ruler, perhaps dying on the battlefield looked less appalling.

Gerin looked up to Ferdulf, who floated over the army light as thistledown. Demigods, unlike the divine half of their parentage, weren't immortal. They commonly outlived ordinary mortals, and they commonly died in ways ordinary mortals might envy, such as dropping off to sleep and never waking up. The Fox wondered if the chance of dying was in Ferdulf's thoughts now. He doubted it; no ordinary four-year-old gave such things a thought.

Then Aragis shouted, "Riders to the right and left. We'll hit the imperials on both flanks this time, and see if we can't cave 'em in."

The horsemen who hadn't joined Rihwin in his assault on the imperials cheered as they rode to take the positions to which Aragis had ordered them. Gerin felt like cheering, too. To his fellow king, he said, "You're learning."

Aragis gave him a wintry look before answering, "The first time your father set a sword in your hand, did you know straightaway everything you could do with it? Now you have given me a new weapon, and I am beginning to discover what it may be good for."

"Fair enough," Gerin said. "Better than fair enough, in fact. A great many people, when they come across something new, will either pretend it isn't there or try to use it as if it were old and familiar, regardless of whether it's really anything like the old and familiar."

"A lot of people are fools." Cold contempt filled the Archer's voice. "Tell me you've not seen that in your years as baron and prince and king and I'll call you a liar to your face."

"I can't do it," Gerin answered. "The difference between us, I think, is that you scorn men for being fools and I find them funny—at least, I do my best to find them funny. The gods know it's not always easy."

"Easy?" Aragis snorted. "It's not worth doing, you ask me." Gerin hadn't expected him to say anything different. The Archer's arrogance had taken him a long way: as long a way as it could have taken him, unless he overthrew Gerin and ruled as king of the whole of the northlands, or unless he crossed over the mountains and cast Crebbig I down from his throne.

"We're all different," Gerin observed with profound unoriginality.

"So we are," Aragis said. "Sometimes I think you're light-minded as a Trokmê. Then I look at what you do, not what you say, and I think you're hiding behind a mask. All these years, and I still haven't figured out what to make of you." He sent the Fox an accusing stare.

"Good." Gerin let it go at that. Keeping Aragis off balance had probably gone a long way toward keeping the two of them from fighting a war.

Before they could take it any further, Ferdulf whizzed down toward them, pointing southwest and shouting, "If that's not the imperial army beyond the next rise, it's a herd of elephants." A moment later, mounted scouts came back with the same news.

Aragis, for once, looked at Ferdulf with approval unalloyed. "He gave us the news faster than the riders did." He took on a thoughtful expression. "Warfare would be a different business if both sides had people up in the air spying on the foe. I wonder if you could fight at all if the other bastard knew what you were going to do as you did it."

"You could, unless I miss my guess," Gerin answered. "You'd just have to make it look as if you were going to do one thing while you really intended to do something else."

Aragis studied him now for some time without saying anything. When he finally spoke, it was in tones of reluctant admiration: "Aye, and belike you'd find some way to do just that, too. You *are* a sneaky demon, no mistake."

He shouted and waved to his troopers and the Fox's, who weren't forming their battle line fast enough to suit him. In the car with Gerin, Dagref said, "How could the Archer not have seen that subterfuge would be necessary if each side could observe the other's preparations for combat?"

"Because he doesn't think as fast as you do," Gerin said, "and he doesn't like to play with hypotheticals in his mind. I'll tell you this, though, son: if he really did have to worry about people spying on him from the air, his dispositions would be the lyingest ones you ever saw."

"That's a fact," Van agreed. "If it's real, Aragis is good with it. If it's not real, he doesn't worry about it."

"Foolishness," Dagref said with a sniff, flicking the reins to bring the horses up to a trot. "The hypothetical has a way of becoming real without warning. Before it happened, who would have thought the Elabonian

Empire would come roaring back over the High Kirs to trouble us?"

"I didn't think that would happen myself," Gerin said, "and I'd be just as glad if it hadn't happened, too, believe me." The Elabon Way swung wide, and he got his first glimpse of the imperial army. "But they're here, and we're going to have to deal with them."

Van said, "By the gods, we've taught them something like respect. They aren't swarming toward us the way they did in the first fight. Then they thought they could ride right over us and make us run. They know better now, the stinking whoresons."

"Yes," Gerin said, not altogether contented with the change in the imperials' tactics. He wanted his enemies to go right on being stupid. It made them much easier to deal with. He also glanced over at the outlander. "And look who's talking about the Elabonian Empire as if he'd been born in the northlands and spent his whole life listening to people running it into the ground."

"Go howl," Van said with dignity. "It's a fight, and I'm on *this* side, so of course the imperials are a pack of bastards. If I were over on *that* side, everybody from the northlands would be a filthy rebel. There. Doesn't that make sense?"

"More than I like," Gerin answered. He watched Rihwin's horsemen swing wide to right and left to take the imperial army in the flank. The imperials didn't send squadrons of chariotry out against them to try to hold them up. They'd learned better than that, too. What they hadn't learned, the Fox saw with rising glee, was that, if they didn't stop the riders, they were going to get both wings of their army smashed up in a hurry.

Dagref saw the same thing at the same time. "What do they think they're doing?" he demanded, like a schoolmaster faced with unprepared pupils.

"They're trying to throw the fight away," Van said. "I'll let 'em. Anybody thinks I'll complain if they make my work easy is plumb daft."

He started to elaborate—Gerin knew it was a theme on which he would be able to elaborate for a good long while—but then grunted in surprise and shut up. Some of the horses had gone down just as they were nearing bow range of the imperials' flanks.

"Is that magic, Father?" Dagref asked.

"Do you know, I don't think so," the Fox replied. "If I had to guess, I'd say the imperials have strewn some caltrops around to either side of their position to help ward their flanks. They work against chariot horses, so I don't suppose there's anything that would keep them from working against horses with men on top of 'em."

Some of Rihwin's riders did get through, and started plying the men of the Elabonian Empire with arrows. But some hung back, and even those who didn't had to ride more slowly. They were an annoyance, then, not a devastation, as they might have been.

Seeing as much, the imperials cheered. Horns blared along their line. Now they rolled forward: they would not receive the attack of the chariots from the northlands while standing still themselves.

Men on both sides shouted, Gerin and Aragis' troopers as individuals, the imperials in the fierce unison that had seemed so effective in the first battle. Arrows flew. As always, the first few fell short. But the range between the two armies closed rapidly. Men began to cry out; horses began to scream. Here and there, chariots overturned, spilling soldiers onto the ground.

"Any place in particular, Father?" Dagref asked as Gerin, arrow set to bowstring, looked around for his first target. "The other king doesn't seem to take much care in the way he arranges things, does he?"

That held an unmistakable sniff. Before Gerin could reply, Van laughed and said, "Being the son of your father has spoiled you, lad. Aragis had given us a decent field and a good chance to win if we fight hard, and I've seen plenty of captains who lived to grow old and fat even though they were in the habit of handing their men a lot less."

Dagref sniffed again. He had high standards, and was too young to have realized the trouble most mortals had meeting such standards. Pointedly, he said, "You still haven't answered me, Father."

"Steer for anybody who looks to have fancy armor or a fine team of horses," the Fox said. "Most men of high rank enjoy showing off."

"Honh!" Van said. His cast-bronze corselet and plumed helm were without a doubt the most distinctive gear on the field.

"You heard me." Gerin's armor was not gilded, nor even polished; the leather that secured the bronze plates in place was scuffed and patched. But all the leather and all the plates were sound. The horses Dagref drove were undersized and rough-coated, but they had more endurance than most. They were descended from a pony off the plains of Shanda for which Van had traded while accompanying Gerin and Elise down to the City of Elabon more than twenty years before. That horse had been even smaller and uglier, but it was tougher than any other Gerin ever knew.

Obediently, Dagref pointed the team at an imperial whose armor was bright with gold paint and who wore a crimson cloak that fluttered behind him. Gerin let fly. The officer of the Elabonian Empire threw both hands in the air and tumbled out the back of the chariot.

"Well shot!" Van shouted. Though refusing to use the

bow in battle, he would not hold back praise from others who used it well.

Dagref guided the horses toward another imperial who looked more splendid than his fellows. Gerin shot at the foe—and missed. However good a shot he was, however much practice he had shooting from the pitching platform of a chariot, he missed more often than he hit. Disappointed but not devastated, he reached over his shoulder for another shaft.

Thunk! An arrow smote the leftward horse of the team, just back of the animal's left foreleg. The horse went down as if clubbed; the arrow must have pierced its heart. Its fall fouled the other horse. The chariot tipped, jounced along on one wheel for a couple of frantic heartbeats, and then overturned, spilling onto the ground all three men in the car.

Gerin heard himself shouting as he flew through the air. He'd gone out of chariots before. He tried to tuck himself into a ball, to land as softly as he could. Even so, the soft ground slammed against him as if it were granite. His helmet spun off his head and bounced away. Pain shot through his right side, which took most of the impact. But, when he tried to scramble to his feet, he discovered he could. Nothing broken, then. That was something—or would be, if he could stay alive long enough to appreciate how lucky he was.

He was, he discovered, still holding his bow. No—he was still holding a piece of his bow. Unlike him, it had broken when it hit the ground. He threw down the chunk in his hand and yanked out his sword. Then he looked around to see how Van and Dagref were. Both of them were on their feet, too, and seemed sound, so for the moment they, like he, were lucky.

How long their luck—and his—would last remained problematical. *Not very long* seemed the likeliest guess.

The chariots of the Elabonian Empire were very close now, and getting closer every heartbeat. One of them thundered straight toward Dagref, who, being slim and beardless and without sword or spear, looked to be the easiest target of the three downed warriors.

Gerin ran—slowly, favoring his right leg—to his son's aid. Dagref proved not to need any aid. With him, as with the Fox, looks turned out to deceive. Though he had no sword or spear, he'd held on to the whip he used to urge on his team (a replacement for the one Caffer had turned into a snake). He waited till the Elabonian chariot was terrifyingly close, then lashed out with the whip, striking one of the horses on its soft, tender nose.

The animal screamed in shock and pain. It stopped dead and tried to rear. The driver kept it from doing that, but the chariot thundered past Dagref instead of riding him down. And, as it went past, the whip lashed out again. The driver screamed as loud as the horse had. He clutched at his eyes. The other two imperials in the car clutched at the reins he'd dropped.

Neither one of them could make a clean grab. That was unfortunate for them, because they got only the one chance. Dagref cracked the whip again. One of them shrieked. He shrieked again a moment later when Van speared him in the side—shrieked and crumpled. Gerin scrambled up into the chariot. The surviving unwounded imperial was an archer who carried only a dagger for self-defense. He didn't stay unwounded long. He scrambled over the rail of the car and ran off howling and dripping blood.

Killing the driver seemed unfair, since he still had both hands clapped to his face. In the middle of a battle, though, *fair* was a flexible notion. Gerin thrust home hard, threw the driver's thrashing body over the side, and seized the reins. He started to shout for Van and Dagref, but they were already up in the car with him.

With a flourish, he handed his son the reins. "I think you know what to do with these," he said.

"He knows what to do with all sorts of things," Van said, an enormous grin on his face. "Don't you, Dagref the Whip?"

"Who, me?" Dagref looked absurdly pleased with himself. A man could get an ekename any number of ways. If he was very fair or very fat, he might have one before he could toddle. Or he might be called his father's son his whole life long. Earning an ekename on the battlefield didn't happen to everyone. It didn't happen to many, in fact.

"Dagref the Whip," Gerin agreed. "Better than Dagref the Surly, or Dagref the Brown Study, or—"

"Since the whip is still in my hand," Dagref remarked pointedly, "a prudent man would save such suggestions for another time."

"A prudent man wouldn't have done a lot of the things I've done over the years," Gerin said.

"You're the most prudent man I know, Fox," Van said.

"That may be true, but it doesn't say much for the rest of the people you know," Gerin retorted. Fand immediately came to mind, but the Fox was prudent enough not to mention her. Instead, he said, "How prudent is it, for that matter, to ride around in a chariot when none of us has a bow?"

"You should have grabbed the one that imperial had before you pitched him out of the car," Van said.

"Aye, that would have been prudent," Gerin agreed, "if only I'd thought of it at the time. Can't think of everything at once, though, no matter how much I wish I could."

Van said, "Well, since we haven't got one, we'll have

to pretend we're some of Rihwin's riders, and see how close we can get to the imperials. I've always liked that kind of fighting better, anyhow."

"Why am I not surprised?" Gerin murmured. Being so big and so strong, the outlander naturally excelled at close-quarters fighting. A man with a bow, though, might hurt him before he had the chance to do damage of his own.

Dagref took the discussion between his father and his father's friend as an instruction for him, and guided the chariot toward the nearest one full of imperials. The men of the Elabonian Empire, seeing a car that looked like their own, took a fatal moment too long to realize the warriors inside were foes. Van speared one of them, Dagref kept using the whip to wicked effect, and, by the time the brief fight was done, Gerin once more had a bow to call his own.

He reached over his shoulder to snatch an arrow out of his quiver. An imperial screamed like a longtooth a moment later, and clutched at the side of his thigh. The Fox shot another arrow. This one missed. He reached back yet again—and found the quiver empty.

He scowled. The quiver had been nearly full before he spilled out of the chariot. Before he . . . He growled a curse. Most of the arrows must have gone flying from the quiver when he hit the ground. He hadn't even noticed. He'd had rather more urgent things on his mind, such as staying in one piece.

"Come on, Fox," Van said. "Why aren't you shooting at the whoresons?"

"I'll tell you what," Gerin answered. "As soon as you figure out how to spear them without any spear, I'll shoot them without any arrows."

"What?" The outlander stared. Then his face cleared. "Oh. Aye. We did go arse over soup-pot there, didn't we? Well, all right, we'll have to keep on doing the way we did just now, won't we?"

"Sooner or later, everyone will start running out of arrows," Dagref said.

"Oh, indeed." Gerin nodded. "The next interesting question is whether people will run out of arrows before one gets stuck in one of us. That's an interesting question in any fight."

"Interesting. Oh, aye. Heh." Van snorted, then spat. In a way, that was disgust. In another way, it was bravado. Not many warriors on the field, Gerin would have guessed, had enough saliva in their mouths to spit. He was a long way from sure he did himself. He worked his cheeks experimentally.

Then he stopped worrying about whether he could spit. There ahead, sure as sure, was a gap in the imperials' line, where chariots had swung right and left around one that had overturned, and then hadn't closed up again. He looked around. Not far from him—how they'd got there, he hadn't noticed—were a good many chariots full of Trokmoi. He waved to them. A couple of the woodsrunners aimed arrows at him. They lowered them when he shouted in their own language: "Through there, now"—he pointed—"and we'll be after carving a great chunk from the southron spalpeens."

"Do you want me to go through that gap and hope the barbarians will follow?" Dagref asked. By his tone, he'd heard ideas he liked much better.

But Gerin said, "That's just what I want you to do."

"Be a mite embarrassing if the Trokmoi decide they'd sooner be rid of you than of the cursed imperials," Van remarked. What he meant was, *If that happens, we're going to get killed*. Gerin couldn't recall the last time he'd heard such a protest so elegantly phrased.

He stopped worrying about that, too. "Go on," he told

Dagref. "Quick, now, before they close up the hole."

"All right." His son urged the horses forward. The Fox shouted when the chariot did force its way between two manned by soldiers of the Elabonian Empire. The imperials hesitated before trying to block his path: as had happened once already, they thought anyone in a chariot from south of the High Kirs was bound to be a comrade.

As had happened once already, they discovered they were mistaken. Gerin laid open the face of one of the imperial troopers on his left, a cut that took the enemy doubly by surprise because he delivered it with his left hand. On the other side of the car, Van speared an imperial archer out of a chariot. The fellow looked comically surprised, or would have had he not also been in agony.

"Well, I think that's drawn their notice," Dagref said.

"I bloody well knew it would draw their notice," Gerin answered as an arrow hissed past his ear. "What I want to know is, has it drawn the woodsrunners in after us? If it hasn't . . ." He let that hang. If it hadn't, Van was right—they would get killed.

He looked back over his shoulder . . . and whooped with glee. The Trokmoi *were* behind him, and more of them than he'd expected. Often, what looked suicidally stupid to an Elabonian looked like fun to a Trokmê. Gerin was heartily glad of that, not least because it meant the imperials wouldn't be concentrating on him alone. They'd have other things on their minds, such as stopping the penetration before it split their whole army in two. Sometimes distraction was better than victory. Sometimes they were one and the same.

Chariots were at close quarters now, everyone hacking and stabbing and shooting at everyone else. The men of the Elabonian Empire seemed to feel a slight superstitious awe of the Trokmoi, who must have been much discussed but never seen during the years when the Empire stayed south of the High Kirs. Superstitious awe, however, had a way of lasting no longer than the first successfully blocked blow. After that, it was just man against man.

For their part, the Trokmoi went after the imperials with almost unholy glee. The woodsrunners had no more use for Elabonians than Elabonians had for them. But, by now, they'd dwelt south of the Niffet for a generation. To them, Gerin's men were only partly hated southrons. They were also neighbors, sometimes friends, sometimes even in-laws.

None of those palliatives applied to the warriors from south of the mountains. They were the enemy, pure and simple. The Trokmoi laid into them with an appalling lack of concern for what might happen to themselves, so long as they could get in a few more licks at the foe.

Because the woodsrunners were so fierce, the imperials needed a disproportionate number of men to hold them in check. And, because they were making a move that would be important if it succeeded, the imperials threw those men at them. That didn't help their position along the rest of the line, which was what Gerin had had in mind.

"There!" As he had before, he aimed Dagref toward a gap between a couple of imperial chariots. "If we get through there and bring a few Trokmoi after us, we really have cut the whoresons in two."

"Aye, Father." Dagref urged the horses forward. Wild whoops proclaimed that the Trokmoi were still following the Fox.

The imperials he faced knew they were holding an important part of the line. They could hardly help knowing it, with so many foes bearing down on them.

One of them let fly with an arrow. Behind Gerin, a Trokmê shrieked. The Fox had a perfect shot at the imperial—or would have had one, with any arrows in his quiver.

And then the imperial cried out and clutched at his flank, from which a shaft sprouted. To have hit him at that angle, it couldn't have come from straight ahead. Gerin turned his head to the right. Recognizing him, some of Rihwin's horsemen waved. He waved back, an enormous grin on his face.

"We've got 'em!" Van shouted. "By all the gods, we've got 'em in the mill. All we have to do now is crumble 'em from grain to flour."

"It'll be harder work than that," Gerin said. "The grain in the mill doesn't try to break the millstones."

"Is this really the time for literary criticism?" Dagref asked.

"Possibly not," Gerin admitted. An imperial who had been thrown out of his chariot flung a stone at him. It clanged off his shoulder, which started to throb. Maybe that was literary criticism, maybe it wasn't. Whatever it was, Van's spear responded to it most pointedly. The imperial was never heard to comment on a metaphor again.

With part of their army cut off and surrounded, the rest of the forces of the Elabonian Empire began falling back. As they had before, the imperials retreated with a professional competence the men of the northlands, Trokmoi and Elabonians both, would have been hard pressed to match. They held their ranks and kept fighting instead of running every which way, which was the more usual response to defeat north of the High Kirs. They didn't seem to be saying, *We're beaten! Gods preserve us!* It was more as if they meant, *All right, you've got the better of us this time, but it was probably just luck. See what happens when we meet again.*

Thinking thus, Gerin said, "What worries me is, this is the second time we've beaten them, not the first. Don't you think they ought to be getting used to the idea that they don't fight as well as we do?"

Dagref said, "They're probably getting used to the idea that they're going to need reinforcements from over the mountains."

"I wish you hadn't said that," Gerin told his son. "Where are we going to get reinforcements if they do? Father Dyaus, where are we going to get reinforcements even if they don't? It's a bloody miracle that Aragis and I are on the same side as things are."

"What do we do if they should send another army over the High Kirs?" Dagref asked.

"Either fight it out or surrender and go back to cheating the Empire out of the tribute it thinks it deserves, the way I did in the old days," Gerin answered. Here he was, winning a battle, and Dagref had managed to make him think he was losing. Pointedly, he went on, "Let's tend to one thing at a time, if you please. If we manage to botch what we're doing now, the Empire won't need to think about sending reinforcements."

"That's sensible, Father," Dagref allowed after his usual pause for thought.

"Nice of him to admit it, eh, Fox?" Van said with a chuckle.

Dagref started to say something else. Gerin cut him off, and the outlander, too. "Take it up *after* the fight's over with," he said. "Meanwhile, let's see what we can do to get it over with faster." He raised his voice to a shout: "Imperials! Give yourselves up and I promise you your lives!"

One of the men in the surrounded pocket of charioteers asked, "And who are you, that we should care about your promise?"

"Gerin the Fox, king of the north," he answered; every once in a while, wearing unobtrusive gear had disadvantages as well as good points. If he'd dressed like a king, they would have known who he was. If he'd dressed like a king, though, they might have done a better job of trying to kill him.

"What will you do with us if we yield ourselves?" the imperial inquired.

That was a good, relevant question. Gerin wished he didn't have to come up with a reply on the spur of the moment. "If you yield now," he said, "I'll disarm you and send you north and settle you in peasant villages— one or two of you in each one, because I don't want you plotting against me. It's the best I can do. Will you take it? Otherwise, you'll die right here, either that or be used as slaves if you give up later and we decide to let you live. What do you say?"

The imperial who'd been asking questions threw down his bow and took off his helmet. "Good enough for me," he said at once.

His comrades started throwing down their weapons, too. Once Gerin saw they were going to yield, he detailed a small number of men to take charge of them, then led the rest south in pursuit of the bigger part of the imperial army.

Before long, he caught up with Aragis the Archer. "Ha!" Aragis said. "I wondered what happened to you, Fox. You disappeared for a while there, and I thought I might be the only king left in the northlands, but I see it isn't so." He plainly wouldn't have been broken-hearted had Gerin died, but he didn't seem broken-hearted to find him alive, either. That struck the Fox as a reasonable reaction. No flies on Aragis, either; the next thing he said was, "That's not the chariot you started out with today."

"So it isn't," Gerin agreed. "They kept trying to kill us out there, and they came closer to doing a proper job of it than I would have liked." Not wearing royal regalia had probably saved his neck.

"Ha," Aragis said again, this time evidently intending it for laughter rather than a greeting. "What they do a proper job of is getting off a battlefield once they've lost the main fight." He waved ahead. "Look at the order they're keeping. If they fought that well *in* the battle, they might win."

Gerin unrolled an imaginary scroll and made as if to read its title: "The triumphal retreats of the Elabonian Empire, being a relation of the manner in which the said Empire was won by its armies' going backwards."

"Ha," Aragis said for a third time. "That's not half bad. If only the bastards would go to pieces once we licked them, we'd drive 'em over the mountains and be rid of 'em once for all."

"Only if they decided not to reinforce," Dagref said.

Aragis studied the youth for a long moment, then shook his head. "He's got as nasty a way of looking at the world as you do, Fox."

"Worse," Gerin answered. He glanced toward his son. Dagref preened. That was the only word for it—he unmistakably preened.

Van pointed ahead to the imperial army. "They *are* going to break away from us, and to your five Elabonian hells with me if I see anything we can do about it."

"Best thing to do is give up the pursuit if we can't break 'em," Gerin said. "If we spread ourselves too thin chasing them, they're liable to counterattack, and then they'd steal a victory on the cheap."

"I hate to say it, but I fear you're right," Aragis said. "We'll gather ourselves up, and then we'll hit 'em another lick in a few days. Sooner or later, they ought to figure out they can't beat us." He gave Dagref a pointed look. Dagref as pointedly ignored it. That made Aragis laugh a genuine laugh. To Gerin, he said, "He will be formidable, won't he?"

"I expect so," the Fox answered. "Of course, he's had practice not paying attention to me." Dagref preened again.

Aragis began shouting orders to bring the army to a halt. When he saw they would be obeyed, he turned back to Gerin. "Where has that Ferdulf of yours got to? I didn't see much of him in the fight."

"Neither did I," Gerin said. "He must have been doing something of his own, unless I miss my guess. He's *his* Ferdulf, not mine; if you don't remember that, he'll make you pay."

Aragis grunted. "I'll remember. Men, now—men you order to do something, and if they don't do it you make them. How are you supposed to make a demigod pay if he doesn't feel like doing it?"

"I've spanked him once or twice," Gerin said, sounding much, much more casual talking about it afterwards then he'd felt doing it.

He succeeded in impressing Aragis. "I always knew you were brave," the Archer said. "Up till now, I never thought you were stupid." Aragis looked Gerin up and down. "Maybe I was wrong."

"Maybe you were," the Fox said. "I'm allied with you, aren't I?" Aragis chewed on that for a little while, then started to laugh. So did Gerin. Why not? They'd just won another battle.

Going back to the field, Gerin found laughter harder to come by. The dead back there, some of them men he'd known most of his life and others, not so old, men he'd known all their lives—they were every bit as dead

as if he'd been defeated. The only consolation he found
was that not so many of them were dead as if he'd been
defeated. That might suffice for him. He didn't think it
would for them.

Nor did victory ease the torment of the wounded. They
still screamed or groaned or wailed or hissed or stood
or lay silent, biting their lips against the pain till blood
ran from the corners of their mouths. There would have
been more of them whom the Fox knew and liked had
the imperials won, but that didn't help the ones who
had been hurt. Moreover, wounded men who'd fought
for the Elabonian Empire didn't look or sound any
different from those who'd followed Gerin or Aragis.

As he had at the earlier battle, Gerin did what he could
to help the wounded, extracting arrows, washing cuts
out with ale despite the curses of the men who'd acquired
those cuts, and, once or twice, quietly cutting the throat
of a man who could not live but would, without help,
be a long, slow, painful time dying. He hated that, but
hated their suffering more.

Presently, he came upon a young fellow with a fuzzy
beard who was limping around with a bloody bandage
on his right calf. No, not a fellow; though his own arms
were bloody to the elbow, Gerin's stomach did a slow
lurch. "Maeva!" he exclaimed.

"Hello, lord king," she said, her voice a little wobbly
but firmer than a lot of others he'd heard. "They wanted
to draw the shaft, but I wouldn't let them. I know you
have a good hand for such things." She sat down on the
ground, pale yet determined.

"I'll do the best I can," the Fox said. She'd given him
a compliment, but not one of a sort he'd ever wanted
to get. In the hope that talking would keep her mind
off the pain, he asked, "How did it happen?"

She looked at him as if he'd asked a very stupid

question. On reflection, he realized he had. "How do you think?" she asked irritably. "I was riding along, doing what I was supposed to be doing, and my leg started to hurt. When I looked down, I saw why—an arrow was sticking out of it."

He nodded. Of itself, one of his hands went to the other shoulder. He'd felt that same absurd surprise when he'd been shot. Then it had started to hurt. He reached down and undid the bandage, saying, "Let's see what we've got."

It was about what he'd expected. Whoever had slapped the bandage on Maeva had also cut the shaft of the arrow off short so it wouldn't be in the way. That was as it should have been, but it kept the Fox from gauging how deep in the meat of her calf the arrowhead lay. "Can you pull it out?" Maeva asked.

"I'd rather not," he answered, his voice troubled. "The imperials use barbed arrowheads, same as we do. Pulling it back will make the wound a lot worse."

"What will you do, then?" Maeva sounded calm, but ragged at the edges. She was liable to start screaming any time. Gerin didn't hold that against her, or blame it on her sex. He'd heard plenty of wounded men scream on the battlefield. He'd been a wounded man screaming on the battlefield.

He used his knife to cut her trousers away from the wound so he could feel of it. He also cut the checked wool on the inner side of her calf. When he gently pressed there, he felt something hard under his fingertip. He grunted. Maeva flinched and hissed and let out a small fragment of a shriek before she could bite down on it.

"It's almost through," he said. "Actually, that's pretty good. If I push it all the way through, the head will be out, and then the rest of the shaft will come with it without much trouble." He was telling the truth. He knew he was telling the truth. He'd had plenty of practice sounding cheerful with wounded men, too. Somehow, this was different. It was harder.

"Go ahead," Maeva said, her voice more ragged now. She set herself. Gerin had set himself, too, before they started working on that shoulder. It hadn't done him much good. He didn't think it would do her much good, either.

He set his hand on the stub of the arrow and pushed hard—soonest over, he'd found, was best. Maeva did shriek then. He'd expected she would; pain deliberately inflicted was harder to bear than that which came by accident.

The barbed bronze arrowhead stabbed out through her skin. Though it was slick with her blood, Gerin seized it and drew the shaft after it. "There," he said. "It's done— well, almost." He carried a jar of ale with him. When he poured it on both wounds in Maeva's leg, she screamed again, and tried to kick him. "Easy," he told her. "Now I'm going to bandage it again."

He did, with fresh rags. Blood started soaking into them from the old wound and the new. Maeva took a long, shuddering breath. "Thank you," she said. "It's . . . better now. I'm sorry I made so much noise."

"I didn't hear anything," Gerin assured her. He knew it wasn't necessarily better yet. The wound could still go bad, in which case she would be very sick and might even die. He'd done what he could do, and made himself sound reassuring: "It won't be long before you're on your feet and running hard again. It didn't cut the tendon; you wouldn't have been on both feet if it had. You should heal nice and clean."

"Thank you, lord king," she said. That made him feel worse rather than better. If he hadn't let her stay and fight, she would have been angry instead of grateful—

but she would have been unwounded. He knew which way he would rather have had her. But, as if picking that thought from his mind, Maeva went on, "I'm glad you gave me the chance to fight, even if it turned out like this. Next time, I hope I'll be luckier."

Gerin looked down at his hands. They had her blood on them, literally and now, he supposed, figuratively as well. He kept trying to think of her as just another warrior; he'd had plenty of wounded young men tell him more or less the same thing she'd said a moment before. Try as he would, it wasn't easy. That thought kept recurring.

"Fox!" a deep voice boomed, from over on another part of the battlefield. "Where in the five Elabonian hells have you gone and got to now?"

"Here!" Gerin answered, and waved. Maeva was frantically shaking her head. Had Gerin thought before he waved, he wouldn't have done it. Too late now: Van was already on the way over, crimson horsehair plume nodding above him to make him even more unmistakable than he was already.

"Hullo, Fox," he called, still from some distance away. "Patching up another—" By the way the outlander's voice cut off, Gerin knew exactly when his friend realized exactly whom he was patching up. Van came the rest of the way at a pounding trot. He stooped beside his daughter. "What happened?" he demanded, a question no more useful than Gerin's had been.

"Arrow," she said, doing her best to make light of it. "The king says it should heal well."

"Through the meat of the calf," Gerin said when Van looked a query his way. "No tendon cut—I'm sure of that. She should heal clean." *The gods willing,* he added to himself. Maybe saying it over and over would help make the gods more willing.

Van was still looking at him, not with a question in

his eyes any longer but with rising anger. Gerin had seen him aim that look at scores, likely hundreds, of enemies over the years. The Fox had never had it aimed at him. *Run* went through his mind, as it was no doubt meant to do. Van growled, "If it hadn't been for you, Fox—"

That Gerin had had the identical thought would have done little to console the outlander. Gerin was sure of it. But, before Van could say anything more, Maeva broke in sharply: "Leave him be, Father. How old were you when you took your first wound?"

"Sixteen or so," Van answered. "I was lucky for a while. I've made up for it since." That was, if anything, an understatement. He bore a great many scars. Gerin wondered how he'd ever survived one wound that had gashed his chest and belly.

"Well, then," Maeva said, as if that said everything that needed saying.

But Van shook his head. "It's not the same, chick," he said: the same thought that had been troubling the Fox.

"Why not?" Maeva said. "I fought well enough—oh, maybe not so well as you, Father, because I'm not the size you are, even though I'm not small. I kept fighting after I got hurt, too; it wasn't bad enough to make me quit the field."

"What am I supposed to do?" Van sounded plaintive, something he very rarely did. He looked to Gerin. "Curse it, Fox, help me. She sounds like I did when I was the same age."

"And why are you so surprised at that?" Gerin asked. "She's your daughter, after all. Dagref sounds more like me than I ever thought anyone could. He sounds more like me than I ever thought anyone would want to."

"Oh, aye, I can see that," Van said. Gerin laughed. Dagref, perhaps fortunately, was nowhere nearby. Van went on, "But it's not the same." He'd said that before, and sounded most sincere. He still did. "Dagref's your son. Of course he'll follow in your track."

"Am I not your child because I have no stones?" Maeva asked.

Before Van could answer, Gerin said, "I've seen men with beards down to their belts who had less in the way of stones than you do, Maeva."

"Thank you, lord king," she said quietly.

Van glared at Gerin. "Fat lot of help you are," he growled, and stomped off shaking his head.

"Thank you, lord king," Maeva said again, more firmly this time. "I think you're a great deal of help."

"I know you do," Gerin answered. "The trouble is, I still don't know whether I'm supposed to be helping you or your father." He gave her a sudden, sharp bow. "And I have other wounded to help. If I am supposed to treat you like a soldier—and I'm still a long way from sure that I am—then I have to go on, as I would from another soldier."

"Why, of course, lord king," she said, as if surprised he could imagine thinking any other way. That surprised him in turn, and made him begin to believe he might in fact be able to think of her as a soldier.

Gerin sat up on his blanket. "Something's wrong," he said, his voice blurry with sleep. He looked around. The campfires were lower than they had been, though sentries still fed them to help hold the night ghosts at bay—not that the ghosts hadn't had their glut of blood earlier that day. Snores rose from sleeping soldiers in an unmelodious chorus. Injured men groaned against their pain.

Everything seemed to be as it should. But Gerin had not been dreaming when he thought something was wrong; he was sure of that. He did not know how he was sure, only that he was. He looked around again. Again, he could find nothing amiss.

He started to lie down once more, then checked himself. He looked around yet again, this time for Rihwin the Fox. Wherever there was trouble, Rihwin usually wasn't far away. That was especially true when wine was involved. Gerin hadn't had to worry about wine for a good many years. Now he did. Worrying about wine meant worrying about Rihwin.

But no: there Rihwin lay, not twenty feet off, snoring as unmusically as anyone else. Gerin let out a small sigh of relief. If Rihwin had no part in whatever trouble brewed, odds were it wouldn't be so bad. Years of experience had led Gerin to believe as much, at any rate.

He yawned and lay flat again. Despite the yawn, despite Rihwin's snores, sleep would not come. "Something's wrong," he said again, quietly this time, and got to his feet. He would not find any rest till he made sure that prickly feeling of unease in his mind was imagination and nerves.

He breathed a little easier when he saw Dagref, too. Dagref probably would not make trouble on his own. He knew precisely what sort of trouble Dagref and Maeva would make together, though. He would not have wanted to make that sort of trouble while wounded, but, with both of them so young, who could tell what they were liable to do? But they couldn't very well do anything with Dagref sprawled asleep on a blanket.

A sentry was laying branches on a fire. He looked up when he heard Gerin's footsteps. "Is everything all right, lord king?" he asked.

"I don't know," Gerin answered. "I'm trying to find out." He prowled on.

Lengyel the wizard was liable to cause trouble, too. Lengyel had already caused trouble, as a matter of fact. Gerin stalked over to where he stayed under guard. The guards were alert. So was Gerin, when he saw that Lengyel, instead of lying there asleep, was sitting up looking at him.

"No, lord king, he hasn't done anything," one of the wizard's guards assured the Fox. "He wakes up in the night sometimes—has to piss, you know. He's often a goodish while dropping off afterwards."

"Is he?" Gerin gave Lengyel a hard stare. "Probably looking for another chance to get away."

"If I found one, I should be a fool not to take it," the sorcerer said. "I regret to admit I have not found it. Your men have been more careful than I had expected." He made a sour face. "Very little on this side of the High Kirs has been as I expected."

"We never expected to see imperials on this side of the High Kirs at all," Gerin said. "We'd have been just as happy if you people had gone on minding your own business, too, instead of poking your snouts into ours."

Even as he spoke, he wondered if he was telling the truth. If the imperial army had stayed south of the mountains, he would have been fighting Aragis instead. By what the men of the Elabonian Empire had shown thus far, the Archer would have made a more troublesome foe. On the other hand, Gerin had no guarantee that the Elabonian Emperor wouldn't send another army over the High Kirs to give this one a hand.

In musing tones, he said, "Tell me what this Crebbig I is like." He chuckled into the darkness, thinking how much he sounded like the imperials asking him about Ferdulf.

"His imperial majesty is bold and valiant and splendid and terrible, beloved of his friends, a terror to his enemies—"

"Wait." Gerin held up a hand. Lengyel sounded as if he could go on like that for days without ever saying anything that mattered. Gerin said, "Let's try it another way: is Crebbig Hildor's son? If he's not, what was he before his backside landed on the throne down there in the City of Elabon?"

"How could you not know these things?" Lengyel asked in surprise.

"No trouble at all," the Fox answered. "Very much the same way as you were ignorant about everything that has anything to do with the northlands. The difference is, I know that I don't know, where you hadn't a clue."

That drew an indignant sniff from Lengyel; wizards, knowing so much about wizardry, naturally assumed they knew a lot about everything else, too. Primly, the sorcerer said, "You exaggerate, I assure you."

"No, I don't." Gerin held up a hand. "Wait. Never mind. It doesn't matter. Just answer my questions about Crebbig."

"Very well." Lengyel did not and would not call him *lord king*, holding to the official imperial view that there were no kings north of the High Kirs, only rebels ruling against the authority of the City of Elabon. The wizard went on, "No, Crebbig is not the son of the Emperor Hildor III, who is now beloved among the gods."

"Dead, you mean," Gerin said, and Lengyel nodded. The Fox asked, "Did Crebbig give him some timely help in becoming beloved among the gods?" Lengyel nodded again. This time, so did Gerin. "Good. Now we're getting somewhere. What was the murderous usurper doing before he slaughtered his way to the top of the heap?"

"I resent the imputation contained within your words," Lengyel said.

"I don't care," Gerin said cheerfully. "Resent all you

like. You serve him. I don't, and I won't. Now answer my question: what was Crebbig the Killer doing before he got to be Elabonian Emperor?"

Lengyel gave him another reproving look for that highly unofficial ekename. He ignored it. He was good at ignoring such looks, having had practice with his children. Seeing it fail, Lengyel said, "The Emperor was formerly commander of the Elabonian garrison occupying the city-states of Sithonia."

"Was he?" Gerin said. "Now, isn't that interesting?" Crebbig would have had a good-sized army behind him when he rebelled; Elabon kept a large garrison in Sithonia for the good and sufficient reason that Elabon needed a large garrison in Sithonia. Down through the centuries of Elabonian occupation, the Sithonians had never given up plotting and scheming and conniving and occasionally rising up against their imperial overlords—and, being Sithonians, had never given up betraying one another to their imperial overlords, either.

It was also interesting, the Fox realized a moment later, because of the Sithonian connections in his own life. He hadn't actually seen a man from one of the city-states east of the Greater Inner Sea since he'd come back from the City of Elabon more than twenty years before, but since then he'd had more dealings with Mavrix than he'd ever wanted, and Mavrix had saddled him with Ferdulf, and . . .

"Father Dyaus," he whispered, and left Lengyel so quickly, the wizard and the guards all stared after him. He didn't care. Something was indeed liable to be wrong, and he thought he finally knew what sort of something, too.

His nostrils twitched when he got close to where he was going. He hadn't smelled that smell in a long time, but he knew what it was. Rich, fruity . . . He couldn't have mistaken it for anything else.

Guards stood around the wine Rihwin the Fox had captured from the imperials, as guards had stood around Lengyel. The wizard's guards hadn't been able to keep him from escaping once, and the guards here hadn't been able to keep somebody from getting into the wine. Gerin's nose told him as much, though the guards didn't seem to notice anything out of the ordinary. "Hello, lord king," one of them greeted him. "What brings you here?"

"Trouble." Gerin pointed. "Don't you see, someone's got past you and in among the wineskins? Can't you smell the spilled blood of the sweet grape?"

Once he showed them they had been befooled, they exclaimed angrily and snatched out their swords. Before then, they'd been oblivious. "Curse the imperial wizard to the hottest of the five hells," said the fellow who'd greeted Gerin. "His spells must have stolen our wits away."

"That's not Lengyel in there." Gerin frowned. "All things considered, I rather wish it were."

Ferdulf looked up from the wine he'd been drinking. "Bother!" he said, glaring at the Fox. "Why didn't my glamour take you, too?"

"It's always harder if someone already knows what he's looking for," Gerin said. "Do you know what you're looking for, there with the wine?"

"My father," Ferdulf said.

"I thought we'd agreed that wasn't a good idea," Gerin told him.

"Aye, we did," Ferdulf, that most unchildlike baritone still as clear as if he'd never begun to drink. "And then I stopped agreeing, and I decided to do something about not agreeing."

"What you should have done was come to me," Gerin

said. "You didn't agree by yourself. You shouldn't have broken the agreement by yourself, either."

Ferdulf shrugged. "It takes two to make an agreement, but only one to be rid of it. You'd have tried to talk me out of this, and—"

"You'd best believe I would," Gerin broke in. Mavrix was the last person—force, god—the Fox wanted to see right now. No one, not Gerin, not Ferdulf, probably not Mavrix himself, could begin to guess what he'd do.

"But I don't want to be talked out of it," Ferdulf said. "The more I thought about that, the more certain I got. And so . . ." He raised a drinking jack to his lips. His throat worked. "That's very fine." It was sure to be only rough army wine, barely worth drinking, but he cared nothing for objectivity. "My father certainly made something better here than boring old ale."

"Ale suits me well enough," Gerin answered sincerely, "though I would be the last to deny wine is fine, too. I've drunk a deal of wine, and drunk it with enjoyment." The last thing he wanted to do was offend Mavrix, if by some mischance the god should be listening and choose to manifest himself here.

He succeeded in offending Ferdulf instead. "Trimmer!" the little demigod sneered, drinking again. "This is good, but that isn't bad—bah! You haven't much time, mortal man. You should be all one thing or all another, not a bit of this and a bit of that."

Gerin shook his head. "I have something of everything in me. If I left something out, that would be the waste."

Ferdulf stared at him. The demigod's eyes caught and reflected what little light there was like a cat's. "You don't answer as you should," he complained. "You don't think as you should. As best I can tell, my father put me on earth where he did for no better reason than to have you torment me."

"I doubt that." Gerin had always thought Mavrix had sired Ferdulf on Fulda for no better reason than to torment him. If Ferdulf hadn't drawn the same conclusion, Gerin didn't intend to point it out to him. Life with the demigod had proved interesting enough as things were.

For his part, Ferdulf was not thinking about about his relationship with the Fox. "I want my father!" he shouted, loud enough that the cry should have awakened the entire camp—but only Gerin and the guards around the wine seemed to hear him. "I want my father!" He poured wine down his throat from a skin almost as large as he was.

Alarm prickled through Gerin. "Don't do that," he said urgently. "Come on, Ferdulf, give me the skin."

"I want my father!" Ferdulf shouted again.

The space around the wineskins seemed to . . . expand. "My son, I am here," Mavrix said.

VII

"Father!" Ferdulf cried in delight.

Gerin trotted out his halting Sithonian: "I greet you, lord of the sweet grape." He bowed low, looking at the Sithonian god of wine and fertility from under his eyelids.

Mavrix, as usual, wore supple fawnskin. A wreath of grape leaves kept his long, dark hair off his forehead. Ferdulf's eyes had flashed; Mavrix glowed all over, raiment and all. The only darkness in him was his eyes, twin pits of deepest shadow in his effeminately handsome face.

"Well," he said now, voice echoing inside Gerin's head as if the Fox heard him with mind rather than with ears, "I have not been north of the mountains in some little while. I cannot say this benighted excuse for a country has improved much since I last saw it, I must tell you."

"What do you mean?" Now Ferdulf sounded indignant. "I'm here, and I wasn't the last time you came to Fox Keep."

"Well, yes," Mavrix admitted. He seemed something less than delighted to make his son's acquaintance. "Even so—"

"The Gradi don't trouble the northlands these days," Gerin put in. He carefully did not add, No thanks to you. Mavrix had tried to stand against Voldar, the ferocious chief goddess of the Gradi, but had not been strong enough. Baivers, the Elabonian god of barley and brewing, had held off Voldar and the rest of the Gradi pantheon, along with considerable help from the fearsome deities of the monsters under Biton's cave. Gerin wondered whether Mavrix despised Baivers or the monsters' gods more.

"Well, yes." If anything, Mavrix sounded even less thrilled than he had with Ferdulf. "Even so—"

Ferdulf ran over to him and caught him by the hand. "Father!" he cried again.

Mavrix inspected him. If the Sithonian god was impressed, he concealed it exceedingly well. "Yes, I am your father," he said. "You summoned me, so I came. Now what do you want?"

He sounded like Gerin granting a brief audience to a man for whom he could not spare any more time: he wanted Ferdulf to come to the point so he could get back to whatever he had been doing. Ferdulf caught that, too. "Here I am, the son you got on my mother," he exclaimed. "Have you no praise for me? Have you no words of wisdom?"

Words of wisdom were the last thing Gerin would have asked of Mavrix. If the Sithonian god had chosen to give him any, he would have reckoned true wisdom likely to lie in ignoring them. Here and now, the issue did not arise, for Mavrix only shrugged; the sinuous motion put Gerin in mind of a serpent. "I may be your father," the god said, "but I am not your nursemaid."

Ferdulf reeled back as if Mavrix had slapped him. However heartless Mavrix's words sounded, Gerin thought they did hold good advice. At least they told Ferdulf in no uncertain terms that he could not rely on Mavrix for anything but his existence.

Whatever else they did, they infuriated the little demigod. "You can't ignore me!" he shouted. His feet came off the ground. He shot through the air at Mavrix like an angry arrow.

In his right hand, the Sithonian god bore a wand wreathed in ivy and vine leaves and topped with a pinecone. The thyrsus looked like a harmless ornament. In Mavrix's hands, though, it was a weapon more deadly than the longest, sharpest, heaviest spear any human warrior could carry.

Mavrix tapped Ferdulf with the wand. Ferdulf groaned and crashed to the ground. "A child who annoys his father gets the stick, as he deserves," the god said to the demigod.

Ferdulf was used to having more supernatural power than anyone around him. He rose into the air again and hurled himself at his sire. "You can't do that to me!" he cried.

"Oh, but I can," Mavrix answered, and tapped his son with the thyrsus again. Again, Ferdulf hit the ground, more heavily this time than before. "You need to understand that. Just because I came when you called, you have not the right to abuse me, nor shall you ever." Ferdulf moaned and lay in a heap. Alert as a longtooth, Mavrix stood there watching him. A faint rank odor, of wine lees and old corruption, floated from the god, making Gerin's nose twitch.

Slowly, with another groan, Ferdulf sat up. "Why did you come when I called?" he asked in a voice full of despair. "I hoped you would see me and be proud of me. I hoped—" He shook his head, as if to clear it.

"What a naive little creature you are," Mavrix said, which brought one more groan from Ferdulf. The Sithonian god turned to Gerin. "I should have thought he would have learned better, dwelling by you as he does. For a mortal, you have a moderate amount of sense."

"Even if he is a demigod, he's only four years old,"

Gerin said, concealing his own bemusement at hearing anything even remotely resembling praise from Mavrix.

Ferdulf heard it, too, heard it and did not like it. "How dare you talk to him, talk to this, this *man*, more kindly than you do to me?"

"I dare because I am a god. I dare because I am your father," Mavrix returned evenly. By early appearances, Ferdulf annoyed him even more than the Fox did. His dark, dark eyes stared at, stared through, his son. "How dare *you* presume to question *me*?"

"I am flesh of your flesh, blood of your blood," Ferdulf said. "If I have not got the right, who has?"

"No one," Mavrix answered. "Now be quiet for a little while."

Ferdulf tried to speak, but produced only squeaks and grunts, not intelligible words. Gerin was impressed he could do even so much; when Mavrix commanded silence of a mortal man, silence was what he got. Seeing Mavrix relatively well-disposed to him, the Fox asked, "Lord of the sweet grape, what aid can you give me against the Elabonian Empire?"

At that, Ferdulf did fall silent. He wanted to hear the answer, too, being anything but enamored of the Empire.

Mavrix looked troubled. That troubled Gerin. Sithonian legend spoke of what a coward Mavrix was. But what was on the god's face did not look like fear to the Fox. It looked like resignation. That troubled Gerin more.

"I can do less than you might hope," Mavrix said at last. "If I could do more than you might hope, do you think I would not have done it for fair Sithonia rather than for this grapeless and otherwise unattractive wilderness?"

"But—" Gerin shook his head. "You Sithonian gods are still very much a part of your own country, while the gods of Elabon hardly seem to notice this world any more: one has to shout to get their attention, you might say."

Mavrix nodded. "That is so. And, once gained, their attention is frequently not worth having." He sniffed scornfully.

"As may be," Gerin said, not wanting to disagree openly with the Sithonian god of wine and fertility. Once he'd summoned Baivers, the Elabonian god had done more for him than Mavrix had. In any case, that wasn't what he wanted to know. He asked, "With the gods of Sithonia immanent in the world while those of Elabon are not, how have the Elabonians"—he carefully did not say *we Elabonians*—"ruled your land so long?"

"That is a cogent question—a painfully cogent question," Mavrix said. "The best reply I can give is that the folk of Sithonia, while they have a great many gifts from their gods, conspicuously lack that of governing themselves. Elabonians, on the contrary, have next to no discernible gifts of any sort . . . save only that of government. It would take a stronger god than any known in Sithonia to make its people unite."

Regretfully, Gerin nodded. That fit too well with what the imperial wizards had told him. "Is there nothing you can do?" he said, wondering, *What good is an impotent god, especially an impotent fertility god?*

"I have already done all you require of me, and more besides," Mavrix answered. "Without my son—who may, by the way, speak again—you would have no hope whatever of repelling the forces of the Elabonian Empire. With him, you have that hope. Nothing in the mundane world is altogether certain, however, either for gods or for men. Do not be smug; do not be overconfident; you may yet lose this fight, too."

"You're talking in riddles," Gerin said accusingly. "I thought you despised Biton."

"And so I do," Mavrix said with a curl of the lip. "But how am I to speak with certainty when I cannot see everything that lies ahead?"

Gerin wondered if he ought to go up to Ikos to hear what the farseeing god had to say. Maybe he'd made a mistake, not doing that when Duren suggested it. He wondered when—and if—he'd have the chance to leave the army and try to puzzle out one of Biton's notoriously ambiguous oracular verses.

Ferdulf said, "But what must I *do* to drive the Empire out of the northlands?"

"*I* don't know," Mavrix answered. "I haven't the faintest idea. I don't much care, either, if the truth be known. That anyone would be mad enough to wish to live in a land where the grape grows not is beyond me." He turned his head toward Ferdulf. "You will manage, I expect—unless, of course, you don't." A sigh rippled out of him. "For some reason, I am frequently disappointed in my offspring. It must be the fault of the mortal women on whom I sire them."

"Nothing is ever your fault, is it?" Ferdulf said, a thought also in Gerin's mind but one he found it politic not to mention. "When things go your way, you take the credit; when they go wrong, someone else gets the blame."

"You, for example, my charming child, are entirely to blame for that unseemly temper of yours," Mavrix returned, which, to Gerin, proved only that the Sithonian fertility god was not so perceptive as he thought he was.

Ferdulf started to curse him. Gerin had heard some fancy curses in his time, but very few to match the ones spewing from the little demigod's lips. When the Fox closed his eyes for a moment, he could easily imagine he was listening to a veteran abusing a man he'd hated for twenty years.

If the abuse bothered Mavrix, he didn't show it. On the contrary: he beamed at Ferdulf as if proud of him. "I love you, too, dear son of mine," he said when the demigod finally paused for breath. He stuck out his tongue even farther than Ferdulf could have—and then he was gone.

Ferdulf kept on cursing for quite some time, even though only Gerin stood beside him near the wineskins. Without warning, he stopped cursing and burst into tears.

"I was afraid something like this might happen," Gerin said, as consolingly as he could. "That's why I didn't want you to try summoning your father."

"He didn't care." Ferdulf spoke in tones of astonished disbelief. "He just didn't care. I am his son—and he didn't care."

"He's a fertility god," Gerin answered. "He's had lots of sons—and lots of daughters, too. He doesn't see much reason why a new one should particularly matter to him."

"I hate him," Ferdulf snarled. "I'll hate him forever. He'd better not show his ugly face around here again, or I'll make him sorry, that's what I'll do."

"Easy," Gerin said. "Easy. You don't want to talk that way about your father, no matter who he is. You especially don't want to talk that way about your father when he's a god."

"I don't care what he is," Ferdulf said, and then began to cry again. "I'll pay him back for not caring about me if it's the last thing I ever do."

"If you try that, it's liable to be the last thing you ever do," Gerin said.

Ferdulf ignored him. The little demigod kept crying as if his heart would break—no, as if it were already broken. The men guarding the wine stared at him. They were Gerin's subjects, and knew about Ferdulf. They no more expected this behavior from him than they expected the Fox to go on a four-day drunk and rumple every peasant girl he could get his hands on.

Gerin stared at Ferdulf, too. After staring, he did what he would have done for any other crying child: he walked over, squatted beside Ferdulf, and put his arms around the demigod. Even as he did it, he wondered how foolish he was being. Like any other crying child, Ferdulf could do all sorts of unpleasant things if he didn't feel like being held. Unlike any other crying child, he could do all sorts of dangerous things if he didn't feel like being held.

But all he did was throw his own arms around the Fox and bawl till he had no more tears left. When sobs subsided into sniffles and hiccoughs, Gerin said, "Why don't you go find your blanket now? I don't think anything more will happen here around the wine tonight." He devoutly hoped—and that seemed to be the right word, too—nothing more would happen around the wine tonight.

"All right," Ferdulf said. "But I will have my revenge. You wait and see if I don't." Off he went, hardly more than half as tall as a grown man but showing a determination few grown men could—or would have wanted to—match.

When the Fox straightened up, his knees clicked. He glanced over to the guards, who were staring after Ferdulf. "The less you talk about what happened just now, the happier I'll be," he said. "The happier I am, the happier you'll be. Do you understand that?"

"Aye, lord king," they chorused.

As Gerin walked back toward his blanket, he was gloomily certain the secret wouldn't hold. He counted himself lucky Mavrix hadn't gone and roused the whole camp. That would have created a fine chunk of chaos, which the Sithonian god often enjoyed.

He lay down. He wondered how he was supposed to go back to sleep after some of that chaos—to say nothing of a despondent demigod—landed in his own lap. He looked up at the stars and the moons. Tiwaz and Elleb were in the sky, both of them moving from full toward third quarter. Even Elleb, which had risen after Tiwaz, floated high in the southeast. Sunrise couldn't be too far away. Gerin yawned. With his luck, he thought, he'd have just dozed off when the sun came over the horizon. And, sure enough, that was exactly what happened.

Rihwin the Fox set hands on hips and looked indignant. He had a good deal of practice looking indignant; along with innocence no sucking babe could match, it was an expression he donned frequently. This time, though, Gerin would have been willing to bet at least most of the ire was real.

"You quaffed the wine without inviting *me*?" Rihwin demanded, as if unable to imagine an act more heinous.

Gerin shook his head. "I didn't quaff a bit of it," he replied. "Ferdulf did. And, sure enough, Mavrix came. Did you really want to make his acquaintance again? Do you think he would have wanted to make yours?"

Rihwin brushed that aside with an airy wave of the hand, a gesture that came from south of the High Kirs. "Wine was quaffed, and I quaffed none of it?" he said. "Where, I pray you, is the justice in that? I found the wine, I brought the wine back to the camp, I—"

"—Pant after the wine the way an old lecher pants after a young virgin," Gerin broke in. "That is what you meant to say, isn't it?"

"Well, possibly I might have chosen other words to the same effect," Rihwin said with a disarming grin— another expression he'd practiced . . . and had need to practice. "But, lord king, unlike the lecher, I have done without for fifteen years—and, now that the wine is a virgin no longer, how can you begrudge my having it, too?"

"I might have known better than to try a figure of speech against you," Gerin said. "Of course you'd turn it upside down and throw it back at me."

Now Rihwin looked smug. He didn't need to practice that expression; it came naturally. "You cannot in logic deny me," he said.

And Gerin nodded. "You're right. I cannot in logic deny you," he admitted. "But I'm going to go right on denying you just the same—and denying myself and Van and Aragis and everyone else. If Mavrix came for Ferdulf, he's liable to come again, and I'd just as soon he didn't."

"But this is unjust!" Rihwin cried. "It has behind it no rational force."

"Yes?" Gerin said. "And so?" Rihwin simply stared at him. Gerin stared back. *He'd* had a lot of practice at keeping his features impassive. What with Rihwin, Ferdulf, his own children, Fand, and many others, he'd needed that kind of practice. Rihwin dropped his eyes. Not smiling, Gerin said, "Go on—get ready to move out. We're not done with the imperials, you know: not anywhere close."

Off Rihwin went. Every line in his body proclaimed mute outrage. Dagref, who had been standing by listening to the exchange, remarked, "He *will* try to get into the wine, you know."

"And the sun will come up tomorrow," Gerin agreed wearily. "Tell me something I couldn't figure out for myself. He stayed away from it as long as he did because no one else could get at it, either. Now that Ferdulf has—"

"But Ferdulf is a demigod, and son to the god of wine,"

Dagref said. "Doesn't Rihwin see any distinction between that case and his own?"

"The only thing Rihwin sees is his own thirst," Gerin answered. "That worries me, too, but I can only do so much about it. The best way I've come up with to make sure he stays away from the blood of the sweet grape is to keep him too busy to get near the wineskins."

That being so, he sent Rihwin out on patrol with a couple of squadrons of his riders. Whatever else Rihwin was, no one had ever accused him of being dull-witted. He had no trouble seeing what Gerin was doing or why he was doing it, and gave his fellow Fox a sour look. But, since Gerin's order also made perfectly good sense in military terms, Rihwin could do nothing about it but obey.

Maeva did not ride out with Rihwin and the others who fought on horseback. Gerin would have given Rihwin a kick in the fundament had he sent any wounded warrior into action without dire need. Maeva still looked offended at being left behind. "How does the leg feel?" he asked her. "Tell me the truth, now."

A more experienced warrior probably would have lied despite that admonition. Maeva was young enough and serious-minded enough to heed it. "Sore," she confessed.

He set a hand on her forehead. "Hold still," he said when she tried to pull away. "You're not feverish. Is your leg hot around the wound?"

"A little," she said, and then, in a very firm voice, "but only a little."

"All right," he answered. "That sounds like it's healing as it should. Stay off it as much as you can. The less strain you put on it, the faster it will get better." *And the sooner you'll have a scar that will startle your husband on his wedding night*, he thought, *or maybe some other young man on a warm spring night a good deal sooner than that*. If he'd said what was in his mind, he would have embarrassed them both. By keeping his mouth shut, he managed to embarrass only himself. Shaking his head, he went off to get the army moving faster as they broke camp.

He soon saw again that the imperials, while they had now lost two battles, were still very much in the fight. They had so many chariots out to slow down the northerners' march, Rihwin sent a rider back to ask for reinforcements. "They'll smash us up if you don't send more men forward, lord kings," the messenger said.

"We'll send more men forward, by the gods," Aragis snarled. "We'll send the whole cursed army forward, see if we don't." He shouted orders.

Gerin frowned. That wasn't how he would have handled things; it struck him as sticking his head into a longtooth's mouth and inviting the beast to bite down. Scouts went ahead of an army to develop the opposition, to see what was out there. Moving up with the entire force meant the scouts didn't have the chance to do their job and invited an ambush.

He started to protest, then made himself keep quiet. This was what he'd bought when he agreed Aragis should have command of the whole host. He could not claim the Archer was holding back his own men and endangering only Gerin's. Aragis was sending everyone into the fight. He was sending everyone into the fight so aggressively that, if the imperials did have an ambush set, it might not do them much good. He didn't seem to have many ideas as a general, but he knew what to do with the ones he had.

And the imperials proved not to have set a trap after all. Their chariots had been skirmishing briskly with Rihwin's horsemen, but drew back when so much support for the riders made its appearance.

"There—you see, Fox?" Aragis said, more than a little complacently. "We *will* drive them back to Cassat, and, once we've done that, we'll drive them over the mountains and out of the northlands for good."

"By the gods, maybe we will." Gerin heard the bemusement in his own voice. He wouldn't have believed it when the war began, but he was starting to believe it now. One more victory over the forces of the Elabonian Empire, and he didn't see how the imperial forces could sustain themselves on this side of the High Kirs any more.

"Of course we will." Aragis didn't seem to have any doubts. Aragis never seemed to have any doubts about anything. Maybe he didn't have doubts because he was right so often. Maybe he didn't have doubts because nobody dared tell him he was wrong, which wasn't quite the same thing.

"What's Cassat like these days?" Gerin asked. "I haven't been through it since just after the Empire closed off the High Kirs."

"You remember what a sad place it was then?" Aragis said. "Remember how it pretended to be the capital of a province that didn't want to have anything to do with it?"

"That I do," Gerin said. "Dyaus only knows what the governor they'd sent there had done to get himself shipped into exile—no, wait, I remember, it was something to do with getting an army chopped to pieces, wasn't it? Whatever it was, he hated everything that had anything to do with the northlands." That wasn't quite true. The imperial functionary had had quite a yen for Elise. So had Gerin, in those days. She'd disabused the governor with a knife to his throat. Disabusing Gerin had taken longer, and hurt worse by the time the job was through, too.

"Didn't he, though?" Aragis said. "Well, like I say, Cassat

was a sad place then, and that was with traffic going over the mountains into the Empire. When the imperials closed the pass, the place didn't have any reason for being at all. What it reminds me of nowadays is a night ghost that wails because it isn't what it used to be—it isn't much of anything, just the remnant of something that was alive once upon a time."

Gerin gave him a look out of the corner of his eye. "You'd better be careful, Archer, or you're going to end up writing poetry."

"Heh," Aragis said. "You're a funny fellow. Order those horsemen of yours forward again, and we'll get on with this business. The gods only know how much I want to get back to my own holdings. Without anybody to keep an eye on 'em, the peasants are sure to be sitting around with their thumbs up their arses."

"They can't sit idle all the time," Gerin said. "They have to eat this winter, too. They know it."

"Aye, and they'll start thinking of that about two days before harvest time, too," Aragis said. "Meanwhile, the weeding and the manuring won't have gone on half so well as they should. Instead of working, they'll be swilling ale and screwing each other's wives."

"They might as well be barons," the Fox murmured.

Van turned a snort into a cough in the nick of time. Dagref's shoulders hunched, as they would have done at the start of a laugh, but he managed to hold it in. "What was that?" Aragis said sharply.

"Never mind," Gerin told him. "You already think I'm too bloody light-minded. Where do we go from here?"

"After the imperials," the Archer replied without hesitation. "We bring them to battle wherever they will stand, either in front of Cassat or behind it, we smash them, and we run them back over the mountains. If they want to come up into our country to trade, well and good. If they come here again with edged bronze in their hands, we'll give them a new set of lumps and send them home again."

"Maybe we will," Gerin said, as he had before. Listening to Aragis made him believe it, anyhow.

Aragis certainly believed it. "We *will*," he declared in such ringing tones that almost everyone within earshot turned his head toward him. "Put your men on the left, Fox; I shall put mine on the right. We'll meet behind the imperials. With the circle closed around them, we'll make sure not many ever do get back over the High Kirs to tell the tale."

He had, perhaps automatically, assigned himself the place of greater honor. "Let it be as you say," Gerin answered; honor mattered less to him, and results more, than to most of his fellows. He was also pleased to see Aragis coming up with a plan more sophisticated than the sort of headlong charge the Trokmoi might have used.

He wondered if he should have been pleased to see the Archer coming up with better plans. Even if they routed the forces of the Elabonian Empire, they would still be left looking at each other across a border that made Aragis acutely unhappy. The more like an idiot Aragis performed, the happier the Fox should have been. And so he would have been, but for the small detail that Aragis' ineptitude, if any, also endangered him.

He did find one question to put to the Archer: "You don't want to start mixing your men and mine together more? They've fought two battles on the same side by now. They should know they can trust one another against the imperials."

But Aragis shook his head. "I don't want to change what's worked well already. Your men have brothers and cousins and friends fighting alongside them, and so do mine. They'll fight better in front of warriors they know, and they'll fight better being certain in their bones the warriors close by them will come to their rescue if they get into trouble."

"I think the Archer has the right of it, Fox," Van said.

"Well, maybe he does," Gerin allowed. "In fact, I suppose he does. His way, the only place we'll have to worry about the kind of trouble he has in mind is at the join of the two armies."

"Just so," Aragis said. "Besides, while your men will obey me and mine will obey you, each force will obey its own sovereign better. Less chance for treachery my way, too. I don't fear it, not after these two fights, but I don't care to leave myself open to it, either."

Gerin started to tell him he was being absurd, but stopped with the words unspoken. Aragis wasn't being absurd. He was being sensibly cautious. Now that Gerin thought about it, he didn't want to leave himself open to treachery from the Archer, either. Keeping his men together reduced the risk of it.

Aragis saw him start to speak and then stop, too. The Archer nodded, as if Gerin had proved his point. In a way, Gerin had. Aragis said, "We are allies against a common danger, not friends. I do not see how we can be friends, you and I."

"Once we drive the Empire back south of the High Kirs—" Gerin began, and then stopped again. The two of them would have been rivals had the Empire not cleared the passes through the mountains; they would have been at war had the Empire not done so. He'd thought as much only moments before. If the Empire left the northlands, what would keep them from being at each other's throats once more? Nothing he could see.

"Allies," Aragis repeated. "Not friends. So long as we

remember it, we should do well enough. We've done well enough so far."

"Allies," Gerin agreed. Did he sound mournful or relieved? Even he couldn't tell. Were Aragis his friend, he might well sleep easier of nights. On the other hand, who could sleep easy knowing he was the sort of person able to make friends with Aragis the Archer?

That evening, after the army encamped, Rihwin fell on his knees before Gerin. "Lord king, I implore you, let me taste of the blood of the sweet grape!" he cried.

"What in the five hells do you think you're playing at, Rihwin? Get up, for pity's sake." Gerin shook his head. "Anyone would think I were a pretty little peasant wench you were trying to wheedle into bed."

"Truly, lord king, I suffer for lack of wine as I would suffer for lack of a friendly wench's caresses," Rihwin replied as he climbed to his feet. He winked at Gerin. "And, as truly, I have wheedled a good many pretty peasant wenches into bed with just such words."

"I don't doubt it for a moment," Gerin said. "They probably lie down with you just to make you shut up."

"It could be," Rihwin admitted, not a bit abashed— but then, Rihwin was seldom abashed. "I did not inquire as to why they did it, I confess." He gave Gerin a sidelong look. "I would not inquire why you did it, either, lord king. You have my solemn word."

Gerin exhaled angrily. "To the crows with your solemn word. You do know, do you not, that Mavrix came visiting when Ferdulf drank of the wine you captured? Of course you do; I told you myself. Now I ask you again, do you want to meet the god?"

"Yes, I do know that." Rihwin looked troubled. "I forgot where I heard it, though, and dismissed it as nothing more than camp gossip."

"Of course you did," Gerin snapped. "It wasn't what you wanted to hear, so you bloody well ignored it. You have a way of doing that with things you don't want to hear. Unfortunately, it happens to be true. One more time, sirrah, and answer me yea or nay, if you please: do you care to try conclusions with Mavrix?"

"I don't care," Rihwin said. "He's taken my magic from me. What more can he do, short of taking my life? And if he should take my life, I shall die happy with the taste of wine on my lips. It's a better way to go than most I can think of."

"That depends on what sort of end he feels like giving you." But Gerin threw his hands in the air. "All right, by the gods, go ahead and drink. You've worn me down— if I were a peasant girl, I'd be taking off my skirt right now. On your head be it, though, and I hope all your bastards are well provided for. If you want to be a cursed fool—if you insist on being a cursed fool—I don't suppose I have the right to stand in your way."

Rihwin seized his hand and kissed it. Gerin yanked it back with a startled oath. Rihwin said, "You are a prince among men—no, a king among men." He winked. "Will you not come and drink with me, that we may greet Mavrix together?"

Greeting Mavrix was about the last thing Gerin wanted to do. Nevertheless, he said, "I'll come with you, all right. If you think I trust you with wine while you're out of my sight, you're even crazier than I think you are—and that, believe me, would take some doing."

"Rail at me and insult me as much as you like, so long as you don't stand between me and the blood of the sweet grape." Rihwin hurried away, to return a moment later with his drinking jack, which dripped. "I have rinsed it in the stream to remove whatever dregs of ale might have remained within."

"Good for you," Gerin said. "Let's go. Let's get this over with."

The guards around the wine began to raise their swords to keep Rihwin away from that which they protected; Gerin had given them very firm orders about that. Then the guards exclaimed in surprise, seeing Gerin stalking along behind him. Gerin countermanded the orders.

"Are you sure, lord king?" one of the guards asked.

"No, I'm not sure," Gerin answered. "The only thing I'm sure of is that Rihwin has wine where his wits ought to be, and he's whined so much I'm going to let him drink some. That will settle that—one way or another."

Rihwin sniffed at Gerin's assessment of him. He poured his jack full, brought it up to his face, and sniffed. His expression grew blissful as he savored the bouquet. "Truly I bless thee, lord of the sweet grape," he murmured. He drank.

Gerin waited for the sky to fall, or at least for Mavrix to appear in all his rather effeminate glory. The sky did not fall. Mavrix did not appear. Nothing whatever out of the ordinary happened, in fact. Rihwin tilted back his head so as to drain the last drop of wine from the jack. He wiped his mouth on his sleeve, a slightly puzzled expression stealing over his face.

"Well?" Gerin demanded. He looked around. Still no sign of Mavrix.

Rihwin kept on looking puzzled. He stared down at the drinking jack, as if it had somehow betrayed him. "It's very fine, lord king," he said slowly. "In sooth, I do prefer it to ale, as I had been certain I should. It's very fine indeed, as I say, and yet . . ." His voice trailed off.

"Not so fine as you remember it, eh?" Gerin said.

"No," Rihwin said in a small voice. "In my mind, I had built up the idea of what it was like, the idea of what it would be like, and, having gone without for so long, I suppose I kept building it and building it, until at the last I had erected a structure taller and wider than the foundation of truth would support."

"And it just came crashing down on you?" Gerin had not expected to find himself feeling sympathetic to Rihwin, any more than he'd expected to find himself feeling sympathetic to Ferdulf when the demigod's encounter with his father failed to turn out as he'd hoped. But Gerin's friend seemed so uncharacteristically crestfallen, he couldn't help himself.

Rihwin let out a small, sad sigh. "Even so, lord king. Have you ever wanted a beautiful woman who would not give herself to you? Your imaginings of what she would be like grow ever more heated, until at last, in them, she puts to shame Astis the goddess of love."

"And if, after that, you do end up having her after all, what do you find out?" Gerin said. "You find out she's only another woman."

"It has happened to you!" Rihwin exclaimed.

"Not since I was very young," Gerin answered. "You always expect great things when you're very young." He sent Rihwin a pointed look. "Most people get over it after a while."

"So kindly," Rihwin murmured. "So generous. So much like finding a wasp by thrusting your foot into the boot wherein it had chosen to pass the night. Well, I shall have my revenge."

"Of course you will," Gerin said. "You come out with four times as many outrageous things as I do. One of them is bound to skewer me before long."

But that was not the sort of revenge Rihwin had in mind. He filled the drinking jack with wine for a second time and, instead of draining it himself, pressed it into Gerin's startled hands. "Here, lord king. You have gone without longer than I. Taste of the sweet grape and measure it against *your* memory."

"Curse you, Rihwin," Gerin muttered. If he drank, he was liable to draw Mavrix's notice, which was one of the last things he wanted to do. But if he refused to drink, he was liable to offend the Sithonian god of wine, which was another of the last things he wanted to do. After a brief mental debate as to which was the worse risk, he decided he had better drink. "I bless thee, Mavrix, lord of the sweet grape," he said in his seldom-used Sithonian, and raised the jack to his lips.

The wine was sweet, not sour like beer. As Rihwin had, he'd remembered that. He did not think it was very good wine; what army was in the habit of sending a fine vintage with its troopers? But, even if it had been good wine, it would have been worth trading for, but not worth ecstasies.

He said as much, looking around warily again lest Mavrix suddenly appear. Wherever the Sithonian god chose to manifest himself, he did not spring into being in the camp.

Rihwin sighed again. "Lord king, I fear you have the right of it. Only wine! What a sad thing to say—every bit as sad, I think, as your, 'Only another woman'!"

"Maybe it is," Gerin said absently. He kept looking this way and that, waiting for Mavrix to appear and do something appalling. The god gave no sign of his presence. Gerin didn't know whether to be relieved or suspicious. He ended up being both at once, as if someone had shot an arrow at him from arm's length and missed.

Rihwin figured out what he was doing. Rihwin was not a fool. No. Gerin shook his head. Rihwin was not stupid—there was a difference. "Waiting for the lord of the sweet grape to come and turn us inside out?" he asked.

"You deserve to be turned inside out," Gerin snapped. He ran his tongue over his lips; a few little drops of wine remained in his mustache. Their taste made him nervous all over again.

"Why?" Rihwin said. "For thinking it would be safe and proving it?"

"For taking the chance," Gerin said. "The risk wasn't worth the reward. You got yourself a jack of wine, but you put your neck on the line to get it."

Rather to Gerin's surprise, that succeeded in embarrassing Rihwin. "I thought the wine was worth my neck," Rihwin said. "Perhaps—I say only *perhaps*, mind you— I was wrong."

"You got by with it," Gerin said. "I don't know that you deserved to get by with it, but you did, so let it go." Hearing Rihwin admit he might have made a mistake made Gerin back off a bit, too.

And then Rihwin said, "Now that we know we may safely partake of the blood of the sweet grape, what say we empty the wineskins as fast as we can, to remove further danger?"

"What say we don't?" Gerin answered dryly. "We don't *know* we can safely drink wine whenever we want. All we do *know* is, we got by with it once." Rihwin stuck out his tongue. Gerin ignored him and let out a long sigh. "And I don't think we'd better get rid of all the wine, whether by drinking it or any other way. We may need to summon Mavrix one day, and wine is best for that." He could hear the reluctance in his own voice, but the words needed saying.

The reluctance got through to Rihwin, but so did the sense of what Gerin said. "Very well, lord king; let that be as you say. My own craving, having been slaked once, shall not be so desperate as it has been till now."

"Here's hoping you're right," Gerin said. "But it's liable

to be as much in Mavrix's hands as it is in yours." Rihwin gave him a horrified look. He pretended not to see it, and slapped his friend from south of the High Kirs on the back. "Let's get what rest we can. I think we may fight in the morning."

They didn't fight the next morning, nor the next afternoon, either. Gerin began to wonder if the imperials were going to fall back not just to Cassat but through it. If that was so, they might have given up on their efforts to reunite the northlands to the Elabonian Empire.

But then, the morning after that, Rihwin's riders came back to report that the imperial army was drawn up in battle array, awaiting attack. "We'll give it to them," Aragis declared. "One more win and they're gone for good." He shouted orders for the advance.

"Do you think he's right, Father?" Dagref asked as he steered the chariot out in front of the warriors who acknowledged Gerin as their overlord.

"As a matter of fact, I do," the Fox answered. "Beating an army once and seeing it keep its spirit—that can happen, no doubt about it. Beating an army twice and seeing it keep its spirit—when the imperials managed it, that surprised me. If we beat them three times running, I don't see how they can keep from running themselves."

Van nodded. "I think you have the right of it, Captain. I don't suppose I've ever seen soldiers with so much discipline in all my days, but discipline only takes a soldier so far. If it keeps taking him into fights where he can't hope to win, it'll break like a dropped pot."

"That does make good logical sense." Dagref looked back over his shoulder at Gerin. "Haven't you tried to thump it into my head that battles don't always make good logical sense?"

"I think I ought to thump your head on the principle

of the thing," Gerin said. "Keep your attention on where we've going, if you please, not on where we've been."

Out ahead of the chariots, and out wide of them as well, rode Rihwin's horsemen. Among them was Maeva, who found sitting a horse easier than walking around. Gerin almost mentioned her to Dagref, because that would have made sure his son looked ahead at all times. He refrained, though, not wanting to remind Van that Maeva was in the fight and had already been hurt once.

Above and ahead of the army of the northlands flew Ferdulf. The demigod had been subdued since meeting his father. He seemed exuberant enough now, though, stabbing out his hand to show the position of the imperial army and then making several lewd gestures in the direction of the men from south of the High Kirs. Gerin's troopers whooped.

The Fox saw the army of the Elabonian Empire a couple of minutes later. He nodded in reluctant admiration. The imperials looked as steady now as they had at the first clash. They'd lost more men than Gerin and Aragis had; having started with an army about the same size as that of the northlands, they were now at a disadvantage. They didn't seem worried, though. As soon as they spied their foes' chariotry, they began their war cry: "Elabon! Elabon! Elabon!"

"Gerin!" the men from the northlands shouted, and "Aragis!" and anything else they could think of. The Trokmoi who rode with the Fox let out a chorus of yips and yowls that might have burst from the throats of wolves.

Maybe those howls were what made Dagref say, "We sound like an army of barbarians."

"And the imperials sound like civilized men?" Gerin asked. His son nodded. The Fox said, "Well, maybe they are. But I'll tell you this: a civilized man doesn't smell any better four days dead than a Trokmê with mustachios that droop down to his collarbones."

"That's a fact," Van agreed. "And another fact is, you'll die just as dead from a civilized man's sword as from a barbarian's—if the silly bugger knows what to do with it, of course."

"Also true," Gerin said. He raised his voice to ask Dagref, "What do you think of these new horses?"

They were still using the team from the imperial chariot onto which they'd forced themselves during the most recent fight. Dagref answered, "They haven't the endurance of the beasts we brought down from Fox Keep—that's certain. But I do think they may run faster for a short burst. That could prove useful. They're easier-tempered beasts than the ponies we had, which is pleasant."

The Fox grunted. If anything, his son had told him more than he'd wanted to know. That was typical of Dagref. He loved detail, and assumed everyone else did, too. With Gerin, that assumption was usually good. Now, though, he had too much on his mind to want a whole lot more rattling around in there.

"Elabon! Elabon! Elabon!" The drivers of the imperial chariots cracked their whips above the backs of their mounts and sent them bounding toward the men of the northlands. Gerin admired their spirit, in the same sort of way in which he admired the courage of the Trokmoi: which is to say, he admired it without seeing that it made much sense. They'd been beaten twice. What on earth made them think the result would be any different this time, especially since they were now outnumbered?

Whatever it was, here they came. Arrows flew toward Gerin and his followers. Some of his men began shooting back, even if they were out of range. He'd told them not to do that, but not everybody thought when he fought.

Nocking an arrow, Gerin waited for a good target to present itself. The imperial officers still persisted in wearing fancy gear to let their men see at a glance who they were. That that also let their foes see at a glance who they were never seemed to enter their heads. Gerin sent two of them tumbling out of their chariots, one right after the other.

Men and horses on both sides went down. One imperial chariot came to grief in front of another, which collided with it and came to grief, too. Along with looking for officers, Gerin sent shafts at drivers and at horses. That last wasn't sporting, and he knew it. He didn't care. If the horses went down, the chariots couldn't roll.

Order and discipline didn't hold long. Once the chariots were in among one another, the tactics of the captains on either side didn't matter much. It was a melee, everyone smashing away at whoever was close by and happened to be shouting the wrong battle cry.

Gerin tried to do something about that, yelling for some of his troopers to overlap the end of the imperial line. The imperials stretched, too, and didn't stretch so thin as to let him shatter them. His mouth twisted. This didn't look like a day on which anything would come easy.

Then Ferdulf dived down to horrify the horses of an imperial chariot. They ran so wild, Dagref had to steer smartly to escape a collision. Van speared the driver out of the enemy car, which meant it would keep right on going wild.

Dagref was no demigod, but he could also make himself unloved by the imperials' horses. His lash made them scream and turn aside from the chariot he drove. One of the drivers who fought for the Elabonian Empire drew back his arm to do likewise to the team Dagref drove. Before he could snap the whip, Gerin shot him in the shoulder. He howled and cursed and dropped the whip, but somehow managed to hang on to the reins. That made Gerin curse in turn.

"How are we doing?" Van shouted. He looked as if he was doing pretty well for himself. His face wore a fierce grin. Blood trails dripped down the shaft from his long, leaf-shaped bronze spearhead. No blood dripped from him.

"Doing well, I think," Gerin answered. He looked around. "The imperials are having to bend back to keep us from getting around behind them, so their line is a bow now—it isn't a line any more. And you can bend a bow only so far. After that, it snaps."

"Aye." Van peered toward the other wing. "Aragis' men seem to be giving the southerners a hard time, too. Say what you will about that fellow, the men he leads can fight."

"I've never doubted that," Gerin said. "He wouldn't be dangerous to me if he weren't dangerous to everyone else who got in his way, too." He hesitated, then admitted, "I suppose I have to say I didn't expect him to be as dangerous as he is."

Dagref said, "If he happened to suffer an unfortunate accident just at the moment when the imperials were routed and running for the High Kirs, I don't think my heart would break."

"Neither would mine," Gerin said. Then, a bit slower than he should have, he realized what else his son had been saying. "If Aragis has an unfortunate accident, it won't be on account of me."

"All right," Dagref said equably. Gerin stared at his son's back. The youth could indeed be formidable to everyone around him when he grew up. As a matter of fact, he was already formidable to everyone around him.

"You keep your eyes open, Fox," Van said, "because I

don't think Aragis' heart would break if you had an unfortunate accident along about the time the imperials were hightailing it for the mountains, either. And Aragis doesn't believe in live and let live, not even a little bit."

Gerin could hardly argue with that. Aragis had about as much forbearance in him as a pike swimming in the Niffet. Any other fish he saw was either his size, bigger . . . or breakfast. But the Fox replied, "I didn't get to be as old as I am by closing my eyes, you know."

"Oh, yes, I do know that," Van said. "But if you want to keep on getting older, don't shut 'em now."

Instead of shutting his eyes, Gerin used them to gape at Ferdulf whizzing around the battlefield, stirring up chaos in the ranks of the imperials. He flew untroubled. Whatever magics the wizards from the Sorcerers' Collegium were using to try to bring him down, they weren't working, not today. And, because they weren't working, the little demigod was making life miserable for the men from south of the High Kirs.

Life, or at least the battle, was pretty miserable for them anyhow. Gerin and Aragis' men did not beat them easily, but beat them they did. Both ends of the imperial line bent back and back now. Gerin began thinking Aragis' dream would come to pass. If his own men met the Archer's behind the imperials, precious few soldiers would have the chance to get back over the mountains and let Crebbig I know what had happened to them. The officers of the Empire realized as much; their shouts grew ever more urgent and desperate.

Gerin shouted, too: "Press them hard! Don't let them have a moment's breather. If we smash them here, they're ruined for good. Press them."

Press them the men of the northlands did. The imperials fought hard, but, though they managed to press forward here and there, overall kept going back and back.

Three arrows, one of them Gerin's, hit an officer who was rallying them. They all struck within heartbeats of one another; the Fox was by no means sure his smote first.

Van whooped as he watched the imperial topple from his car. "He's hit so many times, he doesn't even know which way to fall, the poor sod. You've got your troopers thinking the same way you do, Captain."

"Anyone who can't see that an able officer needs killing is probably too stupid to go on breathing, let alone be worth anything in a fight," Gerin answered with a shrug.

Dagref said, "It would be a wonder, Father, if your followers haven't learned something from you, as long as you've been leading them."

Van whooped again. "Have you ever been called old more politely, Fox?"

"That's not what I—" Dagref began.

"Never mind. I know what you meant," his father said. "I also know Van was trying to rattle you, not me, because he knows you're the easier mark."

"I deny everything," Van said.

"There!" Dagref was triumphant. "Even Van sounds a bit like you, Father, and I'll bet he didn't before he came to Fox Keep."

That was true. Van and Gerin had remarked on it, too. Neither of them remarked on it now, perhaps for fear of making Dagref even more insufferable about his own cleverness than he was already.

Then shouts came from the far rear of the bending imperial line. Gerin leaned forward, trying to make out what they were. A moment later, he let out a shout of his own: "Our men and Aragis' have joined hands. We've got 'em in the barrel—now we pound 'em flat."

His men shouted, too, as they realized they'd surrounded the army of the Elabonian Empire. Most of the shouts were threats aimed at the imperials. But the men from south of the High Kirs stolidly fought on, doing their foes as much harm as they could.

"I think they're too stupid to know how badly beaten they are," Van said.

"You could be right," Gerin allowed. "If you are, though, it's not the worst way for a soldier to be."

Ferdulf kept on flying above the imperials and diving down to dismay them. As before, arrows refused to strike him. He rose on high and dove, rose on high and dove. Then he rose and, instead of diving on the imperials, flew straight to Gerin. "Watch out!" the little demigod shouted, pointing to the southwest. "Watch out!"

"What is it?" Gerin demanded, wishing Ferdulf had been more specific.

And then, when Ferdulf was specific, the Fox wished he hadn't been: "There's another imperial army, as big as this one or maybe bigger, heading straight for us. We're going to get smashed like a bug between two rocks."

In remarkably self-possessed tones, Dagref said, "Well, now we know why the imperials who are already here didn't panic when we surrounded them."

"Don't we?" Gerin agreed sourly. Unlike Aragis, the general in command of the Elabonian Empire's newly reinforced forces was capable of real strategy. He'd set out this tempting army here, certain the men of the northlands would leap on it like a starving longtooth. And the men of the northlands had leaped—and now they were going to pay for it.

Ferdulf hovered in front of Gerin's face like the gadfly he was. "What are you going to do?" he screeched. "What are we going to do?"

"We're going to get licked, that's what we're going to do," Van said.

Ferdulf screeched again, this time wordlessly. "He's

right, of course," Gerin said, which made Ferdulf screech at him. Ignoring the racket, the Fox went on, "Only question left now is how badly we get licked. Ferdulf, go tell Aragis what you just told me. He's on the right; he'll get hammered harder than my troopers will."

"I don't want to talk to Aragis." Ferdulf stuck out his lower lip. "He's nasty."

"Go talk to Aragis!" Gerin shouted. Ferdulf flew off. Gerin hoped he flew off in obedience rather than in a fit of the sulks, but wouldn't have bet anything he minded losing on it.

"We ought to pull back now," Dagref said.

"I know. But we can't." Gerin grimaced. "If we save ourselves like that, we leave Aragis in the lurch."

"Why shouldn't we?" Dagref asked. "He'd do it to us."

"Mm, I think not, not here," Gerin answered. "If he goes under altogether, or if I do, that leaves the other one to face the whole weight of the Empire by himself. That doesn't strike me as something I want to do."

"Well, maybe," Dagref said grudgingly.

Gerin didn't find out whether Ferdulf told the Archer the second imperial army was on the way. It mattered little. Aragis could not have remained in doubt very much longer. The new cry of "Elabon! Elabon! Elabon!" pierced the rest of the battlefield noise like a knifeblade piercing flesh.

"Elabon! Elabon! Elabon!" The surrounded imperials answered the war cry with one of their own.

As soon as he realized he was trapped rather than trapper, Aragis pulled away from the battle without the slightest concern for what that might do to Gerin. The Fox was less infuriated at finding his prediction wrong than he would have been otherwise, for Aragis was the one stuck between the two imperial forces. Most of the pressure fell on him. Gerin was able to break off his part of the fight without too much trouble.

And then, having broken off, he ordered his troopers forward in one last charge against the imperial force he and Aragis had lately surrounded. That made those imperials turn aside from their assault on the Archer to repel him. Van sighed. "Helping Aragis get loose, are you?"

"See any better ideas?" Gerin asked.

The outlander sighed again. "No, but I wish I did. You're hurting yourself while you're helping him."

"Don't remind me." Gerin stared across the field. Aragis did seem to be pulling back, not being surrounded—the fate he and Gerin and inflicted, though not for long enough, on the first army from south of the High Kirs. Seeing that Aragis' men would not be immediately cut off and destroyed satisfied the Fox that he'd done his duty by his ally. "Now back!" he shouted. "Now we get away."

He didn't know how hard the imperials would press his retreating force. They had the numbers now to press him and Aragis at the same time, if they so chose. The lunge they made after his men turned out to be halfhearted. For one thing, they remained intent on trying to break Aragis, against whom they could bring more warriors to bear than against Gerin. For another, most of Rihwin's horsemen—as many as were able—fell back on Gerin's force rather than on Aragis'. The imperial chariotry had great—perhaps even exaggerated—respect for the riders, whose feints and countercharges looked to intimidate them and keep them from pressing harder than they did.

Rihwin himself rode back to Gerin with an anxious expression on his face. "I pray the wine is safe, lord king," he said.

"It's not the biggest thing on my mind right now," Gerin said, in lieu of getting down from the chariot to find a rock with which to hit Rihwin in the head. "I'm more worried about everything else the supply wagons carried. Most of them were on Aragis' side of the field. Without journeybread and sausage and cheese and whatnot, we're going to have to start foraging all over the countryside if we want to stay alive."

"Wine is also important," Rihwin insisted, "it being our best conduit, as you yourself said, to hope and beg for divine aid from Mavrix."

"Not a good hope," Gerin said, but the comment held enough sense to keep him from again wishing to clout his fellow Fox. He sighed. "All right, Rihwin, have it your way. I hope the wine is safe, too. Now let me get back to running this retreat, if you please."

Rihwin sketched a salute. "Lord king, I obey." His eyes twinkled. "When I feel like it, I obey." He rode off before Gerin could find an answer.

The one thing of which the Fox was glad was that his men still showed fight. That let him conduct the sort of retreat the imperials had made before: a retreat with teeth in it. His lines weren't so neat as the ones the men from the Elabonian Empire had maintained, but they weren't pushing him so hard as he'd pushed them. That evened things out. As the imperials had broken free of his pursuit, so his army broke free of theirs.

"Where now?" Van asked. "What now?"

Those were indeed the relevant questions. Gerin took the second one first, not because he had an answer but because he didn't: "I haven't the faintest notion of *what now*, except to get away in the best way we can, so the imperials still have to do some fighting after the battle we just lost. Have to see what sort of shape we're in, have to see what sort of shape Aragis' men are in, have to see if the Empire lets us rejoin them. Maybe I stop being a king and go back to being a baron."

"Would you do that, Father?" Dagref asked, some concern in his voice: if Gerin was not a king, Dagref never would be.

"I might, if I didn't think the Empire would nail me to a cross for taking a title they say I have no right to," the Fox replied. "Being a king—by the gods, even being a baron—never meant all that much to me of itself. The best part of it always has been that it's given me the power I need to make people leave me and mine alone. But I don't think his usurping majesty, Crebbig I, will want anyone around who's dared defy his glory, and so I'm better off to keep on fighting."

"That's the way of it," Van agreed. "You keep standing till they knock you down and you can't get up any more." He looked around. "We'll be on our feet again before too long. Now—the other question I put to you. *Where* now?"

"Northeast, the way we're going," Gerin replied without hesitation. "With all these big villages that are almost little towns around, the farmers down here are plainly growing more than they can eat by themselves. If we have to forage off the countryside, let's forage off countryside that'll give us enough to be worth taking."

"Makes sense to me," the outlander said.

"Besides," Gerin said, "even if I don't know what's happened to most of our supply wagons, I saw taverns in some of those towns. Tonight, I'm going to drink something better than water."

"Not enough better, if you listen to Rihwin," Van said.

"If you listen to Rihwin, you'll hear any number of things that aren't so," Gerin said. "You'll hear any number of things that may be so but probably aren't. You'll hear any number of things that are so but don't matter at the moment. And, I don't deny, you'll hear some things that do matter. But winnowing the grain from the chaff is often more trouble than it's worth."

"You have the right of that." Van rumbled laughter. Then his heavy-featured face grew bleak. "I've not seen Maeva since the fighting started. Have you set eyes on her, Captain?"

"No," Gerin answered. He did not like the way Van looked at him—it was as if the outlander were measuring him for a grave.

But then Dagref said, "She's in the retreat with the rest of us. I saw her off on what would have been our left when we were facing the imperial army; I suppose it's our right now that we've turned our backs on them. She must have been one of the riders who got farthest around the flank of the first imperial force, before the other one made us break off."

"Ah, that's good to hear," Van said, and his features cleared.

"Sounds like your child, too, to be at the fore of the fighting," Gerin said, also more than a little relieved.

"It does, doesn't it?" Now Van looked proud and puzzled at the same time. "Who would have thought a girl child would take after me so, though? I never did, not for a moment."

Dagref looked back over his shoulder. "If you don't mind my saying so, you should have. She's been practicing with bow and sword and spear since she's been big enough to hold them in her hands. She's kept working with them, too, to get to be as good as she is. Why would she do all that if she didn't intend to use them in war one day?"

"When you ask it that way, lad, I have no good answer for you," the outlander said with a sigh. "I thought it was a childish thing in her, I suppose, and that she would put it aside when she turned into a woman, and take up the things of a woman instead."

"That didn't happen," Dagref said. "If you'd been paying attention, you'd have noticed she's been a woman for a year, and she hasn't come close to putting aside her practice. She's worked harder than ever, as a matter of fact."

"Has she?" Van's tone was surprised, not so much at the news, perhaps, as at how emphatically Dagref gave it to him. "You've been paying close attention, haven't you?"

"Well, of course I have," Dagref answered. "I've been practicing a good deal myself, you know. If I didn't notice what people did around me, I wouldn't be much use to anyone, would I?"

Van grunted and subsided. Perhaps he was even convinced. Dagref had spoken most convincingly. He might even have believed what he was saying himself. Over the years, Gerin had seen a great many people talk themselves into believing what wasn't so.

Thoughtfully, the Fox shook his head. He was of the opinion that Dagref was concealing from Van rather than deluding himself. He was also of the opinion that Dagref had made special note of Maeva practicing because she was Maeva, not because she was practicing. He'd also caught Maeva noticing Dagref, which made life . . . less than dull.

The sun sank toward the western horizon. The imperials stopped harassing Gerin's rear guard and drew back. He hadn't thought they would do anything else, but he hadn't thought they would bring a second army over the High Kirs, either. If Aragis had been generous instead of greedy and given the Fox the right instead of the left, the Archer would have had the easier retreat and Gerin would have had to contend with two forces at once. He wondered if Aragis was thinking the same thing at the moment.

Up ahead sat one of those not-quite-towns common here close to the High Kirs. Gerin ordered his men to encamp a couple of bowshots from it. He wasn't worried about feeding them, not tonight. Most of them would have bread or sausage or something on their persons, and those who didn't would be able to get something.

He did need some sort of sacrifice against the night ghosts, though. He walked up toward the village, Dagref at his side. Van stayed behind to talk with Maeva, who'd come through unhurt. Dagref had wanted to do that, too, but Van's presence persuaded him to take himself elsewhere.

When Gerin got to the village, he wondered if anyone would be there at all. His army had passed nearby on the way south, and so had the imperials before them. To his relief, he found that, if the inhabitants had fled as warriors briefly approached the place, they were back now. They were also willing, he discovered, to sell him a couple of sheep.

"How did you keep somebody from stealing them?" he asked.

"Oh, we managed," answered the man who had them. Three words summed up generations of dealing with nobles and warriors, always being the weaker but somehow getting through.

Admiring that resilience, Gerin said, "Well, come to the tavern and have a jack of ale with my son and me."

"I'll take you up on that," the villager said. He led the Fox and Dagref into the tavern, which wasn't too clean but likewise wasn't too dirty. "Three ales," he told the woman who looked to be in charge of the place. He pointed to Gerin. "This fellow here is doing the buying."

She nodded and filled three jacks. She was somewhere in early middle age, brown hair—beginning to go gray—

pulled back from her pale face and tied behind her. In the growing gloom inside the tavern, Gerin couldn't make out what color her eyes were.

She carried the jacks over to the table where he, his son, and the villager sat. She didn't set them down till the Fox put money on the table. Then she nodded and said, "Here you are."

Gerin's head came up, so suddenly that Dagref and the villager stared. He knew her voice. Her eyes were green. He still could not see them, but he knew. Hoarsely, he spoke her name: "Elise."

VIII

She set the tarred-leather drinking jacks on the table very slowly and carefully, as if they were cut rock crystal that might shatter at a touch. Gerin felt as if he might shatter at a touch, too.

"Here, what's this?" the villager said. "The two of you know each other? How in the five hells do you know each other?"

"We manage," Gerin said, his voice still ragged. Dagref's eyes were wide as rounds of flatbread.

"Aye, we do." Elise sounded as much taken aback as the Fox did. Turning to him, she said, "I didn't know your face. I didn't know who you were till I heard you speak."

"Nor I you," he answered. He scratched at his beard. He knew how gray it was. "It's been a long, long time."

"Yes." She looked from him to Dagref and back again. Slowly, some small question in her voice, she said, "Surely this isn't Duren. He would be older."

"You're right." Gerin nodded. "This is Dagref, my older son by Selatre, my wife since a few years after you . . . you left. Did you know that Duren is lord of the holding that belonged to your father?"

Elise shook her head, which meant she was hearing of the death of her father, Ricolf the Red, for the first time. "No. I didn't know," she answered. "News moves slowly, when it moves at all. How long—? How—?"

"Five years ago now," the Fox answered. "A fit of apoplexy. From everything I heard, it was as easy as such things can be. Duren has the holding firmly in his hands these days."

"Does he?" Elise still looked dazed. She had plenty to be dazed about. Gerin was feeling dazed, too. He also felt as if he'd tumbled twenty years back through time, into a part of his life long closed off from that in which he was living now and had been since he'd found Selatre.

The villager who'd come into the tavern with Gerin and Dagref gulped his ale. "Well, I'd best be off," he said, and got up from his stool and hurried out into the sunset.

Dagref, by contrast, stared in fascination from Gerin to Elise and back again. The Fox thought his son's ears curled forward to hear the better, but that might have been his imagination. He hoped it was. Quietly, he said, "Son, why don't you take the sheep back to the camp, so they're sacrificed before the sun goes down?"

"But—" Dagref began. He stopped, then tried again: "But I want to—" Then he realized that what Gerin had phrased as a polite request was in fact an order, and one that brooked no contradiction. The glare Gerin sent his way helped him realize that. Regretfully, resentfully, sulkily, and very, very slowly, he did as his father bade him.

Elise's laugh was nervous. "He wanted to hear everything," she said.

"Of course he did," Gerin said. "And once he'd heard it, he'd know it all, and be able to give back any piece of it you wanted, as near word for word as makes no difference. He'd even understand most of it."

"He takes after you," Elise murmured. By her tone, she didn't altogether intend that as a compliment.

Gerin started to get angry. Before he let the anger show, he saw that half of it—maybe more than half of it . . . no, certainly more than half of it—was all the things he hadn't been able to say since she'd disappeared, now trying to crawl out of his throat at once. With an effort, he crammed them back. "How have you been?" he asked, a question that seemed unlikely to throw oil on the fire.

"How do I look?" she answered. Everything she said seemed to have a bitter edge to it.

"As if you've seen hard times," Gerin said.

She laughed again. "What do you know of hard times? You've always been a baron in a keep, or a prince, or a king. Your belly's been full. People do what you tell them to do. Even your son does what you tell him to do."

"And who says the gods no longer give us as many miracles as we'd like?" Gerin said. Once, a long time before, his sarcasm had amused her. Now she just tossed her head, waiting for him to say something of consequence. Holding back the anger was harder. With an edge in his own voice, he said, "I'm sorry it's been hard for you. It didn't have to be, you know. You could—"

"Could what?" Elise broke in. "Could have stayed? That would have been harder yet. Why do you think I left?"

"My best guess always was that you left because you got bored and wanted something new and didn't much care what it was," Gerin answered. "As long as it *was* new, that would suit you."

"You were the prince of the north," Elise said. "You were having a fine time being the prince of the north— such a fine time, you forgot all about me. I was good enough for a brood mare, and that was that."

One side of Gerin's mouth twisted in what was not a smile. "I needed to do everything I did, you know. If I hadn't done what I did, odds are neither one of us would be here hashing this out now. The Trokmoi would have swallowed up a lot more land than they did."

"That's likely so." Elise nodded. "I never said you weren't good at what you did. I just said you paid more attention to it than you did to me—except when you wanted to take me to bed, of course. And you didn't pay all that much attention to me then."

"Not fair," he said. He hadn't seen her for twenty years, and yet she knew how to get under his skin as if they'd never been apart. "I never looked anywhere else. I never wanted to look anywhere else."

"Of course not," Elise said. "Why would you? I was handy. 'Come here, Elise. Take off your skirt.'"

"It wasn't like that," Gerin insisted.

"Oh, but it was," she said.

They glared at each other. Gerin was convinced he remembered things just as they'd been. Elise, obviously, was as convinced her memory was straight and his crooked. He had no records, not for something like that. He sighed. "It's done. It's over. You made sure it would be over. Have you been happier since than you would have been if you'd stayed with me? I hope so, for your sake."

"Decent of you to say so, though talk is cheap. I've seen how cheap talk is, over the years." She pursed her lips. "Have I been happier than I would have been if I'd stayed behind? Every once in a while, much happier. All together? I doubt it."

The answer held a certain bleak honesty. Gerin sighed again. He was tempted to walk out, walk back to the encampment, and spend the rest of his life pretending he'd never run into the woman who'd borne his oldest son. But that thought brought up another one, one he needed to ask about for Duren's sake: "Do you have any other children?"

"I had two, both girls," she answered, and then looked down at the ground. "Neither one of them lived to be two years old."

"I'm sorry," Gerin said.

"So am I," she said, even more bleakly than before. When she raised her head once more, unshed tears glittered in her eyes. "You know you take a chance loving them, but you can't help it."

"No, you can't," Gerin said. "I've had three since who lived. We lost one."

"You've been lucky," Elise said soberly. She studied him for a moment, then repeated herself in a different tone of voice: "You've been lucky."

"Yes, of course I have," he replied. "I've been steady, too."

He could see she didn't understand what he was talking about. When he'd known her, she'd been ready to turn her world upside down at a moment's notice. That was how the two of them had come together. He doubted she'd changed much since. That made her steady, in an unsteady way.

"You've been lucky," she said yet again. "You sound as if you were even lucky enough to find a woman whose temper matches yours. I didn't think there was any such creature."

"You threw me aside," he said. "Of course you wouldn't think anyone else might want me."

"That's not—" Elise paused. She *was* relentlessly honest. "Well, maybe it is true, but not all true."

"However you like." Gerin shrugged. He could feel how tight a grip he had on his temper. It struggled and writhed in that grip, too, the way Van did when they wrestled together. As the Fox did with Van, he felt it liable to escape at any moment. To try to hold it in check, he asked, "Did you find a man who matched your temper?"

"Several of them," she answered. Given how steadily changeable she was, that saddened the Fox a little but didn't surprise him. Elise scowled. "The latest one threw me over, the son of a whore, for a woman who couldn't have been more than half his age. If he hadn't left this place in a hurry, I'd have slit his throat for him, or maybe slit him somewhere else."

She sounded like Fand. Gerin thought she would have done it if she'd got the chance, as Fand would have. He asked, "How is what this fellow did to you any different from what you did to me?"

He probably shouldn't have said that. He realized as much as soon as the words were out of his mouth, which was, of course, too late. Elise had been scowling at the latest man to disappear from her life. Now she scowled at Gerin. "I never pretended Prillon didn't exist."

"I never pretended you didn't exist," Gerin returned.

"Ha!" Elise tossed her head. The tone flayed meat from the Fox's bones. He hadn't had that tone aimed at him in a long time. She went on, "No one is so blind as the person who thinks he sees everything."

"That's true," Gerin agreed. He saw that she was applying it to him. She had not a clue that it also applied to her. Even after his remark, she didn't apply her own comment to herself. The Fox shrugged. He hadn't expected that she would, not really.

"It hardly seems fair," she said. "I've struggled all this time, and what have I to show for it? Nothing to speak of. And you—you've just gone on and on and on."

"You were the one who left," Gerin answered with yet another shrug. "I didn't put you on a boat in the middle of the Niffet and heave you over the side. I would have . . ." He broke off. He wouldn't have been happier had she stayed. For a little while, he might have been.

Over the long haul of years, he was happier the way things had turned out.

Her mouth tightened. She must have realized what he'd been about to say, and why he hadn't said it. "You may as well go," she said. "There's nothing left at all, is there?"

"No," he answered, even if that wasn't quite true. The thing that had been dead inside him for twenty years stirred, like a ghost at sunset. But even ghosts, drawn by the boon of blood, that tried to give good advice only howled unintelligibly, like the wind. A man who listened to the wind instead of his own mind and heart deserved to be called a fool. Gerin pretended not to hear this ghost, too.

"Would you like another jack of ale?" Elise asked with brittle politeness.

"Thank you, no." He'd seldom been so tempted to drink till he couldn't see. He thought for a moment, then said, "If you like, I'll send a messenger up to Duren, to ask if he wants you to come stay at the keep that was your father's?"

"It's Duren's through me," Elise said angrily. "Why shouldn't I simply go and stay there, if I so choose?"

Gerin ticked off points on his fingers. "Item: I am not the lord of that holding. Duren is. Item: I do nothing to take a hand in his affairs without his leave. Item: you left Fox Keep when he was barely able to toddle. Why are you sure he'd want to see you now?"

"I am his mother," Elise said, as if to a halfwit.

Gerin shrugged.

Her eyes blazed. "I remember why I left Fox Keep, too. You are the most cold-blooded man the gods ever set on the face of the earth."

Gerin shrugged again.

That made Elise angrier. "To the five hells with you,"

she snapped. "What would happen if I left on my own and traveled to my father's holding—my son's holding—by myself?"

She would put herself in danger, traveling alone. After the life she'd lived, she had to know that. After the life she'd lived, she also had to be good at coming through danger. And she might find herself in danger if she stayed here, too. "The imperials are liable to be coming through this place in a few days," he warned.

"I'm not afraid of them," Elise answered. "I have kin south of the High Kirs, too, you know."

"So you do," Gerin said. "If they happen to feel like it, I suppose the imperials could give you an escort to the country south of the mountains—maybe even down to the City of Elabon."

His voice held a sardonic bite. Elise, though, chose to take him seriously. "Maybe they would," she said. "Why shouldn't they? I'm kin to nobles close to the Emperor."

Nobles close to the man who had been the Emperor, Gerin thought. *How they stand with Crebbig I is anyone's guess. How glad they'll be to see you is anyone's guess, too. They weren't very glad when you came calling on them before the werenight.*

He didn't get the chance to say any of those things. Before he could, Elise went on, "And then I'd be living in the capital of the Elabonian Empire and you'd be stuck here in the northlands. How would you like that?"

She was gloating, loving the idea. She knew how he'd longed for the life of the City of Elabon when he'd been together with her. He still longed for it. But the longing wasn't a vital part of him any more, even if it did stir in his heart now and again. Like her, it had become a piece of his past, and he was satisfied to leave it so.

He said, "I've spent most of the time since you left

me trying to make the northlands into the sort of place where I might want to live. Up around Fox Keep, I haven't done too badly. I'm happy enough to stay where I am. If you'd sooner go down to the City of Elabon, go ahead."

Elise glared at him. That wasn't the answer he was supposed to give, nor the way he was supposed to respond. He was supposed to get angry, to shout and act jealous. Elise didn't quite know what to do when he failed to perform as expected.

He got to his feet. "I'm going to go. If you like, I *will* send a messenger up to Duren. I owe you so much, at least. If you want me to, perhaps you'd better come along with me." He didn't like that, not even a little, but saw no other choice. "The gods only know what sort of shape this village will be in after the imperials come through here."

"The only woman in among your army?" she said coldly. "No, thank you. No, indeed."

"You wouldn't be the only woman," the Fox answered. "Van's daughter Maeva is along, riding a horse under Rihwin's command."

That startled Elise. She could fight; Gerin knew as much. She'd never dreamt of making a life of soldiering, though. After a moment, her eyes went hard again. "No, thank you," she repeated. "I'd sooner take my chances with the Elabonian Empire."

"Have it your way," Gerin said. "You were always bound and determined to do that anyhow, weren't you?"

"Me?" Elise exclaimed. "What about you?"

"You know what the trouble is?" the Fox said sadly. "The trouble is, we're both right. That's probably one of the things that helped split us apart."

Elise shook her head. "Don't blame me for that. You did it."

"However you like." Gerin sighed. "Goodbye, Elise. I don't wish you ill. If you're still here after we drive the imperials out of the northlands, think again about finding out whether Duren wants to see you."

"Maybe I'll ask the imperials to take me up to his holding—my holding," she said. "They're going forward. You're not."

His face froze. "Goodbye, Elise," he said again, and left the tavern. At the edge of the village, he looked back over his shoulder. She was not standing in the doorway, watching him go. He hadn't really expected she would be.

"Captain, why in the five hells aren't you getting drunk?" Van demanded. "Something horrible like that happened to me, I wouldn't be able to turn both eyes in the same direction for the next three, four days."

"When I first set eyes on her, I thought that was just what I was going to do," the Fox answered. "But do you know what? It's been so long, she's not important enough to me for me to want to do that."

Van's eyes got wide. "That may be the saddest thing anybody ever said."

Gerin thought about it. "I don't know. *Not* getting over her in all this time would be worse, don't you think?"

"She's . . . not much like Mother, is she?" Dagref spoke very slowly, picking his words with obvious care. He didn't want to offend the Fox, who had, after all, fathered his half-brother on Elise, but he also didn't want to speak well of her. He balanced the one and the other better than most youths his age could have done.

Gerin considered the question as carefully as Dagref had asked it. "Some ways yes, some ways no," he replied at last. "She's a very bright woman, the same as your mother is. But I don't think Elise is ever happy with what she has. If it's not perfect, it's not good enough for her."

"That's foolish," Dagref said.

Van guffawed. "This from the lad who, if you tell a dirty story twice and say the whore was awkward the first time and then that she was clumsy the next, will call you on the difference then and there."

Dagref had the grace to blush, or perhaps the embers got a little more ruddy. He said, "Actually, I think you called her stumblefooted the first time I heard that story, didn't you?"

"Stumblefooted? I never—" Van broke off and glared at Dagref. "You're having me on. Do you know what I do to people who try having me on?"

"Something dreadful and appalling, or you wouldn't be telling me about it," Dagref returned, unabashed.

"What *are* we going to do about him, Fox?" Van said.

"To the five hells with me if I know," Gerin answered. "The way I look at it, it's the world's lookout as much as Dagref's."

"The way I look at it, you're right," Van said.

Dagref didn't rise to that, as he might have a couple of years before. Nor did he let himself be diverted, asking, "If she's different from my mother, why did you marry her?"

"It seemed like a good idea at the time," the Fox replied. Dagref folded his arms across his chest, not about to let an answer like that be fobbed off on him. It was a pose Gerin had assumed many times with larcenous peasants, stubborn nobles, and his own children. Having it aimed at him made him chuckle in spite of everything. He said, "You can't always know ahead of time how you'll get along with somebody. You can't always know ahead of time *if* you'll get along with somebody."

"That's so," Van agreed. "Take a look at Fand and me."

"Oh, nonsense," Gerin said, glad to be talking about someone else's marriage instead of his own. "You knew perfectly well that you and Fand didn't get along."

"Aye, true enough." The outlander's grin was on the sheepish side. "But we make a sport of fighting, if you know what I mean. Most of the time, we make a sport of fighting, I should say. Some of it, now, some of it turns real."

"I don't understand." Dagref turned to Gerin. "Why would you want to fight with someone you love, someone you're living with?"

"Why are you asking me?" the Fox said. "I don't want to do that. He does." He pointed at Van. "It's the first time I've ever heard him say so out loud, though."

"To the crows with you." Van spoke without much rancor. "You want so much peace and quiet, Fox, you want life to be dull all the bloody time."

"No." Gerin shook his head; this was an old argument, and one in which he could take part without bruising. "I just don't want life to blow up in my face, the way a pot of bean stew will if you leave it in the fire with the lid on too tight for too long."

"Sometimes life does blow up in your face, though," Dagref said, a truth as self-evident as any at the moment. "What are you going to do about . . . this woman?" Again, he took a little thought to find the phrase he wanted.

"Nothing," Gerin replied, which made both Dagref and Van stare at him. He went on, "I won't send her up to Duren without finding out whether he wants to have anything to do with her. I offered to bring her along with the army so she'd find out as soon as I did whether he wants her to come up to his holding, but she said no to that."

Van coughed. "If she hangs around here, she won't know for a goodish while what Duren has to say, because the imperials aren't going to stop following us. They'll be here day after tomorrow at the latest."

"I don't think that was the biggest worry in her mind," Gerin answered. "She has relatives south of the High Kirs. You've met one of them—remember?"

"Aye, now that you remind me of it. Some sort of fancy noble, gave the Emperor advice." Van frowned in concentration. "Valdabrun—that's what his name was. He had a mistress I wouldn't have minded tasting at all."

"That's the name," Gerin agreed. "Now me, I'd forgotten about his leman till you called her to my mind."

"You were too busy staring at Elise to have much room left in your mind for other women," the outlander said. Gerin would have got angry at him had he not been telling the truth.

Dagref said, "If her family were advisors to the old Emperor, what does this new Emperor think of them?"

"I don't know," Gerin answered. "That also crossed my mind. I don't think it crossed Elise's, and by then I wasn't going to bring it up. If she goes south of the High Kirs, she's gone, that's all. I won't miss her, not a bit." And that was true, or almost true. He'd missed her more than he'd imagined possible, back in the days just after she first left him. Occasional echoes of that feeling had kept cropping up through the years, even after he'd been happily yoked to Selatre for a long time.

Was one of those echoes cropping up now? If it was, he didn't intend to admit it, even to himself. He waited for Van or Dagref to challenge him. Van, after all, had known Elise, while Dagref had few compunctions about asking questions, no matter how personal.

But neither of them said anything. He realized neither of them was going to say anything. A small sigh of relief escaped him. They'd let him off the hook.

❖   ❖   ❖

Ferdulf flying above them, Gerin's men rolled north through the village the next morning. The Fox wondered if Elise would come out and watch them go, as some of the villagers did. He didn't see her. Once he'd passed through, he decided that was just as well.

Now, instead of screening the army's advance, Rihwin's riders covered the retreat. They did a better job of that than Gerin had thought when he gave them the duty. Rihwin came trotting up to him to report: "The imperials keep dogging us, aye, lord king, but not very hard. We've taught them respect, I think, for they are never sure if we might gallop out at them from some unexpected direction."

"That's good," Gerin said. "If we'd taught them so much respect that they stopped dogging us altogether, that would be even better."

"It would also be too much to ask for," Rihwin pointed out.

"Oh, I wasn't asking for it," Gerin said. "If I did, no one would pay me any attention. But it *would* be better."

"Er—yes," Rihwin said, and soon found an excuse to rejoin his riders.

Van chuckled. "That was well done, Captain. Not easy to confuse Rihwin—not least, I expect, on account of he's so often confused on his own—but you managed." The outlander lost his smile. "Have to tell you, though, I'm a bit on the confused side myself. What are we doing now, and why are we doing that instead of something else?"

"What are we doing?" the Fox repeated. "We're falling back—that's what. Why are we doing it? I can think of three reasons offhand." He ticked them off on his fingers: "If we don't fall back the imperials will smash us here. That's one. If we do fall back, maybe the imperials will string themselves out or give us some chance to hit part of them from ambush. That's two. And, as we're falling back, we're falling back into country that hasn't been foraged too heavily, so we won't starve, which we would, and pretty bloody quick, if we stay where we are. Three."

"Aye, well, there is that." Van looked around. "Falling back toward land Aragis rules, if we're not on that land already. Don't know how happy he'll be if we take everything that isn't tied down and cut the lashings off what is tied down so we can take that, too."

Gerin looked around. "To the five hells with me if I know where Aragis' southern border is. Maybe we'll find boundary stones, maybe we won't. To the five hells with me if I care, either. If Aragis thinks I'm going to starve to death to keep from bothering his serfs' precious crops, to the five hells with him, too."

Over his shoulder, Dagref said, "If the threat lay by the Niffet, he'd eat you out of house and home without a second thought."

"Well, the gods know that's true," Gerin said. Now he looked straight ahead, north and a little east, a thoughtful expression on his face. "Ikos is just on the other side of Aragis' holdings, too. I've never had cause to go to the Sibyl by the southern route, but maybe I will." He nodded, more decisively than he'd thought he would. "Yes, indeed. Maybe I will."

Dagref said, "In the learned genealogies, they say Biton is a son of Dyaus Allfather, but—"

Gerin held up his hand. "But that's Elabonians writing for Elabonians below the High Kirs," he finished. "Biton is truly a god of this land here, and everyone who lives in the northlands knows it."

"Even so," Dagref said. "Compared to the gods of the Gradi, Baivers, god of brewing and barley, is a god of this land, even though we Elabonians brought him here a couple of hundred years ago when we conquered this province. Because he is a god of this land, you were able to use him against the gods of the Gradi. From that, it would follow logically—"

"—that I might use Biton against the Elabonian Empire." Gerin interrupted once more. "Yes."

"I thought you might not have seen it," Dagref said, a little sulkily.

"Well, I did." Gerin clapped his son on the back. "Don't let it worry you. The two of us think a lot alike—"

"You're both sneaky," Van put in.

"Thank you," Gerin and Dagref said in the same breath, which made the outlander stare from one of them to the other. Gerin continued, "As I was saying before we were disturbed by a breath of wind there—"

"Honh!" Van said.

"—the two of us think a lot alike, but I've been doing it longer, so it's likely I'll come up with a lot of the same notions you do," Gerin went on imperturbably. "That shouldn't disappoint you, and it shouldn't stop you from telling me what's on your beady little mind—"

"Honh!" Now Dagref interrupted, doing a surprisingly good impression of Van.

Gerin talked through him as he'd talked through the outlander: "—because you never can tell, you might come up with something I've missed." He took a deep breath, triumphant at finally managing to complete his thought.

"Fair enough, Father." Dagref heaved his shoulders up and down in a sigh. "Hard sometimes, being a smaller, less detailed copy of the man you've already become. It makes me feel rather like an abridged manuscript."

"No, not an abridged one," Gerin said. "You just have a lot more blank parchment left at the end of your scroll than I do, that's all."

"Hmm." Dagref contemplated that. "Well, all right—

maybe so." He flicked the reins and urged the horses up to a better pace.

"By the things you've said, Fox, I know what the difference between you and him is," Van remarked.

"Tell me," Gerin urged. Dagref's back expressed mute interest.

"I will," Van said. "The difference is, Fox, that your father had no more idea what to do with you than a crow would with a chick that came out of the egg with white feathers instead of black. Is that so, or am I lying?"

"It's so, sure enough," Gerin agreed. "My brother was a warrior born, everything my father could have wanted. My father hadn't the slightest notion what to make of me. I might be the first real live scholar spawned in the northlands in better than a hundred years."

"And yet you're a king, while your father died a baron, so you never can tell," Van said. "But my point is, Dagref's the second real live scholar spawned in the northlands. You have a notion of what you've got there, while your father had never a clue with you."

"Ah," Gerin said. "Well, there's some truth in that, sure enough. How about it, Dagref? Do you like it better that I can guess along with you some of the time, or would you rather I had never a clue?"

Dagref looked back over his shoulder at the Fox again. "I can guess along with you some of the time, Father. What in the world makes you think you can guess along with me?" Van guffawed. Gerin felt his ears heat.

Riders and charioteers fanned out through the countryside around the village by which Gerin had chosen to camp for the night. They brought back cattle and sheep and ducks and chickens. "Had to let the air out of a shepherd before he'd cough up his beasts," one rider said, patting his bow so as to leave no possible doubt about what he meant.

Under other circumstances, Gerin would have been angry at him for alienating the peasantry. As things were, the Fox hardly noticed the comment. He had his sword in his left hand, and was wondering if he'd have to start carving chunks off the village headman, who was doing his best to act like an idiot from birth.

"No," the fellow said, "we don't have no grain stored in pits. We don't have no beans in pits, neither."

"That's very interesting," Gerin said, "very interesting indeed. I suppose you get through every winter by not eating during most of it."

"Seems that way, a lot of the time," the headman answered sullenly.

"Well, all right." Gerin's voice was light and blithe. "I suppose we'll just have to burn this place down so all these houses here don't get in our way while we're searching."

The headman sent him a look full of loathing and led him over to the storage pits, which had been concealed by grass growing over them. "I thought you had a name for being soft alongside Aragis," the peasant grumbled.

"Only goes to show you can't always trust what you hear, doesn't it?" the Fox returned with a smile. The village headman's glare held even more hate than it had before. Having got what he wanted, Gerin generously affected not to notice. Keeping his army fed was at the moment more important than keeping Aragis' peasants happy.

That was his opinion, at any rate. He discovered the next day that Aragis had a different one. A chariot bearing the Archer's son, Aranast, came jouncing over a side road toward Gerin's army. When Aranast had made his way up alongside the Fox, he spoke without preamble:

"Lord king, my father forbids you from foraging on the countryside while in lands whose overlord he is."

"Does he?" Gerin answered. "That's nice."

Aranast took off his bronze, potlike helm and scratched his head. "Does that mean you will obey this prohibition?"

"Of course not," Gerin replied. "If he can teach me how to subsist on no food while I cross his lands, I might try it. Otherwise, though, I'll do what I have to do to get through them."

"You dare go against my father's stated will?" Aranast's eyes went round and wide and staring. No one in Aragis' lands had dared go against his stated will for many years. Though Aranast gave signs of being a fairly formidable fellow in his own right, he seemed astonished anyone might imagine going against his father's stated will.

"I just said so. Weren't you listening?" Gerin asked politely. "He's not my suzerain, so I'm under no obligation to obey him, and he's told me to do something impossible, which means I'd be an idiot to obey him. Do I look like an idiot to you, young fellow?"

Aranast didn't answer that, which might have been just as well. His frown did its best to be severe to the point of threatening. People were no doubt much more in the habit of calling him things like *prince* and *heir* and maybe *your highness* than *young fellow*. Taking a deep breath, he said, "My father entered into alliance with you in good faith. He did not enter into it to give you leave to plunder his holdings."

"Oh, don't be a pompous twit," Gerin said, which flicked Aranast on his vanity much harder than *young fellow* had done. The Fox went on, "I told you once, I don't aim to let myself starve. If I were plundering, though, I'd have booty with me, wouldn't I? I'm feeding myself and I'm feeding my men. Would you like some roast mutton?"

"Generous of you to offer me what already belongs to my father," Aranast remarked. Dagref was much younger, but would have done the sarcasm better than Aranast even so. Still, the effort was there.

Gerin rewarded it with sarcasm of his own: "Glad you think so." That drew another glare from Aragis' son. "Where is your father, anyhow?" the Fox asked.

"West of here," Aranast answered. "The imperials still press him hard. Some of them are between him and you. I had to thread my way past them to deliver his word to you, and to have you set it aside as being of no account."

"It was a foolish word to deliver, and you can tell him I said so. He might be better off if more people let him know when he was being foolish," Gerin said. "But he sees no hope of linking with me again?"

"He does not, being too sore beset," Aranast answered. "He hoped you might rejoin him, and also expressed the hope that you would use your skill at magic to good effect in the struggle against the Empire."

"I'll do everything I can," Gerin said with a sigh. Aragis persisted in believing he could do things he couldn't. He held up a forefinger. "Has Aragis also forbidden the imperials from plundering his holdings?"

Aranast shook his head. "No, for he did not think it would do any good. You, however, are not his enemy, unless you choose to make yourself so."

"Or unless he makes me one by insisting I do things I can't," Gerin said. "A man who asks too much of his friends starts finding out he doesn't have so many friends as he thought he did."

"I will take your words back to my father, that he may judge them for himself," Aranast said stiffly.

"Fine," the Fox told him. "Tell him this, too: if he wants to fight a war against me after we beat the Empire,

I'll be ready, the same as I was ready to fight a war against him before I knew the imperials were on this side of the High Kirs."

He kept astonishing Aranast. "You challenge my father?" Aragis' son said. "No one challenges my father."

"I've done it for more than twenty years, as he's challenged me all that time," Gerin answered. "Tell him I'm doing what I have to do here, no more—and no less."

Still scowling, still muttering to himself, Aranast Aragis' son got back into his chariot and rattled off toward the west, toward whatever was left of Aragis' army. "Well, he doesn't lack for nerve, that's certain," Van said, eyeing the dust the horses' hooves and the chariot's wheels kicked up from the track along which it traveled.

"Who doesn't?" Gerin asked. "Aragis or Aranast?"

"Both of 'em, now that I think on it," the outlander replied. Gerin watched that receding plume of dust, too. After a moment, he nodded.

Getting livestock and grain from the peasants who lived under Aragis' rule turned out to be, for the most part, easier than Gerin had expected. The majority of village headmen had lived so long under the Archer, they seemed to have forgotten the possibility of cheating an overlord. "Take what you will, lord," one of them told Gerin. "Whatever you take, you'd do worse to us if we tried to hide it from you." The men and women who came up to listen to him talking with the Fox nodded. Aragis, evidently, had given lessons of that sort.

A few villages, though, appeared to have no substance whatsoever: only huts and whatever was ripening in the fields. Gerin's men found no livestock even on searching the nearby woods, and the headmen at such places staunchly denied having grain pits anywhere by their huts.

"Do what you want with me," one said. "I can't give you what I haven't got."

"You should be careful saying things like that," Gerin told him. "If you said them to Aragis or his men, they'd do it."

The headman pulled off his tunic and stood there in his wool trousers. He turned his back on the Fox. Long, pale ridged scars crisscrossed it. "Laid the whip on himself, he did," he said with something that sounded almost like pride. "He didn't come away with anything here, either, on account of there isn't anything to come away with."

After seeing those scars, Gerin gave up and went on to the next village, whose headman proved more tractable. The Fox remained unconvinced the serfs he'd just left had as little as they'd shown, but lacked both time and inclination to check as hard as he might have otherwise. He also knew a certain amount of admiration for their headman. Anyone who could stand up to Aragis had more than the common amount of nerve.

Every so often, the imperials hounding the Fox's force would press forward. A couple of the skirmishes were sharp, but the men from south of the High Kirs made no effort to get close to his army, stay close to it, and hound it to death, which was what he would have done to theirs had it not been reinforced. He wondered how Aragis fared, with more imperials after him. The Archer had sent no more messengers to him after Aranast's unsuccessful mission.

Keeps dotted the landscape, as they did throughout the northlands. Most of the nobles who dwelt in them had gone to fight under Aragis. These days, the castles housed striplings, graybeards, and noblewomen who were often more determined than the menfolk left behind. Some of the keeps opened their gates to share what they had and let Gerin and some of his officers sleep in real beds. Some—very often, those where petty barons' wives seemed to be in charge—stayed shut up tight against his force, as if against enemies.

"If you're friends, you won't be offended that we don't let you in, because you'll understand why we don't," one of those women called from the walkway around the wall of the keep she was running. "And if you're foes masquerading as friends—well, to the five hells with you, in that case."

Gerin didn't push her any further. For one thing, he would have had to lay siege to the keep to get inside if she wouldn't let down the drawbridge. For another, what she said made perfectly good sense from her point of view.

Van thought so, too, saying, "By the gods, if Fand were running a keep, that's the sort of defiance she would shout."

"You're likely right." Gerin raised an eyebrow. "Maybe Maeva gets it from both sides of the family."

"Aye, maybe she—" Van broke off three words too late, and gave the Fox a dirty look. "And maybe you talk out of both sides of your mouth."

"Maybe I do, when there's a need, but not this time," Gerin said. "I've said the same thing all along here."

Van rumbled something, down deep in his chest. Maybe it was just a discontented noise; maybe it was an oath in one of the many languages he'd picked up in his travels. Whatever it was, he changed the subject: "What's the road up to Ikos from the south like?"

"I've never taken it myself, so I can't tell you for certain," Gerin answered. "I hear, though, that it's easier than jogging west off the Elabon Way because it doesn't go through that haunted forest in the hill country there."

"I won't miss that forest a bit, thank you very much,"

Van said with a shudder. "There's things in there that don't think men have any business going through on the roads. The gods help you if you wander off under the trees, or if you're stupid enough to try spending the night there."

"You're right," the Fox said. "I wouldn't want to do either of those things."

"Sounds like an interesting place," said Dagref, who'd never been through the forest.

Van laughed. So did Gerin, as much in awe as in mirth. "A lot of places sound interesting, when you hear people talking about them at a nice, safe distance," he observed. "Visiting them, you'll find, is a lot less interesting than hearing people talk about them at a nice, safe distance."

"You've been into the forest," Dagref said. "You've been in it a good many times, and you must have always come out the other side, or else you wouldn't be here at a nice, safe distance talking about it."

"Logic," Gerin agreed gravely. "But doing it once, or even doing it a few times, doesn't mean I'm anxious to do it again. Unlike some people I could name, I've never been wild for adventure for adventure's sake. One of the things that make adventure adventure is that somebody or something is trying to kill you, and I'm usually against that."

"Oh, I'm against anybody or anything trying to kill me, too," Van said. "Best way to stop it, I've always thought, is to kill whoever or whatever it is first."

Gerin shook his head. "The *best* way to stop it is not to put yourself in a place where anybody or anything can try to kill you in the first place."

"A long life and a boring one," Van said with a sneer.

"This argument strikes me as being moot, seeing that we have an imperial army on our tail and another on our left that's dogging Aragis—that we hope is dogging Aragis," Dagref said.

"A long, boring life," Van repeated. "Nothing to do but futter women and sit around drinking ale." He paused, as if listening to what he'd just said. Then he stuck an elbow in Gerin's ribs, almost hard enough to pitch him out of the chariot. "Well, it could be worse."

Aragis' holdings ran up close to the southern end of the valley in which lay the village of Ikos and Biton's shrine. Not even Aragis had been so arrogant as to claim that valley as his own.

Guardsmen from the temple patrolled the road that led up into Ikos. They did not bother on the road that ran west off the Elabon Way; the strange trees and stranger beasts of the forest through which that road ran guaranteed its safety better than men with bronze weapons and armor of leather and bronze could hope to do. Here, though, on an open dirt track, they were needed.

One of them recognized Gerin. "Lord king!" he exclaimed in no small surprise. "Why do you come to Ikos by this route?" After a moment, he phrased that differently: "*How* do you come to Ikos by this route?"

"Having an army from south of the High Kirs on my trail might have something to do with it," the Fox answered, at which the temple guards exclaimed in dismay. Biton might have—surely would have—seen that, but he hadn't told them anything about it. Gerin went on, "Aragis and I made alliance, as you may have heard, which is what I was doing down in the direction of the mountains in the first place."

"We had heard you had he had made common cause, aye, but rumors of the foe have been many and various," the soldier answered.

"It's the Empire. Even though we'd forgotten about it up here, it never forgot about us, worse luck," Gerin said. "The imperials have beaten Aragis, too, and they're chasing him somewhere off to the west of here. How do you suppose the farseeing god would feel about being shoved back into a pantheon headed up in the City of Elabon?"

"If the Empire tries such a thing, there will be trouble," the guardsman said positively. He himself looked to be an Elabonian in blood, but several of the soldiers with him were plainly of the folk who had lived in the northlands before the Elabonian Empire first came over the High Kirs a couple of centuries before. They were slimmer than Elabonians, with wide cheekbones and delicate, pointed chins. Selatre, who had formerly been Biton's Sibyl at Ikos, had that look to her.

One of those men asked, "And why do you come to Ikos now, lord king?" His Elabonian was fluent enough, but had a half-lisping, half-hissing accent to it: traces of the language the folk of the old blood still sometimes spoke among themselves.

"Partly because I'm in retreat," Gerin admitted, "but also partly because I would hear what the farseeing god has to say about this—if lord Biton has anything to say about it."

The guardsman who had spoken first said, "You cannot bring your whole host into the valley to camp. It may be that they shall be permitted to traverse the valley, but they may not encamp in it."

"Why not?" Gerin asked. "Biton protects his own shrine. Even if we wanted to plunder, we wouldn't dare."

"But Biton's protection reaches less certainly to the villages around the sacred precinct," the temple guard replied. "We would not have them plundered. Surely, with your numbers, you can overcome us here, but what sort of welcome will you have from the god if you do?"

"A point," Gerin said. "A distinct point. Very well. It shall be as you say. I'd sooner have my men foraging off Aragis' lands than those here in the valley, anyhow."

"So, lord king, would we," the guardsman said. "You being allied to him, I hope you will forgive my saying so, but Aragis the Archer has not always made the most comfortable of neighbors."

"He hasn't always made the most comfortable of neighbors for me, either," the Fox answered, "and he has fewer reasons to keep from stepping on my toes than to keep from stepping on Biton's. Or rather, Biton can do a better job of stepping on Aragis' toes than I can."

"If he's not gone to war with you in all these years, lord king, he thinks you can do something along those lines," the guard said.

"You flatter me outrageously," Gerin said. He enjoyed flattery. There was, he told himself, nothing wrong with enjoying it. The trick was not to take it too seriously. When you started believing everything people told you about how clever you were, you proved you weren't so clever as they said.

He gave his army their orders. The men seemed content enough to rest where they were. "If the imperials try to bring us to battle, lord king, we'll make 'em sorry they were ever born," one of them said, which raised a cheer from the rest. Since the bulk of the force from south of the High Kirs was chasing Aragis, the Fox thought his men did have a decent chance of doing just that.

When he started forward, up into Biton's valley, Adiatunnus surprised him by coming ahead, too. "By your leave, lord king, I'm fain to be after seeing the Sybil myself," the Trokmê chieftain said. "The oracle here was a famous one, you'll know, even back in the days when I and all my people dwelt north of the Niffet."

"Yes, I did know that." Gerin nodded.

"But there's summat else you might not ha' known," Adiatunnus said. "Back before Balamung the wizard, the one you slew, now, back before he led us south over the river, some of our chieftains came down to Ikos to hear whether 'twould be wise to go with that uncanny kern. But they were never heard of again that I recall, puir wights."

"As a matter of fact, I knew that, too," the Fox answered. "They tried to kill me here. Van and I—and Elise, too—killed all of them but one. He decided moving against me wouldn't be a good notion, but Balamung caught him and burned him in a wicker cage."

"Ah, I mind me I heard summat o' that, now that you speak of it," Adiatunnus said. "But you'll not mind if I come with you the now?"

"Not unless you plan on trying to murder me inside the temple, the way those other Trokmoi did," Gerin replied.

"Nay, though I thank you for the offer," Adiatunnus said, which made Gerin snort. Adiatunnus went on, "I've had my chances, that I have, and the putting of you in the ground for good and all, I've found, is more trouble nor it's turned out to be worth."

"For your sweet and generous praises, far beyond my deserts, I thank you most humbly," the Fox said, and Adiatunnus snorted in turn. With a sigh, Gerin turned to Rihwin. "If the imperials do pitch into us, you're in command till I can get back. Send word to me straightaway, and try not to wreck the army till I can come and join the celebration."

Rihwin gave him a sour look. "For *your* sweet and generous praises, lord king, I thank you." Gerin chuckled and dipped his head, conceding the round to his fellow Fox.

When Dagref drove the chariot up toward the temple to Biton, Adiatunnus followed close in his own car. Above them floated Ferdulf. The temple guardsmen stared up at him with interest and curiosity. So did Gerin. He said, "Are you sure you want to visit the Sibyl and the farseeing god? Biton and your father don't get on well." That would do for an understatement till a better one came along, which he didn't think would happen soon.

Ferdulf turned a fine semidivine sneer his way. "Why should I care what my father thinks or does?" he returned. "Since he has no room in his life for *me*, do his views on others—even other gods—matter?"

"I told him he shouldn't have got into the wine," Gerin murmured to Van.

The outlander rolled his eyes. "A man's own children don't listen to him. Why should anyone else's children?"

"Whose son is that?" one of the guardsmen asked, pointing up to Ferdulf.

"Mavrix's," Gerin answered. "The Sithonian wine god got him on one of my peasant women."

"Is it so?" The warrior's eyes widened. "But Mavrix and the lord Biton worked together in driving the monsters off the surface of the earth and back into the caverns under Biton's shrine."

"So they did," Gerin agreed. "And it was the most quarrelsome cooperation you've ever seen in all your born days."

They drove past several neat little villages and the fields surrounding them. The peasants in the valley of Ikos were all freeholders, owing allegiance to no overlord save Biton. That arrangement had always smacked of anarchy to the Fox, but he, like Aragis, fought shy of trying to annex the valley. If Biton tolerated freeholders here, Gerin would, too.

Ferdulf flew down and hovered alongside Gerin like a large, bad-tempered mosquito. In confidential tones, he asked, "Do you think the farseeing god will be able to tell me how to take vengeance on my father?"

"I have no way of knowing that," Gerin said. "If I were you, though, Ferdulf, I wouldn't get my hopes too high."

"He's all god," Ferdulf muttered. "It's not fair."

"No, it probably isn't," Gerin admitted, "but I don't know what you can do about it, either."

White against greenery, the marble walls of Biton's shrine gleamed ahead. The earthquake that had released the monsters had also overthrown it, but Biton's own power restored it at the same time as Biton and Mavrix recontained the monsters.

"Isn't that pretty?" Adiatunnus said, and then, in speculative tones, "Doesn't look so strong as the wall of a proper keep, though. And I've heard the god keeps all manner of pretties inside, though."

"So he does," Gerin said, "and it's worth your life to try to steal any of them. Biton has a special plague he uses to smite people who walk off with what's his. I've seen one or two he's killed with it. It's not a pretty way to go."

Adiatunnus looked thoughtful, but no less acquisitive, as they drew near the temple compound. Back in the days when he was newly over the Niffet, he likely would have assumed Gerin was lying and tried to steal. He would have paid for it then. He would pay for it now if he tried it, too. Gerin didn't think he would be so foolish.

Outside the gates, attendants took charge of the two chariots. No others waited there. The shrine did not draw the crowds it had before the earthquake, let alone before the days when folk came from all over the

Elabonian Empire, and even from beyond its borders, to gain the Sibyl's oracular responses.

A plump priest with a eunuch's smooth face led the travelers into the temple compound. Ferdulf had been drifting along a couple of feet off the ground. As soon as he passed through the entranceway, he descended to the earth with a thump that staggered him. He glared toward the temple ahead. "He's a full god, too," he growled resentfully, "so I have to do what he wants. Not what I want. Still not fair."

Adiatunnus and the couple of Trokmoi with him paid no attention. They were gaping at the treasures on display in the courtyard, chiefest among them the statues of the Elabonian Emperors Ros the Fierce, who had conquered the northlands for the Empire, and of his son, Oren the Builder, who had erected the temple now standing above the entrance to the Sibyl's cavern. Both statues were larger than life, both starkly realistic, and both made of ivory and gold.

Gerin's voice was dry as he gave Adiatunnus good advice: "Pull your tongue back in, there, and stop drooling on the grass."

"Och, 'tis no easy thing you ask of me, Fox darling," the Trokmê chieftain said with a sigh. His eyes flicked from the statues to stacked ingots to great bronze bowls supported on golden tripods. "I'd heard of these riches, but the difference between the hearing of them and the seeing of them with the eyes of a man himself, it's the difference 'twixt hearing of a pretty woman and lying with her. And these won't be all the gauds, either, I'm thinking."

"You're right about that, too," Gerin said. "There's plenty more in the caverns off the route to the Sibyl's throne." Adiatunnus sighed again, as at the thought of the pretty woman he would never meet.

He glowered at the frieze on the entablature above the colonnaded entrance to the temple itself. It showed Ros the Fierce driving back Trokmoi with Biton's aid. Adiatunnus did not approve of anything depicting Elabonians beating Trokmoi. Gerin didn't suppose he could blame his vassal for that.

They went into the temple. Adiatunnus and the two woodsrunners with him exclaimed again, this time at the rich marbles of the columns, the fancy woods that had gone into the pews, and the gold and silver candelabra throwing sheets of light over them.

Ferdulf exclaimed, too, but he was pointing at the cult statue of Biton that stood near the opening into the caverns below the shrine. The statue was not an anthropomorphic representation of the farseeing god, as were the rest of the images in the compound. Instead, it was a column of black basalt utterly plain except for scratches that might have been eyes and a jutting phallus. "How old is it?" Ferdulf whispered; in this place, even he showed a certain amount of respect for the god who ruled here.

"I wouldn't even try to guess," Gerin answered. "It's been a shrine for a long, long time, even if it didn't used to be as pretty as we Elabonians made it after we came up here."

"Not *we* Elabonians," Ferdulf said testily. "I am no Elabonian, for which I thank all the gods, Biton very much included."

Gerin made his voice sweet as clover honey: "On your mother's side, you are." He cherished the horrible look the demigod gave him. Perhaps he shouldn't have yielded to the temptation; reminding Ferdulf of his background was liable to make him less willing to oppose the Elabonian Empire. Turning aside every temptation, though, made life too dull to stand.

The priest waved the suppliants to the pews. "Pray to the lord Biton," he urged. "Pray that your question will be phrased in such a way as to make his answer, which shall be true, also meaningfully true for you."

That, Gerin thought, was good advice. The Sibyl's oracular responses were often obscure, clearer after the event than beforehand. He tried to clear his mind of all his worries so he could ask a question that would have as unambiguous an answer as possible.

Just for a moment, he looked up at the cult statue. He'd done that on other visits to Biton's shrine. Those crudely carved eyes would seem to come alive for a heartbeat, to look back into his. He wondered if that would happen again. It did—and then some. For an instant, no more, he saw the god as he had seen him in the little shack back at Fox Keep where he undertook his sorceries. Biton might have been a handsome man, but for the eye in the back of his head that showed when he twisted his neck preternaturally far. And then he was gone, back into the basalt.

"That statue—that *is* the god," Ferdulf whispered—had he seen the apparition, too? "That's not his image—that *is* the god. It's how he looks when he isn't thinking about how he looks, and when people aren't thinking about how he looks."

"Maybe it is," Gerin said. Philosophers had always wondered whether gods were as they were because people conceived of them as being that way, or if people conceived of gods as they did because the gods essentially were like that. The Fox suspected such arguments would go on forever.

"Have you composed your mind?" the eunuch priest asked. Gerin nodded. The priest smiled. "Then come with me. We shall go down below the ground, down to the cave of the Sibyl, where Biton shall speak through her."

He tried to make it sound mysterious and exotic. It *was* mysterious and exotic, but Gerin had gone many times into the cavern below the temple to see the Sibyl— and for other, darker, purposes. He climbed to his feet, saying, "Let's get on with it." The plump eunuch in his fancy robes looked disappointed that the Fox and his comrades were not trembling with awe, but took a torch and led them all to the mouth of the cave.

Elabonian workmen had put steps down from the cave mouth after a prominent visitor years before tripped, fell, and broke his ankle. Soon, though, Gerin's feet trod the natural stone of the cavern. Generations of suppliants seeking guidance from the Sibyl had worn a path in the rock, but it was a path more visible in torchlight than smooth beneath the feet.

Every so often, torches flaming in sconces added their light to that of the burning brand the priest carried. A cool breeze made the flames flicker. "Isn't that strange, now?" Adiatunnus murmured. "I always thought the air inside a cave would be still and dead as a corp."

"It is the power of the god," the priest said.

"Or else it's something natural that we don't understand," Gerin put in. The priest glared at him, eyeballs glittering in the torchlight. Gerin looked back steadily. Biton didn't seem inclined to smite him for blasphemy. With a disappointed sniff, the priest resumed the journey down to the Sibyl's cave.

Other paths led off that one; other caverns opened onto it. Biton's priesthood used some of them to store treasures. The Trokmoi exclaimed at the gleaming precious metals the torches briefly revealed. Of course, they also exclaimed at the beautiful but largely worthless bits of shining rock crystal set here and there in the walls of the cavern.

And some entrances to Sibyl's underground chamber

were bricked up and sealed not only with masonry but also with potent magical charms. Some of the bricks, baked with round tops like loaves of bread, were almost immeasurably ancient.

Ferdulf shivered as he came to one such wall. "Monsters dwell behind these bricks," he murmured.

"That's so," Gerin agreed: "monsters like Geroge and Tharma. They have an understanding of sorts with us now, which is why some of these charms have been set aside here. They could come forth, but they don't: their gods are in our debt for launching them against the gods of the Gradi."

"A mad venture," the priest said. Adiatunnus nodded; the torchlight made the shadow of his bobbing head dip and swirl. Since Gerin was inclined to agree with them, he didn't argue.

Before he was quite ready, they came to the Sibyl's cave. Biton's priestess sat on a throne that looked as if it had been carved from a single black pearl, which glowed nacreously when light fell on it. She herself wore a plain tunic of undyed linen. The eunuch priest went up to her, set a hand on her shoulder, and murmured something too low for Gerin to catch. Had the fellow been a whole man, he would not have been permitted to touch her; not only did Sibyls remain lifelong maidens, they were not allowed even to touch true men.

The Sibyl looked something like Selatre—not close enough to be near kin, but plainly of the same blood. She eyed Gerin with curiosity; perhaps the priest had told her who he was—no reason for her to remember his face, with his last visit five years in the past—and reminded her that he was wed to the woman who'd preceded her on the Sibyl's throne. Was she wondering what that would be like?

If she was, she didn't show it. "You have your question?" she asked the Fox.

"I do," he answered. "Here it is: how may the Empire of Elabon be made to give up its claims to the northlands and withdraw its forces south over the High Kirs?" He'd phrased it carefully, not asking what he could do to make that happen. Perhaps it would happen without him. Perhaps it would not happen at all. He forced himself to shove that thought aside.

He had scarcely uttered the last word when the Sibyl stiffened. She thrashed on the throne, limbs splayed awkwardly. Her eyes rolled up in her head till only the whites showed. When she spoke again, it was not in her own voice, but in Biton's, a deep, virile baritone:

> *"The foe is strong, up to no good—*
> *To rout him will take bronze and wood.*
> *You must not find the god you seek:*
> *'Twould make your fate a sour reek.*
> *They snap and float and always trouble,*
> *But without them fortune turns to rubble."*

IX

As soon as Ferdulf left the temple compound, he hopped into the air and let out a luxurious sigh of relief. "My feet were getting tired," he said, and then, to Gerin, "Well, was that obscure enough to suit you?"

"And to spare," the Fox answered. "I've had difficult omens from Biton and the Sibyl before, but never one close to that."

"As best I could see, it was meaningless, not difficult," Dagref said.

"But can you see as far as the farseeing god?" Gerin asked.

Dagref only shrugged. Adiatunnus said, "I'm with the colt, lord king. When you hear summat without plain sense in it, more often the reason is that it's senseless than too clever for words, I'm thinking."

More often than not, Gerin would have made the same argument. Here, he said, "I've seen Biton be right a good many times when everyone would have thought he was wrong. I'm not going to say he's wrong here, not now."

"Why do we hope we don't find a god?" Van demanded. "If we're seeking one, shouldn't we hope we do find him?"

"And which god would you be seeking?" Adiatunnus added. " 'Twouldn't be Biton his own self, or we're ruined or ever we start. But he wouldna say who it was, did you see?"

"Obscure. Ferdulf had the right word for it," Gerin said. "Sooner or later, we *will* have the meaning laid out before us."

"Aye, likely when it's too late to do us any good," Van said.

"That is the way of oracles sometimes," the Fox agreed. "But you never know till you try."

"And now that we have gone and tried and got nothing to speak of for it, what are we to be doing next?" Adiatunnus asked. "Shall we bring our army through the valley of Ikos?—on the promise we willna linger, mind."

"I don't want to do that," Gerin said. "I don't think the god wants us to do that. If it's that or stay out and be destroyed, then I might, but not before. I still have a fighting chance of beating the imperials, and no one who opposes a god straight up will do anything but lose."

"You say that," Dagref said, "you who have probably outdone more gods in more different ways than anyone else alive."

"But never straight up," Gerin said. "The way to deal with gods is to trick them, or else to make them do what you want by showing them it gives them some advantage, too, even if that's just that it lets them score off a rival; or else to use a rival either to beat the god who's angry at you or to distract the other god so he doesn't care about you any more."

"That's what you did with the Gradi gods," Dagref said, and Gerin nodded.

"So it is," he answered. "The brawl I got them into has worked out better—which is to say, it's lasted longer—than I ever dared hope."

"Puts me in mind of something that happened to me

a good many years ago, back in my wandering days," Van said as they waited for the attendants to bring back their chariots.

"Probably something that didn't happen," Ferdulf said, "if it's anything like most of your stories."

Van glared at him. "I ought to pop you like the blown-up pig's bladder you are," he growled.

Ferdulf rose into the air. "I am the son of a god, and you would be wise to remember it, lest we discover who pops whom." He was not much more than half as tall as the outlander, and couldn't possibly have weighed a quarter as much, but that little body held power of a different sort from Van's brute strength.

Glaring still, Van said, "I don't care whose son you are, you bigmouthed little weed—I'd like to see you show that even one of my stories, even one, mind you, has the smallest bit of falsehood in it."

Ferdulf fell a few inches, a sign of dismay or chagrin. "How am I supposed to show that?" he demanded. "I wasn't born yet when you were having these adventures you tell lies about, and I haven't been to the preposterous places where you had them."

"Then why don't you shut up?" Van asked sweetly. "Why don't you shut up before you open your mouth so wide, you fall right in?"

Now Ferdulf glared. Before he could say anything, Adiatunnus said, "I'm fain to hear the outlander's tale. He's never dull, say what else you will of him." His comrades nodded; Van's stories had long been popular along the border.

"Shall I go on, then?" Van asked. When even Ferdulf did not say no, go on he did: "This was out in the Weshapar country, east of Kizzuwatna and north of Mabalal. The Weshapar have the most jealous god in the world. He's so crazy, he won't even let them call him by his name, and he has the nerve to claim he's the only real god in the whole wide world."

"Foosh, what a fool of a god he is," Adiatunnus than. "What does he think of the gods of the folk who are lucky enough not to be after worshiping him?"

"He thinks they aren't real at all—that the people around the Weshapar country are imagining them," Van answered.

"Well! I like that!" Ferdulf said indignantly. "I'd like to fly over his temple and piss on it from on high. Maybe he would think that was his imagination, too. Or else I could—"

"Do you want to say what you would do, or do you want to hear what this god and I did do?" Van gave Mavrix's son a dirty look. The attendants fetched the chariots then; everyone but Ferdulf got into them. He floated along beside the one Dagref drove.

"Oh, go on." Now Ferdulf sounded very much like his father, which is to say, petulant.

"Thank you, most gracious demigod." From living with Gerin, Van had learned to be sardonic when it suited him. It didn't suit him very often, which made him more dangerous when it did. While Ferdulf sputtered and fumed, the outlander went on, "This god of the Weshapar put me in mind of a jealous husband. He was always sneaking around keeping an eye on his people to make sure they didn't worship anyone but him, and—"

"Wait," Dagref said. "If this strange god said none of the other gods around him was real, how could people worship them? They wouldn't be worshiping anything at all. Logic."

"I don't think this god ever heard of logic, and I'm starting to wish I'd never heard of you," Van said. "Between you and Ferdulf, we'll be all the way back with the rest of the army before I'm through. Anyhow,

there I was, on the way through the Weshapar country—
it's hills and rocks and valleys, hot in the summer and
cold as all get-out in the winter—trading this for that,
doing a little fighting on the side to help keep myself
in food and trinkets, when one of the Weshapar chieftains
got on the wrong side of this god."

"How'd he do that?" Gerin asked.

"To the five hells with me if I know," Van answered.
"A god like that, any little thing will do the trick, same
as a jealous husband will think his wife is sleeping with
somebody else if she sets foot outside the front door."
He sighed. Maybe he was thinking of Fand, though he
wasn't a jealous husband of the type he'd described—
and though he gave her plenty of reason for jealousy,
too. Gathering himself, he went on, "Like I say, I don't
know what Zalmunna—this Weshapar chief I was talking
about—did to get his god angry at him, but he did
something, because the god told him he had to cut the
throat of his son to make things right—and to show he
really did reverence that foolish god."

"And did this Zalmunna spalpeen tell him where to
head in?" Adiatunnus asked. "I would ha' done no other
thing but that."

"But you and your people hadn't been worshiping this
god for who knows how many generations," Van said.
"Zalmunna was in a state, I'll tell you. He was in an
even worse state because his son was all ready to let
himself be used like a goat or a hog, too. If the god
wanted him, he was ready for it. Ready?—no, he was
eager as a bridegroom wedding the loveliest wench in
the countryside."

"You would think he would have had better sense,"
Dagref said.

"No, lad—you would think he had better sense,
because you have better sense yourself," Van said. "What

you haven't figured out yet is how many people are fools, one way or another. What you haven't figured out is how many people are fools one way *and* another."

"I wonder why they are," Dagref said, a question aimed not so much at Van as at the world around him.

The world around him did not answer. Van went on, "Like I say, the lad was ready to be offered up like a beast. Most of the Weshapar were ready for him to be offered up, too. They were used to doing what their god told them. He was their god. How could they do anything else? Even Zalmunna was thinking he might have to do it. He didn't want to, you understand, but he didn't see that he had much choice.

"We got to talking the night before he was supposed to go into this overgrown valley where that god had his shrine and kill the boy. He'd got himself drunk, the same way you would have if this was happening to you. He knew what I thought of his god, which was not much, so he came to me instead of to any of the rest of the Weshapar.

"Well, since their god was as jealous as he was, and as stupid as he was . . . like I say, we got to talking. When the time came for him to take his son down into the valley, I went along. His son didn't want me to come. He was fussing and fuming like anything. Sometimes, though you can't pay much attention to what these brats say."

Dagref ignored him. Ferdulf stuck out his tongue at him. Van grinned. "Miserable little excuse for a shrine this god had, too—nothing but a few piled-up stones and a shabby stone table for the throat-cutting business. We got there, and the god's voice came from out of the stones. 'Get on with it,' he said, and he sounded like my old grandfather about two days before he died.

"Zalmunna laid his son down on the stone table. He

took out his knife. Before he used it, though, I hit his
son in the side of the head with a little leather sack full
of sand and pebbles. The lad went out like a torch you'd
stick in a bucket of water. I'd led a sow along, too. I
lifted her up onto the table instead of Zalmunna's son,
and Zalmunna cut her throat."

"What happened next?" Gerin asked. "The god didn't
strike you dead." He took a long, careful look at the
outlander. "At least, I don't think he did."

"Honh!" Van said. "What happened was, that god said,
'There. You see? Next time you'd better pay attention
to me.' He felt Zalmunna's son stop thinking, you
understand, and then there was blood all over the place.
It was just like we'd hoped: he thought Zalmunna really
had killed the boy. I slung Zalmunna's son over my
shoulder and carried him back to the Weshapar village
we'd started out from."

"What happened when he woke up?" Gerin asked.

"To the five hells with me if I know," Van repeated.
"I clouted him a good one; he was still quiet as a sack
of mud when we got back to the village. Zalmunna started
shouting up a storm about what an idiot their god was
and how he'd fooled him and how they should all quit
worshiping him and on and on and on. Me, I thought
that looked like a pretty fair time to find somewhere
else to go, so away I went."

"And what might that ha' been, pray?" Adiatunnus
asked. "Are you after telling us you were fain to keep
clear o' the quarrels 'twixt a god and his folk?"

"Now that you mention it, yes," Van said. "The Fox
will tell you I've done a stupid thing or three in my time,
but he'll also tell you I've never done anything outright
daft in all my born days."

"Oh, I will, will I?" Gerin said. "This, I have to let
you know, is news to me."

"Go howl," Van said. "Anyhow, a couple of days after that, I felt myself a pretty fair earthquake—say, about like the one that turned Ikos topsy-turvy and let the monsters out, though I was right on top of that one and a ways away from the one I'm talking about now. It would have hit hardest in the Weshapar country, unless I miss my guess."

"You think the god caused it?" Dagref said.

"Well, Zalmunna couldn't very well have done it," Van replied, "though he was angry enough to, if only he could. I can't tell you, even now, whether the Weshapar still follow their nasty little jealous god, or whether they've all gone over to the ones their neighbors follow."

"I would that," Adiatunnus said. "If you must be worshiping gods, now, better to follow the bunch that let you have a good time, I'm thinking."

Dagref had another question: "If all these—Weshapar, was it?—did fall away from the jealous god, would he shrivel up and die for lack of worship?"

"It's a good question," Van said, "but I'd be lying if I claimed I knew the answer to it, for I don't. But if it's not what Zalmunna was hoping for, I'd be astonished."

"It's not a good question," Ferdulf growled. "Not even slightly. It's a wicked question, and a wicked idea. Gods are immortal—it's one of the things that make them gods. How can an immortal die?"

Gerin asked a question of his own: "Suppose you're a god, and no one worships you for a thousand years or so—how would you like that? Would you be hungry? If you weren't dead, wouldn't you rather be?"

Ferdulf considered that. "It's not something my father need fear," he said at last. "People will always worship a god who gives them wine, a god who gives them the pleasures that go with fertility, a god who aids them in all manners of creation."

"That's so," Gerin said, understanding from Ferdulf's answer why the little demigod had been so upset. The Fox thought Ferdulf's father would live forever, too; Ferdulf had named good reasons he would stay popular among men. Wistfully, Gerin wished Dagref's father would live forever, too.

"Bronze and wood." Van touched his sword hilt, then set his hand on the chariot rail. "Here we have the one thing and the other. Now we have to go forth and lick the cursed imperials."

"You make it sound so easy," Gerin said, his voice dry.

"It *was* easy," Van said. "Twice in a row, it was easy. Why shouldn't it be once more?"

"You're forgetting something," Gerin replied, even more dryly than before. "The two battles we won, Aragis and I were together, and together we matched the number of imperials we were fighting. They have more men now, and they've split us in two. Attacking when you're outnumbered doesn't strike me as the best idea I've ever heard."

"And have you got a better one?" the outlander asked.

And Gerin didn't. The imperials had not pressed the pursuit so hard as they might have. While he wasn't eager to attack them, they still weren't eager to attack him, either. Those two victories he and Aragis had won over them made them wary even with the advantage of numbers. Even so . . .

"We're going to get hungry pretty soon if we don't do anything but stay where we are," Van said, driving home the point. "It's either knock 'em back and find some new land to forage over or else fall back into the valley of Ikos—and farseeing Biton isn't going to be happy about that."

"I know." Now Gerin's voice was somber. "His guardsmen

couldn't have made that much plainer, could they?" He sighed. "If it's fighting the Elabonian Empire or fighting the farseeing god, there's not much choice, is there?"

Rihwin's riders in the van, the Fox's army moved out the next day. Those of Aragis' vassals who had not gone to war along with their king held their keeps shut tight against Gerin. They were holding their keeps shut against everyone. They no doubt wished Gerin and the imperials would all go away and leave them at peace, or as close to it as they had known while living under Aragis' rule. No matter what they wished, they had not the strength to enforce their wishes.

The Fox's forward move seemed to catch the imperials by surprise. The riders drove back the scouts the forces of the Elabonian Empire had posted to keep an eye on them. They killed a few, too, and captured several more.

Maeva, beaming from ear to ear, brought one of those prisoners back to the Fox—and, not coincidentally, to her father and Dagref. "I caught him myself," she said, pride ringing in her voice.

The prisoner looked indignant, perhaps at being captured by a woman, perhaps at being captured at all. The latter, it proved, for he burst out, "You cursed rebels are a tougher nut to crack than they told us you were going to be when we came over the mountains. They said some of you would want to come back under the City of Elabon, and the rest wouldn't be able to fight."

"People say all sorts of stupid things," Gerin answered. "The trick is knowing whether they're stupid. For instance, I'll know if you lie, because I've already asked these questions to other prisoners. How many men have you got? . . ."

He got the answers he wanted. They largely agreed with the answers he'd had from other imperials his men had captured. The soldiers of the Elabonian Empire outnumbered his own men, but not overwhelmingly. He had some reason to hope he could knock them back on their heels.

"What will you do with me?" the prisoner asked.

"What will you do with me, *lord king*?" Dagref and Maeva spoke together, in the tones they would have used to reprove younger siblings who'd said something stupid. They looked at each other, both seeming surprised and pleased.

"What will you do with me, lord king?" For his part, the prisoner seemed grateful enough to be corrected with words rather than with something hard slammed against the side of his head.

"Take him back that way, Maeva," Gerin said, pointing over his shoulder. "Don't do anything to him as long as he behaves himself. If he doesn't behave himself . . . well, the ghosts will have fresh blood to drink tonight." To the captured imperial, he went on, "I don't quite know what we'll end up doing with you. We may let you farm on a peasant village, but I won't lie to you— you may end up in the mines. It depends on where we can get the most and the most useful work out of you."

"Lord king, if it's use you're after, I know something of smithcraft," the prisoner said.

"If that turns out to be true, you won't go to the mines," Gerin said. "And if it turns out not to be true, you will, for having lied." The imperial didn't quail, from which Gerin concluded he was either telling the truth or had some small practice lying. "Take him away, Maeva."

"I do thank you for getting her out of the brawling for a while," Van said.

"You're welcome, for whatever it may be worth," Gerin answered, his voice mild; he understood what was in the outlander's mind.

Dagref, on the other hand, spoke to Van in the same hectoring tones he'd used on the prisoner Maeva had taken: "You do understand, don't you, that she gets to go out of the brawling now because she was in it before?"

"Oh, aye, I understand that, lad," Van said, manfully resisting the temptation to break Dagref over his knee or offer him some other form of great bodily harm. "Now if you want to ask me whether I like the idea or not, I may just have a different answer for you. Aye, I may."

For a wonder, the brittle edge in his voice got through to Dagref, who suddenly made himself very busy steering the chariot. Gerin caught Van's eye and raised an eyebrow. Van coughed a couple of times. They both laughed.

"Stop talking about me," Dagref said without looking back, which only made his father and Van laugh harder.

More prisoners came back as the Fox's advance drove in the scouts the imperials had set up to keep an eye on him. He was mournfully certain his horsemen and chariots were not capturing all those scouts. He pushed south and west harder, to hit the main imperial army before the foe was ready for him.

Instead of finding the imperial force concentrated to receive his men, he found it scattered in detachments. He hit them one after another, glad of his good fortune. They would skirmish with him and then draw off, retreating toward the west every time. The peasants in the eastern part of Aragis' kingdom did not seem delighted to have him foraging from the countryside rather than the soldiers of the Elabonian Empire.

Some of them, in fact, probably would have preferred to have the imperials remain. Being strangers in the northlands, and unused to some of the ways of the peasants there, the men from south of the High Kirs missed stores that Gerin and his men had no trouble sniffing out. They'd dealt with the local peasants all their lives, and knew their tricks.

Flatbread made from coarse-ground flour baked in the hot ashes of a campfire was not the most appetizing meal, but it kept a man going. Van said, "We may run those buggers right out of here yet. If they keep giving us ground, by the gods, we'll take it."

"So we will," Gerin said, gnawing on flatbread. He kept looking toward the west. His expression was glum.

Van noted that. "You ought to be glad we've broken out of that cramped little stretch of ground where they'd pinned us back. If you are, you've not told your face of it."

"I am glad. We would have got hungry after a bit. But I'm not delighted. You see what they're doing, don't you?"

"Running," Van said with a sniff.

"Running, aye," the Fox said. "But running with a purpose." Van let out an interrogative grunt. Gerin explained: "They're keeping themselves between Aragis and us. They don't want us joining up with him until their other force has hit him hard, unless I miss my guess."

"Ah." Van took a bite of flatbread, too. He chewed on the bread and the idea at the same time. By the look on his face, he didn't much care for the taste of either. He tried to make the best of things: "Well, they'll be the ones with the harder foraging now."

But the Fox shook his head. "I have my doubts about that. If they can bring two armies up over the High Kirs, they'll have a supply train with 'em, too, to keep them fed." He listened to his own words. A smile slowly stole over his face. "And they've gone and let us out."

Van's smile spread till it matched Gerin's. "Wagons and wagons full of good things to eat—that's what you're saying, isn't it, Fox?"

"Good things to eat," Gerin agreed. "Probably more

wine, to help Rihwin get drunk. Probably arrows and such, too. All sorts of things we could use. All sorts of things we'd be happier if the imperials didn't have. And they're falling back toward the west, to keep us away from Aragis the Archer."

"Don't they realize you'd think of the supply train?"

"Do you know, I don't believe they do," Gerin said. "To them, after all, I'm just a backwoods half-barbarian." He winked. "But I'll tell you something: I'm going to show them they're wrong."

"This will be grand fun," Van boomed as the chariot jounced along the stretch of the Elabon Way Gerin's counterattack had opened up. "Grand fun for us, I should say—the imperials won't like getting a door slammed on their prongs even a little bit."

"Wouldn't much care for that myself." Gerin had all he could do not to clutch at himself at the very idea. "But aye, if it goes as we hope, it'll do us some good and make life harder for our chums from south of the mountains."

He'd taken as many of Rihwin's riders as he could while still leaving enough to scout for the main mass of warriors he'd left behind. He'd also taken the chariots with the fastest horses and those with the fiercest crews, including a good many of Adiatunnus' Trokmoi. Set the prospect of booty in front of the woodsrunners and they'd go after it the way a pack of hounds would run baying down the scent track of a stag.

He glanced east. Somewhere not far over there, beyond forests and low hills, lay the village where Elise had her tavern. Gerin wondered what had happened when the imperials went through there after him.

A rider came galloping north up the Elabon Way toward his force. "Wagons!" the fellow was shouting. "Wagons!"

When he was sure the Fox had heard him, he pointed in the direction from which he had come.

"Let's go," Gerin said, and waved his men forward. They whooped with glee. The troopers in chariots urged their teams ahead. The riders booted their mounts up from slow trot to quick. Sure enough, as soon as the paved highway rose a little, the Fox saw the ox- and donkey-drawn wagons coming toward him. The riders were already whooping and reaching over their shoulders for arrows.

The drivers saw Gerin's oncoming men at about the same time as he spotted them. They had a few chariots along to protect them against bandits, but not nearly enough to hold back a force like the one Gerin had assembled. The charioteers did what they could: they rolled up the highway in a spoiling attack to try to give the wagon crews time to form a defensive circle.

Gerin was having none of that. "Roll past them!" he shouted. "Don't let them slow us down. Once we get in among the wagons, we'll be able to throw the chariots into the bag, too."

Arrows flew as the imperials tried to delay his troopers. A couple of men on either side tumbled out of their cars. But then, despite shouts of scorn and dismay from the warriors from south of the High Kirs, the Fox and his followers were by, speeding on toward the wagons.

A fierce grin stretched his mouth wide: the circle remained incomplete. His men knew they had to make sure it stayed incomplete, too. They broke in among the wagons. Some of the men from the chariots dismounted and set upon the wagon drivers. The drivers fought back as best they could, but they were not armored, and many of them carried nothing more lethal than knives.

Pointing to the havoc the dismounted chariot crews were wreaking, Van said, "Wouldn't be so easy for riders to do that."

"You're right—it wouldn't," Gerin agreed. "But men on horses can do things men in chariots can't, too: more things, unless I miss my guess." He raised his voice. "There go a couple, Dagref. See if you can run them down before they make it into the trees."

"Aye, Father." Dagref steered the chariot after the closer of the two fleeing drivers. As it pulled alongside the fellow, Van swung his mace. Its wicked spiked bronze head slammed home with a meaty thunk. The driver shrieked and crumpled.

"I would have let him yield," Gerin said mildly.

"He wasn't yielding," the outlander answered. "He was running."

As if the other driver had heard him, he stopped running and threw up his hands. Gerin waved for him to head back toward the Elabon Way. He obeyed, but, as soon as Dagref turned the chariot aside, he whirled and sprinted for the trees and got in among them before the chariot crew could do anything about it. Gerin shot an arrow at him, but missed.

"There, you see?" Van said. "Try and be generous and look at the thanks you get."

"He's not as smart as he thinks he is," Gerin said as the chariot bounced back to the highway. "If he comes out, either we'll scoop him up or Aragis' peasants will put paid to him. He'll have a thin time either way."

"That's not the point," Van said. "The point is, we should have put paid to him, and we cursed well didn't."

Since he was right, Gerin didn't try to argue with him. Instead, he said, "Let's see if we can keep their chariot escort from getting away and letting the rest of the imperials know we've made their wagons disappear."

His shouts pulled other chariots from the northlands away from the wagons and into the pursuit. He and his men caught up with what he thought was the last imperial

chariot a mile or so up the Elabon Way. Seeing they
would be overhauled, the driver and the two warriors
with him jumped out and ran for the woods, as the wagon
drivers had done. Unlike the wagon drivers, they didn't
get there.

"Now, let's get these wagons back to our camp," the
Fox said. "We haven't got time to waste. The faster we
move 'em up along the road, the less the chance the
Empire will have of getting them back."

Some of the wagon drivers had surrendered. Gerin
was glad of that, because his own men, while skilled
with horses, had less practice with donkeys and oxen.
The animals obeyed better when they saw what their
fellow beasts were doing under drivers who knew how
to make them work.

Rihwin rode up alongside Gerin. "I wonder what all
we've captured." For a wonder, he didn't say, *I wonder
how much wine we've captured.*

"Same sort of things we'd have along for our own
troopers, I expect," Gerin answered. "Journeybread and
sausage and onions and cheese—anything that keeps
well. Dried fruit, too, maybe. There's a name for dried
grapes." He snapped his fingers. "Raisins, that's what
they call them."

"Raisins," Rihwin agreed. "It's been a very long time
since I've had raisins." He still didn't say anything about
wine, which Gerin had made a point of not mentioning.
Gerin eyed him suspiciously, as if wondering whether
he was coming down with some peculiar ailment.
Maturity? Gerin wondered, trying again to find a name.
He shook his head. If Rihwin hadn't caught that yet,
he probably never would.

Van said, "Have to see what they've got in these
wagons besides food, too. Sheaves of arrows, like you
said. Those'll come in handy for us. Maybe swords.

Maybe metal fittings for chariots, too. Those'd be nice."

"Let's move faster," Gerin said again.

"Captain, trying to hurry a donkey bothers you more than it does the donkey," Van said. "The only way I know to hurry oxen is to fling 'em off a cliff. What's that the Trokmoi say? Don't fash yourself—there you are. We're making the best time we can."

"It's not good enough," Gerin fretted. He knew his friend was right. He couldn't help worrying and barking and snapping anyhow. Eventually, more of his own riders came down to screen the wagons from any possible imperial revenge. Only then did he relax.

His troopers cheered when the wagons came into camp. When they started going through them, they found about what they'd expected, including one wagon full of wineskins. Gerin stalked around that wagon, glum as a man with a toothache. "What in the five hells do we do with it?" he asked the air.

Dagref was close enough to hear him. "My view is, we ought to drink it. If Mavrix didn't come up to the northlands in a cloud of purple smoke when Rihwin drank, why should he care about Widin Simrin's son drinking, or Adiatunnus, either, for that matter?"

"I don't know why he might care about Widin or Adiatunnus," the Fox answered. "I haven't the faintest idea. If he does care, though, is the risk in drinking worth the chance we're taking?"

"No way to tell ahead of time, of course," Dagref admitted. "But then, Mavrix would surely be insulted if we spill the wine, and might be insulted if we *don't* drink it. Risks everywhere."

"You so relieve my mind," Gerin said, at which Dagref bowed, as if to a compliment.

Ferdulf came swaggering up to the wagon, walking with his feet far enough off the ground to let him look

Gerin the the eye. "You've found more of my father's spoiled grape juice, have you?" he demanded.

"If that's what you want to call it, yes," Gerin answered cautiously. "Why?"

"Because I still aim to pay him back, that's why," Ferdulf said. "And now I know how to do it, too."

"Wait!" Gerin said, and grabbed at the demigod. He missed—Ferdulf must have known he was going to try it. With a mocking laugh, Ferdulf floated up into the air. Gerin leaped after him, which proved how alarmed he was. He didn't leap high enough or fast enough.

From above his head, Ferdulf mocked him. "You can't stop me this time. Nobody can stop me this time." He pointed a forefinger at the wine and muttered under his breath. Gerin couldn't hear all of it, but part of it was, "Take that, Father, and I hope you choke on it!"

"*Stop* it!" Gerin said urgently, but Ferdulf had no intention of stopping it, not for him, not for anybody. He was going to do what he was going to do, and if the Fox didn't like it, too bad for the Fox.

What if Mavrix didn't like it? That, obviously, was what Ferdulf hoped would happen. He wanted the Sithonian god of wine to come up to the northlands. Maybe he even wanted Mavrix to punish him. Getting a rise out of his father might have looked better to him than the indifference Mavrix had shown at their first meeting.

He drifted down to the ground, a brat doing an imitation of a snowflake. "Go ahead," he told Gerin. "Drink all the wine you like. I hope you and your troopers enjoy it."

"What have you done?" the Fox demanded.

Ferdulf gave him a nasty smile. "You'll find out." And off he went, before Gerin could make up his mind to try to shake some truth out of him.

"What do you think he's done?" Dagref asked.

"Something horrible," Gerin snapped. "What does he ever do? I ought to make Rihwin open a skin and find out what's gone wrong: he's wild for wine, so he should be the one to see how wild the wine's got. Doesn't that sound like justice to you, Dagref?"

His son didn't answer. With a question like that, a long answer meant *no*. No answer at all meant *no*, too. With a sigh, Gerin went and got a tarred-leather drinking jack. He took a wineskin out of the wagon, undid the tie at the neck, and poured the jack full.

He hadn't raised it to his lips when Rihwin called, "Oh no you don't, my fellow Fox. I was all but supernaturally patient, not even speaking of the blood of the sweet grape, but if you're going to go ahead and quaff—"

"Justice," Dagref said, and sighed.

"Here." Gerin pressed the jack into Rihwin's outstretched hand. "Since you want it so much, it's only fitting that you should have it. Go right ahead, my fellow Fox. Quaff."

Rihwin should have been suspicious when Gerin yielded so easily. But he wasn't. "I not only want it," he declared, "I deserve it." He took a big mouthful—and then sprayed out as much of it as he could, coughing and choking on what had gone down his throat. "Feh!" he said. "Vinegar!"

"Well, that's something of a relief," Gerin said. "I was afraid it would be donkey piss."

"Thank you so much," Rihwin snarled. "And you went ahead and let me drink it."

"No," Gerin said. "I did not *let* you drink it. You insisted on doing it. 'I deserve it,' you said. In my opinion, you were correct. You did deserve it. If you hadn't been so greedy, you would have let me taste, or you would have let me tell you Ferdulf had done something to the wine. But no—you went ahead and took what you wanted and enjoyed it less than you might have done. I'd say, both as your friend and as your king, that you have no complaint coming."

Rihwin wiped his mouth on his sleeve, which couldn't have done much good. "And I'd say, both as your friend—for some indecipherable reason or other—and as your subject, that you haven't the faintest notion of what you're talking about." He wiped his mouth again.

"Maybe you should go drink some ale," Dagref suggested. "That would get rid of some of the taste."

"Aye, maybe I should go and—" Rihwin gave Gerin's son a horrible look. "You take altogether too much after your father." He strode away, his back as stiff as an offended cat's.

"Thank you," Dagref called after him, which only made his back grow stiffer—it wasn't what he'd wanted to hear. Dagref turned to Gerin. "He'll be a while getting over that."

"So he will," Gerin agreed. "So he ought to be." He scowled at the wagon, then let out a long sigh. "We can pickle all the cabbages and cucumbers we like, but we're not going to be drinking wine."

"That's so," Dagref agreed. "I wonder why Mavrix hasn't descended on us in a cloud of fury. He's not usually one to ignore insults, is he?"

"No, he's usually one to pay them back," Gerin answered. "That's why my heart fell into my sandals when Ferdulf decided to take his petty revenge."

"Well, why isn't Mavrix here, then?" Dagref demanded, as if his father were somehow responsible for the absence of the Sithonian god of wine and fertility.

"If I knew, I would tell you," Gerin answered. "Maybe he's finally decided he doesn't care what happens here in the northlands any more. That would be nice, wouldn't it? Or maybe he's raising a rebellion down in Sithonia, and doesn't have time to fret about this part of the world for a while."

"But didn't you say he told you he didn't think the Sithonians *could* successfully rise against the Elabonian Empire?" Gerin asked.

"Yes, I did say he told me he didn't think they could," Gerin answered, and stuck out his tongue at his son. "Doesn't mean he wouldn't try to raise one anyhow. The Sithonians have revolted against the Empire a good many times over the years, even if they've always lost."

"If the Sithonians are revolting," Dagref said, both thoughtfully and with malice aforethought, "that could be very convenient for us."

"We're guessing, you know," Gerin said. Dagref nodded. Gerin went on, "We're guessing with our hearts, not our heads." He sighed. "It would be nice, but we don't dare believe it. It's like believing a pretty girl you've never seen will come looking for you. It happens every once in a while, maybe, but not often enough that you can expect it for even a heartbeat."

"I understand," Dagref said. "What happens anywhere else doesn't matter anyhow, not unless we beat the imperials here."

"That's also true," Gerin said. "In fact, that's *the* truth about this war. And we were on the point of doing it, too, till they threw another army into the fight. Nasty and rude of them, if anyone wants to know what I think. They want to win, too, worse luck. Very inconsiderate."

"Can't trust anyone any more, can you?" Dagref asked.

"Who said I ever did?" the Fox returned.

The next morning, Ferdulf was loud and triumphant and obnoxious: in other words, not far removed from his usual self. "I gave my father a proper black eye," he boasted, "and he hasn't had the nerve to come do

anything to me. I guess he sees who's boss in the
northlands now."

"You've done better guessing," Gerin told him.

Ferdulf stuck his nose in the air. Following that nose,
the rest of him floated off the ground. "I do not have
to stay here to listen to myself being insulted," he said
haughtily, and drifted away like an indignant dandelion
puff.

"He hasn't the faintest notion how big a fool he is,"
Van said.

"Fools never do," Gerin answered. "That's what makes
them fools."

"Strange, thinking of a half-god as a fool," the outlander
said, "but Ferdulf gives us plenty of chances to do it."

"So he does," Gerin said. He could easily think of a
few gods he'd met whom he considered fools, but he
didn't mention that. Whether gods were fools or not,
they were vastly stronger than mortals. A man insulted
a god, even a god as cowardly as Mavrix, at his peril. A
demigod insulted a god, even a god who was his father,
at his peril. Ferdulf hadn't figured that out—another
proof Ferdulf was a fool.

"What now?" Van asked.

"I don't know what we can do but keep on with what
we've been doing," Gerin answered. "If we can keep
riders moving along the Elabon way, the imperials are
going to have a harder time supplying their armies up
here. And if we can keep pushing back the outposts of
that force that was dogging us, maybe we'll be able to
join hands with Aragis."

"Aye, maybe we will," Van said. "And maybe, once
we do, we ought to count the fingers on the hand we
join with his, too."

Gerin, once more, would have argued with his friend
more had he agreed with him less. The men from the

northlands did drive in a couple of more imperial positions, which gave them new land from which to forage. The men from the Elabonian Empire hadn't been on the land long enough to pick it bare, nor were they as good at the job as Gerin and his followers. Combining what they took from the land with what they captured from the imperial supply column, the warriors from the northlands were for the moment comfortable.

He ate sausages and gnawed on chunks of journeybread and tried to decide what to do next: probably about the same thing as his imperial opposite number was doing.

He could do one thing his opposite number couldn't: he could send riders west to slide around the imperial forces between him and Aragis. Men on horseback could go at least as fast as men in chariots, and could go crosscountry on tracks and through fields and woods chariotry couldn't use.

Maeva was not one of the riders he sent toward Aragis. As she had before when she wasn't chosen for a duty, she complained. He did his best to look down his nose at her; it wasn't easy, not when they were very much of a height. "You're right," he said. "I didn't pick you. So what?"

"It's not fair," she insisted. "I deserve to go into danger the same as any other rider."

"You deserve to have your backside walloped," the Fox said, now truly starting to get annoyed. "And 'It's not fair!' is the battle cry children use. I'm tired of it from you. If you want to be a warrior, act like one when you're not in the middle of a fight, not just when you are."

"You're holding me back because I'm a woman," Maeva said.

"No, I'm holding you back because you're a girl," Gerin said. She stared at him, astonished and furious at the same time. He went on, "This is your first campaign, remember? Take a look at the riders I sent west. What do you notice about them, pray tell?"

"They're all men," Maeva said angrily.

"That's right," Gerin agreed. "They're all men. There isn't a boy among them. They've all been riding horses as long as you've been alive; a couple of them have been riding horses as long as anyone in the northlands has been doing it. They've all done a lot of fighting, and a lot of fighting from horseback. If you're still in the army ten or twelve years from now" —*if I'm still alive ten or twelve years from now*— "you'll have a real chance of getting sent on a ride like this."

He wondered how Maeva would take that kind of dressing-down. Fand would have flown into a fury at him. Van would have been angry, too, but not with the same sort of deadly rage. But Gerin had a great many years on Maeva, which made her take him more seriously than either of her parents would have done. "Very well, lord king," was all she said before going off disappointed but not obviously irate.

Watching her go, the Fox nodded in reluctant approval. He almost wished she had thrown a tantrum; that would have given him the excuse he needed to send her home. But she offered him no such excuse, however much having one would have pleased him and delighted Van. All things considered, she'd taken the tongue-lashing . . . like a soldier.

No sooner had that comparison crossed his mind than he wished it hadn't. Too late. He'd started thinking of Maeva as a soldier even before he saw how well she handled herself when she was wounded. He couldn't very well change his mind now.

Not all the riders he sent out came back. Before any of them came back, he had to try to withstand an assault from the imperials, who had begun to concentrate against him once he started rolling up their outposts. Their commander was about as unsubtle as Aragis the Archer. He simply gathered his force and rolled toward where he thought Gerin had the bulk of his army. He turned out to have a pretty good notion of that, too.

Mounted scouts brought the Fox the word. "They can't be a quarter of an hour behind us, lord king, coming down that road there," one of the riders said, pointing west along the dirt road up which he'd come.

"Well, all right." Gerin's grimace held annoyance, but no real surprise. He'd poked the men from south of the High Kirs; they were going to hit back if they could—and they could. He surveyed the ground through which the road ran. It was mostly open country—grain fields and and meadows—with a forest of oaks and elms off to the left. "We'll stay right here," he said. "It's as good a spot as any, and better than most."

"I think you're doing the right thing, Father," Dagref said. "We've shown that, man for man, we're more than a match for the imperials."

"So we have," Gerin agreed. "Unfortunately, they've shown they've got more men than we do."

He started shouting orders, shaking his men out from line of march into line of battle. He barely had time to post a couple of dozen chariot crews in among the trees, with orders to burst forth against the enemy's flank and rear when the time seemed ripe, before a rising dust cloud and horn calls through it announced the imperials were at hand.

"Elabon! Elabon! Elabon!" the men of the Empire shouted, as if to leave no doubt who they were. Gerin's men were not in any doubt: his riders plied the leading chariots from the Elabonian Empire with arrows and javelins. The horsemen in front of them kept the imperials from charging as ferociously as their commander probably would have liked. The men from south of the High Kirs were still learning how to face mounted foes.

One thing they'd learned was that, when there were enough of them, their foes had to give way. Archers shooting from tightly bunched chariots put enough arrows in the air to discourage anyone—on foot, on horseback, or in other chariots—from doing much to hinder their passage.

Seeing their numbers—sure enough, they were going to have more men in the fight than he did—Gerin waved and yelled to extend his line to either side and lap round them. If he could hit them from three sides at once, those numbers wouldn't do them much good: his troopers could slay men in the middle of that rumbling herd of chariots without their having the chance to do him any harm.

"There's a lot of them, Captain," Van said.

"I'd noticed that myself," Gerin answered. "We scraped together all the men we could, Aragis and I. The Empire of Elabon is bigger than the northlands, and has more people, too. They've sent a bigger force over the mountains than we can hope to equal."

"Most places, that's a recipe for a lost war for the side that doesn't have the big army," the outlander said.

"Thank you so much," the Fox snapped. "I never would have realized that if you hadn't pointed it out to me."

"Glad to help, Captain," Van said imperturbably.

He did not stay imperturbable after an arrow ticked off the side of his helm, scratching a brighter line on the brightly polished bronze. He cursed and bellowed and brandished his spear at the imperials, though he couldn't have had the slightest idea which of them had shot at him.

Gerin started shooting at the soldiers and horses of the

Elabonian Empire in front of him. One way to reduce
the odds his men faced was to kill or disable as many of
the imperials as he could. One of his shafts struck the
right-hand horse of a team square in the breast. The horse
went down. The chariot slewed leftwards, colliding with
the car and team next to it. They slewed away in turn.
Because the main body of the imperial was so tightly
packed, they ran into the team on their left, too: one arrow
fouling three chariots, half a dozen horses, and nine men.

"Well shot," Van said, seeing what the Fox had done.

"Thank you." The Fox sounded modest, letting the
shot speak for itself. "Come on, men!" he shouted. "Lay
into them."

Lay into them the men from the northlands did. The
imperials' charge slowed as collisions and casualties took
their toll of the cars in the front ranks. The fight became
a melee, the sort of struggle in which Gerin's troopers
had consistently proved to own the advantage.

Gerin shot an arrow at an imperial officer with a red
cloak draped around his shoulders. The fellow was
inconsiderate enough to lean to one side at the moment
the shaft hissed past him. Gerin cursed. "How in the
five hells am I supposed to get rid of the imperials if
they keep trying not to get killed?" he demanded of no
one in particular.

Dagref, as usual, had an answer: "Pretty rude of them,
isn't it, Father? They aren't behaving the way the
enemy—whoever the enemy is—usually does when the
minstrels sing their songs."

"To the five hells with the minstrels, too," Gerin
growled. He had a couple of reasons for despising
minstrels. First and foremost was that one who had
practiced that calling had kidnapped his eldest son fifteen
years before. But the way they distorted the truth to fit
into what made a good song grated on him, too.

He wondered how the historians who recorded events down in the City of Elabon would mention this clash. To them, of course, he and his followers would be that highly variable creature, the enemy—*rebels*, they'd call the warriors of the northlands, and *semibarbarians allied to true barbarians*. He knew their style. Being the enemy, he probably wouldn't get any credit from the historians no matter what he did. If he lost, that he was the enemy would be enough to explain a great deal. If he won, they'd chalk it up to guile or trickery, not courage.

As long as he won, he didn't care how they chalked it up. He wondered what sort of guile or trickery he could use to rouse the future historians' ire.

Looking around the crowded field, he didn't see much opportunity for anything of the sort. His men did have some advantage of position, but the imperials had the advantage of numbers. They seemed at least as liable to win as did the men of the northlands.

He sighed. He hadn't wanted this particular battle, not here, not now. He sighed again. Life had given him any number of things he didn't want. The trick was to get through them as well and as quickly as he could, to have the best chance to return to what he did in fact want.

He shot at that imperial officer again—and missed again, at a range from which he should not have missed. He cursed in disgust. The fellow seemed to lead a charmed life, though Gerin knew of no magic that would keep an arrow from piercing a man if properly aimed.

Arrows would not pierce Ferdulf, but Ferdulf's immunity was not the sort to which an ordinary man could readily aspire. Ferdulf swooped down on the officer from the Elabonian Empire, for all the world like a ill-mannered hawk. He shouted in the officer's ears. He waved hands in front of the officer's face. He flipped

up his tunic in front of the driver's face, giving the fellow
a charming view of a semidivine backside.

With such distractions, the officer couldn't do much
in the way of commanding and the driver couldn't do
much in the way of driving. Both men, and the soldier
in the car with them, did their best to grab, shoot, or
otherwise get rid of Ferdulf. They paid so much attention
to him, they didn't notice their chariot was about to collide
with another till it did. The officer and the soldier fell
out the back of the car. The driver got yanked over the
front rail and under the horses' hooves. Ferdulf flitted
off to work more mischief elsewhere on the field.

Gerin looked toward the forest in which he'd placed
those couple of dozen chariots. He wished he had them
in the fight, either bursting from ambush or simply in
the line with the rest of his men. The imperials weren't
doing anything fancy, but he didn't have enough men
to drive them back. That was becoming more and more
obvious as the fight wore along. All the imperials had
to do was stolidly keep on fighting and odds were he'd
lose unless he came up with something spectacular. For
the life of him, he had no idea what that might be.

He looked toward the oaks again. He didn't want to
send a messenger over there; that was liable to draw
the imperials' attention to the wood, which was the last
thing he wanted.

A moment later, he changed his mind about that. Truly,
the last thing he wanted was to be hacked to bloody
pulp in the chariot. A car full of imperials pulled alongside
of his. One of them cut at him with a sword. The blade
turned slightly, so that the flat thudded against his ribs.

He hissed in pain anyhow, and snatched out his own
sword. He and the imperial traded strokes till their
chariots pulled apart from each other. He thought he
would have beaten the fellow had they fought longer;

being left-handed, he hadn't had to bring the sword across his body as they battled. But what might have been didn't matter. The truth was, the trooper remained alive and hale to fight someone else.

Gerin wondered how hale he was himself. Breathing hurt but didn't stab, so he doubted he'd broken ribs. He could go on fighting. He laughed, which also hurt. Even if he had broken ribs, he had to go on fighting.

Dagref snapped his whip at one of the horses harnessed to another imperial chariot drawing near. The horse screamed and reared and flinched aside, despite the driver's best effort to force an attack.

"You *are* getting good with that thing," Van said in admiring tones, and then half spoiled the compliment by adding, "You must have got the practice flaying the hide off folk with your tongue."

"I haven't the faintest notion what you're talking about," Dagref replied with more dignity than a stripling had any business owning.

"I know, lad," Van said. "That's the trouble." Dagref's dignity, this time, consisted of pretending he hadn't heard. He didn't bring that off quite so well as he had the dispassionate answer.

More seriously, Gerin said, "Maybe you ought to start practicing with a longer lash than most drivers carry, son. You're better with it than most, that seems plain, so you ought to get as much advantage from it as you can."

"Now that's not a bad idea, Father," Dagref said. "I've had the same thought myself, as a matter of fact."

Had he? Gerin studied his back, which was remarkably uncommunicative. Maybe he had. One thing Dagref was never short on was ideas. He seldom lied, either, unless he found an immediately expedient reason for doing so. The Fox couldn't see one here.

He also couldn't see anything that looked like victory—
certainly not for his side. The soldiers of the Elabonian
Empire kept on fighting, no matter what he did to them.
Every once in a while, in fist fights, Gerin had seen a
man whom no blow would put down. Sooner or later,
even if that kind of fellow wasn't a particularly good
fighter, he would win by wearing down his foe.

That, he thought worriedly, was what he faced here.
He was hurting the imperials worse than they were hurting
him—he could see that much. The trouble was, they could
afford it better than he could. Their captain had brought
more men to the battle than he'd thought at first, and
he'd known from the beginning he was outnumbered.

He looked over toward the trees again. He waved,
on the off chance that anyone over there was looking
in his direction and could recognize him at a considerable
distance through the dust the chariots and horses had
kicked up. A sudden thrust at the flank and rear of the
imperials would be extremely welcome about now. The
longer the men he'd concealed in the forest delayed,
the greater the effect of that thrust would be. He knew
as much. If they delayed much longer, though, the battle
would be lost.

Van looked in the same direction. "Maybe they're
waiting for an invitation, like shy maids hanging back
from the dance."

"There won't be any dance left if they don't come soon,"
Gerin said.

Then he shouted. Out from among the oaks burst the
chariots he'd stationed there. On toward the imperials
they thundered, picking up speed with every lengthening
stride of their horses. The crews in the cars shouted
like men possessed. Arrows flew ahead of the chariots.

The imperials shouted, too, in dismay. Their whole
line shook as Gerin's men took them from an unexpected

direction. "Come on!" the Fox shouted, to all his warriors whom the men of the Elabonian Empire had been pressing back. "Now is our chance to beat those bastards!"

As soon as the words were out of his mouth, he wished he'd phrased that differently. It was all too accurate for comfort. He'd hoped the flank attack would win him the battle. Instead, it was doing exactly what he'd said— it was giving him a chance to win. That it was doing no more than giving him a chance told him with unpleasant clarity how much trouble he'd been in.

"Forward!" he shouted. Forward his line went, instead of moving back. Forward—for a little while. Then the imperial resistance stiffened. Had he had a hundred chariots in the wood, he might have thrown the men of the Elabonian Empire into confusion enough to let him crush them. But, had he had a hundred chariots in the wood, he was likelier to have weakened the rest of his force so much, the battle would have been lost before they could think about a flank attack.

Dagref drove the chariot past a car full of imperials. Van speared the horse closest to him. Spouting blood, the beast screamed and foundered. Dagref's slash made the driver scream, too, and clutch at his neck. Gerin shot one of the archers in the car. The other dove out before anything dreadful could happen to him.

"That's as near a clean sweep as makes no difference," Van said as the archer ran for his life.

"You'll talk differently if he shoots you from ambush," Gerin said.

"If he shoots Uncle Van from ambush, he probably won't talk at all," Dagref said over his shoulder.

"To the five hells with logic, and with both of you, too," Van said. He looked around. "Now we get down to it. Are we going to lick these whoresons, or are they going to lick us?"

Gerin looked around, too. What had been an advance was stalled. The imperials had managed to contain the band that had attacked them from the forest. Without much fuss, without much style, but with plenty of men, they pressed ahead with the fight. He'd mauled them. He had indeed hurt them worse than they'd hurt him, much worse. They kept coming anyhow.

He didn't know what he was supposed to do about that. It wasn't how warfare usually worked up here in the northlands. Finding foes stubborn enough to keep fighting no matter how badly battered they were wasn't easy anywhere. A lifetime of experience and as much reading as he'd been able to do convinced him of the truth there.

He had just reached that unhappy conclusion when Dagref said, "I don't think we can force them back, Father."

"I don't, either," Gerin said. "They have too many men—that's all there is to it. Anything even close to equal numbers, and we'd beat them. We've proved that. But we haven't got equal numbers, and we can't get them."

"Well, what do you aim to do, then, Fox?" Van asked.

"I've got two unpleasant choices," Gerin answered. "I can give up this battle, admit we've lost, retreat, and yield the field to the imperials. Or I can keep on fighting, do the best I can, and watch them chew my army to pieces one bite at a time."

"You're right—those are both nasty choices," Van said.

"If you see any others, please let me know," Gerin said. Van grunted while he thought, then shook his head. Gerin sighed. "Too bad. I was hoping you would."

Dagref said, "What will you do, Father?"

"What would *you* do?" Gerin returned. The battle was lost, one way or the other, but he might at least get a lesson out of it. It wasn't so dreadfully lost that a moment spent here would matter one way or the other.

"I'd hold the army together," Dagref answered at once. "Maybe they'll divide their force or send out detachments we can pick off, the way they did before, or leave themselves open to ambush. If we still have an army, we can take advantage of that. If we let them grind us here like flour, we're finished."

"You're my son, all right. For better and for worse, we think alike. I'm going to see if the imperials will the satisfied with a win and let us go." Gerin raised his voice in a reluctant shout: "Pull back, men of the northlands! Pull back!"

The imperials made no more than a token pursuit—certainly less than he would have made were roles reversed. He thought the commander facing him was the one who'd led the first imperial force into the northlands. The other one, with the larger part of Crebbig I's army, had more drive and more imagination—and was facing Aragis, who, while surely a driver, imagined very little.

Gerin had scant time to worry about Aragis. He had scant time to worry about anything except making certain he put enough distance between his army and that of the Elabonian Empire to let his men camp safely. That, with some effort, he managed.

Adiatunnus came up to him after the army halted. "And what do we do now?" the Trokmê chieftain asked.

"To the crows with me if I know," Gerin answered.

X

What the army did, over the next several days, was retreat. Gerin fought a number of sharp skirmishes with the imperials. He never had any trouble pushing back their advance parties. Whenever the main force came up to support the scouts, though, he had to fall back himself.

Before long, he found himself with no choice but to abandon the swath of Aragis' country in which his army had been foraging. He cursed at having to do it, but it was either that or move south and let the imperials get between him and his own homeland. He resolved not to do that no matter what. If the Elabonian Empire wanted him out of his own holdings, the imperials would have to come and dig him out one keep at a time, just as Aragis would have had to do if he'd beaten him in the field.

"Good thing we stole their supply train," Van said as he gnawed sausage of an evening.

"Anything that keeps us going is good," Gerin said. "We'll have a hard time doing it again, worse luck—they've pushed us a long ways back from the Elabon Way now."

"See any chance of turning loose a decent counter-attack?" the outlander asked, taking another bite.

"I wish I did," Gerin said. "This fellow isn't leaving

himself open, though. He doesn't fight like a Trokmê or one of our crack-brained barons up here. I wish he would just charge straight ahead without looking where he's going. It would make life a lot simpler. But he doesn't want to do that. Slow but sure, that's him."

"Doesn't seem stupid, anyhow," Van said. He looked back over his shoulder, toward the northeast. "If he keeps coming, he's liable to push us back into the valley of Ikos whether we want to go there or not."

"That thought had also crossed my mind," Gerin said unhappily. "If we have to go back through there, we'll go back through there, that's all. Biton is the farseeing god. If he can't see far enough to figure out that we're doing what we have to do, not what we want to do, he's not as smart as I think, nor as smart as he thinks he is, either."

Van grunted. "Gods aren't gods because they're smart, Fox. They're gods because they're strong."

"I wish I could say you were wrong," Gerin replied. "The trouble is, I know too well you're right."

He looked around. Where was Dagref? Last time he'd noticed his son, the lad had been eating sausage and journeybread not far away. He didn't see Dagref now. He'd waited for some pungent comment from him about gods and whether they were strong or smart, and now, almost disappointed, realized he'd have to do without.

A moment later, he stopped worrying about Dagref, for Rihwin the Fox strode importantly up to him and said, "Lord king, I'm sure I know how all our troubles may be solved."

Rihwin was enough to worry about any time. Rihwin sure was sure to make Gerin worry. "I'm glad you're sure," he said, his voice as polite as he could make it. "That doesn't necessarily mean you're right, of course. Some people have trouble understanding the difference."

Rihwin looked wounded, an admirable artistic effort. "Lord king, you have no call to make fun of me."

"Why doesn't he?" Van asked in tones of genuine curiosity. "You leave yourself open to it often enough."

"And to the five hells with *you*," Rihwin replied with dignity.

Gerin held up a hand. "Never mind. Enough wrangling. How, my fellow Fox, may all our troubles be solved?"

Rihwin raised an eyebrow. He knew irony when he heard it. For that, if not for a number of other things, Gerin gave him credit. But he answered as if Gerin had meant his sardonic question soberly: "We need divine aid against the men from south of the High Kirs."

"You're a man from south of the High Kirs," Van pointed out.

"Wait." Gerin forestalled the outlander. He fixed Rihwin with a baleful stare. "Why do I think I already know the god whose aid you are going to tell me we must seek?"

"Because he is one of the gods whom you know best, perhaps?" Rihwin said. "Because he has come to your aid and to the aid of the northlands before? Because he is a god who has no reason to love the Elabonian Empire and a great many reasons to loathe it? Those must be the reasons you have in mind—is it not so, lord king?"

"Mm, possibly," Gerin allowed. "That Mavrix is also lord of the sweet grape and what comes from the sweet grape also enters my mind, for some reason or other. Why do you suppose that might be?"

"I haven't the faintest notion," Rihwin replied.

Van guffawed. "If you were as innocent as you sound, you'd still be a virgin at your age, and that, at least, you're not."

Rihwin ignored him, which wasn't easy. "Lord king,"

he said, addressing himself directly to Gerin, "do you deny, can you deny, Mavrix is our best hope among the gods?"

"Of course I deny it," Gerin answered. "So would you, if you had any sense, though all the gods know *that's* too much to ask for. Biton is a god of this country. Mavrix is even more an imported interloper than we Elabonians are."

"Biton is also aloof," Rihwin said. "The only way you got him to move against the monsters was with Selatre's help and with the added irritation of an appeal to . . . Mavrix." He looked triumphant.

Gerin let out a long, exasperated breath. "Rihwin, if you want another cup of wine, take another cup of wine. If you think the risk is worth it, go ahead. If you get away with it, well and good. If Mavrix tears your head off, my view is that you bloody well asked for it. But don't go wrapping your own desires in a scheme you claim will benefit all of us."

"I should like to drink wine again, aye," Rihwin said, "but I am no longer mad for it, as I was before I slaked my thirst and my desire not long ago. And when I slaked my thirst not long ago, let me remind you, Mavrix made no appearance of any sort, your jittery predictions to the contrary notwithstanding. I propose enlisting him in our cause regardless of whether or not, in the accomplishment thereof, I once more taste the blood of the sweet grape."

"Well—a disinterested Rihwin. Now I've seen everything," Gerin said. Rihwin looked—no, not indignant. Rihwin looked angry. Gerin, for once, did not think the expression was donned for the occasion, to be casually discarded at need. He thought he'd struck a nerve.

All Rihwin said, though, was, "Are you sure *you* are disinterested in this matter, lord king, or are you prejudiced against me because of events now past?"

"Honh!" Van said. "Who wouldn't be? Some of the things you've done would make the hair stand up on a bald man."

But Rihwin's question brought Gerin up short. He prided himself on viewing the world around him as disinterestedly as he could. Anyone who could be anything close to disinterested about Rihwin, though, needed divine detachment, not that afforded to mere mortal men. Slowly, Gerin said, "You're like the boy who says that, just because he's pushed his sister into the mud half a dozen times, there's no reason to think he'll do it again."

"Not so," Rihwin said. "Unlike that boy, whom some of my bastards assuredly resemble, I have learned my lesson. I urge you to summon Mavrix, regardless of whether I play any role whatever in the summoning, and also regardless of whether I get to drink wine then or afterwards." After a bow to Gerin, he strode off.

"Bugger me with a pine cone," Van said. "Now I've seen everything, too."

"If I thought you were wrong, I would argue with you," Gerin answered. He scratched his head. "Much to my own surprise, I'm willing to believe my fellow Fox means what he says. That brings me to the next question on the list: is what he says a good notion or a foolish one?"

"Having the help of a god is is better than not having the help of a god," Van said. "That's a general working rule. Of course, Mavrix is the sort of god who has a way of showing you that general working rules aren't all they're cracked up to be, isn't he?"

"That's putting it mildly," the Fox said. "And there's this foolish feud Ferdulf has chosen to pick with him, too. If Mavrix does come here, it's more likely to be to warm Ferdulf's backside than to give us a hand against the Empire."

"But if he did come to help us—" Van said.

"Aye," Gerin said. "If he did." He looked around again for Dagref. When he realized why he was doing that, he blinked in surprise. He admired the wits of few men enough to ask them for their views. Without his quite noticing it, his son had become one of that small, select group.

Dagref did come back to the fire. "Mavrix?" he said when Gerin asked him about trying to summon the Sithonian god. "Mavrix . . . hmm." It was almost as if he had never heard of the god of wine and fertility.

Gerin clicked his tongue between his teeth in annoyance. "Yes, Mavrix. You remember—fawnskins, thyrsus, tongue like a frog's."

"Oh, yes, of course I remember," Dagref said. But even that sounded absent-minded, nothing like the sharp comeback he would usually have given. He yawned, rubbed his eyes, and yawned again.

"Oh, by the gods!" Gerin snapped. "Did you go and jump into an alepot? Is that why you're acting as if you haven't got two sticks of sense to rub together?"

"I'm not drunk," Dagref said. Gerin eyed him. With some reluctance, he decided his son was telling the truth. After one more yawn, Dagref went on, "I am tired. Am I allowed to be tired?"

"You weren't acting that tired before you went off to wherever you went off to," the Fox grumbled. "Since you weren't, you can give me an answer to my question before you lie down on your blanket: should I seek Mavrix's aid or not?"

"I don't see why you shouldn't *seek* it," Dagref answered. "You might be better off if you don't get it, though. That's what the oracle Biton gave would seem to mean, wouldn't it?" He hesitated. "If, of course, Biton was talking about Mavrix and not some other god altogether."

Gerin grunted, then said, "All right, go to sleep. You've earned it. You've given me something new to think about, I admit."

Dagref unfolded his blanket, wrapped himself in it, and was snoring very shortly thereafter. Gerin eyed him and scratched his head. His son didn't reek of ale, and had spoken and thought clearly enough when he decided to put his mind to it. But that mind had been somewhere else, somewhere far away. The Fox let out a puzzled grunt. That wasn't like Dagref.

But his son, once he chose to pay attention—some attention—to what he was saying, had indeed given him something new to think about. The idea of summoning a god in the hope that he would ignore the summons hadn't occurred to the Fox. He doubted it would have occurred to him, either. Dagref had a sideways way of looking at the world that could come in handy sometimes, no doubt about it.

"Ah, but the next question is, what happens if we summon dear Mavrix and he does decide to lend a hand?" Gerin murmured. That could prove embarrassing. Biton had plainly said—as plainly as the god ever said anything, anyhow—he would be better off if he got no divine help when he asked for it. What *would* he do if Mavrix pitched in against the forces of the Elabonian Empire?

After some thought, Gerin smiled. If Mavrix did decide to aid him, he could summon some other god, so that his failure there would bring him into conformity with the oracle. He glanced over to Dagref. That had an underhanded quality to it his sleeping son would appreciate.

Then he glanced over at Dagref again, in sudden sharp

suspicion. If a young man disappeared for a while and then came back tired and with his mind far away from whatever his father was talking about, one obvious explanation sprang to mind.

That it was obvious didn't make it true. Gerin looked this way and that to see if he could spy Maeva. He couldn't, which proved nothing one way or the other. The only ways to prove anything would be to catch the two of them in the act (if there was any act in which to catch them) or to have her belly start to swell—and even that wouldn't prove who the father was.

Van lay snoring a few feet from Dagref. For Dagref's sake, Gerin hoped Van's mind didn't work the way his own did.

Next evening, Rihwin's eyes got big and round. "Do you mean what you say, lord king?" he breathed.

"Of course not," Gerin snapped. "I'm lying to build your hopes up." He snorted in exasperation. "Yes, I mean what I say, curse it. I've thought things through, and I've decided you had a good idea there after all. We shall try to summon the lord of the sweet grape to our aid."

He wished he'd looked up before he spoke. Ferdulf, drifting overhead, had been close enough to hear. The demigod dove down to screech in his face: "You want my father here again? I forbid it!"

"You can't forbid it," Gerin said. "You can make my life difficult—the gods know you do make my life difficult—but you can't stop me. Ferdulf, I *am* going to do this. What you do afterwards is your affair and Mavrix's."

"He'll be sorry if he comes here," Ferdulf said darkly.

"You'll be sorry if he comes here and you try annoying him," Gerin answered. "He's stronger than you are, and you'd do well to remember it."

Ferdulf stuck out his tongue. "I'm not afraid of him. Bring him on. He'll regret it, he will."

Gerin shrugged and forbore to argue any more. People had an amazing ability to put unpleasant truths out of their minds. The Fox saw that also applied to demigods. For that matter, it probably applied to gods, too.

"Shall we now summon the lord of the sweet grape to the northlands without any further delay?" Rihwin said with a sidelong glance at Ferdulf.

Ferdulf sneered. "I'll delay you, all right. I'll turn all the wine you have left into vinegar, the same as I did with that wagonload you captured from the imperials."

"No, you won't," Gerin said, much as he might have told Blestar he wouldn't jump off the palisade walkway back at Fox Keep.

"And what's to stop me?" Ferdulf said, sticking out his tongue again.

"If you turn that wine to vinegar," Gerin said deliberately, "I will use the vinegar to call your father, it being the best I have for the purpose, and I will tell him why I could use nothing better. Then we can all find out what he chooses to do about that."

Ferdulf's glare came close to scorching him where he stood. "How could a mere mortal prove so hateful?" he demanded.

"Practice," Gerin answered. "Come on, let's get on with this."

He had Rihwin do the actual honors, drinking a cup of wine and imploring Mavrix to appear. His fellow Fox was the one who most wanted the Sithonian god to come forth. Gerin himself would have been just as glad—gladder—to have Mavrix stay down in Sithonia. The only reason Ferdulf wanted to see his father was to harass him.

"We summon thee, lord of the sweet grape," Rihwin

called, sipping the wine he and his riders had captured from the warriors from south of the High Kirs. He didn't shudder with ecstasy, as he had before he'd drunk his first cup of wine in so many years. He simply drank, without making a fuss about it. Gerin took that for a good sign.

"Well, where is he?" Ferdulf said nastily when Mavrix did not forthwith appear. "Is he asleep? Is he drunk? Is he off buggering a pretty boy, or perhaps a pretty lamb?"

"You would do well, I think, to watch your tongue," Gerin said.

Ferdulf stuck it out farther than any man could have, and, for good measure, waggled the end of it. "There," he said indistinctly—he didn't bother pulling it back in before he started talking. "I'm watching it. It isn't doing very much, though."

"Heh," Gerin said—the sound of a laugh, without the mirth.

Rihwin drank more wine and called on Mavrix again. The Sithonian god stayed wherever he was; he did not come to that part of the northlands. Rihwin looked unhappy. So did Gerin, though he did not feel that way.

"Maybe he won't come. Maybe he won't hear us." Rihwin sounded as disappointed as he looked

"Maybe he won't." Gerin also sounded as disappointed as he looked, but, again, he did not feel that way.

"Maybe he's afraid of me." Ferdulf sounded arrogant. He was a demigod. He had reason to be arrogant most of the time. He did not, in Gerin's view have reason to be arrogant when he was talking about making a god afraid. Maybe, when he was older, Ferdulf would figure that out for himself. Maybe he would stay arrogant as long as he lived. Maybe, if he stayed arrogant around gods, he wouldn't live so long as he expected.

Rihwin drank yet again. "We implore thee, lord of the

sweet grape, to favor us with thy presence," he said.

When nothing happened, Gerin began, "Well, all right, you've had yourself some wine, Rihwin, but the lord of the sweet grape doesn't—"

And then the lord of the sweet grape did. Glowing softly, Mavrix appeared before Gerin, Rihwin, and Ferdulf. The Sithonian god did not look happy. Mavrix, in fact, looked intensely annoyed. "Well, what is it now?" he asked in a peevish voice. "You keep bellowing in my ear until I can hardly hear myself think. Rudeness, that's what it is."

"Welcome, lord of the sweet grape," Gerin said. Now that Mavrix was here, he had to make the best of it. "We have summoned you to the northlands once more to implore you for aid against the Elabonian Empire, and—"

"And to take your much-used backside out of here, and never come back again," Ferdulf broke in.

"Is that so?" Mavrix said. Between *that* and *so* he moved from where he had been to right next to Ferdulf, apparently without crossing the intervening space. He seized his son. Ferdulf squalled and tried to get away, but could not. Mavrix gave Ferdulf a harder, more thorough spanking than Gerin had ever dared administer. "This is for the filthy tongue in your head." After a brief pause, he walloped his son again, harder than ever. "And this is for presuming to tamper with the blood of the sweet grape—so much wine wasted, so much wine men will never drink."

In an aside to Gerin, Rihwin muttered, "I'd do that to Ferdulf for wasting a wagonload of wine, too, if only I dared."

"Mavrix has the power to do it," Gerin whispered back.

Presently, Mavrix left off chastising Ferdulf, who collapsed in a weeping puddle. The Sithonian god turned his fathomless black eyes on the Fox. "What were you saying before we endured that tasteless interruption?"

"Lord Mavrix, I was saying that I hoped you might change your mind and aid me against the forces of the Elabonian Empire," Gerin replied.

"No," Mavrix said. He then repeated himself several times, at increasing volume: "*No. NO. NO!* Does that adequately acquaint you with my feelings in this matter?"

"But why not, lord?" Rihwin asked.

"Why?" Mavrix screeched—yes, he was exercised, and Gerin felt a certain amount of relief that Rihwin had beat him to the question. Since this whole summoning had been his fellow Fox's idea, let the oh-so-clever fellow take the heat for it. And heat there was. Mavrix continued, high and shrill, "I am not required to tell you anything, you pustule on the backside of this backwoods nest of barbarians!"

"I know you are not required to do anything of the sort, lord," Rihwin said: for a wonder, he had the sense to walk very small. "I thought you might, in your great generosity, deign to tell me, that's all."

"Well," Mavrix said, somewhat mollified by a mortal's flattery. "You are trying. But then, you are trying, too, if you take my meaning." He stuck out his tongue at Rihwin, but then drew it back in. "All right. All right. If you must know, if you *must*, one reason I have no interest whatever in coming to your aid is on account of what this little wretch did." He dug his foot into Ferdulf's ribs in what was half a poke, half a kick.

"I didn't do half of what I wish I could," Ferdulf snarled.

Mavrix ignored him, which was probably his good fortune. The Sithonian god went on, "Don't you think there's a basic rudeness involved in insulting a deity and then beseeching him for aid? Don't you?"

"Lord, I did not insult you," Rihwin said. "Gerin the

Fox did not insult you. We are the ones who seek your aid, not your son."

Gerin would have been just as well pleased—better than just as well pleased—had Rihwin not mentioned him. But, when Mavrix turned those deep, deep black eyes his way, he found he had no choice but to nod. "Assuredly, lord, I offered you no insult," he said, and that was true—he, unlike Ferdulf, knew better than to insult a god.

"I don't care," Mavrix said sniffily. "My son insulted me, and he associates with you. Therefore, you might as well have insulted me."

That was breathtakingly unfair. Had Gerin really wanted Mavrix's aid, he would have protested loud and long. Since he didn't, he contented himself with saying, "I myself would never do such a thing, and I cannot control everyone who associates with me." He gave Rihwin a pointed stare.

"I don't care," Mavrix repeated. "I am insulted, and one of yours insulted me. You get nothing from me in return."

"I'm not one of his!" Ferdulf shouted. "I'm yours."

"He showed me a pleasant peasant wench to tempt me to his keep," Mavrix answered, pointing at Gerin. "I let myself be tempted . . . and then I let myself be tempted. You, Ferdulf, are the result."

Ferdulf's curses, aimed impartially at Gerin and Mavrix, were loud and fierce and vile. In point of fact, Rihwin, who had a more intimate acquaintance with the charms of peasant women than did Gerin, had chosen Fulda, who'd proved tempting to Mavrix. Gerin refrained from mentioning that. Ferdulf was quite upset enough as things were.

Rihwin said, "What other reasons have you for refusing, lord?"

"None I need discuss with you," Mavrix said haughtily. "None I intend discussing with you. Whatever they may be, they are mine, and no business of yours in any particular."

He'd said pretty much the same thing about his first reason, which made Gerin, whose curiosity never rested, ask, "Can we not persuade you to explain yourself?"

Maybe Mavrix would have explained himself, maybe he wouldn't. Before he could speak, though, Ferdulf broke in: "Can we not persuade you to bugger off? Can we not persuade you to take a flying futter at fast Fomor, as the Trokmoi say? Can we not persuade you to—?"

Gerin did not get a chance to find out what else Ferdulf might have wanted to persuade his father to do, because Mavrix gave the demigod another licking, more savage than either of the first two. Demigod Ferdulf might have been, but he was not strong enough to withstand punishment from a god. He wailed and shrieked and made noises not far different from those any child might have made after a drubbing from its father.

Through that racket, Mavrix said to Gerin, "You see how it is. This north country is unpleasant enough without the insults. With them, it is intolerable. I go, and, if fate be kind, I shall not return." He vanished.

"Well," Gerin said to Rihwin, "so much for that."

"Er—yes, lord king," Rihwin answered. "I think it shall be some long while before I once more seek to have aught to do with Mavrix, lord of the sweet grape." He sketched a salute and strode off, shaking his head.

That left Gerin alone with Ferdulf, not a position he would have chosen. But the choice was not his to make. He thought about walking off, as Rihwin had. Ferdulf, after all, had been the author of his own troubles. The Fox was mildly surprised to discover himself not

hardhearted enough to leave the battered little demigod
by himself in his pain.

"Are you all right?" he asked Ferdulf.

"You can bugger off, too," Ferdulf growled. "You're
laughing at me. You hate me. Everybody hates me."

"Not quite everybody," Gerin answered, "though that
certainly isn't from any lack of effort on your part. You
seem to go out of your way sometimes to make yourself
hateful."

"Go away," Ferdulf said. "You're not my father. I haven't
got a father. As far as I'm concerned, he isn't real. He
doesn't exist."

"You were scandalized about the foolish god of the
Weshapar, who said the same thing about his neighbor
gods," Gerin said. "Do you. think it sounds any wiser
coming out of your mouth?"

"I don't care," Ferdulf said. "I just don't care. You
had a proper father, a father who cared about you."

Gerin burst into laughter so bitterly raucous, it made
Ferdulf stare. The Fox said, "What in the five hells do
you know about it? My father thought he could cure
me of books and make me a warrior with the back of
his hand. It was only when he finally figured out he was
wrong that he shipped me over the High Kirs to be rid
of me."

"But you ended up a warrior anyhow," Ferdulf said.

"So I did," Gerin said. "But that was my doing, not
his—and I didn't waste his time and mine with a pack
of childish tricks and tries for revenge."

"I am not a child," Ferdulf said. "I am a demigod."

"You are a demigod," the Fox agreed. "But you're also
a child. That's what makes things so difficult for everyone
around you."

"Good," Ferdulf said, and drifted away, apparently none
the worse for wear from the beatings Mavrix had given

him and just as apparently intent on taking no notice whatever of Gerin's sermon. The Fox sighed. He didn't suppose he should have been surprised.

"Aye, lord king, that's how it is," Fandil Fandor's son said as he rubbed down his horse. "I got around the imperials with no great trouble, but it didn't do me as much good as I would have liked. It didn't do you as much good as you'd like, either." He patted the horse's neck. "I will tell you this, though—I had no trouble getting through the bastards and back again."

"Wonderful," Gerin said sourly. "But, once you did get through, you found that Aragis had gone to earth?"

"That's what I said, lord king." Fandil returned to rubbing the horse's back. Gerin sympathized with the animal. Fandil's father had been called Fandor the Fat. Fandil was more along the lines of *the Chubby*, but Gerin wouldn't have wanted to try carrying him on his back.

"He doesn't plan on doing any more fighting out in the open, then?" Gerin persisted.

"Not if he can help it," Fandil answered. "He and his army are holed up in the strongest keeps they can find, and he doesn't think the imperials can pry him out of them before winter comes and they get too hungry to stay in the field. If they tear up the countryside but then go home, what does he care? He's ahead of the game."

"His peasants aren't," Gerin said, but that only made him laugh at himself. As long as the imperials went away, Aragis didn't care what happened to the peasantry. Gerin supposed he had to sympathize with that, but Aragis didn't care what happened to the peasantry any other time, either.

Fandil said, "Looks like the imperials are settling down

to the sieges, too. Don't know whether they'll try knocking
down walls or just sit there and starve the places out
one at a time—if they can."

"If they can," Gerin agreed. "The one thing I'm sure
of is that Aragis wouldn't put his men into castles that
are easy to take, and he wouldn't put them into castles
that don't have plenty in their cellars, either."

"You know best about that, lord king," Fandil said.
"But what it looks like to me is, we're on our own over
here."

Gerin sighed. "It looks that way to me, too, Fandil.
We've been on our own over here all along, and we
haven't done any too well so far."

"You'll come up with something." Gerin might not have
confidence, but Fandil, like a lot of his men, did.

"I hope so," Gerin said. "To the crows with me if I
have the faintest notion what it is, though." Fandil didn't
seem to hear that, any more than Aragis had heard Gerin
when he said he wasn't a sorcerer. Not for the first time,
nor for the five hundredth, either, he wondered why
people didn't pay more attention to what other people
said. They already had their own ideas, and that seemed
to be enough for them.

The next morning, he and Van and Dagref rode out
along the picket line of horsemen he kept west of his
force to warn him if the imperials decided to come at
him again. For the moment, the men of the Elabonian
Empire were holding back. They had pickets out, too,
in chariots, to warn of any sudden move Gerin might
make against them.

"They're not bad fellows," one of Rihwin's riders said,
pointing toward an imperial chariot perhaps a quarter
of a mile away. "For business like this, they don't bother
us and we don't bother them. When the time comes to
really fight again, they'll really go after us, I suppose,

and we'll do our best to fill 'em full of arrow holes, but what's the use till then?"

"None I can see," Gerin allowed. "It's a pretty sensible way of going about things, when you get down to it."

He glanced over at Van. In the outlander's younger days, odds were he would have thundered out something about killing the foe whenever you found any chance to do it. Had Gerin had Adiatunnus with him, the Trokmê chieftain probably would have said the same thing now. But Van only shrugged and nodded, as if to say the horseman's words made good sense to him, too. Little by little, he was mellowing.

A couple of riders farther along the line, Maeva patrolled a stretch of meadow. "No, lord king," she said when Gerin asked her, "I haven't seen anything out of the ordinary." As the earlier rider had, she pointed toward an imperial chariot out of arrow range to the west. "They're keeping an eye on us, same as we're keeping an eye on them."

"All right," Gerin said. "Right at the moment, I'm not sorry things are quiet. We need the time to pull ourselves back together."

"They're probably thinking the same thing about us, lord king," Maeva answered seriously. "We had to pull back, aye, but we bloodied them."

"They have more room to make mistakes than we do, though," Van said. "By the gods, we didn't make any mistakes I could see in that last fight, and we lost it anyhow."

Dagref said nothing at all. That was unusual enough to make Gerin keep an eye on his son, as Maeva kept an eye on the force from the Elabonian Empire and as the imperials kept an eye on Gerin's army. For his part, Dagref was keeping an eye on Maeva. As best Gerin could tell from watching the back of his son's head, Dagref's eyes did not leave her.

She kept looking at him, too. *Well, well*, the Fox thought. *Isn't that interesting?* Gerin looked over at Van again, too. The outlander was also eyeing his daughter, but not, Gerin judged, with that kind of suspicion. Van was still trying to figure out why in blazes she wanted to take the field, and not worrying about anything else.

Life would get even more interesting if Maeva's belly started to bulge. Gerin had had that thought before. He wondered whether Dagref worried about such things. He might well not have himself at that age. A man and a woman—or a boy and a girl—could enjoy each other a good many ways without running the risk. Did Dagref know about them? He had little in the way of real experience, but who could guess what all he'd heard, what all he'd read? Who could guess what all Maeva knew, either?

Still shaking his head, Gerin tapped Dagref on the shoulder. "Let's get moving," he said. With obvious reluctance—obvious to the Fox, at any rate, and probably to Maeva, too—Dagref flicked the reins. The horses began to walk, and then to trot.

Dagref was not so unsubtle as to look back over his shoulder at Maeva. Gerin, however, could look back with no fear of rousing Van's suspicions, and he did. Sure enough, Maeva was staring after the chariot. Maybe that was because it held her father. Gerin wouldn't have bet on it, though, not anything he couldn't afford to lose.

After he'd finished the tour of his pickets and convinced himself the imperials weren't going to take him by surprise, he had Dagref drive back to camp. When he returned, Rihwin and Ferdulf were in the middle of a screaming row, each plastering the other with names that stuck like glue. Van descended from the chariot and tried to break up the fight, with the result that both Rihwin and Ferdulf turned on him.

Gerin hadn't tried to interfere between his friend and the little demigod, knowing that was what would happen if he did. He'd had a sufficiency—indeed, an oversupply—of people shouting at him lately, and saw no need to encourage more. If Van was of the opinion he hadn't been getting his own fair share of abuse, he was, in Gerin's view, welcome to it.

Van's furious bass roar blended with Ferdulf's baritone and Rihwin's higher, lighter voice to produce discord in three-part disharmony. Dagref rolled his eyes. "You'd think Uncle Van would have better sense than to get mixed up in that," he said.

"Aye, good sense is hard to come by among these parts, isn't it?" Gerin said.

He didn't think he was being much more than his usual sardonic self. His son's mind, though, worked in the same channel as his own. Dagref whirled around and gave him a look half stricken, half relieved. "You know, don't you?" he said.

"I *know* now," Gerin said. "I'd wondered for a while, aye."

"You don't think Van knows, do you?" Dagref asked in some alarm—not enough, as far as Gerin was concerned, but some.

"If he did know," the Fox answered, "do you think he'd waste his time yelling at Rihwin and Ferdulf?"

"A point," Dagref said, still not happily.

"You had better be careful," Gerin said—useless advice to most youths, but Dagref was not—in some ways was not—cut from the usual cloth. "If you get her with child, you'll think the five hells had come crashing down on you, no matter how much fun you're having now."

"Another point," Dagref admitted. "There are—" He paused and coughed and might have blushed a little as he searched for words. "There are . . . ways of doing things where we don't have to worry about that."

"Yes, I know about those ways," Gerin said, nodding. "I wasn't sure whether you did."

"Er—I do," Dagref said, and stopped there.

Gerin was content to stop there, too. He couldn't very well keep an eye on his son, not in this matter he couldn't. He could—and did—hope Dagref and Maeva would stay content to stop with substitutes when they found themselves alone together. Whatever Maeva did, she threw herself into it wholeheartedly. In that, she very much resembled both her parents. That meant Gerin would have to rely on Dagref's good sense, and on Dagref's having good sense at a time when good sense was supposed to go flying out the door.

With any other lad of Dagref's age, it would have been the most forlorn of forlorn hopes. Gerin studied his son. He still didn't think the odds were any too good, but he didn't think they were hopeless, either. He sighed. Whatever the odds were, he had no choice but to accept them.

He rubbed his chin. That wasn't strictly true. "Maybe I ought to send Maeva home, to keep this from getting any further out of hand than it is already."

Dagref looked stricken. "Don't do that, Father. You didn't send her home for anything she did, so it wouldn't be fair to send her home for anything I'm doing."

"Unless you're violating her by force, which I doubt you would do and doubt you could do, you're not doing it altogether by yourself," the Fox pointed out, at which Dagref blushed again. In musing tones, Gerin went on, "Maybe I should send you home instead."

"I hope you don't send either of us," Dagref said. "If you have to send one of us, though, send me."

Gerin slapped him on the back. "That's well spoken,

for I know you aren't trying to get away from the fighting. But I do think I'll leave you both here." He found one other question to ask: "What will you do if Van finds out?"

He didn't think Dagref would be able to come up with any answer for that. But Dagref did, and promptly, too: "Run."

"Well, all right," Gerin said with a startled laugh. "That's probably the best thing you could do, though I don't know if you'll be able to run far enough or fast enough."

"Have to try." Dagref risked a wry smile that reminded Gerin achingly of himself. "Maybe he won't be able to decide whether to set out after me first or Maeva, and we'll both be able to get away."

"Maybe." Gerin laughed again. Van, though, was too automatically competent a warrior to dither at a time like that. He would settle on one of Dagref or Maeva—probably Dagref—first and then the other. The Fox hoped his son wouldn't have to learn that from experience.

After a few days, scouts brought back word that the imperials looked to be getting ready to push forward again. Gerin clicked his tongue between his teeth, far from a happy sound. "I knew it was coming," he said with a sigh. "I'd have been happier if it hadn't come so soon, though."

"What will we do, lord king?" a scout asked.

"Fight, I suppose." Gerin sighed again. "The only other choice we have is letting ourselves get pushed back into the valley of Ikos, and I don't want to do that. With everything else that's gone wrong in this campaign, I don't need to have Biton angry at me, too."

"We lost the last time we tried to withstand the imperials," Dagref pointed out. "Why should this time be any different?"

"Last time, they picked the ground—or they didn't leave me much choice, which amounts to the same thing," the Fox answered. "They struck faster and harder than I thought they would. We have better warning this time. I'm going to fight where I want to fight, by the gods."

"What sort of ground are you thinking of?" Dagref asked.

"I have a place in mind, as a matter of fact," Gerin said. "It's a long, thin stretch of meadow, with really heavy woods on either side. Off to the left, beyond the woods, there's a little hill I intend to screen off with a good many of Rihwin's riders. Do you see what's in my mind?"

"I think so," Dagref answered. "You want to put men back there and trap the imperials between your two forces, don't you?"

"That's what I'm planning, yes," Gerin agreed. "Now I have to hope the imperials don't see it as clearly as you've done."

But the imperials, to his loud, vehement, and profane dismay, did see the trap, and refused to fall into it. When his riders picked off one of the scouts from south of the High Kirs, he found out why. "We've got Swerilas in command of us now," the prisoner said. "Swerilas the Slippery, men call him. He sent Arpulo Werekas' son back west to take charge of the sieges against Gerin—"

"I'm Gerin," Gerin said.

"Against Aragis, then. I can't keep you rebels straight," the captured imperial said. "Swerilas figured that was the easier part of the job, so he gave it to Arpulo. You've caused Arpulo trouble; Swerilas decided he needed to deal with you himself."

"Were it not for the honor he shows me, it's a compliment I could do without," Gerin murmured, and then,

"Swerilas the Slippery, eh? He'd be the fellow who was in charge of your second army, wouldn't he?"

"Aye," the prisoner said. "Arpulo led the first."

Gerin scowled. His life had just got more difficult. He had Arpulo's measure, even if he'd lacked the manpower to beat him in their latest clash. But Swerilas . . . an ekename like *the Slippery* was all too close to *the Fox*, and Swerilas had shown that he had more than a few ideas of his own. Gerin would have been happier fighting a bruiser who didn't think very well.

After he sent the prisoner away, he decided he might have been lucky that Swerilas had stayed out of his trap rather than letting himself go in with his eyes open and then smashing out in both directions at once. Gerin's force was inferior to his in numbers. Against an average commander like Arpulo, the Fox had no qualms—well, few qualms—about dividing even an inferior force. Against someone who knew what he was doing, as Swerilas plainly did, dividing his force was asking to be destroyed in detail.

With another scowl, Gerin did his best to come up with a new plan. Against Swerilas, he had fewer options than he'd had against Arpulo. And Swerilas, no doubt, would be able to think of more unpleasant things to do to him than would have crossed Arpulo's fierce but unimaginative mind.

Gerin dispatched all his horsemen to harass Swerilas' scouts, to drive them back on the main body of imperials, and to disrupt the imperials' foraging as much as he could. "You riders are the one force we have that the imperials don't know everything about," he told Rihwin the Fox. "We'll wring every particle of advantage we can out of that."

"Aye, lord king," Rihwin said. "We shall fall on the men of the Elabonian Empire like a whirlwind. We shall trouble them with continuous attacks from all directions, until they weepingly regret ever having stirred north of the High Kirs."

That was as grandiloquent as anything Gerin had heard lately, even from Rihwin. But Rihwin, fortunately, was almost as long on fighting talent as he was on bombast. Gerin thumped him on the shoulder. "Aye, that's good. That's what I want from you. The harder he has to work against your horsemen, the less leisure he'll have to do anything against the main army here."

"I shall think on this with gratitude as the imperials chew my force to pieces," Rihwin replied, bowing.

"Go howl," Gerin said. "I don't want you to get chewed to pieces. I'm counting on you not to let yourself and your force get chewed to pieces. By the gods, I don't want to fight a pitched battle with this Swerilas. I want you to keep him running every which way, so he's too busy and hot and bothered to come and fight a pitched battle with the whole army."

"Oh, I understand you, lord king," Rihwin said. "Whether what you want and what Swerilas wants are one and the same remains to be seen."

"That's true in any fight," Gerin said. "I'll move forward as far as I can with the bulk of my force. If you do get in trouble, I'll support you as best I can." He set a hand on Rihwin's shoulder again. "Do your best not to get in too much trouble, would you?"

"How can you say such a thing about me?" Rihwin drew back in an artful display of indignation. "Have I ever been anything in all my days save staid and sedate?" He had an excellent straight face.

"No, never," Gerin agreed soberly. Both men laughed then.

Rihwin said, "Will you let Ferdulf come along with me? It will be easier to annoy the imperials if I have the best notion I can of where they are, where they're moving, and what they want to try to do to me."

"If you can talk Ferdulf into going with you, you're welcome to him," Gerin answered. His grin was distinctly sardonic. "In fact, you're welcome to him as a general principle."

"As a general principle, I don't want him, thanks." Rihwin's grin closely matched Gerin's. "Didn't you hear us going at each other a few days ago?"

"Most of the northlands heard you, I should think," Gerin said.

"I daresay. You can understand me, then. As a flying spy, though, he has his uses."

"Whether he'll want anything to do with you, of course, remains to be seen," Gerin said. "He's liable not to be very happy with you, you know, after the rough handling Mavrix gave him—you were the one who was bound and determined to summon the Sithonian god."

"Yes, that's what Ferdulf was screeching about before," Rihwin said, "but I'll take my chances now."

"You certainly will," Gerin agreed, at which Rihwin gave him a dirty look. Gerin went on, "Talk with him, though. If, after he's done insulting you some more, he decides to go along, I think you're right—he'll be quite useful to you as a flying spy."

"After something close to half a lifetime with you and Van of the Strong Arm, I shan't let insults from a bad-tempered baby demigod faze me," Rihwin said. Off he went, ostentatiously ignoring the sour stare Gerin sent after him.

Sure enough, he managed to persuade Ferdulf to accompany the force of riders. After the shouting Ferdulf put up when he made the request, though, Gerin wouldn't have blamed Rihwin if he'd buried Mavrix's son upside down in the ground. That, at least, would have made Ferdulf shut up.

Watching the little demigod wheel and swoop above the horsemen, Gerin was also just as well pleased not to be under there, in the same way he would have been just as well pleased not to be under a flock of crows with griping bowels. The crows would have let fly—or let fall—at random. Ferdulf, if the evil mood took him, could aim.

Van was not watching Ferdulf as the riders trotted away. He was trying to spot Maeva among the warriors on horseback, and not having much luck. Turning to Gerin, he said, "I still wish you'd made her go home."

"She's doing what she wants to do, you know," the Fox answered. "You couldn't stop it more than another couple of years at the most."

"That would be good," Van said. "In a couple of years, likely enough, we wouldn't be worrying about the imperials any more."

"Unless we'd already lost to them, of course," Gerin replied. "No, wait—I take your point. But we would be worrying about Aragis or the Trokmoi or the Gradi or *somebody*, by the gods. If Maeva wanted to fight somebody, she'd find somebody to fight. And if you didn't feel like letting her, she'd fight *you*."

"Maybe. Maybe." The prospect didn't make Van look any happier. "But that's not the only thing I fret about. Come on, Fox—you know what soldiers are like."

"Well, what if I do?" the Fox said. "Anyone who tried to take anything she didn't feel like giving would regret it as long as he lived, and that might not be long, either. We've been over this ground before, you know."

"Oh, aye." The outlander let out a long, sad sigh. "Why couldn't she have just stayed home and come to notice Dagref, say? We could have married them off, and that would have been an end to it."

Gerin didn't gape like a fool. He didn't burst into hysterical laughter. He didn't even suffer a coughing fit. The effort he needed to keep from doing any of those things would have let him lift the temple at Ikos over his head and throw it from one end of the valley to the other.

In an offhand tone that somehow wasn't more elaborately casual than it should have been, he answered, "If they like the idea, you wouldn't see me complaining. We'll have to see if we can make it seem as if they're the ones who came up with it, not us."

"Truth that," Van said, one of the turns of phrase he'd learned from the Trokmoi that still occasionally showed up in his speech. "If anybody older than I was came up with a notion back when I was a sprat, I didn't want anything to do with it." He cocked his head to one side and studied the Fox. "And you! You must have been a terror when it came to listening to your elders."

"Who, me?" Gerin did his best to look like innocence personified. His best, evidently, wasn't good enough, for Van guffawed.

"Aye, you, Captain," he said. "Go on and look sweet all you fancy. My guess is, you weren't any more ready to pay the least bit of attention to what your father told you than Dagref is for you."

"My father hit me harder and more often than I've hit Dagref," Gerin said after a brief pause for thought. "That made me more likely to listen, but I think less likely to agree."

Van smacked a fist into the palm of his other hand. "Sometimes you'll settle for getting them to listen that way."

"You say that *now*," Gerin said. "What did you say *then*?"

"Ahh, what difference does that make?" the outlander

replied with a grin. "I was just a brat then, wet behind the ears. Of course, I wouldn't have believed that if anybody told it to me, mind you."

Rihwin began sending back prisoners and the occasional wagon pilfered from the imperials and news of what Swerilas the Slippery was up to. "The Empire's general looks to be pulling all his men back into a knot," one of Rihwin's riders reported, "the same way a snail will go back into its shell if you poke it in one of its little horns." He held up a couple of fingers, imitating a snail.

"The creatures have their eyes at the ends of those stalks," Gerin said, a fact he'd picked up in the City of Elabon. He'd never had occasion to trot it out in all the many years since, but his fiendishly tenacious memory hadn't let him forget it.

Now that he finally did get to use it, he discovered the horseman didn't believe him. With a laugh, the fellow said, "That's funny, lord king."

"I mean it," Gerin said indignantly. "If those little black dots on the ends of the stalks aren't eyes, where would a snail keep 'em?"

"How am I supposed to answer a question like that?" the rider said. "The whole world knows snails have no eyes."

"But they do," the Fox insisted. He couldn't persuade the horseman he wasn't joking. Finally, in disgust, he sent him back to Rihwin. Gerin was still fuming when he turned to Van, who had listened to the last part of his exchange with the scout. "Can you believe the stubborn ignorance of that man?"

Van chuckled. He shook his head, but not in the way Gerin would have wanted. "Oh no you don't, Captain," the outlander said. "You can try and confuse a rider from some backwoods keep as much as you like, but you're not going to do it to me, by the gods. When you come right down to it, that fellow was right—everybody knows snails don't have any eyes."

Gerin snarled a curse and stalked off.

He snarled another curse a couple of days later, when the imperials mauled a detachment of Rihwin's riders. The damage done was bad enough that Rihwin felt he had to come back himself to explain. "They outwitted me," he said, sounding angry and embarrassed at the same time. "They had a small band showing, making their way through wheatfields. But more of them were lurking in the trees. As soon as we were well engaged with the decoys, out they swarmed."

"That's . . . unfortunate," Gerin said. He looked down his nose at Rihwin. "It's also unfortunate that you let yourself be fooled by the sort of trick we've used so often ourselves."

"I didn't expect it of the imperials," Rihwin said, a little sullenly. "One of the reasons I came north of the High Kirs all those years ago, if you'll remember, is because interesting things happen here while all stays stodgy south of the mountains. The way the Emperor's men fought in this campaign had given me little reason to change my view."

"Except for the forces commanded by this Swerilas the Slippery," Gerin said. "He beat us when we were almost down to Cassat, and he did it the same way he did here: he stuck out one force, and then he struck with another one we didn't expect. If bait looks too juicy to be true, my fellow Fox, it likely is."

"But it didn't look too juicy to be true." Rihwin angrily kicked at the dirt. "By the gods, you would have sent in the riders with no more hesitation than I showed. It was a chance encounter, nothing more."

"No, it *seemed* a chance encounter—or you wouldn't

have been ambushed," Gerin said. "He must have set it up by gauging where your detachment was, which way they were headed, and how fast." He kicked at the dirt, too. "Which means Swerilas is very slippery indeed."

"I want another crack at him," Rihwin said. "No one does that to me, not without paying for it."

"Unfortunately, someone did do it to you," Gerin answered, "and I don't want you charging after the imperials all wild for revenge. Swerilas will be waiting for something like that."

For a wonder, he got through to Rihwin. "Aye, belike you're right," Rihwin said. "It's just what a man from the City of Elabon would expect in the northlands— let the locals make fools of themselves, and then count on them to make bigger fools of themselves trying to recover."

"Of course, odds are he didn't know he was facing another man from south of the High Kirs," Gerin said.

"Go ahead—rub salt in the throbbing wound." Rihwin struck a pose of affronted dignity. Then it collapsed, and he chuckled. "Speaking of men from south of the High Kirs, lord king, did I tell you we've captured my cousin?"

"No." Gerin raised an eyebrow. "How did that happen?"

"Usual sort of way," Rihwin answered. "He got wounded in the shoulder—doesn't look too bad—fell out of his chariot, and we scooped him up. When I found out his name was Ulfilas Batwin's son, I asked about his family, because my uncle's son Batwin is a man of about my age. And sure enough, we are first cousins, once removed."

"You've been removed by twenty years and a mountain range, too," Gerin said. He sighed and put an arm around Rihwin. "All right. You walked into this one. It's over. Don't do it again." He laughed. "I sound as if I'm talking to one of my sons, don't I? One of these days, maybe, just maybe, you'll grow up. One of them has done it, and the second is on the way."

"I resent the imputation." Rihwin looked affronted again.

"Go ahead," Gerin said cheerfully. "I'll probably have to keep right on lecturing you till they shovel dirt over one of us or the other."

"You could shut up instead," Rihwin suggested. They laughed, both knowing that Gerin shutting up was about as likely—or rather, as unlikely—as Rihwin growing up.

Ferdulf came flying toward Gerin's main force. "Here he comes!" the demigod shouted. "That cursed horse turd of a Swerilas is heading this way, and I don't think he's coming to invite you to take ale with him."

"Well, I can't say I'm surprised," Gerin answered. He couldn't say he was truly ready to meet Swerilas' assault, either, but volition didn't play any great role here. "How far away is he, and how are the horsemen doing at holding him back?"

"He'll be here in a couple of hours' time, maybe less," Ferdulf answered. "The riders are doing what they can, but they can't stop the son of a sow all by themselves. He's got too many men. He's got too many chariots, too."

"I know that," Gerin said discontentedly. "He's got too many men and too many chariots for this whole army."

"Well, what are you going to do about it?" Ferdulf screeched.

"The best I can," Gerin answered.

"*That's* not good enough," Ferdulf said. "You have to beat him. If you don't beat him, the northlands are ruined."

"If I don't beat him, I'm ruined," the Fox said. "The possibility remains that I may not beat him." He clicked his tongue between his teeth. "If I don't, I'll just have to go on from there."

"You make it sound so easy." Scorn laced Ferdulf's voice. "Where will you go on from there, pray tell?"

"I don't know," Gerin admitted. "I hope I don't have to find out." Ferdulf stared at him. A trifle irritably, he went on, "I'm not a god, Ferdulf. I'm not even related to a god. I don't know what's going to happen next. All I can do is the best I can, and see what happens. I told you that already."

"What a sloppy arrangement," Ferdulf said. "And what, if you would be so generous as to tell me, is the best you can do?"

Gerin had been thinking it over while the demigod carped at him. "I'm going to keep my men in one compact mass and hit the imperials as hard a blow as I can. I don't dare divide my army against Swerilas. He has too many men and too many brains for me to take the chance. What I hope is that I'll catch him trying to do something fancy and punish him before he can pull all of his forces together." He brightened a little. "Go fly off and tell me how he's deploying. That way, I'll have some notion of what I'm up against."

"You're out of your head," Ferdulf replied with mournful certainty, but away he flew. Gerin sighed and began shouting orders.

The men formed up as quickly as he could have wanted. None of them showed any particular eagerness for the fight ahead, not even Adiatunnus' Trokmoi. Maybe that meant they were veterans who didn't need to scream like fiends to go out and fight well. Maybe it meant they had no particular hope of victory. Gerin hoped it was the one and not the other.

Far faster than he should have, given where Swerilas' force was, Ferdulf came whizzing back. "What now?"

Gerin asked in alarm. Had the imperial general stolen a march on him?

But Ferdulf answered, "If you're going to fight in one large, ugly lump, are you fain to have me tell Rihwin bring his horsemen back so they can take their lumps with the rest of you?"

"Oh, by the gods!" Gerin exclaimed, mentally kicking himself for having sent the demigod off too soon. "Yes, and thank you, Ferdulf. I'm in your debt. I admit it."

"You're in my debt, you owe your son a promise, you owe the imperials a thrashing—do you think you can deliver on any of these?" Ferdulf flew away before the Fox had a chance to reply.

He sent his men forward, toward that field he'd found that was well suited to the size of his force. As the main force advanced, Rihwin's riders began joining them. Gerin posted the horsemen as a screen in front of the main body of chariotry and on either flank.

"Is that Maeva?" Van pointed off to the right. He answered his own question: "Aye, it is." He waved, then muttered in disappointment. "She didn't see me, curse it."

Dagref's head was turned in that direction. He nodded. "It is Maeva, though, and she seems all right." He was better than he had been a little while before at sounding casual about it.

Gerin looked west down the dirt road that ran through the field. he nodded. Here came the imperials, exchanging arrows with the last of his horsemen. Like his own troops, the men of the Elabonian Empire were already deployed in line of battle, sweeping down the road and along the open country to either side. Catching them in column would have been sweet, but Swerilas, with his sobriquet, was too alert to have let that happen.

"Elabon! Elabon! Elabon!" the imperials shouted.

Gerin, for one, was heartily sick of that battle cry. His own men yelled the usual northlands assortment of war cries and insults back at their foes.

"Forward!" Gerin put everything he had into his own shout. He wanted to be moving to receive the imperials' charge, not standing still, waiting to be overrun.

Dagref flicked the reins and cracked the whip above the horses' backs. They went from walk to trot to gallop. One wheel of the car hit a stone. The chariot flew into the air and came back to earth with a crash. Neither Gerin nor Van nor Dagref did anything more than shift weight back and forth.

Gerin looked to see if he could pick out Swerilas the Slippery among the imperials. He couldn't. Swerilas was slippery enough not to deck himself out in raiment that made him a target. The Fox shook his head in disappointment. He hadn't seen any other imperial officers that canny.

He started shooting anyhow. If he couldn't find the best target, he'd hit what he could. He didn't think Swerilas had sent an outflanking party off to either wing; if the imperial general had done such a thing, Ferdulf would have reported it—or so the Fox devoutly hoped. That made it a straightforward slugging match, army against army: the same sort of fight Arpulo had waged. Like the general he'd replaced, Swerilas had greater numbers.

But Swerilas quickly proved himself a better general than Arpulo. Arpulo had let Gerin's men get round his flanks and attack his force from three sides at once. Swerilas, by contrast, made his own battle line wide and kept trying to lap round Gerin's force to the right and left. Very much unlike Arpulo, he knew what he had and what to do with it.

Unhappily, Gerin extended his own line. He knew what

Swerilas was trying to do: make him thin his force enough to let the imperials find or create a weak spot and punch on through. If they did that, they could split his army in two and destroy one of the parts at their leisure.

Other than retreat, the only counter he could find was doing it to them before they had a chance to do it to him. That meant thinning his line even more than he'd done already, to collect a force with which he could strike. Crew by crew, his chariotry remained better than that of the Elabonian Empire. Without that being true, he couldn't have done what he did. Even with its being true, he gripped the rail of the chariot hard, knowing the risk he took.

"Forward!" he shouted again. Dagref steered the car toward what looked like the weakest part of the imperial line.

For a brief, shining moment, he thought his striking force would break through. The imperials still had a respect for the Trokmoi just short of dread. Adiatunnus' howling warriors did make them hesitate. But Swerilas, unlike Gerin, did not have to stint one part of his line to send reinforcements to another. He brought enough men in against Gerin's striking force to keep it from piercing his army through and through.

"Well, what do we do now?" Van yelled in Gerin's ear once the attack had plainly bogged down.

"Good question," Gerin answered. Dagref maneuvered smartly to keep the imperials from getting a chariot to either side of his own at the same time. The maneuver brought the horses around so they were facing more nearly the way they had come than the way they'd been going. Gerin shot an arrow at one of the imperials closest to him, and wounded the trooper in the arm. But there were still too many soldiers from the Elabonian Empire close by. With a weary curse, the Fox said, "Now we go back. I don't see what in the five hells else we can do, not if we want to keep the army in one piece."

He managed the retreat as well as he could. By then, he'd had more practice managing retreats than he'd ever wanted. He'd never had to manage one against Swerilas the Slippery before, though. Swerilas did what he would have done himself in the same place: pushed hard and tried not merely to beat the army from the northlands but to wreck it.

Gerin had hoped to be able to make a stand back at his camp, but the leading imperials were too closely mingled with his rear guard to make that possible. They were pressing Gerin and his men too hard to make any stand possible for some time. Gerin had everything he could do to keep the imperials from getting ahead of his men and cutting off their line of retreat.

He did succeed in doing that much—that little, he thought of it at the time—but Swerilas drove him almost to the southern opening of the valley of Ikos before the light finally failed. By all indications, Swerilas aimed to keep right on driving him when morning came, too. He looked north. Temple guards no doubt waited at the mouth of the valley. He didn't care. But for Ikos, he had nowhere to go.

XI

A guardsman held his shield horizontally across his body to bar the road into the valley of Ikos. "The lord Biton forbids the entry of large bodies of armed men into the land surrounding his sacred precinct," the fellow said.

Gerin answered, "If the lord Biton punishes me for bringing my army into his land, then he will, that's all." He turned and waved his battered army forward. "Get moving, boys!"

"The god will know of your action!" the guard bleated as chariots began rolling past him and his spear.

"He's the farseeing god, so of course he will," the Fox replied. "He'll also know why we're doing it, which is more than you do. Swerilas the Slippery and the Elabonian army are on our tail. You're going to have more company than us, and worse company than us, too."

"Biton preserve us!" the guardsman said.

"That would be nice," Gerin agreed, "but don't count on it too much, because it's liable not to happen."

The guard glared at him. "Why did you have to lead the imperials here? Why couldn't you have fled in some other direction than this one?"

"It's hard to flee straight toward the fellow who's just made you do it," Gerin pointed out. "And it was either come here or head off east toward the plains of Shanda. Somehow, I don't think I'm cut out to be a nomad."

"But we've been free of the Empire for many years," the temple guard moaned. "Will the officious priests from south of the mountains stick their long snouts into the way we run our affairs, as I have heard they did in the long-ago and far-off days?"

"Very likely they will," Gerin said. "That's what they're good for: sticking their noses into things, I mean. That's what they'll do if they win, anyhow. But my army is still in one piece, even if we have lost some fights. We may beat the imperials yet."

"Farseeing Biton grant it be so!" the guard answered. "Very well, then: I give you leave to pass into this valley, unless the farseeing god should himself choose to overrule me."

"Thanks," the Fox said. He'd intended to take his army into the valley of Ikos whether the guardsman gave him leave or not. If the temple guard had been so foolish as to refuse to give his leave, Biton's temple probably would have had to get along without him from then on. Gerin figured he could square it with the god; what use would a farseeing deity have for such a stupid guard?

"We shall not grant leave to the imperials," the temple guard declared. "If they enter, they shall enter in Biton's despite, and shall face his punishment."

"Will you fight against the men of the Elabonian Empire?" Gerin asked. "Will you fight alongside us to protect the northlands?"

"That will be Biton's judgment to make, not mine," the guardsman said. "If the god orders it, we shall assuredly fight. If the god orders otherwise, we shall likewise obey him."

I haven't the faintest idea, was what he meant, though his phrasing was a good deal more polished than that.

He hadn't come right out and said no. Gerin supposed that would have to do.

Into the valley of Ikos rode his battered troopers. Had the imperials been a little luckier—and he knew it would have taken no more than that—his army would have been cut off before it got to the valley, cut off and destroyed. The imperials would have more chance to do that soon enough.

For now, though, rest. Time to see to the wounded, time to see to the horses and chariots, time to curl up in a blanket and sleep a sleep that seemed not far removed from death. Gerin looked forward to that kind of sleep—looked forward to it with a hopeless longing, because he would be too busy to enjoy anywhere near so much of it as his men did.

As usual after a battle, he did what he could for the men who had been hurt. He did some horse-doctoring, too. That was harder, and in a way more discouraging. His men had a notion of why and how they'd taken wounds. To the horses, everything was a nasty surprise.

Gerin was washing a cut on a horse's rump with ale when Rihwin came up to him. The horse quivered and let out a whuffling snort, but did not try to bolt or kick. "That's a good fellow," the Fox said. The rider holding the horse's head stroked its nose and murmured, "There's a brave fellow. That's my beauty." The words meant little, the tone much.

With a sigh, Gerin turned to Rihwin. "And what can I do for *you*?" His tone meant much, too, but in a far less gentle way.

Rihwin answered, "Lord king, I should like to know what our next movement against the imperials will be."

"Should you?" Gerin said. Rihwin nodded. With a grimace, Gerin went on, "Well, by the gods, so should I. The only thing I can think of doing, though, is to keep on with what we're already doing, which is to say, retreating."

"Back toward our own lands, you mean," Rihwin said.

Gerin exhaled in exasperation. "You must have been listening to that lackwit of a temple guard. It's very hard to retreat *toward* the enemy; the technical term for that is *advance*."

"For which wisdom I thank you, O font of knowledge," Rihwin said, not about to be outdone in sarcasm, "but that was not precisely what I had in mind. As you know, only one road leads from the valley of Ikos to lands under your illustrious suzerainty, and it is a road perhaps something less than conducive to rapid travel."

"Ah," Gerin said, and nodded. "Now I understand. You're not happy about the notion of traveling through the haunted woods, eh?"

"To put with as much abridgment as I can muster, lord king, no," Rihwin said. "Are you?"

"Not so you'd notice," Gerin answered. "But if it's a choice between that and staying here so the imperials can finish wrecking us, I know which direction I'll go. All I can do is hope my men and I come out on the other side. If we do, maybe we can smash in the head of the imperials' column as they come after us."

"That would be good," Rihwin said without much conviction. He didn't think it would happen, then.

"Better still," Gerin said in a spirit of experimentation, "would be meeting the imperials here in the valley of Ikos and driving them back."

Plainly, Gerin didn't think that would happen, either. "Yes, that would be better, lord king," he agreed. "Not likely, perhaps, but better without a doubt. How do you aim to produce a victory when lately we've known nothing but defeat?"

"I don't know," Gerin admitted, which seemed to

nonplus Rihwin more than anything else he might have said. "The best we can hope for now, it seems to me, is to hope the imperials haven't the stomach for a long, hard campaign and give up and go home."

"We might have had a better hope for that had we gained the aid of the lord of the sweet grape," Rihwin said.

"That's not what Biton said, but then you've never been much interested in any opinion but your own."

Rihwin scowled at him; a moment later, though, the eyes of the man from south of the High Kirs widened. "You demon from the hottest hell," he whispered. "You let me go through the danger of summoning Mavrix hoping and expecting I would fail, and you said never a word."

"I understand how surprising it must be for you to discover there are people who can on occasion keep their mouths shut," Gerin replied sweetly. "You really should try it sometime. It can be useful."

"To the crows with utility, and to the crows with you, too," Rihwin said. His effort to stalk off in impressive fury was hampered when he bumped into Van. Like everyone else who bumped into the outsized outlander, he bounced off. He kept stalking after that, but it wasn't the same.

Van shook his head. "I see you were rattling his cage again."

"Twice," Gerin answered. Then he corrected himself. "No, I take that back. He rattled his own cage once, when he figured out I wasn't too unhappy that he hadn't managed to get Mavrix to help us after all."

"What did he do, say you were trying to use him as a sacrifice, the way the god of the Weshapar wanted Zalmunna to sacrifice his son?"

"He didn't use that example, no, but that was the

general tone, as a matter of fact." The Fox laughed.
Laughing felt good. It also let him take his mind off
the unpleasant fact that he still had no idea how to stop
the imperials. But when he stopped laughing, that fact
remained—and it seemed to be laughing at him, laughing
and showing fangs as long as sharp as those of a longtooth.

Maybe it was laughing at Van, too. He said, "Come
morning, that Swerilas the Slimy is going to start nipping
at our tails again."

"Slippery," Gerin said. "Swerilas the Slippery, no matter
how slimy he is. But . . ." He hesitated, then spoke in
some surprise: "I may just know what I'm going to do
about him. Aye, by the gods—and by one god in
particular—I may just."

Sure enough, Swerilas pushed his men forward not
long after the sun came up. The temple guards did resist
them. So did a rear guard of Gerin's men. But the
imperials were too many to be withstood for long, and
in Swerilas had a leader who grew angry with anything
less than victory.

Gerin fed more men into the fight, not so much in
expectation of stopping Swerilas as to slow him down.
And, had Swerilas not already been a suspicious sort,
failure to try to hold him off would have made him one.
Slowing him down also let Gerin's main force forage
among the prosperous villages of the valley of Ikos as
they retreated toward the Sibyl's shrine.

The temple guards peeled off to defend the temple
from its marble outwalls. Gerin ordered his own men
to keep on retreating. Dagref gave his father a curious
look. Then, all at once, it vanished from his face. "Biton's
temple holds a lot of rich things, doesn't it?" he remarked.

"Oh, there might be a few in there, I suppose," Gerin
answered, his voice elaborately casual. "Why? Do you

think that might be interesting to the imperial soldiers and their officers?"

"It just might," his son said, imitating his tone with alarming precision. "The one thing about which the men of the northlands always complain is how the Elabonian Empire squeezed wealth out of them like a man squeezing whey out of a lump of cheese."

"Biton isn't the sort of god who fancies being squeezed," Van put in.

"You know that," Gerin said. "I know that. The question is, does Swerilas the Slippery know that? And the other question is, if he does know, does he care? He has wizards with him. He has the backing of the Elabonian gods, or thinks he does. Maybe he won't care a fig's worth, and think he can take whatever he pleases."

"Wouldn't that be nice?" Van said dreamily. "We've seen the plague Biton sends down on people who try robbing his shrine. All those blisters and things—it's not pretty, not even a little bit. Fox, don't you think this Swerilas would look mighty fine all blistered up?"

"Since I've never met him, I don't know how ugly he is already," Gerin replied. "But any old imperial covered in blisters would look pretty good to me right now."

North of the Sibyl's shine lay the town that catered to visitors to the valley who came seeking oracular responses. The town was not what it had been in Gerin's younger days. Traffic for the Sibyl had diminished when the Elabonian Empire severed itself from the northlands, and diminished again after the earthquake that loosed the monsters on the earth. Many of the inns and taverns and hostels that had served travelers were empty. Some were wrecks that had gone unrepaired since the quake fifteen years before. Grass grew where others had once stood.

The innkeepers whose establishments survived viewed

the arrival of Gerin's army with the same delight that serfs would have shown over the arrival of a swarm of locusts, and for similar reasons: they feared the troopers were going to eat them out of house and home, and they were right.

"Is this justice, lord king?" one of them wailed as Gerin's soldiers gobbled bread and roasted meat and guzzled ale.

"Probably not," the Fox admitted. "But we're hungry and we're here and we're bloody well going to eat. If we win this war, I'll pay you back next year—by all the gods I swear it. If we lose, you can send the bill to Crebbig I, the Elabonian Emperor."

"Then I'll root for you," the innkeeper said. "You have a good name for not telling too many lies. I wouldn't wipe my arse with a promise from somebody on the far side of the mountains, not that I even have a promise from the whoreson to wipe my arse with."

Gerin thought it likely the innkeeper would see the imperials at first hand before too long. As he'd hoped, Swerilas had slowed his aggressive pursuit of the men from the northlands when he came in sight of Biton's shrine. Rihwin's riders had no trouble holding the imperials away from the town of Ikos, not for the time being.

Taking advantage of that, the Fox put as many of his men in real beds as he could. The summer's fighting had worn down his troopers; the more rest they got now, the better they would perform when they had to climb into their chariots again.

He slept outside rolled in a blanket himself, which perplexed Adiatunnus. "Where's the point to kinging it if you canna be after enjoying yourself?" the Trokmê chieftain demanded. He hadn't been slow about claiming the pleasures of a bed.

Gerin shrugged. "I'm all right. Some of the men with small wounds need mattresses worse than I do."

"Maybe that's so, and maybe it's not," Adiatunnus said. "Most o' these lads are half your age—half my age, too, forbye—and think naught of a night in the open. If you say you don't creak of a morning, you're a better man than I am—or else you're a liar."

"I do creak," Gerin admitted, "but I don't creak too badly. And half the time I'll creak when I get up out of a bed in the morning, too. I'm at the age when creaking is part of being alive. I'm used to it. I don't love it, but I can't do anything about it."

"Nor I," Adiatunnus said sadly. "Nor I. But I creak less if I'm rising from soft straw or wool, sure and I do, and so I'll take a bed when I find one. A bed is better when you're after finding a friendly barmaid, too."

"However you like," Gerin said with another shrug. Like Van, Adiatunnus wenched whenever he found a chance.

He laughed at the Fox now. "You canna be saying you're so old, it stirs in your breeches no more. When it does, why not let it out to play? Plenty o' girls'd lie down with you just for the sake of saying they'd bedded a king."

"I don't want—" Gerin stopped. What he'd been about to say wasn't true. He wasn't immune from wanting an attractive woman when he was away from Selatre. What he did, or rather didn't, do about it was something else again. He changed the direction in which the sentence had been going: "I don't want to complicate my life. How many bastards have you got?"

"A good many, I'll allow," the Trokmê answered, laughing again. "Not so many as Rihwin, I expect, but I had fun getting every one of 'em."

"All right," Gerin said. "I don't begrudge you the way

you live your life. Why can't you let me lead mine as suits me best?"

Adiatunnus scowled again. "How can I be having a proper quarrel with you when you willna get angry?"

"My quarrel is with Swerilas the Slippery, not with you," Gerin replied. "You're my ally and my vassal; he's my foe." He grinned a lopsided grin. "And when we were young, neither of us would have believe that could be so, not for a minute we wouldn't."

"Truth that," Adiatunnus said. "Och, how we hated the very name of yourself on the far side of the Niffet! Too good you were, too good by half, at tying us all in knots whenever we thought to raid over the river. And then, we we did at last lodge ourself on this side, who but you did so much against us and kept so many from crossing? And now you are my overlord, and we have the same enemies, as you say. Aye, 'tis strange and more than strange."

"If I can put up with the likes of you," Gerin said, "I shouldn't—and I don't—mind putting up with a blanket on the ground."

"Sure it was for your kindness and sweet spirit I first named you king," Adiatunnus said. He walked off shaking his head and laughing.

The next morning, Maeva, her face glowing with self-importance, came riding back from the line against the imperials with the fat eunuch who had taken Gerin down to the Sibyl's cave. "He says he must have speech with you, lord king."

"I'm glad enough to speak with him," Gerin answered, and turned to the priest. "How now?"

Awkwardly, the eunuch prostrated himself before Gerin, as if before an image of farseeing Biton. "Lord king, you must save the god's shrine from desecration!" he cried.

"Get up," the Fox said impatiently. When the priest had risen, Gerin went on, "Who says I must?"

"If you do not save the shrine, lord king, the arrogant wretches from south of the High Kirs will plunder it of the accumulated riches of centuries." The priest seemed on the point of bursting into tears.

For his part, though, Gerin had hoped the accumulated riches in and around Biton's temper would make Swerilas forget about him for a while. And so he repeated, "Who says I must save the shrine? Is it a command sent straight from Biton himself?" If it was, he might have to obey it, however little he wanted to.

But the priest shook his head, the loose, flabby flesh of his jowls swinging back and forth. "Biton has been mute in this matter," he said in his sexless voice. "But you, lord king, are well known for the great respect you have always shown the farseeing god."

"If the farseeing god ordered me to try to drive the men of the Elabonian Empire from his temple, I would do it, or do my best to do it," Gerin answered, on the whole truthfully. "Since he does not, though, let me ask a question of my own: why do you think I retreated past the Sibyl's shrine and made my base here in the town of Ikos?"

"I wondered, lord king," the eunuch priest replied. "I thought surely you would defend us with all your power."

"With all my power." Gerin heard the bitterness in his own voice. "If I had the power to stop the imperials, why would I have retreated into the valley of Ikos in the first place? Why would I have retreated through it? Why will I have to retreat out of it if the imperials attack me again?"

The priest stared at him. "But you are the chiefest warrior in all the northlands. How could you be beaten?"

"More easily than I'd like, as a matter of fact," Gerin answered. "When the Elabonian Empire sends more men against me than I can withstand, they beat me. Nothing complicated about it at all. And you can be glad Aragis the Archer isn't here to hear you call me the chiefest warrior, too. He'd disagree with you, and he isn't pleasant when he disagrees."

He might as well not have spoken. The priest didn't interrupt him, but plainly didn't pay any attention to his words, either. The fellow went on, "And you are the favorite of the farseeing god as well. How could it be otherwise, when you are wed to Biton's former Sibyl?" He sighed, perhaps admiring the close relationship with Biton he thought being married to Selatre gave Gerin, perhaps—as he was a eunuch—admiring Gerin for being married at all.

And, where he had not before, he gave Gerin pause. *Did* being married to Selatre give him any special obligations? It had given him advantages in the past, and accounts had a way of balancing. Even so, he hardened his heart and shook his head, saying, "If the farseeing god wants anything from me, he can tell me himself. I'll do what I can then. Without orders from the god, though, I'm not going to throw myself and my army away. Have you got that?"

The eunuch stared at him out of large, dark, tragic eyes. "I have indeed, lord king," he said. "I shall take your words back to my comrades in Biton's holy priesthood, that they may learn nothing shall suffice to rescue them from the rapacious clutches of the Elabonian Empire."

Gerin's children sometimes tried to make him feel guilty by taking that tone of voice. It didn't work for them, and it didn't work for the eunuch priest, either, though the Fox didn't laugh at him as he often did at his offspring. "If Biton wants his temple to stay unplundered, I expect he can manage that without me."

"I console myself with the hope that you are right," the priest replied, "but I have seen little to persuade me of it." He turned and waddled south, back toward the temple.

"Thanks, Maeva," Gerin said, watching him go. "You did the right thing to bring him to me, even if we can't help him now."

"I wish we could," Maeva said.

"So do I," Gerin said, "but if we could beat Swerilas' army any time we chose, don't you think we would have done it by now? Go on back and keep an eye on the imperials. They did slow down for the temple, the way I hoped they would. Sooner or later, they'll start again."

"Aye, lord king." She sketched a salute and rode after the eunuch priest.

The imperials did not move that day. Gerin hoped for thunderbolts from the temple, but none came. Glad at least for the respite, he wrapped himself in his blanket and went to sleep. While he slept, he dreamt.

It might have been the strangest dream he'd ever had. He kept seeing everything in it from an enormous distance, so he could make out nothing clearly. At the same time, he felt an overpoweringly strong sense of urgency. It was almost as if he were seeing the very edge of an important dream truly intended for someone else.

He kept trying to get closer to the center of the dream, to learn why it seemed so important. Try as he would, though, he could not. His dream-self ground its teeth in frustration. He might have stood at the bottom of some deep, smooth-sided hole too deep from him to climb out of it. But he had to climb out of it, no matter what.

When he woke, he was on his knees, his hands up

over his head. He stared around in confusion at the inns and houses of Ikos, and at the campfires around which most of his soldiers slept. For a moment, they seemed far less real than the dream he'd just lost.

He bit his lip. He'd missed something important. He knew he'd missed something important. He hated missing anything important. In the straits he was in, he couldn't afford to miss anything important. He couldn't do anything about it, though.

Maybe if he lay down and fell back to sleep, the dream would return. They sometimes did. Maybe, too, he would find himself closer to the heart of the matter. He bit his lip. He didn't like maybes. But, with no better choice, he lay down. Eventually, he slept. So far as he remembered, he dreamt nothing more for the rest of the night.

In the morning, Dagref and Ferdulf were missing. Gerin didn't fret so much over the demigod. For one thing, he thought Ferdulf likely able to take care of himself. For another, the camp was a good deal quieter without Ferdulf around.

But Dagref—for Dagref to run off struck Gerin as highly unlikely. And then, all at once, it didn't. Dagref could have had a perfectly good reason for slipping out of camp, a reason named Maeva. That he should have been so foolish as not to come back before things started stirring was another matter, one over which Gerin intended to have some pointed conversation with him.

The Fox couldn't even lose his temper, not so thoroughly as he would have liked, unless he wanted to alert Van to the reason he was upset. The outlander, seeing he was worried but not fully grasping why, said, "To the five hells with me if I like the notion of Dagref and Ferdulf going off together. Who can guess what mischief they're liable to get into till they go and do it?"

And that gave Gerin something new to worry about. He'd been thinking so much about Dagref and Maeva together, the prospect of Dagref and Ferdulf together had entirely escaped his mind. That was an oversight on his part, he realized. "You don't suppose they've gone off to conquer the imperials all by their lonesome, do you?"

He hadn't intended Van to take him seriously. But the outlander said, "The gods only know what they've gone off to try and do. *I* don't think they *can* conquer the bloody imperials by themselves, seeing as the whole lot of us haven't been able to do that. What *they* think they can do—who knows?"

"Who knows?" Gerin echoed mournfully. Dagref was at the age where he thought anything was possible. As for Ferdulf, almost anything *was* possible around him.

Since his driver had gone off, Gerin borrowed a horse from Rihwin's men and rode, slowly and carefully, down to the horsemen who were holding the line against Swerilas' imperials. The Fox wished he'd put in more time on horseback over the years. He managed a simple ride well enough, but wouldn't have wanted to try to fight while mounted.

One advantage of going by horse rather than by chariot was that he went by himself. Without Van along, he didn't have to come up with fancy and fanciful explanations for why he wanted to see Maeva. But he got no satisfaction from seeing her, nor did it seem that Dagref had got any satisfaction from her the night before.

"No, lord king," she said, her eyes widening. "I haven't seen either Dagref or Ferdulf. Why do you think Dagref would have come to me?"

"For the obvious reasons," he answered, and watched her flush. "He's not back at the camp, and he didn't tell me he was going anywhere. My first guess was that that meant a tryst with you."

"If it meant a tryst, it wasn't with me." Now Maeva sounded dangerous for reasons that had only a little to do with warfare.

"If it didn't mean a tryst with you, I don't think it meant a tryst with anyone," Gerin said. Maeva relaxed—a little, and grudgingly. The Fox scratched his head. "If it didn't mean a tryst with you, I don't know what it did mean."

All at once, he remembered the peculiar dream he'd had, the dream where he'd been on the fringes of things and unable to figure out what was going on no matter how important figuring out what was going on was. Maybe he'd had to stay on the fringes of things because the dream had truly been aimed at Dagref. The two of them had both remarked on how much they thought alike; Gerin didn't find it unreasonable that he should catch the edge of a dream meant for his son. That, though, only raised the next interesting question: who or what was aiming dreams at Dagref?

Two answers came to mind—the imperials and Biton. No, three, for Mavrix might have done it, too, which would, or could, have accounted for Ferdulf's absence—assuming, of course, Ferdulf's absence was connected to Dagref's.

"Too much I don't know," Gerin muttered with a sigh.

"What's that, lord king?" Maeva asked. "Is Dagref all right?"

"I don't know that, either," Gerin said. Awkwardly, he swung up onto the horse and rode back to the town of Ikos.

He hoped against hope Dagref would be there when he got back. He even hoped Ferdulf would be there when he got back. If that wasn't a mark of desperation, he didn't know what was.

But neither Dagref nor Ferdulf was there. "Where in the five hells have they gone? What in the five hells do they think they're doing?" he asked of Van, who had already shown he didn't know the answers, either.

"We'll just have to see if the imperials ask us for ransom," the outlander said. "If they've got Ferdulf, as far as I'm concerned they can keep him."

"There are people who would say the same about Dagref," Gerin said gloomily, "but I'm not any of them. If they have him, I'll pay what they want to get him back."

"The price they want is liable not to be gold or copper or tin," Van said. "It's liable to be a bended knee."

"Whatever the price is, I'll pay it," Gerin answered. "Do you think I'm so much in love with having people call me 'lord king' that I'd throw away my son so they'd keep on doing it?"

"No," Van said at once. "And if you were fool enough to throw your son away, no one would call you 'lord king' afterwards anyhow, for everybody would sicken at being led by such a man."

"Here's hoping you're right," Gerin said. He had his doubts, but did not pass them on to the outlander. Van would surely sicken of being led by such a man, but plenty of truly vicious people had gone on to long and successful reigns. The Fox, though, had no desire to emulate them.

He wondered if Dagref and Ferdulf hadn't gone south after all, if instead they'd chosen to head west along the track through the haunted woods back toward lands within Gerin's suzerainty. He had trouble imagining why they would want to do such a thing—the fighting here would be over long before they could bring back reinforcements—but he had trouble imagining why they would go see the imperials, too.

He slammed one balled-up fist into the palm of the other hand. What *had* that dream been? If he'd been able to see more of it . . .

Some time in the middle of the morning, his son and Ferdulf came walking into the town of Ikos: up from the south, not from the forest and hills to the west. No one escorted them, which Gerin took to mean that no one had seen them while they were coming from wherever they had been.

That was his first to the two of them: "Where were you?"

Neither answered right away. Dagref's silence was thoughtful. Silence from Ferdulf struck Gerin as most uncharacteristic. At last, Dagref said, "We went down to see Swerilas the Slippery."

"Just like that?" Gerin said. "You didn't have any trouble getting through my pickets? You didn't have any trouble getting through the imperials' pickets? You went right ahead and walked in to have a chat with Swerilas?"

"Aye, we did," Ferdulf said. The unemphatic nod he gave lent credence to his words.

"We did," Dagref echoed, sounding a bit surprised about it. "We had no trouble doing it. I knew we would have no trouble doing it. I had a dream that told me we would have no trouble doing it, and it was a true dream."

"Ha!" Gerin said. "I was right. The dream was aimed at you. I had it, too, or rather the ragged fringe of it."

"Did you?" Now Dagref looked interested. "I thought you might have, or someone might have. I thought someone on the outside was trying to look in, you might say."

"I didn't notice anyone else when I had the dream,"

Ferdulf said with more than a trace of hauteur. "I was alone, communing with the god."

"Which god?" Gerin asked. "Your father?"

"Not likely," Ferdulf exclaimed. "My wretch of a father communes with his hand on my fundament, not with a dream in my mind."

"With whom, then?" the Fox demanded.

"Why, with Biton, of course," Ferdulf said, and Dagref nodded. "He did indeed tell us to go to see Swerilas the Slippery—who is truly as oleaginous an article as I have ever set eyes on—and so we did. Biton has more power than I could hope to oppose, and I daresay more power than my father, too."

Gerin didn't know whether that last was true or not. Either way, it wasn't his problem. He kept on trying to find out about the things that were his problem: "And what did you tell Swerilas when you saw him?"

"Why, we told him to attack your army, of course, and not to waste any more time doing it." Ferdulf and Dagref spoke together, smilingly confident they had done the right thing.

"You told him *what*?" Gerin shouted. "How could you tell him that? Why would you tell him that?"

"It was what farseeing Biton told us to tell him," Ferdulf and Dagref chorused. Only after the words were out of his mouth did Dagref's smile slip on his face. "I wonder why Biton told us to tell him that."

"To ruin me?" Gerin suggested. "I can't think of any other reason, can you? If Swerilas attacks me, he'll push this army right along the path through the haunted wood west of here. He'll probably push us to pieces, too, trying to get onto that one path. How are we supposed to hold him off? We haven't got the men to hold him off. Don't you know that?"

"We do know that," Dagref said. "Of course we know

that. We knew it then, too." Ferdulf nodded. "It didn't seem to matter then, though," Dagref added in some perplexity, and Ferdulf nodded again.

"Why does Biton hate me?" Gerin didn't direct the words at his son and the little demigod, but at the indifferent sky.

"He doesn't hate you, Father." Now Dagref tried to sound reassuring. "Why would he hate you? My mother was his Sibyl on earth."

"Maybe he hates me for taking her away from him." But Gerin frowned and shook his head. Biton had never shown any sign of disliking his match with Selatre. But if this wasn't such a sign, what was it? He couldn't answer that question, so he found another one to ask Dagref and Ferdulf: "What else did the farseeing god tell you to tell Swerilas?"

"Nothing much," Dagref answered. "We were supposed to make it plain to him that we came with Biton's message, but we didn't have any trouble convincing him of that."

"I'll bet you didn't," Gerin said. He thought for a while, then asked, "Did Biton tell the two of you to tell *me* anything? Why he decided to do this to me might be interesting to learn, in a morbid sort of way."

"You?" Ferdulf had some of his arrogance back. "Why on earth would the god want us to speak to *you*? If he had wanted you to know anything, he would have sent you a dream. But he didn't, did he? He left you on the outside looking in, didn't he? No, he wanted nothing to do with the likes of you."

Gerin didn't get insulted, as he might have done. He just shrugged and said, "Well, the god might have sent a dream straight to Swerilas the Slippery, too, but he didn't choose to do that, so I thought I'd ask about this."

"Nothing for you," Ferdulf repeated. "Nothing, do you hear?"

"Ferdulf, you need never doubt that, when you say something, people do hear you," Gerin said. "They may sometimes—they may often—wish they didn't, but they do."

He'd hoped that would make Ferdulf glower at him. Instead, the little demigod's childlike face took on an altogether unchildlike look of satisfaction. As far as Ferdulf was concerned, the Fox had paid him a compliment.

Dagref frowned. "Wait," he said. "There was something. I think there was something."

"No, there wasn't," Ferdulf said indignantly. "I just told him there wasn't. I ought to know. I'm half a god myself, and the better half at that. If I say there wasn't anything, there wasn't, and that's flat."

"Maybe we didn't have exactly the same dream," Dagref said. "Maybe I got this because I'm my father's son."

"Maybe you think you have this because what's really between your ears is rock, not brains," Ferdulf retorted, and stuck out his tongue.

Dagref remained unperturbed, which perturbed Ferdulf. "Whatever the reason, there was something," the youth said. He turned to Gerin. "Here it is, for whatever it maybe be worth: it's something like, *Pick the right path, stay on the right path, don't go off the right path no matter what.*"

"What a stupid message," Ferdulf said. "You must have made that up yourself. Why would a god say anything that foolish?"

"I don't know," Dagref answered. "I've certainly heard a demigod say a good many foolish things lately."

Ferdulf did glower at that. Gerin said, "What path?"

His son shrugged. "I couldn't begin to tell you. Until you asked, I didn't even know I had any message for you at all."

"Maybe it's the path through the wood west of here," Gerin said. But then he shook his head. "I really don't see how it could be. There's only the one path through that wood. No right or wrong about it: you're either on the path or in the forest, and if you're in the forest, well, too bad for you. So what in the five hells is Biton talking about?"

"Something you're too ignorant to understand," Ferdulf said.

"I'm too ignorant to understand a great many things," the Fox said. "Why I put up with you immediately springs to mind."

Before Ferdulf could find a retort to that, a horseman came galloping up from the south. "Lord king!" he cried. "Lord king! The imperials are attacking, lord king!"

After that, everything seemed to happen at once. The Fox shouted for his men to form a battle line in front of the town of Ikos. They were still forming it when Rihwin's riders came back to them. "Sorry, lord king," one of the horsemen said, wiping at a bleeding cut on his forehead. "There's just too many of the cursed buggers for us to hold back, and they're coming hard, too."

"Swerilas has a way of doing that," Gerin answered absently.

"Now what?" Ferdulf exclaimed. "Now what?" He hopped up into the air. Anyone might do that while excited. Ferdulf, though, was not just anyone. He didn't come down again.

Dagref answered him before Gerin could: "Now we fight. What else can we do? Even if you float like a pig's bladder, you wits should be better than the ones a bladder, or even a pig, comes with." Ferdulf's venomous glare showed that even the Fox would have had a hard time being more pungently sarcastic.

"Aye," Gerin said. "Now we fight. Now we . . ." His voice trailed away. He looked from Dagref to Ferdulf and back again. After stroking his beard for a moment, he walked over to Dagref and kissed him on the cheek. Then he did the same with Ferdulf.

"What was that in aid of, Father?" Dagref asked. Ferdulf's comments were a good deal more pungent, but had the same general meaning.

"Understanding," Gerin answered. "At least, I hope it's understanding." *If it's not understanding, if it's anything but understanding, I'm in even more trouble than I was already—and here I'd been thinking that couldn't possibly happen.* He didn't say that out loud. What he did say was, "Come on. We have to meet that temple-robbing whoreson of a Swerilas with edged bronze before—"

"Before what, Father?" Dagref broke in.

"Before anything else happens," the Fox said—not the sort of reply calculated to satisfy his son. Satisfying his son was not the most urgent matter on his mind right then, though.

Dagref gave him an irked stare. "You're being as deliberately obscure as the Sibyl when Biton speaks through her," he complained. "You're . . ." And then, as his father's had done, his voice trailed away. "Wouldn't that be interesting?" he murmured.

"What *are* the two of you talking about?" Ferdulf sounded even more irritable than usual.

"You're a demigod. Use your semidivine wisdom to figure it out," Gerin told him. "While you're at it, why don't you fly up and tell me what Swerilas is trying to do to us?"

"You don't need me for that. You can see him from here," Ferdulf answered, which was depressingly true. But the little demigod did pop into the air, perhaps as much for the chance that gave him to wave his backside at Gerin and Dagref as for any other reason. Off he flew.

"I hope you're not wrong, Father," Dagref said.

"So do I," Gerin said. "Believe me, so do I."

Before the Fox could say any more—not that there was much more to say—Van came rushing up demanding to know why in the five hells he and Dagref weren't in the chariot yet, and why they weren't charging forward to smash Swerilas into some large number of small pieces.

"We do have to try, Father," Dagref added.

"I know we do," Gerin answered. "Well, let's be about it, then." He stepped up into the chariot, where Van was already waiting and fuming. So did Dagref, who flicked the reins and got the horses moving.

Van gave Gerin a dubious look. "Are you going fey on us, Captain?" he demanded. "Do you think we're as done as a slab of beef over a fire? Are you riding out expecting to be killed?"

Gerin shook his head. "No. Very much the opposite, as a matter of fact. I don't think we're going to win this battle, but I haven't lost hope for the war. In fact, I have more than I did a little while ago."

Now the outlander's stare was quizzical. After a moment, he shrugged. "All right—you've got some sort of scheme cooking in that beady little mind of yours. I don't need to know what it is right now. As long as it's something, and you haven't given up on us."

"I've never quite done that," Gerin said. "I've come close a few times over the years, but I've never given up."

Ahead of his force of chariotry, Rihwin's riders and some of the temple guards were righting to slow the force Swerilas the Slippery led. "Elabon! Elabon! Elabon!" the imperials shouted, their war cries ringing through those of the men from the northlands.

"Let's hit 'em!" Gerin yelled to his own troopers. He plucked an arrow from his quiver, let fly, and pitched an imperial out of the chariot. His men cheered. They didn't seem to have any particular hope of victory, either, but they went into the attack with a will.

And, for a while, they drove the imperials back toward Biton's shrine. "Temple robbers!" was the shout Biton's guards raised. They fought with a fury that made them stronger than their numbers. Rihwin's riders strove mightily to keep the warriors from the Elabonian Empire off balance. Gerin began to wonder what he would do if his army beat the foe. That would mean he'd been wrong in the way he'd thought things would go.

He shrugged. "It wouldn't be the first time I've been wrong," he muttered.

"What's that, Fox?" Van asked.

"Nothing much, believe me," Gerin answered.

Just out of bowshot of the wall of the temple, the momentum of his counterattack faded. Swerilas had too many men and was too good a leader to let an inferior force beat him. His men rallied and began to push not only forward but out to either wing. The Fox's troopers had to fall back to keep from being outflanked and cut off.

Gerin stayed calmer about this retreat than he had during earlier fights in which the imperials had used their numbers to gain the upper hand. "You know something," Van said. "What is it?"

"Saying I *know* something probably pushes things further than they should go," the Fox answered. "I have some ideas, though."

"Ah, that's good. That's fine." Van beamed. He didn't even ask what the idea were. Instead, he stuck a finger in his friend's face. "There, you see? Didn't I tell you you'd come up with something. And you, walking around with a rain cloud over your head, you told me I was wrong. You told me I was crazy."

"I don't know whether you were wrong or not," Gerin said. "In case you're wondering, though, I still think you're crazy."

When he ordered the army to fall back through the town of Ikos without making a stand protected by the houses and other buildings, Van shook his head and said, "You don't need to wonder if I'm crazy. I'm the one who needs to wonder whether you're daft."

"Maybe I am," Gerin said. "We'll know pretty soon."

North of the town, he had two choices left: he could fall back to the top of the valley and try to break out through the rugged hills to either side, or he could swing to the west and take the one narrow, winding road through the ancient wood that lay between the valley and the Elabon Way. Without hesitation, he swung his men to the west.

"Stay on this path!" he shouted to the warriors. "By all the gods, and by farseeing Biton most especially, stay on this path!"

"What other path could they go on, Fox?" Van said. "There's only the one, after all. We've been along it, going east and west, often enough to know."

"Take another look," Gerin suggested.

Van did, and his eyes widened. As soon as he'd finished staring to either side, he stared at Gerin. "I'm *not* daft," the outlander said. "I know I'm not daft that particular way, anyhow. If you tell me there used to be half a dozen roads climbing up toward the forest, I'll call you a liar to your face. I know better. They didn't used to be here."

"Unless I'm the one who's gone mad, they weren't here yesterday," Gerin answered. "That doesn't mean they're not here now, though." He raised his voice to shout again: "Stay on this road, men! No matter what happens, stay on this road!"

"How do you know this is the right one, Father?" Dagref asked.

Gerin gave him a harried look. "I don't," he answered in a low voice. "But I think it is, and that will have to do." He let out another yell "Stay on this road, by the gods!"

"But, lord king, they're outflanking us!" one of his men cried in a frightened voice. The trooper pointed to either side. Sure enough, Swerilas the Slippery, with the luxury of numbers, was dividing his force, sending parts of it along the new paths that had appeared to either side of the one on which Gerin and his men traveled. Never having been in the valley of Ikos before, Swerilas did not, could not, know they were new.

"Stay on the path!" Gerin shouted again. He looked ahead. The wood was getting closer and closer. A few imperials—enough to plug the gap should his army try to reverse its course—followed the men of the northlands along the road they were using. Most, though, hurried along the other paths that led into the wood.

Van chuckled, but even the bluff outlander sounded a little nervous now. "I know what Swerilas is thinking," he said. "I know just what he's thinking, the son of a pimp."

"So do I," Gerin said. "He's thinking these roads will all come together inside the forest. He's thinking he'll rush men along some of them, get ahead of us, cut us off, and wreck us once and for all. If you look at things from his point of view, it's a good plan. It's better than a good plan, in fact. Or it would be."

"Aye," Van said in a hollow voice. "It would be."

As he spoke, Dagref drove the chariot in under the trees. It was one of the last cars that belonged to the men of the northlands to enter the wood west of the valley of Ikos. "Stay on the path," Gerin called to the riders and chariot crews ahead. "For your lives, stay on the path! Ride through to the end of the wood, and we'll see what happens then."

He hoped they heard him. He hoped they *could* hear him. He didn't know, not for certain. Sound had a different quality here under these great, immeasurably ancient trees. The rattle and squeak of the chariot axle, the clop of the horses' hooves, seemed distant, attenuated, as if not quite of this world. He could hardly hear the noise from other cars at all.

Light changed, too. As it filtered down through the branches interlaced overhead, it became green and shifting, making distances deceptive and hard to gauge. Gerin imagined seeing underwater would be something like this. The green was not the usual shade it would have been in a forest, either. The Fox could not have said how it was different, but it was. He noticed that whenever he entered this strange place. Maybe it was because so many of the trees and bushes in this place grew nowhere else in the world. But maybe, too, it was because the rest of the world did not fully impinge on this place.

Gerin tapped Dagref on the shoulder. "Stop the car," he said.

His son obeyed. The last few chariot crews who had been behind them went past. The men in those cars gave Gerin curious and alarmed looks. Dagref looked curious, too, and perhaps a little alarmed. "If we wait here very long, Father, the imperial vanguard will be be upon us," he said.

"Will they?" Gerin shook his head. "You may be right, but I don't think so. Listen."

Obediently, Dagref cocked his head to one side. So

did Van. So did the Fox. He could hear, ever more faintly, his own men hurrying west through the old and haunted wood. That was all he could hear, but for a few soft padding noises from beasts he had heard before but of which he had never seen anything save, once or twice, green eyes.

"Where are the imperial whoresons?" Van sounded indignant. "They should be rattling along close behind us. Dagref is right; they ought to be coming upon us any time now. And they're racing along those other paths, too, the funny ones to either side of us. We should hear them there, too. By the gods, how could we miss 'em? But I don't hear a bloody thing." He dug a finger in his ear, as if that might help. "Where are they?"

"I don't know." Gerin didn't hear the imperials, either. As Van said, he should have. Nor could he hear his own men, not any more. All he heard now was his own breathing, that of Dagref and Van, and the horses' panting and the jingle of their harness. "Turn back," he told his son. "Swing the chariot around and go back toward Ikos."

"I will, Father," Dagref said, "but only if you're sure you want me to."

"Go on," Gerin said. Shaking his head a little, Dagref flicked the reins and clucked to the horses. He was obviously reluctant. So were the animals. They rolled their eyes and snorted and flicked their ears. But they obeyed Dagref, and he obeyed Gerin. The chariot turned on the path, which was barely wide enough to let it do so, and rolled back toward the east.

It did not roll far. No sooner had it rounded the first turn in the road than there was no more road. Trees and bushed blocked the way, looking as if they'd been growing there for the past hundred years. Dagref stared. "How could we have come up this path if there's no path to come up?"

Before Gerin could answer, Van said, "The trees in this wood aren't to be trusted, and that's a fact. They move around some kind of way—I've seen it before. Never like this, though. Never like this."

"He's right," the Fox said. "I've never seen it like this, either, though, because . . ." His voice trailed off. *Something* was watching him from the cover of the bushes. He couldn't tell what—or who—it was. He couldn't even make out its eyes, as he could sometimes spot those of the strange creatures that dwelt inside this haunted wood. But he knew it was there.

Something passed from it to him—and to Dagref and Van. It wasn't a message in words. Had it been, though, it would have required only two: *go away*. Dagref swung the chariot back toward the west. Now the horses seemed glad to run. They scurried away from that new-risen barrier. Gerin blamed them not in the least.

Softly, Van said, "I wonder what's going on behind those trees. I wonder what's going on other places in the forest. Something quiet, but not something, I'd guess, that's making the imperials very happy."

"I'd say you're likely right," Gerin agreed. "No matter how slippery Swerilas the Slippery is, I think he's just run into something he's not going to be able to slip out of again."

"I wish I knew what was happening to the imperials," Dagref said.

He had every bit of Gerin's relentless itch to know. He had only a small part of his father's years to temper that itch. Still, Gerin found the right question to ask: "Do you want to know badly enough to step off the road?"

Dagref thought that over, then shook his head. He didn't spend much time thinking, either.

Gerin wondered what would happen if, quite suddenly, the road ahead closed off as the road behind had done.

Whatever it was, he didn't think he would be able to do much about it. He hoped it would be quick.

But then he heard the rattle and squeak of chariots in front of him. Without his saying a word, Dagref urged the horses up to a quicker trot. They soon caught up with the cars at the rear of his force. The men in those chariots exclaimed to Gerin and his companions. "Lord king!" one of them said. "We didn't think you'd be coming this way again when you stopped there."

"Well, here I am," the Fox answered, determinedly making his voice sound as normal as he could. "Now, are you glad or sorry?"

"Oh, glad, lord king!" the trooper said, and others echoed him. "How far behind are the imperials, would you say?"

Dagref and Van both looked at Gerin. He, in turn, looked for the best reply he could give. "Farther than you'd think," he said at last, and then, liking the sound of the words, repeated them: "Aye, farther than you'd ever think."

The warriors took the literal meaning and missed his tone. "That's good," one of them said. "Maybe the bastards'll take a wrong turning and get lost in these stinking woods."

"Maybe they will," Gerin said, again with irony his men did not catch. When he spoke again, though, he was not being ironic at all: "I only hope we don't get lost in them ourselves."

"Don't see how we could," a trooper said. "It's just the one road, and it looks like it runs straight on through. Doesn't get much simpler than that." Gerin didn't say anything. He and Van and Dagref looked at one another again. Then that trooper spoke once more, in puzzled tones: "I wonder what happened to the rest of the imperials, the ones who went down those other paths."

"So do I," Gerin said solemnly. "So do I."

He was relieved when the trooper turned out to be right: the road stayed straight, and the men of the northlands emerged from the wood into bright afternoon sunshine. Rihwin, who had been one of the first men out, was forming them into a line of battle to resist the imperials. "If we hit them hard," he was shouting when Gerin came out of the wood, "we'll have the effective advantage of numbers, for most of them will still be back under the trees."

"Are you going to tell him, Father?" Dagref asked softly.

Gerin shook his head. "I don't know for a fact, not yet," he said. "The event will tell better than I could, anyhow."

Ferdulf came flitting over. "Do you know that I had to ride in a chariot like an ordinary mortal all the way through those ugly woods?" he demanded. "Well? Do you?"

"You seem to have survived," Gerin answered dryly. Ferdulf glared, then floated off in a snit.

The army waited, and waited, and waited. At last, as the sun began to set, the troopers made camp. No imperials came out of the wood, then or ever.

When morning came, the Fox rode into the forest again. He had no trouble traversing it. It seemed as normal as it ever did, perhaps even a little closer to normal than he'd ever known it before. Or perhaps the strangeness that dwelt within was sated for a time.

Presently, Van said, "We're farther in now than we were yesterday when we turned around and the track was gone, aren't we?"

"Aye, I think so," Gerin answered, and Dagref nodded. After a moment, the Fox added, "It's still here now. Or rather, it's here again now. Anyhow, it's as if the thing never went away, isn't it?"

"Isn't it, though?" Van fixed Gerin with an accusing stare. "You knew this was going to happen, didn't you?"

"This?" Gerin shook his head. "I had no idea *this* would happen. I did hope *something* would happen if the imperials came into this forest, and I was lucky enough to be right."

"Not, *if the imperials came into this forest*," Dagref said. "The proper phrase is, *if the imperials came into this wood*."

"What in the five hells difference does it make?" Van said. "The forest—the wood. So what? You're not a bard, to complain the one doesn't scan and the other does." He paused. Dagref looked very smug but didn't say anything, rare restraint for a lad his age. Gerin didn't say anything, either. That extended silence warned Van he was missing something. Though not quite so quick as either Gerin or Dagref, he was nobody's fool. After a moment, he snapped his fingers. "The oracle!"

Dagref grinned. Gerin just nodded. "Aye, the oracle," he said.

Van slapped him on the back, almost hard enough to pitch him out of the chariot. "You sneaky son of a whore," he said in admiring tones. "You *sneaky* son of a whore. When the Sibyl talked about 'bronze and wood,' I thought sure she meant swords and spears and arrowheads on the one hand and chariots on the other. Who wouldn't have thought that?"

"It's what I thought first, too, and I'm not ashamed to admit as much," Gerin said. "And we kept fighting the imperials, and they kept kicking us in the teeth. It's not surprising, when you get down to it—they had twice as many men as we did, near enough."

"Nothing like being proved wrong over and over again to make you think you might have misinterpreted an oracle," Dagref observed, sounding appallingly like his father. "You had already fulfilled one condition of the verse, when Rihwin summoned Mavrix but the god refused to aid us."

"Even so," Gerin said, nodding.

"One piece of the verse still puzzles me, though," Dagref said. " 'They snap and float and always trouble'? What on earth was the farseeing god talking about there?"

Gerin looked at Van. The outlander was looking back at him. He couldn't have said which of them started laughing first. Dagref let out an indignant snort. Laughing still, Gerin said, "That part of the oracular response seemed pretty plain to me, even at the time."

"To me, too," Van added.

"Well, I don't follow it," Dagref said, getting angrier by the moment. "And furthermore, let me tell you—"

"No, let me tell you," the Fox broke in. "You're doing the snapping now. You don't float, but someone you know does."

Dagref stopped and stared. "Ferdulf and me?" he said in a voice much smaller than the one he usually used. Gerin nodded. Dagref's eyes got even wider. "How did the god find a place for Ferdulf and me in his prophecy?"

Van laughed. "You're not the most promising material, lad, but there's no accounting for what a god's liable to do."

Dagref turned his head to give the outlander a dirty look over his shoulder. He opened his mouth. By the expression on his face, Gerin knew what he was going to say: something along the lines of, *You may not think I'm so much, but your daughter has different ideas*.

Without the least hesitation, Gerin kicked Dagref in the ankle. Instead of saying what he'd been about to say, Dagref let out a startled yip. "On this road of all roads," Gerin said, "you'd better keep your eyes ahead of you and your mind on what you're doing—and nowhere else."

He couldn't have been much less subtle if he'd walloped Dagref over the head with a branch. For a wonder, Van didn't notice that he was giving a ponderous hint. For an even bigger wonder, Dagref did.

Then, a moment later, the Fox forgot all about the indiscretion from which he'd saved Dagref. Through the clop of the horses' hooves, though the squeak of the axle and the rattle of the wheels of the car, he caught the noise of another chariot—a chariot headed west, straight toward him.

"Stop the chariot," he told Dagref, and reached over his shoulder for an arrow. His hand shook as he set the shaft on his bowstring. His heart pounded. Cold sweat burst out on his forehead. After the disaster that had befallen the army of the Elabonian Empire in this haunted wood, who was—who could be—riding through it now? Or was the right question, what could be riding through the haunted wood now?

On came the other chariot, steady and confident as if it owned not just the road but the rest of the wood, too. Van muttered something under his breath. It wasn't in Elabonian. It wasn't in any language Gerin understood. Beneath his sun-bronzed skin, the outlander was pale. He didn't know who or what was liable to be in that other car, either, and he didn't seem to like any of the possibilities that occurred to him.

Dagref clutched the whip till his knuckles whitened. "Is it—the master of this place, Father?" he whispered.

"I don't know," Gerin whispered back. "I don't know if this place *has* any one master. If it does, I don't know if he's the sort of master who rides in a chariot. But I think we're about to find out."

Around a slight twist in the path came the other car.

Gerin, Dagref, and Van all shouted the instant they spotted it. The driver of the other team shouted, too, in horrified surprise. So did his passenger, who threw his hands in the air, bleating, "I yield! Spare me, by the gods!"

"Why, it's only a couple of imperials," Gerin said in slow wonder. "Did you lugs come into this wood yesterday?" Could they have survived when all their comrades . . . disappeared?

But both imperials shook their heads. "By the gods, no!" the passenger said. "We are not fighting men; we are but harmless couriers."

Gerin stared. The imperial couriers he'd known had been ready-for-aughts who delivered their messages come what might. These fellows were a disgrace to the breed— either that, or it had gone badly downhill over the generation during which it hadn't operated north of the High Kirs.

"And what message were you delivering to Swerilas the Slippery?" he asked. When the couriers hesitated before speaking, he went on, "You can tell me now, or we can take the message pouch off your body and read what's inside it." He aimed his bow at the driver's face. "Which will it be? You haven't got much time to make up your minds."

Neither courier was armed with anything more than a knife at his belt. They must have thought they were traveling through safe country, and that Swerilas had crushed Gerin by now. The Fox grinned. They hadn't known everything there was to know.

"We'll talk," the passenger said at once. The driver might have said something different if he hadn't been looking at an arrow from a range almost short enough to make his eyes cross. As things were, he nodded glumly. The passenger went on, "You'll probably like the news anyhow."

"How do we know till we hear?" Gerin didn't lower the bow. "Speak up."

And the courier did: "We were sent here to recall both lord Swerilas and lord Arpulo to duties more urgent than suppressing these semibarbarous northlands. All the empire's forces are needed in more vital provinces, for the Sithonians are risen in furious revolt."

XII

Back at the encampment west of the haunted wood, Gerin examined the order the imperial couriers would have given to Swerilas the Slippery. The one of them had summed up that order well enough: Crebbig I was abandoning the reconquest of the northlands because, as he wrote, "the wicked, treacherous, underhanded Sithonians and their effete and effeminate gods have banded together in a malicious conspiracy to overthrow our rule in Sithonia, an effrontery we do not propose to and shall not tolerate."

If ever two men had been bewildered, the couriers were they. That Swerilas' opponents had captured them was one thing, and quite bad enough. That Swerilas' army had vanished off the face of the earth was something else again, and a great deal worse, too.

Gerin wasted no time on explanations with them. For one thing, he was far from certain of explanations himself. For another, he had matters more urgent to worry about than whether a couple of prisoners were contented.

"Do you see?" he said to Rihwin the Fox. "Mavrix did have other things on his mind besides the northlands. No wonder he didn't feel like helping us, and no wonder he didn't thank you for jogging his elbow."

"Very well, lord king," Rihwin said. "Seen in retrospect, you plainly have the right of it. But you could not see in retrospect at the time, and neither could I. Why twit me over it, when I was doing the best I could?" That was such a good question, Gerin didn't answer it.

He did ask Ferdulf, "What do you think of your father now?"

"I think he is an odious, sniveling, drunken degenerate who chanced to do you a good turn for reasons that had nothing whatever to do with you, but only with his own selfish desires," Ferdulf answered.

That was nothing if not forthright. It was so forthright, in fact, that it pitched the Fox into a coughing fit. "Oh, come now," he said when he could speak again. "I've hardly ever heard Mavrix snivel."

Ferdulf pondered that for a few heartbeats. When he was done pondering it, he laughed one of the few laughs Gerin had ever heard from him. Then he floated away, a contented little demigod—contented, typically, because someone else had just been insulted.

Dagref came up to Gerin. "Father, between our army and Aragis', we outnumber the imperials. And, since Arpulo is ordered to withdraw anyhow—"

"—We can beat him about the head and shoulders while he's going," Gerin broke in. "Yes, I intend to do that. If the imperials lose one of their armies here in the northlands and have the other cut to pieces, it's likely to be a good long while before they poke their noses over the High Kirs again, regardless of whether they put down the Sithonian uprising or not."

"Ah, that's fine. That's very fine." Dagref looked relieved. "I was just wondering if, with so many things going on so fast, that one might have slipped past you. I'm glad it didn't."

"No, I managed to keep up there," Gerin answered. "Haven't moved against Arpulo yet, but I do intend to. After that, I have two other things on the list, and then, the gods willing, I think we can head back up toward the Niffet."

"Ah." Dagref raised an eyebrow. "And those are—?"

His father started ticking them off on his fingers. "First, I need to see how things stand with Aragis the Archer. Don't forget, we came south to fight a war with him, not with the Elabonian Empire. If the imperials have hurt his lands enough, it'll be a good long while before he can think of tangling with us again, too. If not, we'll start a new verse of the old song next spring."

Dagref nodded. "Aye, I saw that one myself. It's the only one I saw, as a matter of fact. What's the other?"

"I want to send someone to that village off the Elabon Way and find out what Elise intends to do," the Fox answered. "If she wants to go to Duren's holding, I'll send her. If she's gone there on her own, she's liable to be aiming to stir up trouble between your half brother and me."

"Do you think she could?" Dagref asked, wide-eyed. He'd always been slightly in awe of Duren, as younger brothers often are of older ones.

"I don't think so," Gerin answered, "but I don't know. Nor do I want to be unpleasantly surprised. Now that I know where she is, I want to keep an eye on her." He didn't think Elise would like that, but he wasn't going to lose much sleep over whether she did or not.

He'd finished his explanation, but Dagref didn't go away. Instead, the youth took a deep breath and said, "Father, I know how I want to use the promise I won from you as we were coming south."

"Do you?" Gerin said, hoping, he was doing a good enough job of disguising apprehension as polite curiosity.

"I do." Dagref sounded very determined. Hearing how determined he sounded should have made the Fox proud.

As a matter of fact, it did make him proud. It also made him more than a little frightened.

"I suppose you intend to tell me," he said when his son showed no sign of doing anything of the sort.

"Oh. Yes. Of course." Dagref snapped his fingers and looked annoyed at himself. "That's right. You do need to know." He took another deep breath; maybe he too was less steady than he wanted to seem. After letting it out and inhaling again, he said, "When the time comes, I want you to speak to Van about Maeva for me."

"Is that all?" Gerin asked, now trying to hide surprise. Dagref nodded. The Fox set a hand on his shoulder. "I'll do it." He took a deep breath of his own. "I'd do it anyhow. If you like, you can have your promise back and save it for something else you want."

Dagref weighed that. "You've been worried about what I'd ask for, haven't you?" he asked. The Fox nodded; he could hardly do otherwise. Dagref rubbed his chin, on which some of the down was beginning to darken. "And yet you'd let me hold on to the promise and still speak to Van?"

"I just said so, didn't I?" Gerin wondered how much he'd regret it.

But Dagref was shaking his head. "That wouldn't be right. I gave it up freely, for something that matters to me—well, you know how much it matters to me."

"Yes, I do." Whether it would matter so much to Dagref in half a year, or in five years . . . who could tell, before the event? Farseeing Biton, surely, but no one of lesser powers.

Dagref made motions as if to push his father away. "That wouldn't be right," he repeated. "Do what I asked you to do, and that will put us at quits."

"No." Now Gerin shook his head. "That will make us square. I don't want the two of us to be at quits."

"That's fair enough, Father. Neither do I." Dagref looked at Gerin out of the corner of his eye. "If I did, I could easily have asked for something else." He didn't say *something more*, not with Maeva on his mind, but that was what he meant, and Gerin knew it.

"So you could." Gerin admitted what he could scarcely deny. "Since you decided not to, can we get on with the business of running the imperials back to their side of the mountains?"

"Oh, I suppose we can," Dagref said, so magnanimous his father felt like kicking him in the teeth. Then they both laughed. Why not? They were both getting what they wanted.

Arpulo Werekas' son was still in the process of pulling together the detachments he had on Aragis' lands when Gerin struck him. The Fox's army drove in a series of Arpulo's bands and siege parties; the last thing Arpulo had expected was that Swerilas and his whole force would completely disappear from the scene. Whether he had expected it or not, though, it had happened. His withdrawal became an undignified scamper.

As Arpulo fell back from one keep he had been besieging after another, Aragis' soldiers who had been trapped inside those keeps came forth and joined Gerin in pushing the imperials ever farther south. They accepted the Fox's orders without complaint, and obeyed him far more readily than his own troopers often did.

"I know why that is," Van said with a sly grin. "They're still used to the Archer, who'd have their guts for garters if they tried telling him no. They don't know how soft you are."

"Hmm," Gerin said. "How am I supposed to take that?" He held up a hand. "Never mind. I don't really want to know. I'll just ask you this: if I'm so soft, why has no one ever raised a successful revolt in twenty-odd—and a lot of them were very odd—years?"

"Nothing hard about that, Captain," the outlander answered. "Who'd follow a rebel against you? Whoever the son of a whore was, he'd be more trouble than you ever were. And so everyone's been on your side all along."

"Oh, indeed," the Fox replied. "And that, of course, is why I've never fought a single, solitary war in all the time since I became baron of Fox Keep."

"Well . . ." Van paused to think. At last, he said, "Not all your neighbors know you as well as they should, that's what it is." Gerin snorted. Van was unabashed, but then Van was usually unabashed.

The next day, Arpulo's men withdrew from around the castle where Aranast Aragis' son was leading the defenders. Aranast was glad to be able to come out. He was glad to join in helping to chase the imperials out of his father's dominions. He was appalled at the way his father's vassals obeyed the Fox.

"You are not their sovereign, lord king," he told Gerin that evening as the army encamped. "You have no business requiring them to act as you desire."

"Fine," Gerin said cheerfully. "In that case, you can go back to your keep and stay there, too."

"That is not what I meant." Had Aranast's back got any stiffer, he would have turned to stone. "These men are vassals to my father, King Aragis the Archer. It is fitting and proper for your own vassals to grant you all due obedience. It is neither fitting nor proper for the vassals of another sovereign to grant you the aforesaid obedience, nor for you to claim it."

Gerin felt like marching around behind Aranast and giving him a boot in the arse, that being a likelier avenue to admit sense than his ears. Regretfully abandoning the idea, the Fox said, "When we were campaigning against the imperials before, I acknowledged your father as the overall commander. I wasn't his vassal when I did it. The world didn't end. It won't end now, either, if his men obey me for a while."

"My father will not approve," Aranast said.

"If he has any sense, he will," Gerin replied. "I don't know how much that proves, I will admit. Besides, your father is still besieged down there"—he pointed south— "and so they can't very well obey him for the time being. Do please remember, I'm the one who got rid of Swerilas the Slippery and won my half of the war. I did that before the imperials retreated, before they knew they were even supposed to retreat. What did your father do? Locked himself up in a keep, that's what."

"That's unfair," Aranast said. "He was heavily beset, and facing the larger half of the imperial army—against which he struck some strong blows."

"Good for him," Gerin said. "I have no complaint about anything he did. No, I take that back—for him to send you to tell me not to presume to forage off the countryside struck me as excessive, and does to this day. When he comes out of his castle, he's welcome to take his men back, for all of me. In the meanwhile, I intend to get some use out of them."

Aranast sputtered and fumed. He remonstrated with some of his father's vassals. "Gerin the Fox has a higher rank than yours, Prince Aranast," one of them told him. "If you expect us to obey you, shouldn't you also expect us to obey him?" That made Aragis' son sputter and fume even more, but he gave the noble no answer.

The imperials had trampled down a good many fields of wheat and barley in Aragis' dominions, and stolen a lot of livestock. Now that they were withdrawing from the northlands, they set fires in the fields behind them, both to hamper Gerin's pursuit and to leave Aragis' vassals and serfs as hungry and weak as they could.

Aranast cursed Arpulo with bitter hatred. So did Aragis' retainers who rode with the Fox. So did Gerin. Arpulo was conducting a coldbloodedly vicious retreat, doing as much harm as he could before he finally went south over the High Kirs.

But only the Fox's long experience as a ruler, a man whose every action was on display before his fellows, let his curses sound sincere. Inwardly, he was something less than downhearted at seeing how much Aragis would have to do in the lands he already ruled before he could contemplate going to war against anyone else.

Just before sunset, the riders Gerin had sent to the village where Elise was keeping a tavern caught up with his army. "You haven't got her with you," Gerin noted. "Did she refuse to come?"

"No, lord king," one of them answered. "She wasn't there."

Gerin scowled. "Where did she go? Did any of the villagers know? Did she go south into the Empire, or north to Duren's holding?"

"No one knew, lord king," the rider said. "One day she was there, as she'd been for the past little while. Next morning, she was gone. The villagers made it plain she was not in the habit of telling them what she intended doing before she did it."

"I believe that," Gerin said. "She was never in the habit of telling anyone what she intended doing before she did it."

He paced back and forth, discontented with the world. He'd hoped to have an unambiguous answer about the woman he'd once loved, but the world hadn't been generous enough to give him one. For her sake and his own, he hoped Elise had gone down over the mountains, not up to her son's holding. Not only would the road up to Duren's be full of refugees and brigands and deserters from Aragis' army and Gerin's and the imperials', and thus dangerous for her, she might make the road dangerous for Gerin if she reached the keep and inflamed Duren against him.

Gerin wondered again if she could do that. In the end, he had to shrug and shake his head. He simply did not know.

By that time the next day, he'd stopped worrying about a woman he'd seen for an hour or so over a twenty-year span. He had more urgent—perhaps not more important, but more urgent—concerns: his army came up to the keep in which Aragis the Archer had been besieged.

Aragis proved not to be in the castle. "Oh, no, lord king," said the steward, a pudgy fellow named Wellas Therthas' son. "He went south in pursuit of Arpulo when the imperials broke off their encirclement yesterday."

"Sounds like him," Gerin agreed. He eyed Wellas. "You could have stayed besieged a lot longer before they starved you out, couldn't you?"

"Oh, aye, lord king," Wellas answered. "But how could you have known that, to bring it out so sure and certain?" He eyed the Fox, too, with a mixture of respect and wonder.

"Call it a good guess, if you like," Gerin said. If Wellas was still plump after a good many days shut away from the outside, the siege couldn't have caused the defenders too much in the way of hardship. Gerin didn't want to come right out and say that, though, having no reason to hurt the steward's feelings.

The Fox rode after his fellow king. Wellas thoughtfully helped supply the army with journeybread, sausage, and smoked meat from the castle storerooms, proving the keep had indeed been far from running out of supplies. Gerin was quickly glad to have the extra food: the imperials had set more fires behind their line of march, and he could have done little in the way of foraging.

For that very reason, he met Aragis coming back up the Elabon Way. The Archer looked disgusted. "Good to see you, Fox," he growled, though *good* was not a word that would have fit his humor. "We can do this better together than I could by myself—I haven't the men for a proper pursuit, and I just went after that bastard of an Arpulo as soon as he pulled out: didn't realize he'd burn everything behind him as he went." His lean face—not much leaner than when Gerin had seen him last—was streaked with soot and smoke.

"He does seem to be doing that," Gerin said, nodding. "A farewell present since he can't stay, you might say."

"So I gather." Aragis looked more disgusted than ever. "I've been penned up in there, away from everything that looks like news. What in the five hells happened? Did Crebbig I, his ever so illustrious majesty, have the generosity to drop dead?"

"No such luck, I'm afraid," Gerin answered. "The Sithonians are revolting again, and he's called his men back over the mountains."

"Ah, is that what it is? So we'll be rid of Swerilas as well as Arpulo, eh?" Aragis nodded, too. "I won't miss either of them a bit, and that's the truth." His gaze suddenly sharpened. "What are you doing here, Fox? I mean *here* in particular. Why aren't you chasing Swerilas' men instead of Arpulo's? For that matter, where are Swerilas' men? Why didn't they come down and join their friends?"

"They were chasing me," Gerin answered. "They tried chasing me through the wood west of Biton's shrine in the valley of Ikos. Do you know that wood?" Aragis' eyes widened in his filthy face. Gerin took that for agreement. He went on, "They rode into the wood. They didn't ride out." He explained the oracular response he'd had from Biton's Sibyl, and how he interpreted it.

" 'Bronze and wood,' " Aragis repeated. "I would have taken that to mean swords and chariots, or maybe spearheads and spearshafts. That the wood might be *a* wood . . . I doubt I'd have thought of that."

"I almost didn't, either," Gerin said. "Even when I did think of it, I was a long way from sure I was right— but I was in so much trouble, I had nothing to lose by finding out."

Aragis pointed at him. "Did I not say that, when the time came, you would have some sorcery ready to wreck the foe?"

"You said it," Gerin agreed. "That you said it doesn't make it true. Rihwin summoned Mavrix, except that Mavrix didn't feel like being summoned. Biton gave his oracular response—all I did was hear it. When Dagref and Ferdulf went off to see Swerilas, I didn't know anything about it. If I had known anything about it, I would have stopped it if I could. I don't know exactly what happened in the haunted wood, and I don't think I ever will know. By the gods, I don't think I want to know, either. The only thing *I* did in all of that was ask Biton for the oracular response, and I didn't know what I'd get when I did."

"Everything you say is true—taken one thing at a time." Aragis let out a long, angry breath. "But it's only true taken one thing at a time. Put it all together and you were at the center of it, the way a spider sits at the center of its web. Tell me that, when Rihwin summoned Mavrix, you weren't hoping he would fail. Go ahead and tell me—I want to see how good a liar you are."

"Not good enough, evidently," Gerin said. "If you already know the answers, why ask the questions?"

"Because I wanted to find out if what I thought was true: that you were in the middle, taking advantage of everything that happened around you." He glared at the Fox like an angry wolf. "And you were, and I curse you for it."

Calmly, Gerin folded his arms across his chest. "I haven't taken advantage of *every* tiny thing that happens around me. I hope I am on my way toward doing that, though. In aid of which, shall we discuss the matter of suzerainty over the holding of Balser Debo's son?"

Aragis looked around. Had more of his men been close by than Gerin's, the Fox thought he would have ordered them to attack on the instant. But more of Gerin's troopers stood near the two kings, and they looked alert. Aragis' earlier glare had been mild to the point of benignity compared to the one he gave Gerin now. "You see what the imperials have done to my lands," the Archer ground out.

"Yes, I see that," Gerin said.

"You see they've hurt my fighting force worse than yours," Aragis persisted.

"Yes, I see that, too," Gerin said, nodding.

"And so, because I am weakened, you think to gain at my expense," Aragis said.

"Of course I do," Gerin said. "I'm not gaining anything I didn't think was rightfully mine beforehand, though. How hard would you have squeezed me if things were the other way round? You know the answer to that as well as I do: you'd take as much as you could get away with. I've said it before, Aragis: unless you make yourself so, you're not my enemy. You've spend twenty years not believing me. Will you believe me now?"

"Because I am hurt here, you think to drop the hammer on me," Aragis said, as if the Fox had not spoken.

"You're repeating yourself," Gerin said. "The words are different; the meaning is the same. You ought to try listening to me instead. If you don't want to listen to me, by the gods, I'm tempted to drop the hammer on you just to get you to pay attention for once in your life."

Aragis turned the color of molten copper. "No one has presumed to speak to me in that fashion for a very long time," he growled.

"Oh, I believe *that*," Gerin said. "You're the sort who hands a fellow his head if he has the nerve to tell you something to your face. That will make your vassals shut up around you, I must say. But it'll also make you miss things you ought to hear. You're not strong enough to hand me my head if I tell you something to your face, so you can bloody well listen to me instead."

He wondered if he oughtn't to hurt Aragis as badly as he could, to keep the Archer from trying for revenge as soon as he saw the chance. The only sure way of doing that, though, was killing Aragis now. He didn't have the stomach for it. Murder was not a political tool he kept in his chest.

Just for a moment, Aragis' hand dropped down toward the hilt of his sword. He checked the movement before he touched the hilt. Like a bear bothered by bees, he shook his head. "Slaughtering you might solve the problem, but you haven't—quite—done anything to deserve it," he said.

"For which polite qualification I do thank you," Gerin said. "I thought about stretching you out bleeding on the ground, too." He grimaced. "This being a king is a nasty business sometimes."

"So is being a baron. So is anything above being a

serf," Aragis said, "and being a serf is a nasty business, too, in a different way. It's a nasty business all the time, with no letup ever. If I have a choice between taking orders and giving them, I know which one's for me."

"If I had a choice, I'd sooner do neither," the Fox replied. Aragis stared at him in blank incomprehension. He'd been sure Aragis would do something like that: as the Archer himself admitted, he liked giving orders. With a sigh, Gerin went on, "Since I don't have a choice, I'd sooner be on the top than on the bottom. I won't say different."

"You'd better not," Aragis said. "And I'll tell you one other reason I didn't try to let the air out of you there."

"You'd answer to Dagref," Gerin said.

He'd meant it for a joke, or mostly for a joke. Aragis, however, gave him a very odd look, a look as nearly frightened as the Fox had ever seen on his face. "How did you know that?" Aragis whispered. "How *could* you know that? To you, he'd be only a youth."

"Oh, Dagref is a youth, all right," Gerin answered, "but it's been a long time since I thought of him as *only* an anything. If I don't strangle him in the next two or three years, he'll go far, that one will."

He scratched his head. Did that mean he'd made up his mind about the succession? Maybe he had. Duren was doing a perfectly fine job as baron of the holding that had been his grandfather's, but how much did he look beyond it? Dagref had a wider view. But Dagref was also much younger, and had never actually ruled a barony or anything else. Who could tell what he'd be like when he was seventeen? So maybe Gerin hadn't made up his mind about the succession after all. Maybe.

"Back to matters at hand," he said, as much to himself as to Aragis. "Balser Debo's son wants me as his overlord. I have accepted him as my vassal. I don't want a war, but I was ready to fight to keep that holding as part of my domain before the imperials came, and I am still ready. So." He turned away, picked up a long, thin broken branch that had fallen out of a load of firewood, and used it to draw a circle in the dirt around Aragis' feet. "Shall we have peace, or shall we fight? Answer me one way or the other before you step out of that circle."

Aragis' eyes looked about ready to bug out of his head. "Of all the high-handed—" he spluttered. "You have not the right to use me so. No one has the right to use me so."

He started to stride out of the circle, but stopped when Gerin held up a hand and said, "I have the right, and it's one even you understand."

"What is it?" Aragis demanded.

"Simple—I'm stronger than you are," Gerin answered. "Now—peace or war? If you step out of the circle without naming one or the other, we shall have war right now, I promise."

To some degree, he was running a bluff. He was far from sure that, if he suddenly shouted for his men to attack the Archer's, they would obey him. But he was also far from sure how many of Aragis' men would fight hard for their overlord.

Aragis must have been making the same calculations, and coming up with answers not far removed from his own. "You are an arrogant son of a whore," he ground out, to which the Fox bowed as at a compliment. "May you toast your toes in the hottest of the five hells forever." Gerin bowed again. Aragis bared his teeth in another wolf's smile before going on, "But you *are* stronger than I am, curse you. Take the holding of Balser Debo's son. Keep it. I hope you choke on it, but I will not fight you for it." He stepped out of the circle.

Gerin wondered if he was lying. If he was, he would

be made to pay for it, that was all. He had done as the Fox required. Trying to hold him to more—even trying to get an oath from him—would be too much in the way of arrogance.

"We've beaten the imperials," Gerin said. "Now, if the time does come, we can settle things that have to do with the northlands between ourselves—and, if the Empire puts down the revolt in Sithonia and decides to have another go at us, we can still fight side by side. Remember, I am not taking anything that was yours; you weren't Balser's suzerain. You wanted him to become your vassal, aye, but he never did."

"Hmp." If Aragis was mollified, he wasn't about to let Gerin know it. Had the sandal been on the other foot, Gerin wouldn't have let him know it, either. But the Archer had got a better deal from him than he would have got from from the Elabonian Empire, and he had to know as much. If Crebbig I sent another army north, the Archer was unlikely to be inclined to throw in with it.

"We aren't friends—we've never been friends," Gerin said, "but we've had our borders march for a lot of years without going to war against each other, and that's something a good many friends can't say. I'd sooner see it go on than end."

"Hmp," Aragis said again. He turned and walked away. He'd said he wouldn't fight the Fox over Balser's holding. If he meant that, everything would be fine. If he didn't . . . Gerin sighed. If he didn't, there would be another war, that was all.

Another war. Gerin was mildly amazed at how little the prospect bothered him. After so many wars, what would one more be? And maybe Aragis would live up to his word after all. Stranger things had happened. "Not many," Gerin muttered, "but a few. They really have."

He might even have meant it. He hoped with all his heart that he did mean it.

As Gerin's men began pulling back from the lands over which Aragis the Archer ruled as king, Aragis said not another word about his foraging on the countryside. Gerin took that for a good sign. He did not take the state of the countryside for a good sign. Aragis and his vassals were going to have a hungry time of it over the winter. Maybe that would leave the Archer too weak to fight come spring. Maybe, on the other hand, it would leave him with no choice but to fight come spring.

"How will you know, Father?" Dagref asked.

"Oh, it's a simple enough business," the Fox answered. "If he attacks me, he does. If he doesn't, he doesn't, that's all."

"Yes, that is simple," Dagref agreed, "but what I meant was, how will you know beforehand?"

"If he does choose to attack me, I may not know beforehand," Gerin said. "I may get signs beforehand that tell me he isn't going to war, though. If his harvest is as it looks now, his serfs are liable to rise against him. If they do, he'll be too busy dealing with them to worry about me."

"I'll say he will," Van put in. "He's been grinding his peasants' faces in the dirt for a long time. If they rise up, they'll try to pay him back all at once."

"Some of his vassals may decide to rise against him, too," Gerin went on. "He's a demon of a warlord, but that's not all that goes into the mix for making a good king. Maybe some of his barons will decide as much, anyhow."

"Maybe you'll help some of them decide as much," Dagref said.

"Hmm. Maybe I will, if I can do it so that Aragis

doesn't figure out I'm doing it," Gerin said. He thumped his son on the back. "One fine day, you're going to make all your neighbors, whoever they may be, very uncomfortable." He was liable to make all his friends very uncomfortable, too, but that was another matter.

Gerin sent riders north to Duren, not only to let him know what had happened in the war against the Elabonian Empire but also to tell him the Fox had met Elise. That was, of course, something Duren was liable to know already. Gerin instructed the riders to bring word back to him if Elise was at Duren's keep. He wondered what he'd do if she was. He wondered whether he could do anything if she was. He had his doubts.

Balser Debo's son received him like a hero. Gerin listened to his new vassal's fulsome praise with but half an ear; he'd heard such praise delivered many times before, and heard it done better, too. As often as not, he knew what Balser was going to say three sentences before he said it. That let his mind dwell on more interesting things.

There were some. Chief among them was the way Rowitha the serving girl had come out into the courtyard and was staring so intently at Dagref. Dagref might have stared back at Rowitha, too, if Maeva hadn't been standing by Van, only a few feet away. As things were, Dagref alternated between a polite smile and doing his best to pretend Rowitha didn't exist.

That was a tricky bit of juggling; a man three times Dagref's age would have had a hard time bringing it off with aplomb. He did about as well as could have been expected: better than most his age would have done, Gerin thought, because he habitually showed less of what was in his mind than most.

Maeva was watching Rowitha, too, watching her, not

much liking what she was seeing, and liking it less by the moment. She'd slept out with the rest of the riders when Gerin's army was on its way south. Only a couple of people, Gerin certainly not among them, had known what she was then. Things were different now.

But Maeva couldn't very well keep Dagref from going over and talking with Rowitha after Balser finally finished blathering, not without giving more away to Van than would have been wise. She had to stand and stare and do her best not to fume too openly. Her best wasn't so good as Dagref's had been.

Rowitha, now, Rowitha didn't have to hold anything back, and she didn't. She listened to Dagref's low-voiced explanation, or part of it, and then hauled off and slapped him, a ringing report that made all heads in the courtyard turn his way. He stood, his cheek turning red—actually, his whole face turning red, but his cheek turning redder—while she stomped away.

"Haw, haw, haw!" Van boomed. "Well, there's something that'll happen to most men a time or twelve before they shovel dirt on 'em. The lad may be starting a little early, but then, thinking back, he may not, too."

Maeva, by contrast, hurried over and put her arm around Dagref's shoulder. Remembering his promise to his son, Gerin spoke to Van: "You said you'd hoped her eye might fall on Dagref if she'd stayed back at Fox Keep. Maybe it's fallen on him anyhow."

"Maybe it has," Van agreed, in tones polite but imperfectly delighted. He was probably wondering how long ago Maeva's eye had fallen on Dagref, and what might have happened since. Turning a thoughtful frown toward Gerin, the outlander continued, "We'll have to speak of this further when we get back to Fox Keep, I expect."

"I expect we will," Gerin agreed. He also expected

he would have to dicker with Fand. As if in anticipation, his head started to ache.

Dagref came over to him, the mark of Rowitha's palm and fingers still printed on his cheek. "Father," he said, "would you mind if I asked you to spend as little time here in Balser's holding as you possible can?"

"No, I wouldn't mind that." Gerin hid a smile. "We *do* have to head north."

"That's good," Dagref said. "That's very good." He looked around to see if the serving girl had reappeared. Not spotting her, he relaxed a little.

"You know, if you ask Balser to make sure your lady love—excuse me, your former lady love—doesn't come inside the castle as long as you're here, he'll likely find her something else to do," Gerin said.

"Do you think so?" Dagref looked astonished. Gerin felt pleased with himself, though he didn't show it: Dagref wasn't used to asking special favors just because of who he was. Then his son went on, "Would you do it for me?"

Gerin was less pleased with that. "If *you* do it, I said," he replied. "You're the one who wants the wench out of your hair. When we were here last, I didn't do anything to get any wenches into my hair."

"You are the soul of virtue," Dagref said sourly. "Besides, Mother would be in your hair if you did anything like that. I didn't have anyone special in my life when Rowitha and I—" He coughed a couple of times, finishing, "But I do now, you see." Gerin only shrugged, which left his son dissatisfied.

Maybe Dagref talked to Balser and maybe he didn't. In either case, Maeva ate in the great hall with Gerin and Van and Dagref, and Rowitha did not make an appearance there. Dagref did his best to pretend Rowitha had never existed. Maeva, by contrast, kept looking around for her. She still dressed like a warrior, with a sword on her belt. Maybe Rowitha had noticed that instead of getting orders from Balser. Gerin did not inquire. It was not his business.

Van kept watching Maeva watching out for Rowitha. He kept muttering things that weren't quite words and that didn't quite get past his beard and mustaches. He was, it seemed, drawing his own conclusions, and not much caring for the pictures they made. Every now and then, he would glance over toward Dagref, too, and then mutter some more.

"This was a match you said you wanted," Gerin reminded him, continuing to keep his promise. "I think it's a good one, too, for whatever it may be worth to you."

"Eh?" Whatever Van had been thinking, it wasn't about how good a match Dagref and Maeva might make. Now, very visibly, he did. He grunted instead of muttering— progress, of a sort. At last, he came out with real words: "Oh, aye, Fox, I don't doubt you're right, or I don't doubt it too much, anyhow. But good match or bad, I didn't look for it so bloody *soon*."

"That I understand. Neither did I, though I might have noticed a sign or two even back at Fox Keep." Gerin slapped his friend on the back. "There isn't one cursed thing in life that doesn't happen too bloody *soon*, especially when it happens to our children."

Van thought that over. He'd had enough ale to make thinking take a while. Slowly and deliberately, he nodded. "Tell your fancy Sithonian philosophers to go on home, Fox," he said. "Once you've said that, you don't need to say any more."

Gerin approached Duren's keep with more than a little apprehension. His riders had come back to let him know Elise hadn't been there then, but he would still have to tell his son by her about their meeting. And strife between Duren and Dagref was one more thing that was liable to come too bloody soon. If it *ever* came, that was too bloody soon for him.

Duren's vassal barons had been anything but delighted about accepting him as their overlord. Gerin had wondered if they would see his own preoccupation with the south as an opportunity to rise against his son. That hadn't happened; everything looked peaceful as he led his army up the Elabon Way toward Duren's keep. Either Duren's vassals had thought the Fox would win and punish them for rebelling against his son, or else they'd figured Duren could put them down by himself. Gerin hoped for the latter.

"Who comes to the castle of Duren Ricolf's grandson?" a sentry shouted as the Fox's army drew within hailing distance. The question had a certain formal quality to it—either it was Gerin, or someone was about to lay siege to the keep. But, Duren not owing his father homage and fealty, he treated with him as one equal with another.

"I am Gerin the Fox, king of the north, returning from my campaign against the Elabonian Empire," Gerin answered, again as one equal to another.

"Congratulations on your victory, lord king," the sentry said. The Fox's messengers would have told of that. Without any orders Gerin heard, the drawbridge began to lower. "Enter into the keep of Duren Ricolf's grandson. The baron eagerly awaits you."

Sure enough, Duren stood just inside the wall. He looked to be about ready to burst, waiting for Gerin to dismount from his chariot. When the Fox and Van and Dagref did get down, Duren couldn't at once ask Gerin what was so plainly on his mind, either; he had to go through polite greetings first.

Then those greetings turned more interesting than Duren might have thought they would be. He gave Dagref a long, long look as the two of them clasped hands. "You were on your way to turning into a man when you came down from Fox Keep. Now, unless I'm much mistaken, you've gone and done it." Duren sounded almost accusing.

Dagref answered, "Well, now I've done more of the things men do than I had then, anyhow." He looked at his half brother out of the corner of his eye. "I even picked up an ekename. I don't know if it will stick, but I don't know that it won't, either."

"What is it?" Duren asked warily. He used no ekename— styling himself *Ricolf's grandson* had helped him gain control of the holding formerly his grandfather's.

"Dagref the Whip." Dagref was still holding the lash he'd used to urge on the horses and with such effect against the imperials. He hefted it, to show the source of the sobriquet. Duren looked something less than delighted. Then he looked astonished, for Maeva came up and placed herself alongside Dagref in a marked manner. Gerin, who had become something of a connoisseur of astonishment, and who had seen—and caused—a great deal of it over the years, judged that Duren's had at least three flavors: seeing Maeva there at all, seeing her there as a warrior, and seeing her there so solidly beside Dagref.

When Duren turned away from Dagref and Maeva, he spoke plaintively to his father: "Fall out of touch for even a little while, and things go all strange by the time you get another look at them."

"Even if you don't fall out of touch, things have a way of going all strange behind your back," Gerin answered, also more than a little plaintively.

"Father, you speak nothing but the truth," Duren said.

"Come into my great hall—come into my great hall, all of you—and have some ale. And then"—he looked toward Gerin—"then I will hear about my mother." He spoke the last word slowly, and with some hesitation, for which the Fox could hardly blame him.

As they were walking into the castle, Gerin said, "Elise didn't come up here, then? She told me she might."

"She didn't." Now Duren's voice was flat, uninflected. He went on, "If she set out this way, she never got here. Do you suppose something happened to her along the way? That would be terrible."

Gerin wasn't convinced it would be so terrible as all that, but he understood how his son had to feel. The idea that something might have happened to Elise when she was on her way to see him for the first time since abandoning him as an infant had to eat at Duren. As consolingly as he could, Gerin said, "She's been traveling through the northlands for a lot of years, and she's always been able to take care of herself. I think it's likelier that she went south to visit her kin down in the Empire. She was talking about that, too."

He did not mention the other possibility that had occurred to him: that Elise might have suffered misfortune at the hands of the imperial warriors who'd come through her village after his own army retreated out of it. Some soldiers did whatever they pleased in their foes' country. Elise was no longer young and beautiful, but she wasn't ancient and ugly, either. She might not have gone—she might not have had the chance to go—anywhere at all.

Perhaps fortunately, Duren's mind was running in a different channel. In an indignant voice, he said, "I'm her kin, too."

"That's so," Gerin agreed, "but one thing about your mother was always plain, as long as I knew her—and now, too, from the little I saw of her—and that is that she was going to do what she was going to do, and she wasn't about to listen to anyone who tried to tell her anything different."

"What would she say about you?" It wasn't Duren who asked the question but the avidly curious Dagref.

"Most likely, she would say that I never cared what she wanted to do, and that I never wanted to do anything interesting myself," Gerin answered, doing his best to be just.

"Would she be telling the truth?" Dagref asked.

"Well, I don't think so," the Fox said, "but I don't expect that she thinks I'm telling the truth about her now, either. Truth is easy enough to find when you're talking about things you can see or count on your fingers. It gets a lot harder when you're trying to figure out why people are the way they are and how they truly are. Half the time, they don't know themselves."

"Hmm," Dagref said, plainly unconvinced. "I always know *precisely* why I do what I do."

Maeva nodded vigorous agreement, as much because he was very young as because she was enamored of Dagref. Gerin and Van laughed. Duren looked thoughtful, as if wondering which side was right.

"Is that so?" Van rumbled. Dagref nodded. He might not always have been right about such things, but he was always sure. Van cocked his head to one side and said, "Then tell me *precisely* why you've formed an attachment with my daughter." He stared down at the Fox's son.

Dagref did *precisely* what Gerin could have done in the same circumstances: he spluttered and turned red and said nothing intelligible. Maeva set her hand in his. Most times, that would have steadied him. Here, it only seemed to make matters worse.

"Well, Father, how, *precisely*, did you beat the imperials?"

Duren asked. "Not everything your couriers told me was as clear as it might have been." Maybe he was helping ease his half brother off the hook, in which case he had more charity in him than his father would have had at the same age. Or maybe, having learned everything he could—surely not close to everything he wanted—about his mother, he was just moving along to the larger events that had taken place down toward the High Kirs.

Gerin told him the oracular verse the Sibyl at Biton's temple had delivered, how he'd interpreted it, and the role Dagref and Ferdulf had played in fulfilling it. That made Duren give Dagref another sharp look. Dagref looked back with a bland, blank expression he might have stolen from Gerin's face. He wasn't immune to discomfiture, but he got over it in a hurry.

Getting no satisfaction there, Duren turned to Gerin and said, "By what I have seen and heard of Dagref and what I have seen and heard of Ferdulf, the two of them must be . . . lively together."

"And so they are," Gerin agreed. "They're pretty bloody lively apart from each other, too."

"I can see that." Duren gave Dagref another measuring, speculative stare, which his half brother returned. Duren turned back to the Fox. "We need to talk, the two of us."

"The three of us," Dagref corrected.

Gerin shook his head. "I need to talk to both of you. I need to do it with each one separately. My mind's not made up about any of these things, and I don't expect it to be any time soon."

"It should be—I'm your eldest," Duren said. With no small bitterness, he went on, "But I'm not your son by Mo—by your wife, who raised me. I can see how that makes a difference."

"Less than you think," Gerin answered. "Selatre has

never once pushed me to shove you aside and put him in your place. She knows you'd do well. And I know you'd do well, come to that. I'm also coming to know Dagref would do well, too."

"If no one shortens him by a head, he would," Van put in.

"And what will you do?" Duren asked. "Split the kingdom between us?"

"I couldn't find a better recipe for civil war if I brought a cook up from the City of Elabon," Gerin said with a shudder. "Remember the barony north of you that used to be Bevon's, and how all his sons squabbled over it for years? Whatever else I do, I aim to make sure that doesn't happen with or to everything I've spent so long building up."

"What does that leave, then?" Duren asked. "What will one of us do if you leave the whole kingdom to the other?"

"It could be that you'd stay content with this barony if Dagref held the kingdom." Gerin held up a hand before either of his sons could say anything. "And it could be that Dagref might want to study down in the City of Elabon while you took on the burden—and it *is* a burden, believe me—of ruling. That would depend on what the Empire decides to do about the northlands, of course."

"And there's Blestar to figure into all this," Dagref said. "He's only a little fellow now, but I was only a little fellow when you went off to take over this holding, Duren."

"I'd almost forgotten about Blestar," Duren admitted. "Not forgotten he was there, but forgotten he could mean something in all this."

"I hadn't," Gerin said. "The gods only know now how he'll turn out when he's a man, though. As a boy, he's better natured than either of the two of you was, not that that's saying much."

Duren and Dagref joined in giving their father a dirty look. That didn't bother the Fox, who wanted the half brothers as united as they could be: if in annoyance at him, fair enough.

Dagref said, "Do you really suppose, Father, that the Empire would let me go down to the City of Elabon to study?"

Before Gerin answered that, he let his eyes flick to Maeva for a moment. By her expression, she didn't realize she had a rival in learning, very possibly a rival more dangerous than any woman, no matter how beautiful, no matter how passionate. Gerin smiled a little. If she didn't realize it yet, she would before too long.

And Dagref had asked a good question. The Fox gave it the best answer he could: "If the Empire decides to take another shot at conquering us, then you won't be able to go south of the High Kirs, no. But the revolt in Sithonia and the drubbing the imperials took up here are liable to make them think twice. My guess is, that's more likely. Crebbig I may never recognize Aragis and me as kings, but I don't think he'll come up and try to knock us over again, either."

Dagref and Duren both thought that over. Duren said, "What do you expect from Aragis after this?"

"I hope he'll lick his wounds for a while," Gerin answered. "He has plenty of them. He also has plenty of vassals who've seen me, which means they've seen that a man doesn't have to be a bronze-arsed son of a whore to make a proper ruler. If some of them rise up, or if the serfs on Aragis' land decide they've had enough of being squeezed to bits, then Aragis will find he has the same sorts of troubles as Crebbig."

"You'd weep and wail over that, wouldn't you?" Van said, setting a finger by the side of his nose.

"So I would," Gerin said dryly. "I'd weep till my eyes were all red and swollen." He let out an exaggerated sob. Everyone laughed.

Some time later, after roasted mutton and fresh-baked bread and berry tarts and a good many jacks of ale, Duren waved for Gerin to walk out from the great hall into the court between the outer wall and the castle itself. Darkness had fallen. Tiwaz, a medium-fat crescent, hung low in the southwest; ruddy Elleb, just past first quarter, shone in the south; pale Nothos, nearly full, climbed above the eastern wall. Math would not rise for another hour or two.

Duren said, "I wish you'd found out more about my mother—either more, or nothing at all."

"I understand," Gerin said, setting a hand on his shoulder. "But we do what we can do, not what we wish we could do. I didn't expect to find out anything at all. I didn't even know her till she spoke, nor she me." He started to add, *Maybe she'll turn up one day*, but decided that would do more harm than good. Duren was no doubt thinking it, too, but the gulf between thinking something and saying it yawned wide and deep.

"Now I wish I'd come along with you," Duren said.

"Maybe it's just as well you weren't there. We've all changed a good deal, these past twenty years. Last time your mother saw you, you were making messes on the floor." That was not his principal concern. His principal concern was how much damage Elise might do if she turned Duren against him. He still didn't know whether she could, but he still didn't want to find out, either.

"I've changed," Duren said. "My mother must have changed, or she wouldn't have gone away from you."

"Honh!" Gerin said, borrowing the useful not-quite-word from Van.

Before he could add anything to it, Duren went on, "But you, Father, you've hardly changed at all."

"You only say that because you're watching me with a son's eyes," Gerin answered. "I'm like anybody else. I'm soup in a pot, and the years boil away more and more of the water, so my flavor gets stronger and saltier, the same way my beard keeps right on getting grayer. The longer you live, the more you go about the business of turning into yourself."

Duren didn't fully follow that. Gerin hadn't expected that he would. Duren said, "I suppose I'll have to go on as best I can. I don't see what else I can do. Do you, Father?"

"I don't think there is anything else you can do," Gerin told him. "Nothing useful, anyhow: pining away over might-have-beens doesn't help." He clicked his tongue between his teeth. "Other thing I'll say is, you're Elise's son, aye, but you're my son, too, or you wouldn't think that way. Remember it."

"I always do," Duren answered. Not quite for the first time, Gerin thought that, whatever happened to his kingdom, he'd leave some good behind.

Dagref urged the horses up from a walk to a trot. The chariot swung around the curve in the road that brought Fox Keep into sight. "It's still there, and it's still mine," Gerin said.

"A lot of people have tried taking it away from you," Van said. "You've made 'em all sorry. They mostly know better now."

"I wish they did," Gerin said. "I wish they had for a long time. I'd have lived a more peaceable life if it were so." Van snorted, a wordless expression of his opinion about what a peaceable life was worth. Gerin ignored him.

The drawbridge swung down over the ditch around the palisade as soon as the folk inside Fox Keep recognized Gerin and the warriors who still accompanied him: those who did not dwell at his keep had already peeled off and headed for their own homes. As he had to Duren's keep, he'd sent riders ahead to his own, so people knew he was returning, if not in triumph, at least in something close to it.

Men and women—and Geroge and Tharma with them—came spilling out over the drawbridge. Van pointed. "There's Fand," he said gloomily. "Now I'm for it. She'll have to hear about every time I dropped my drawers for some hussy since I rode out of here, and she'll make me pay for all of 'em."

Sure enough, Fand charged out ahead of most of the rest of the people, so far ahead that Ferdulf, feeling mischievous, dove on her—and just missed spitting himself on a knife she pulled from her belt and thrust at him. He darted away, shouting abuse. Fand screeched back.

But, for once after an army returned from campaign, she did not screech at Van. Instead, she ran toward Rihwin's riders and screeched at Maeva for going off and fighting without letting her know she'd done it.

"Well, isn't this nice?" Van said, beaming. "I come home to peace and quiet, at least aimed at me." The smile slipped. "It won't last. It can't last. It never lasts—but I'll enjoy it while it does."

Maeva, plainly, did not enjoy it. "Mother," she said, "I'm home safe. I've killed a couple of men, and I'm home safe." Gerin noted she did not mention taking a wound of her own.

She did not impress Fand, either. "Och, you've killed,

have you now? If that was all you wanted, you could have waited till some lustful young spalpeen tried putting his hands where they don't belong, then stuck a knife 'twixt his ribs whilst he was after trying to stick summat else 'twixt your legs."

"I have no trouble taking care of myself there, either," Maeva answered. "No one will ever do anything to me that I don't want."

Van rumbled something deep in his chest. In front of Gerin, Dagref's ears turned pink. And Fand, who though hot-tempered was far from a fool, exclaimed, "And who's been doing things to you that you do want, now?"

Maeva did not answer, not in front of everyone. But Gerin had no doubt she would before too long—and Van knew, and a good many others who could tell Fand. Maybe she would approve of the match. Maybe she wouldn't, too. Gerin would find out in due course.

"Ride on into the keep," he told Dagref. "Easier to sort everything out in there than out here."

"Aye, Father," Dagref said. As the chariot made its slow way forward through the crowd, he and Gerin both waved to Selatre, and to Clotild and Blestar as well. Van waved to Kor. His son looked furiously jealous of Maeva, who'd had the chance to go out and fight and kill. Maeva let her hand fall to the hilt of her sword, which only infuriated Kor even more. Gerin, who'd had his older sibling flaunt privileges, too, knew a certain amount of sympathy for the boy.

He jumped down from the chariot as it slowed to a halt. Not too far away, Fand was still shouting at Maeva: "Why couldn't you go saving yourself for a nice lad like that Dagref, say, instead of letting some rough soldier ha' his way with you? The shame of it, now!"

Dagref jumped down after Gerin, as soon as a stable boy had taken charge of the horses. "Well, we won't have too much trouble there, will we?" he murmured. "Not if she wishes Maeva had saved herself for me, I mean."

"There's always going to be trouble with Fand," Gerin answered, also quietly. "The only question is, how much? By the sound of that, there shouldn't be too much. Of course, when she finds out you and Maeva are already . . . well, something more than friends, there'll be a row over that, too, I expect."

Dagref sighed. "You're probably right—people get so excited over these things."

Before Gerin could respond to that, Selatre and Clotild flung themselves onto him, while Blestar was flinging himself onto Dagref. Gerin kissed his wife and daughter. Blestar didn't want kisses. He wanted every single solitary detail of Dagref's adventures, he wanted the details on the spot, and not even his older brother's astonishingly retentive memory looked likely to be good enough to satisfy him.

Clotild, having got her share of kisses and hugs from her father, tried to get some from Dagref, too, which put him off his stride in his narration, which made Blestar shout at Clotild. Gerin laughed. "It's so *good* to be home," he said.

Selatre laughed, too. Then she glanced at him sidelong. "I hope you'll say that tonight and sound more as if you mean it," she said, adding, "If we can find somewhere to be alone, that is."

"The library," Gerin whispered in her ear, "even if Ferdulf is liable to fly up and peek through the window, and even if Dagref is liable to figure out why we keep that rolled-up bolt of cloth in there. But the library, even so. Yes indeed." He slipped his arm around her waist. She molded herself to him.

"Dagref will figure that out, will he?" Selatre asked.

Gerin nodded. His wife clicked her tongue between her teeth. "Time does go on, doesn't it?"

"Doesn't it, though?" Gerin said. He hesitated, then spoke of something he had not entrusted to the riders who'd come up to Fox Keep ahead of him: "I was passing through a village down in the land Aragis rules, and I happened to run into Elise there."

Just for a heartbeat, the name did not register with Selatre; it was not one the Fox had been in the habit of using often. Then it did, and her eyes widened. "Duren's mother," she said in a voice that showed nothing whatever.

"Aye, Duren's mother," Gerin said. "I don't know where she is now, or what she's doing." He explained how he'd told Elise of Ricolf's passing, how she'd spoken of going south over the High Kirs, and how she had not come back to the barony that had been her father's and now was her son's. "And if you think I'm sorry that she hasn't, you're very much mistaken."

"No, I don't think that." Selatre still held her voice under tight restraint. That restraint was revealing in itself. After a little while, she said, "I never thought you would see her again."

"Neither did I," Gerin answered, "and I would have been just as well pleased if I hadn't, believe me."

Something in Selatre eased. The Fox hadn't noticed how tensely she was holding herself—almost like a bow strung and drawn—till she stopped doing it. She said, "I'm sorry, but I can't help worrying about these things. You did find her before you found me, after all."

His hand still rested on the curve of her hip. He squeezed, just for a moment. "And do you want to know what she taught me?" he asked. Selatre's nod was wary. He said, "She taught me to know when I was well off, because she gave me a standard of comparison, you might say."

Selatre thought about that for a moment, then threw her arms around his neck. After she finished kissing him, she said, "You just made me want to drag you up to the library right now."

"Why?" Gerin asked innocently. "Did you come up with a new codex while I was away on campaign?"

Selatre snorted and planted an elbow in his ribs. "When you choose, you can be most absurd," she said. Best of all, and one of the many reasons he was so fond of her, was that she made it sound like a compliment.

"How have things been while I was gone?"

"On the whole, very well," Selatre answered. "The weather has been good, and the harvest looks promising." She and Gerin both glanced toward the west. The Gradi still had their foothold in the northlands, out where the Niffet flowed into the Orynian Ocean, but they'd stayed quiet since their gods got embroiled with Baivers and the gods of the monsters who dwelt in some of the caves below Biton's shrine. If that fight ever ended, the gods of the Gradi and the Gradi themselves might prove troublesome again. It hadn't happened yet, though. With luck, it wouldn't happen for many years to come.

"On the whole, you say." Gerin knew when his wife had things to add, even if she tried to paint as bright a picture as she could.

She nodded now. "Yes, on the whole. The one worrisome thing I can think of is that, if Tharma isn't carrying pups— and I don't think she is, right now—it's not from lack of effort, if you understand what I'm saying."

Gerin sighed, loud and long. "Well, we've been waiting for that to happen for quite a while, so I can't say I'm surprised. The gods only know what I'll do about it if she does bear pups or cubs or babies or whatever you want to call them, but I can't say I'm surprised."

"The gods who may know best what you should do if

Tharma gives birth are busy fighting the Gradi gods," Selatre said.

"Oh, the monsters' gods?" Gerin said, and his wife nodded. He went on, "I was thinking of them in a different connection a moment ago. I suppose you're right. And, for that matter, Maeva's lucky—or careful, one—not to be coming home great with child herself."

Selatre's eyes widened. "You mean Fand wasn't just shouting to hear herself shout, the way she does so often?"

"Not this time," the Fox answered. He hesitated, then spoke one word more: "Dagref."

Selatre's eyes got wider still. "But he's not old enough. She's not old enough, either, come to that." Then she counted on her fingers and frowned. "Time does run away, doesn't it? They could, I suppose, but I wish they wouldn't."

"So do I," Gerin said. "Outside of wishing, though, I haven't the faintest idea what to do about it but let it run its course and see what comes of that. Van and Fand both seem to think a match between the two of them would be good, and I don't mind one, either. How about you?"

"If it's what they want, I don't mind," his wife said. "I wouldn't want it right away, though. They aren't old enough to know their own minds. Let's see what they think two or three years from now."

"That sounds good to me," Gerin agreed. "My guess is, Van and Fand won't mind, either. Whether Dagref and Maeva will put up with waiting two or three more years, though, is another question. If they stay attached to each other, they'll just get more attached, if you know what I mean."

"I suppose so," Selatre said. "When I was their age, though, I was waiting for the old Sibyl to die. I was to be a maiden, and had no chance to form an attachment to any male." She took his arm in hers, so that his also brushed against the side of her breast. "I've made up for it since."

"That's good." Gerin let it go there. He couldn't say he wondered if he would be around in two or three more years, because saying as much would bring up the question of the succession, and the succession was the one thing he'd ever found that he did not care to discuss with Selatre.

No, she'd never urged him to name Dagref over Duren. He didn't think she would urge him to do that, but he didn't want to set temptation in front of her, either. If Dagref kept growing as well as he had lately—and if no one hit him over the head with a rock for being so maddeningly right all the time—the decision might shape itself. If Dagref made everyone want to hit him over the head with a rock, even if no one did, the decision would shape itself, too, the other way.

If neither of those things happened, Gerin would have to shape things himself. He shook his head. He would have to try to shape things himself. Whatever choice he made, by the very nature of things he wouldn't be around to enforce it. That would be up to his sons, and to Selatre if she outlived him, and to all his vassals: many of them, these days, the sons of the men who'd first given him homage and fealty, some the grandsons.

"No matter how long you last," he murmured, far more to himself than to Selatre, "sooner or later things fall from your hands."

His wife thought along with him, as she often did. "They don't fall and break, though. Someone catches them and carries on. You did, when the Trokmoi killed your father and your brother." She said no more than that. She didn't suggest that someone would catch the affairs of Gerin's kingdom when they did fall from his hands. Suggesting such a thing was as much as implying that someone should be Dagref.

Gerin thought about Duren competently running his barony, about Dagref fighting well and also falling in what might be love with Maeva. "You're right," he said. "One way or another, things do go on. Pretty soon, they'll be in someone else's hands."

"Not pretty soon, I hope. And whosoever hands they're in, your mark will be on them," Selatre said.

He considered that, then slowly nodded. "I suppose it will. I helped keep the Trokmoi from overrunning all the northlands—and the ones who did settle south of the Niffet are mostly my vassals these days. I kept the monsters from breaking out, too: all except Geroge and Tharma, anyhow. If I didn't drive the Gradi from the northlands, I pinned them back against the ocean. And I could be wrong, but I don't *think* the Elabonian Empire will trouble us again any time soon. The gods know I haven't been perfect, but I've done pretty well. When you think how things can go for a man, I'll take that." He nodded once more. "Aye, I'll take that."

PRAISE FOR
LOIS MCMASTER BUJOLD

What the critics say:

The Warrior's Apprentice: "Now here's a fun romp through the spaceways—not so much a space opera as space ballet.... it has all the 'right stuff.' A lot of thought and thoughtfulness stand behind the all-too-human characters. Enjoy this one, and look forward to the next."   —Dean Lambe, *SF Reviews*

"The pace is breathless, the characterization thoughtful and emotionally powerful, and the author's narrative technique and command of language compelling. Highly recommended."   —*Booklist*

Brothers in Arms: "... she gives it a geniune depth of character, while reveling in the wild turnings of her tale. ... Bujold is as audacious as her favorite hero, and as brilliantly (if sneakily) successful."   —*Locus*

"Miles Vorkosigan is such a great character that I'll read anything Lois wants to write about him. ... a book to re-read on cold rainy days."   —Robert Coulson, *Comics Buyer's Guide*

Borders of Infinity: "Bujold's series hero Miles Vorkosigan may be a lord by birth and an admiral by rank, but a bone disease that has left him hobbled and in frequent pain has sensitized him to the suffering of outcasts in his very hierarchical era. ... Playing off Miles's reserve and cleverness, Bujold draws outrageous and outlandish foils to color her high-minded adventures."   —*Publishers Weekly*

Falling Free: "In *Falling Free* Lois McMaster Bujold has written her fourth straight superb novel. ... How to break down a talent like Bujold's into analyzable components? Best not to try. Best to say 'Read, or you will be missing something extraordinary.'"   —Roland Green, *Chicago Sun-Times*

The Vor Game: "The chronicles of Miles Vorkosigan are far too witty to be literary junk food, but they rouse the kind of craving that makes popcorn magically vanish during a double feature."   —Faren Miller, *Locus*

MORE PRAISE FOR
LOIS MCMASTER BUJOLD

What the readers say:

"My copy of *Shards of Honor* is falling apart I've reread it so often.... I'll read whatever you write. You've certainly proved yourself a grand storyteller."
— Liesl Kolbe, Colorado Springs, CO

"I experience the stories of Miles Vorkosigan as almost viscerally uplifting.... But certainly, even the weightiest theme would have less impact than a cinder on snow were it not for a rousing good story, and good storytelling with it. This is the second thing I want to thank you for.... I suppose if you boiled down all I've said to its simplest expression, it would be that I immensely enjoy and admire your work. I submit that, as literature, your work raises the overall level of the science fiction genre, and spiritually, your work cannot avoid positively influencing all who read it."
— Glen Stonebraker, Gaithersburg, MD

" 'The Mountains of Mourning' [in *Borders of Infinity*] was one of the best-crafted, and simply best, works I'd ever read. When I finished it, I immediately turned back to the beginning and read it again, and I can't remember the last time I did that." — Betsy Bizot, Lisle, IL

"I can only hope that you will continue to write, so that I can continue to read (and of course buy) your books, for they make me laugh and cry and think ... rare indeed." — Steven Knott, Major, USAF

What Do You Say?

<u>*Send me these books!*</u>

Shards of Honor	72087-2 ◆ $5.99	☐
Barrayar	72083-X ◆ $5.99	☐
Cordelia's Honor (trade)	87749-6 ◆ $15.00	☐
The Warrior's Apprentice	72066-X ◆ $5.99	☐
The Vor Game	72014-7 ◆ $5.99	☐
Young Miles (trade)	87782-8 ◆ $15.00	☐
Cetaganda (hardcover)	87701-1 ◆ $21.00	☐
Cetaganda (paperback)	87744-5 ◆ $5.99	☐
Ethan of Athos	65604-X ◆ $5.99	☐
Borders of Infinity	72093-7 ◆ $5.99	☐
Brothers in Arms	69799-4 ◆ $5.99	☐
Mirror Dance (paperback)	87646-5 ◆ $6.99	☐
Memory (paperback)	87845-X ◆ $6.99	☐
Falling Free	65398-9 ◆ $4.99	☐
The Spirit Ring (paperback)	72188-7 ◆ $5.99	☐

LOIS MCMASTER BUJOLD
Only from Baen Books

If not available at your local bookstore, fill out this coupon and send a check or money order for the cover price(s) to Baen Books, Dept. BA, P.O. Box 1403, Riverdale, NY 10471. Delivery can take up to ten weeks.

NAME: _____

ADDRESS: _____

_____

I have enclosed a check or money order in the amount of $ _____